Aitanga Nui	enemy iwi
Arakura	Kiri's mother
Ēpa	Kai's aunt
Hae	Aitanga Nui warrior chief
Haere	Tāwae & Kiri's daughter
Hara	one of the kai-rākau at Kō Pā
Hinewehi	Tūterangi & Poka's daughter; Tui's wife
Hīraia	Tūhoro's wife
Kaiora	tohunga/priest
Kaitanga (Kai)	Tāwae & Kiri's eldest son
Kapua	Aitanga Nui chief; Ringa-mutu's son
Kere	Kai's friend (part Ngāi Haere, part Ngāti Ira)
Kiri	Tāwae's wife
Kōrihi	Kai's cousin and nemesis
Kū	Tāwae's father, killed at Te Maniaroa
Kuharu	Ēpa's husband
Kura	Tāwae & Kiri's daughter
Manu-pōkai (Manu)	Tāwae & Kiri's eldest daughter
Ngāheru (Ngā)	Kai & Wairere's eldest son
Ngāi Haere	iwi/tribe
Oha	Tūterangi & Poka's youngest daughter
Parakore	tohunga/priest
Poka	Tūterangi's wife
Pona	Roro's grandson
Rākai	Pona's mother; Roro's daughter-in-law
Ringa-mutu	superior chief of Aitanga Nui
Roro	Kiri's paternal grandfather
Tāmō	Tūterangi & Poka's son
Taniwha	Aitanga Nui leader (also Ngāti Ira)
Tare	chief at Poko Pā
Tāu	Hara's son

Tāwae	chief of Whānau-a-Mate (at Kō Pā)
Te Ika	Roro's son by Rākai
Te Ratu	senior chief at Tūranga
Te Tau	Kū's older brother and once chief of Whānau-a-Māte
Te Wī-o-te-rangi (Tui)	Tāwae & Kiri's son
Tū	Kiri's maternal grandfather
Tuameko (Tua)	Kai & Wairere's son
Tūhoro	Tū's son
Tukua	Wehe's father
Tupaea	Tahitian wayfinder aboard *Endeavour*
Tūterangi	chief at Kauae-nui Pā
Ue (Old Ue)	Tāwae's grandmother
Ūkaipō	Tūterangi & Poka's eldest daughter; Kere's wife
Wairere	Tūterangi & Poka's daughter; Kai's wife
Wehe	leader of the kai-rākau; Kai's great-uncle
Whai	Tūhoro and Hīraia's son
Whakaata	Arakura's twin sister
Whānau-a-Mate	hapū/subtribe
Whiwhi-rangi	Taniwha's son

8

KĀWAI

In memory of Mum (d. Sept 1982) who set me on this path.

KĀWAI

FOR SUCH A TIME AS THIS

A Saga from the Uttermost End of the Earth —
Aotearoa New Zealand

MONTY SOUTAR

This saga is loosely based not on one true story, but on many true stories. The sequence of events has been conflated and much of the dialogue is imagined. Some names and other particulars have been changed for dramatic purposes, and out of respect for the descendants of the ancestors mentioned.

© Monty Soutar, 2022

The moral rights of the author have been asserted.

Typographical design © David Bateman Ltd, 2022

Published in 2022 by David Bateman Ltd,
Unit 2/5 Workspace Drive, Hobsonville,
Auckland 0618, New Zealand
www.batemanbooks.co.nz
ISBN: 978-1-77689-047-7 (Hardback)
ISBN: 978-1-77689-030-9 (Paperback)

A catalogue record for this book is available from the National Library of New Zealand.

ARTS COUNCIL OF NEW ZEALAND TOI AOTEAROA

The *Kāwai* series has been supported through the prestigious Creative New Zealand Michael King Writer's Fellowship, which Dr. Monty Soutar was awarded in 2021.

Recipient of a 2021 Contestable Fund Grant from Copyright Licensing New Zealand.

Front cover design: TORO Studios and lead illustrator Raukura Riwaka; conceptual design by Te Tuhi Soutar; front cover photograph by Siobhan Houkamau; back cover photograph of Mt Hikurangi from Ihungia by Te Tuhi Soutar. Text design: Katrina Duncan
Printed in China by Toppan Leefung Printing Ltd

FAMILY TREE
(WHAKAPAPA)

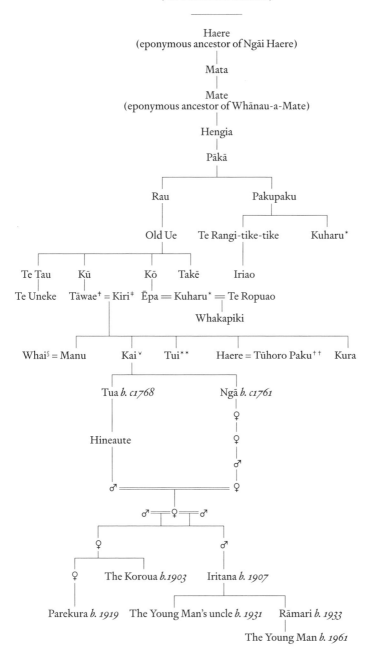

Haere
(eponymous ancestor of Ngāi Haere)

Mata

Mate
(eponymous ancestor of Whānau-a-Mate)

Hengia

Pākā

Rau   Pakupaku

Old Ue   Te Rangi-tike-tike   Kuharu*

Te Tau   Kū   Kō   Takē   Iriao

Te Uneke   Tāwae† = Kiri‡   Ēpa = Kuharu* = Te Ropuao

Whakapiki

Whai§ = Manu   Kai˅   Tui**   Haere = Tūhoro Paku††   Kura

Tua b. c1768   Ngā b. c1761

Hineaute   ♀

                            ♀

                            ♂

♂ ══════════════════ ♀

♂ ═ ♀ ═ ♂

♀   ♂

♀   The Koroua b.1903   Iritana b. 1907

Parekura b. 1919   The Young Man's uncle b. 1931   Rāmari b. 1933

The Young Man b. 1961

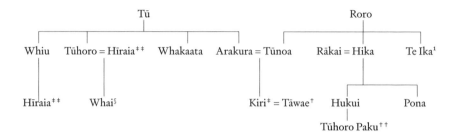

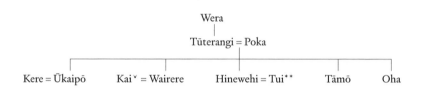

1 Te Ika's mother was also Rākai

PROLOGUE

———

I unlatched the gate and stepped onto the stone path that led up a small rise to the ancestral meeting house, anxious now about having come here alone. Aside from the rattle as the gate latch closed, the only sound was my shoes crunching on the gravel. A disquieting spirit seemed to emanate from the tall pines that stood guard around the pā. My walk along the isolated valley that morning, accompanied by the sound of cicadas, had only increased my apprehension about meeting the old man. A warm breeze caressed my face, momentarily soothing my nerves.

I had just finished the first year of an education degree — I was a typical nineteen-year-old uni student focused on sport, studies and girls. My father was a teacher with a passion for the profession and I had grown up assuming I would follow in his footsteps. I wasn't up on my iwi connections; I didn't see any need for it in the city. And anyway, as Dad said, 'Knowing Māori won't get you a job.' Here, however, standing outside our pā, I was suddenly conscious of my ignorance.

My family had left this valley a decade ago. It was strange to be back, to see how much it had changed. I felt like I didn't belong. Glancing over to an adjacent paddock I spotted the dilapidated remains of my great-aunt's house. Two of the walls had collapsed and the remaining lean-to looked as if it served as a shelter for stock. There was an empty shepherd's cottage nearby, but no signs of life.

Toitū te whenua, whatu ngarongaro te tangata. *The land remains, but people pass on.* I had heard the old people say that often enough when I was a child. Now, as I stood looking at the derelict meeting house and its overgrown marae courtyard, the old proverb made sense. Nūpe was virtually deserted, save for the old man who allegedly lived in the whare puni. The families had long since relocated to nearby towns and cities.

I followed the path up to the marae, feeling the weight of the building's past as I drew nearer. An ancient mustard-coloured Vauxhall, covered in rust, was parked in the grass. Alongside it stood a commemorative stone, its granite obelisk pointing to the sky. I had seen similar memorials during the bus ride the previous day. The inscription on this one was illegible, with lichen obscuring many of the letters.

My eyes were drawn beyond the obelisk to a distant hill. On its crest I could make out headstones. One, I knew, must be my grandmother's. Momentarily, I envisioned a winding trail of mourners, draped in the dark garments of grief, making their way up to the cemetery. I was part of that procession fifteen years earlier, along with my brothers, clinging to the pleats of our mother's long black skirt, puzzled by all the weeping and wailing.

Then a flashback to the inside of the house: four small boys standing in a line. A church minister of the Ringatū faith[1] had deposited a teaspoonful of seawater into each gaping mouth and anointed us with olive oil, while mumbling a prayer in Māori. My brothers and I had looked to our parents for reassurance.

'Hei ārai atu i te mate Māori,' our mother whispered. *To ward off Māori illness.*[2] Mate Māori — shivers still run down my spine when I hear that term.

As quickly as it appeared the vision faded, and I found myself stepping over a patch of freshly turned soil onto the wooden veranda. The paint was peeling below the front window and one of its side carvings was lying in the grass, its pāua-shell eyes missing. The sign above the door, bearing the ancestor's name, was marred with bird droppings.

KAI-TA-NGA. I read the syllables aloud, then shrugged. A quick mental translation didn't shed much light either: *The Eating*. Slipping off my shoes, I rapped my knuckles on the open wooden door and, clearing my throat, called into the gloomy atmosphere.

'Kia ora, Koroua!' *Hello, old man!*

I peered inside the large single-room building, my eyes adjusting to the dim light. Bed, ramshackle furniture, food and utensils, books, general clutter . . .

Eventually a faint, raspy voice replied from the far end of the building. 'Tomo mai!' *Come in!*

Gingerly I wove my way through the room, doing my best to avoid knocking over the piles of books and paper and other objects around me. A sea of framed faces covered every wall — relatives long gone, I assumed. Many were in khaki uniforms, their images hung below the black, red and white of the numerous painted kōwhaiwhai or scroll panels that decorated the ceiling.

Then I saw the old man, who was sitting on the edge of his bed, sipping from a white enamel mug. He smiled as he used his tokotoko or carved walking stick to stand up slowly. His stature impressed me. Although now stooped with age, he must have been big and broad-shouldered in his youth. We shook hands while pressing our noses and foreheads together in a hongi.

'Nā wai koe?' *Who do you belong to?* he enquired, scrutinising me through his thick, black-rimmed glasses while he reached to open the back door. As the light came flooding in, I was able to see him more clearly. His eyes were magnified by the heavy glasses, his cheeks sagged and his neck was deeply wrinkled. He was unshaven and his hands were ingrained with dirt. Despite his somewhat dishevelled appearance, there was an aura of nobility about him.

'Nā Rāmari, tamāhine a Iritana,' I said. *I belong to Rāmari, Iritana's daughter.* The old man's eyes lit up as he realised his visitor was his cousin's grandson.

'E noho, e noho,' he said warmly as he offered me a seat, now obviously pleased to have company.

'He tī māhau?' *Would you like some tea?* On a small table I saw steam coming from the spout of a well-used stainless-steel teapot. I had timed my visit well.

'Yes, thank you.' As he reached for another cup I mentally berated myself for not bringing a koha. How many times had my parents told me to take food to share when visiting the old people?

'Kei te aha tō kōkā?' *How's your mother?* he asked as he poured the tea.

A week earlier I had been on the other side of the country talking with my mum about her relatives. For as long as I could remember there had been a constant procession of visitors that she introduced to us children as 'uncle' or 'aunty'. Recently something had piqued my interest in my roots and I asked her if they had all actually been blood relatives. I wanted to know the connections. Over two evenings my mother, often through tears, painted a vivid picture of a large family that included many whāngai or adopted children.

I was fascinated and kept probing, but once my questions got beyond her grandparents, my mother's answers became hazy. That's when she mentioned the old man. The koroua held the key, she said, that would unlock a door into the distant past for me.

Until recently I had thought of the past as so remote as to be beyond the reach of my imagination, or my interest. Who cared? They were all dead and gone. But, hearing my mum's stories, I became gripped by the idea of finding out more. And here was someone who had kept aglow the embers of the family history. *My* history.

I took a day's train ride to Tūranga³ on New Zealand's east coast, from where I rode a bus north for two hours into the heart of our tribal territory, below Mt Hikurangi — the first place in the world to see the sun. I spent that night at the home of my mother's brother, not far from Nūpe. It seemed to me that the closer I got to Nūpe, the further back in time I was travelling.

Now I was finally here, and I sensed my host was keen to know why I had come so far. With my hand clammy against my bouncing knee, I got straight to the point.

'My mother said you would be able to tell me something about our past — who our people were, and where they were from.'

The old man didn't answer right away. He just smiled and topped up our cups of tea. Eventually he spoke.

'E moe i te pō.' *Spend the night.*

Ever since the koroua's mother, my great-great-aunt, had overseen the building of this whare puni in the 1930s, one or more of her descendants had lived in it. Still, it didn't feel like home to me, and I couldn't imagine sleeping under the gaze of all those photos. I took a sip of tea while I tried to think of an excuse.

'Oh, Uncle is expecting me for dinner, but I can come back again tomorrow.'

'E tā!' *Is that so!* the old man replied with a hint of scorn.

I admit to feeling a little embarrassed. At that stage I did not understand that the invitation was more than an offer of hospitality. It was wise advice to someone operating on city time to *slow down*, and to realise that the information he sought could be shared neither casually nor quickly. The koroua looked apprehensive.

'Why do you want to know about the past anyway?' he asked. 'Young fullas your age should be running after girls, not chasing ghosts.'

I was unsure what to say to this. He was right. My lectures had finished for the year, exams were over. All my mates were pretty much doing what the old man was describing. But I also knew he was testing me. Why was I here? I wasn't entirely sure. All I knew was that the recent conversation with my mother had fanned the flames of something burning inside me. Perhaps I recognised that this old man was my one chance to grasp at the dust motes of my own history before they swirled away forever.

I was still formulating my reply when the koroua spoke again.

'I have to go into town today for groceries.'

'I can wait,' I quickly replied.

'Then I've got the marae lawns to mow.'

'I'll do them,' I said eagerly.

'No, no, the grounds are far too big.'

'It's okay. If you show me how to work your mower, I can get started while you're away.'

The corners of his mouth turned upwards. I could tell he was mulling something over. When he took me to the mower, I realised what it was. The area behind the house was enormous and the grass was long — *really* long. I had never seen a mower of that vintage but I was sure I'd manage.

+

The koroua was gone for a couple of hours. When he returned I was only halfway through. The midday sun was baking my dark hair and I was down to my sweat-drenched singlet and shorts. I had grass all over my legs, as the mower had no catcher and I had to tie up the rear flap to stop the chute blocking. It was mid-afternoon when I eventually finished.

The koroua beckoned me to the veranda where, on a table, he had set a plate of hot mutton chops and scrambled eggs and a jug of cool orange cordial.

'I thought you couldn't eat in front of a whare puni?' I said, sitting down gratefully. The kai smelled delicious.

'Nā wai tēnā kōrero?' *Who told you that?*

'The priests at boarding school. They said the front of the house was tapu.'

The old man screwed up his eyes and shook his head.

'I rue the day that the Pākehā teaches me my own culture.' He continued as he sat down. 'When I was a child we didn't have dining rooms. All the meals on big occasions were at the front of the house. The kai was laid out on food mats on the ground.' Then he bowed his head and said grace in Māori. I closed my eyes too.

As I salted my food, the koroua gestured to the carved wooden mask on the gable of the house.

'Now that's somebody you ought to know about — the fulla on this house, Kaitanga. He's a big chief, a real warrior, you know? Tō tipuna hoki.' *Your ancestor too.*

'Nē rā?' *Is that right?* I had not heard of this warrior chief whose name I had made out in faded paint when I arrived. I looked up to the apex of the reddened barge boards. The face had an owl-like appearance and its bulbous eyes and lolling tongue seemed to be grinning defiance at any visitor.

'Kaitanga was here when that fulla Cook came, you know.'

'Really? Captain Cook? Here at Nūpe?'

'Not right here. Out at sea.'

I wondered how the koroua knew that. 'There are histories hidden on this coast,' he said, 'that you won't find written in any of those books in that school of yours. But be warned — you might not like what you hear.'

'I'm sure I'll be all right, Koroua,' I said quickly. I was keen to hear any information the old man might have to offer.

'E kī, e kī!' he said as he grinned. *You think so!*

We ate in silence, the only sound being that of his false teeth clicking as he chewed. Only after I had washed and dried the dishes did the koroua finally speak again.

'Now, you come back early tomorrow and I'll tell you a bit of your tipuna's story. Don't forget — early.'

+

I arrived at 7.30 a.m., expecting the koroua to be still in bed, only to find that he had been out in his vegetable garden for an hour.

'Aa, mōrena, e tama. Kei te aha?' he said perkily. *Ah, good morning, boy. How you feeling?*

'Kei te pai.' *Fine.* I smiled.

'Go inside and make yourself comfortable while I get cleaned up.' The koroua shuffled along the side of the house to the kāuta, the dirt-floor lean-to kitchen, where there was an outside basin with cold water. Other than the men's and women's whare paku or longdrops, it was the only other structure near the house.

The mustiness of the whare puni and the haunting faces in the frames, whose eyes seemed to be following me, made me uneasy. I walked slowly along the walls, stopping to peer closely into the faces in the hand-coloured daguerreotype portraits, quietly reading out the neatly painted names on each frame.

Suddenly I heard creaking on the veranda and the sound of chanting. The old man must have company. I went over and peered out the front door. No one there. Then I heard the strange intoning again, deep and distant. It sounded like Māori but I couldn't be sure. Whatever it was, it was unsettling.

Then I heard 'Ki te mate au': I recognised that much. *Should I die . . .* I felt goosebumps all over my arms. I squeezed my eyes shut and slowly counted to three.

When I opened my eyes again I still saw no one. I could still hear the disembodied voice but it was growing fainter. The hairs on the back of my neck began to bristle. The sound seemed to be coming from beyond the stone memorial and was trailing off towards the hill cemetery. It dwindled to nothing and there was silence. I stood at the edge of the veranda feeling bewildered. Was I dreaming?

'Haramai, e noho.' *Come and sit down.* The koroua's words brought me back. I made my way back inside, repeating the words that I thought I heard.

The old man glanced at me with a look of fleeting surprise.

'Kei te pararāwaha koe te aha?' *What's that you're mumbling?*

'I heard some voices outside.'

'Ko tāua anake kei kōnei.' *There's only us here.*

'Perhaps I was imagining things. It sounded so real.'

'What did you hear?'

'Ki te mate au.'

The koroua's eyes widened and fixed directly on mine.

'Ko wai ka mōhio — tērā pea ka pērā tonu i te wā kei kōnei koe.' *Who knows — you might be here for just such a time as this.*

But before I had a chance to analyse his cryptic words, the koroua began his story, which transported me to another place and time.

PART ONE

CHAPTER ONE

He aha mōu mō te kotahi?
What can you alone do?

Te Maniaroa, 1734 AD

It was late afternoon. The sound of waves crashing on the distant shore was barely audible. The voices around the boy chief sounded muffled, as if he was covering his ears. As he struggled to gather his wits about him, Tāwae, son of Kū, detected a familiar smell. Hika mā? *What the hell?* His head was pounding and he was still woozy, but the mist in his eyes was beginning to fade. Where am I? What's going on?

He tried to move one arm but it was pressed into the warm, sandy soil. His limbs were constrained under the weight of other near-naked bodies. As his eyes adjusted to the light he realised he was staring into the tattooed face of another man. The warrior's eyes were open, but when Tāwae looked into them there was nothing there. The man's mauri, his life force, had been taken from him.

The indistinct images on the sandy plain gradually became clearer and Tāwae realised he was lying on his stomach among several corpses, his head turned to the side. It was death he had smelt. There was blood everywhere. In the next instant he remembered. He had been watching the battle from afar, where his father had told him to stay put. He was too young to take part, and it was inappropriate, too,

19

given that he was closely related through his mother to the enemy. His father had only brought him along to sample the victuals of victory after the battle.

Four hundred warriors, led by a phalanx of chiefs, had set off across the alluvial plateau just before midday, while another hundred had gone by the shoreline to be met by an equal number of foes at the other end of the long stretch of beach. The fighting raged for hours, the advantage swinging back and forth.

Although he had seen only thirteen winters and had just begun his warrior training, when Tāwae saw his father in trouble he had wasted no time in grabbing a spear and racing to his aid. As he reached the edge of the battlefield he was quickly mired in the great melee. The last thing he recalled was a club glancing off his tao before grazing the side of his head. He could not remember hitting the ground.

One thing seemed clear now as he cautiously looked about him. His father's warriors had fled the scene. He lay very still.

He heard a burst of laughter in the distance as a party of women approached, making their way among the lifeless bodies.

'Auē! E hika mā, e moumou rā ia, te ure nei e!' one of them exclaimed. *Oh! Friends, what a waste! Look at this penis!*

'Ōkau is not so great a pā after all!' another woman retorted. 'Te Rangi-tike-tike's penis could smash through its palisades on its own!' Again, they broke into raucous laughter.

'Auē, kua hinga taku tāina,' Tāwae whispered to himself. *Oh, my cousin's dead.* How many more of his relatives were among the slain? Just as sorrow began to grip him he told himself: No time to grieve — I'm alive. Now I have to get out of here.

He slowly wrestled one arm free and reached up to touch his throbbing temple. Coagulated blood. Extracting his other arm from under a corpse, he propped himself on an elbow and peered cautiously over the dead warrior's chest. The sand was covered with bloodied bodies — there must have been at least a hundred of them, and probably more down on the beach.

He could see enemy warriors on the far side of the battlefield.

No doubt they were despatching the maimed and cutting up the corpses, while at the same time retrieving their own dead and wounded. Tāwae caught a whiff of roasted flesh on the wind. His nostrils would recognise that smell anywhere. Smoke rose from several cooking fires at the end of the beach.

He resisted the impulse to vent his fury there and then at the massacre of his whānau. Quivering with anger, he knew he had to think clearly. Surely it would take them until the following day to remove all the bodies, so he was safe for a few hours. Wait until nightfall, he told himself. Don't panic. Sunset will come soon enough. Then make a run for it.

He positioned his head so he could just see over the chest of the dead warrior. He watched a group of men standing at the spot where Tāwae had last seen his father.

'Wāhine mā! Mauria mai ā koutou nā pīkau!' an older man yelled. *Women! Bring your packs over here!*

'Who does Taniwha think he is, summoning us like servants?' one of the women said as they put on their packs again.

Tāwae was curious. He peered over at the men, squinting into the late afternoon sun. The older man was the shortest and darkest of the group, thickset with muscular legs that looked like the main posts of a palisade.

So that's Taniwha, Tāwae thought. The man my father insulted.

The women headed back to the group of men. The youngest of the warriors was the tall, red-haired, fair-skinned fighter that Tāwae had watched annihilate one of his uncles.

One of the women slipped off the straps of her pīkau kete and placed something on the ground. It looked like a block of wood. Taniwha turned to address the deceased in a loud voice, as if they were still alive.

'Ha! Kātahi te manu āta pōkai, ngā kurī paakā a Ue!' *There you lie huddled like a bevy of birds, the brown dogs of Ue!*

When Tāwae caught these words, he couldn't help but let out a small yelp. He knew then that his father and his two uncles were among the fallen, Ue being the name of their mother. The group looked up momentarily and Tāwae froze. Their eyes scanned the landscape of bodies. They saw no movement but they were unconvinced.

'Whiwhi-rangi, haere ki te mātaki,' Taniwha ordered the young red-haired warrior. *Whiwhi-rangi, go and check.*

Patu in hand, the young man strode quickly towards where Tāwae was lying. Tāwae closed his eyes and held his breath. He heard the young warrior stop a few metres short of him, presumably examining the scene.

Tāwae could hear every move the young warrior made. He sensed that this Whiwhi-rangi was very close as he lay there, frozen. There was a long silence. No movement. Then Tāwae felt the corpse next to him being turned over. A blowfly took off and circled, wings thrumming the empty air. The low buzzing seemed amplified until it stopped; the insect must have landed on the open flesh of another body. Then there was a low moaning sound, perhaps as air was expelled from a dying man's lungs. A loud thump reverberated, reminding Tāwae of the dull thud of a wooden pounder on fernroots. The young warrior must have struck the corpse. He was right there.

The boy chief awaited his own death blow, but it did not come. Eventually the footsteps retreated. After what seemed like hours, Tāwae slowly opened his eyes. The wide-eyed corpse was no longer facing him. Tāwae was now looking at a gaping wound in the back of the dead man's skull.

In the distance Tāwae saw the retreating figure of Whiwhi-rangi signal something to the others. Taniwha, apparently satisfied, recommenced his kōrero with the dead. Tāwae's fear was overshadowed again by anger. He was barely able to contain his rage and stay hidden. He clenched his teeth, which made his head throb painfully. It was all he could do not to scream his father's name.

Taniwha, with what Tāwae imagined was a vile smirk, reached down and took hold of one of the limp arms of a corpse.

'E! Ka eke hoki i ngā pikitanga o Kōrau-whakamae, ka motu ngā kawe,' he snarled. *When we ascended the Kōrau-whakamae ridge, these hands severed our straps.*

He laid the arm, palm up, across the block of wood. Tāwae knew what was coming. His blood ran cold and his hands tightened into fists.

Taniwha took hold of an adze.

'Toroa mai tōna ringa.' *Stretch out his arm.*

Whiwhi-rangi did as he was ordered. Without a moment's hesitation, Taniwha raised the wooden handle above his head. Then, with all his might, he brought the adze down to meet the forearm at the wrist.

With a sickening crunch, the hand toppled off. Whiwhi-rangi picked up the mutilated limb and tossed it into one of the pīkau kete. Tāwae closed his eyes again and muted the wailing that threatened to escape his throat by biting into the fleshy part of his own arm. Over and over he had to endure the sound of hands being severed. It was as if each impact was hacking his own heart into pieces. Tears trickled down his face as his jaws remained locked on his arm. After an age, when all was quiet again, he opened his eyes and saw one of the women hurrying off with the kete.

Time slowed down as Tāwae lay there, wretched and wild with silent fury, tortured by the sound of these sons of wild beasts dismembering his kin and preparing their corpses to be cooked in the umu or steam ovens.

He would rather have died a gruesome death in battle than endure this, but his strong spirit kept him mindful of his duty.

Ki te mate au, ko wai he mōrehu hei kawe kōrero ki te iwi e auhi ana? *Should I die, who will report what has happened here to our grief-stricken people?*

As soon as the sun set, Tāwae began to crawl out from the mound of bodies that had hidden him, careful to stay low. Once he thought he was far enough away, he started running and didn't look back. The moon will be out soon, he said to himself. Head for cover, run as fast as you can and no matter what, don't stop.

He felt the gritty sand squeeze between his splayed toes. Then suddenly he was aware of a distant commotion. Had they spotted him? Seized by fear, he raced into the bush, not daring to look behind — stumbling, slipping and tripping, barely able to see his way forward in the growing dark. Deeper and deeper into the bush he plunged, breaking twigs, pulling aside branches. His heart was thumping and his lungs howling. He paused for a second here and there to gasp for breath, then ploughed on.

Tāwae eventually staggered into a waterway, which he calculated must be the Karaka Stream, meaning he was about halfway back to where they'd started from that morning. He remembered crossing where it spilled out onto the plains. Dropping to one knee, his head and shoulders dripping with sweat, he gulped water from his cupped hand as he scanned the surrounding bush on high alert. Every one of his senses was heightened. Even the breeze on his skin felt like a tempest.

On and on Tāwae ran, well into the night, until his muscles ached and exhaustion finally overwhelmed him. Unable to take another step, he lay down on the forest floor under a low tree canopy to rest. He tried to stay awake, straining to listen for any sign of his pursuers, but sleep soon consumed him. Even the mosquitoes could not rouse him now.

+

The first rays of light to reach through the branches awakened the boy chief. He sat up, trying to dodge the low branches he had slept under. Tāwae's brain was frazzled from lack of sleep — his exhaustion would make him easy prey. He crawled slowly out from under the bush and looked up to see splashes of gold playing on leaves in all shades of green. He was in a majestic forest brought alive by the sounds of hundreds of chattering birds.

How could such beauty co-exist with man's contempt for life? He felt momentarily overcome by despair. *I could hang myself from a vine tied to one of these branches*, he thought. *Or scale a cliff and leap* to my death. He pulled himself back from such desperate thoughts. What use would he be to his people if he was dead?

Orienting himself to the coastline, he set off again, skirting the base of inaccessible cliffs, keeping under bush cover but avoiding the denser foliage. Eventually Tāwae began to wonder if he was on the right path after all. In the frenzied dark the previous night his only objective had been to get himself as far away as possible. He hadn't really been focusing on where he was going. Now he could hear the sea below, so he realised he must have gone well past the point where his father's warriors had formed up the previous morning. If he could just make it down to the beach without being seen, he thought, he would be able to find his way to Ōkau Pā. It was not home, but it was safe.

At the edge of the bush Tāwae was relieved to see the green sea. The beach was deserted. He knew the way now. He crouched down, alert, pausing momentarily to rest. He could see no one, hear no one, in any direction. He took several steady, deep breaths, in and out. Then, with a final half-breath, he sprang out onto the sand and sprinted in a wide arc down the beach. Sand flicked up behind him as the balls of his feet pounded the surface beneath him. From time to time he glanced over his shoulder, and although he saw no one, he kept going as if his life depended on it. His life *did* depend on it.

It was not long before he reached the Tere River, on the other side of which stood Ōkau Pā. Someone spotted him and called to others who began rushing down from the broad spur on which the fortress stood to meet him. Safety at last.

Tāwae slowed to a jog, then a walk, as relief turned to weariness. He waded across the stony river, his frame slouching forward, every step taking its toll. When the reception party finally reached him on the other side, Tāwae sank to his knees, beating his fists on the ground. Turning around, the boy chief shouted back across the river, 'E koa koe āianei, otirā māku hoki apōpō!' *You rejoice today, but tomorrow will be mine!*

CHAPTER TWO

He pounamu kākano rua.
A highly prized treasure.

Ngāpō Village, six years later, 1740 AD

Kiri's labour was brief but intense, her robust young body having brought forth the infant vigorously. Perspiration ran down her face as she watched her tapuhi carefully raise the newborn by its legs.

A watery emission seeped from the baby's mouth and nose, so Kiri's mother, Arakura, daughter of the old warrior chief Tū, gave instructions to the young attendant.

'Ruia taku mokopuna kia heke te ngaru.'

Immediately the tapuhi shook the newborn gently to expel the secretion. On seeing the baby's gender, Kiri beamed with delight and the other two joined her.

'Ā, taku tama.' *Ah, my son.* Kiri's tears kissed her baby's skin as she took him from the tapuhi, lifted him onto her chest and placed her hand gently on his back to give him some warmth. He was still blue and mottled and covered with mucus, a whitish waxy coating and small streaks of blood, but to his exhausted mother he was perfection.

+

It was the beginning of spring, a generation before the Tahitian wayfinder, Tupaia, and the first Europeans set foot on Aotearoa.[4] The newborn had announced his arrival with loud howls, just before hundreds of white-tufted tūī and sweet-sounding kōpara gave voice to the breaking dawn. The tapuhi, suddenly aware of the bellbirds' clear, liquid song, glanced out from the thatched whare rauhi to see the orange-red skyline above the ocean give way to the first rays of sunlight. The birds' operatic duet ceased as quickly as it started, and the attendant gasped audibly at the fleeting sight of Mercury disappearing in the sun's glare.

'Whiro is returning to his house of darkness,' the attendant murmured. Kiri looked at her. What sort of sign, if any, might the young woman receive when she herself gave birth crouching alone in the bush someday, she wondered. As the sun's golden ball came free of the horizon and its reflection threw a path across the gentle swells, the tapuhi pointed out a second significant omen in the sky — a clump of reddish cloud trailing a long, narrow strip of vapour.

'E hika! He manawarangi, he kohoka, e Kiri!' *Gosh! A roasted heart on a spit, Kiri!*

Kiri glowed with pride, not for this sign of victory in future battle, nor for the relief that the baby was out, but because she knew the gods had gifted her and Tāwae a redeemer. She unfastened her smooth greenstone pendant and placed it around the infant's neck.

'Take this heirloom, my son, long ago plucked from the waters of Te Wai-pounamu,' she whispered. 'Let it remind you of your grandfather who wore it before me.' The infant's small opaque eyes opened slightly and for a moment he seemed to grin at the face looking down at him. Kiri touched her cheek to his tiny melon-shaped head before his eyelids closed again. She wiped her own eyes, then softly asked Arakura, 'Kūmea mai te ārai, e Kō.' *Draw back the screen, Mother.*

The bright sunlight forced Kiri's eyes to close tightly as she experienced the first flush of the morning. She inhaled the fresh salt air, recognising the sound of a passing pod of whales slapping their tails on the water's surface, and a herd of seals barking from the rocks.

'Mmm,' she murmured before taking another deep breath and squinting at the shoreline. 'Oh, for a morsel of kōura mara.'

'The cooks will have fermented crayfish,' her mother said before turning to the tapuhi. 'Take word to the cooks that your mistress craves kōura mara. Tell them the delicacy will ensure her breasts have plenty of milk for the chief's son.' As the tapuhi crawled out the opening of the birthing hut, Arakura cautioned her. 'Make sure you stand well back when you speak to them.'

After the tapuhi had gone, Arakura turned to Kiri. 'You endured your birth pains in silence, tamāhine, as is expected of young mothers of our rank,' she said approvingly. Kiri offered a courteous nod but her smiling eyes remained fixed on her newborn.

'If I had to describe the agony, Mother, it was the kind where everything disappears and there's nothing but you and this terrible pain. At times I couldn't even have told you my own name.'

Arakura placed her hand on her daughter's forehead and brushed back a stray lock of hair.

'I know. You were always the stoic one, my dear. May your son inherit your courage.'

In truth, stoicism was but one of the eighteen-year-old's many appealing qualities. Kiri was statuesque and beautiful, with penetrating eyes. Had she been born a male she would surely have been the commander of the tribe's warriors.

First light revealed the periphery of Ngāpō village, a community that was about to be forever changed by the birth of its future chief. The village was full of reed-thatched huts and a population of about one hundred and fifty. The sun crept over the low roofs, seeped along the dirt paths and lit the tiny dewdrops that clung to each blade of grass and every leaf at the edge of the bush. Home to the Whānau-a-Mate people, Ngāpō was closed in on three sides by wooded hills, and open to the ocean on the other. Of the misty inland mountains, Hikurangi was by far the highest.

Howling dogs were the first sounds of village life that morning, leading to a reverberation of cries from some of the forty or more awakening infants. Then came the usual *thud-thud-thud* of mallets as the pononga pounded aruhe or fernroot to supplement the children's meal. These slaves — captives taken in battles or raids — were always early risers, but not by choice.

Smoke from the first cooking fires soon snaked upwards outside the compounds of several huts. Straight-backed men, fighting weapon in one hand, digging implements in the other, keen to make the most of the cooler part of the morning, took several gulps of water before heading out along ferny tracks to their clearings to turn the soil. It was only a fortnight until planting time. A group of women, youth and pononga followed. The gait of the party, like that of all barefooted people, was marked by heavy, plodding steps, their disposition indifferent.

The Whānau-a-Mate were a handsome people, though few, if any, were without scars; many of the older people, women as well as men, bore gruesomely large gashes on their chests or limbs. They were lean but big-boned, their black curly hair often tied in tousled topknots. Some were tall, with aquiline features and of a light complexion but tanned by constant exposure to the sun and a life spent mostly outdoors. Others tended to be shorter and darker-skinned. All were equally impressive in build.

The Ngāpō Stream wound its sluggish course down from the hills and along the southern edge of the village before flowing into the sea. It ran close by the whare rauhi, its rippling sound having soothed Kiri during the night. The stream was fed by deep, pristine bush creeks teeming with sweet-tasting eels and freshwater crayfish.

On the south side of the stream, overlooking the village, stood Kō Pā, where Kiri and Tāwae lived. If ever attacked, everyone in the village would withdraw to the safety of its steep, terraced pā, for its palisades had never been breached. A guard of thirty experienced warriors, the kai-rākau, maintained this dry and airy hill fortress.

Kiri and Tāwae married young, three years after the bloody massacre of Te Maniaroa, their marriage arranged by their elders. They fell deeply in love and their daughter was born less than a year later. The couple were close in age, and although Kiri grew up in a neighbouring pā, she was always aware of who Tāwae was. He, on the other hand, was oblivious to her before their betrothal, his total focus being on learning to lead the tribe. They were so alike in their thinking that they could have been mistaken for siblings, even though there was no obvious likeness in their physical appearance.

Before long, the shrill cries of karoro were heard circling the pā, while more seagulls squawked noisily as they dashed pipi along the flat, sandy beach to break the shells open. The lush bush, which stretched from the western edge of the village to the mountains some thirty kilometres distant, was suddenly alive with the vibrant trill of all manner of crawling and flying insects. It seemed as if nature too was heralding the birth.

The whare rauhi or birthing hut, being tapu, had been placed outside the village to ensure its sanctity and to maintain physical hygiene. Entry to it was forbidden to most because birth was considered sacred.

On the tapuhi's return, Kiri instructed her to adjust the whāriki beneath her, allowing the young mother a better view of the rising sun. As the flax mat was moved, a piece of folded kōwhai bark was revealed. Kiri picked it up and opened it to remove the kawakawa leaf she knew was there. Her mind flashed back to early summer. The tohunga, an elderly man of high rank to whom villagers entrusted all the important religious ceremonies, had stood at her feet.

'I lay on a mat, next to a small fire,' she told her mother as her thumb and forefinger smoothed out the heart-shaped leaf. 'My cloak was opened down to my navel. He held the stem of the leaf while he recited a charm. You can still make out the human figure he cut into it. See — it has a penis.'

Tāwae had enlisted the tohunga's services after Kiri heard about the success other couples were having in ensuring male births. Kiri had totally forgotten about the leaf until that moment but now leaned towards her mother and, in a half-whisper, began describing the ritual to her. The tapuhi seemed to be listening intently too.

'I hardly understood him, he spoke so fast,' Kiri told her mother. 'He laid the kawakawa leaf face down between my breasts, then closed my cloak and started chanting, which seemed to go on forever. Both Tāwae and I saw a short rainbow appear in the smoke coming from the fire. It only faded when the tohunga stopped.

'Then he told Tāwae to bite the big toe of his right foot and the thumb of his right hand! My love didn't hesitate, despite the tohunga's feet being dirty. After this, the tohunga sprinkled water on me, Tāwae and himself, before emptying the rest of the water in the fire. "Kua mutu", he said.' *It is finished.*

The baby, who had been asleep on his mother's abdomen, let out a soft cry. Kiri sat up, lifting him to rest his head on her shoulder, gently patting between his shoulder blades and shushing him.

'I was relieved Tāwae was with me,' she continued. 'Like the other women, I . . . I get agitated when I'm alone with the tohunga. I'm sure it's because he has the power to direct negative forces.'

'Against people of other villages, not our own,' Arakura clarified.

'Oh, don't get me wrong, Mother. I have every confidence in his foretellings. He told us we would have two sons, about two summers apart, and that they would both be redeemers. The elder of the two would be both hero and rogue, and he said he (the tohunga) would not know the younger.' Kiri gave her mother a quizzical look. 'Then he put this leaf inside the bark and said he would put it in a sacred spot in the pā. It was supposed to serve as a sort of medium to influence conception.'

Kiri didn't tell her mother the bit about the tohunga instructing her and Tāwae to consummate the ritual on their takapau-whara-nui, ensuring the leaf was beneath it. Despite it being the middle of the day, the young couple had needed no encouragement and retired to their hut, placed the leaf under their marriage mat and were soon entwined in deepest intimacy. Phrases from the tribe's phallic haka pervaded Kiri's thoughts as Tāwae thrust inside her:

Nā wai parehua taku hope
kia whakakā te rangi kia tare au?
Hā!
He roha te kawau! Hā!
Kei te pou tara
Tū ka tetē, ka tetē! Tau, hā![5]

Who is it that gnaws and bites deep at my loins
until in pain I see the heavens ablaze, 'ere I faint?
Hah!
Like the shag with outspread wings! Hah!
The labia minora is plunged through
Erect, grinding, grinding! Until zenith is finally reached, haaah!

Kiri could still picture Tāwae smiling as drops of sweat fell from his face and body, mingling with hers. 'Taku kare-ā-roto,' he murmured. *My soulmate.* She stroked his chest and he drifted into sleep while she was left marvelling at the words and rhythm of the haka, deftly veiled as a tribute to the earthquake god, Rūaumoko.[6]

Kiri conceived during early summer and their son had come forth in the lunar month of Mahuru, when new growth was about to sprout.

She held her prize to her shoulder and inhaled his special scent. With tears welling in her eyes, she spoke softly to him.

'E taku tama, kia ora tōu ngākau i tōu taitamarikitanga. Hei te tau tītoki rā anō ka tuku whakarere i to tinana ki te mate.' *My son, enjoy your childhood. For one day you will hand your body over to the clutches of death.*

CHAPTER THREE

Tū mai e tama, te whakaata o oū mātua, te moko o ōu tīpuna.
Stand strong, oh son, the reflection of your parents, the emblem of your ancestors.

'He tama! He tama!' *A son! A son!*

Tāwae let out a shout as news of the birth was delivered to him at Kō Pā. His immediate thought was to give thanks to the gods, so with his two-year-old daughter Manu-pōkai swaddled on his back, he raced up to Kai-namu-namu, the highest point in the pā. As he ascended the terraced rise he could see four other distant hill pā, all about the same size, their summits cleared of bush, and all within a day's walk.

Each of these hills was the stronghold of a separate hapū or clan who, when united, brought together a huge swathe of territory and formed the tribe known as Ngāi Haere. All that Tāwae surveyed in this tranquil, lush environment where his ancestors had lived and died, from the far side of the mountains all the way to the sea, including its bounteous fishing grounds, was under his stewardship, and now there had come news of a healthy son.

Facing the ocean, which was clearly visible from the pā, he lifted his eyes to the rising sun and spoke to the sea:

'Haramai, e tama!
I haramai nei koe i Tawhiti-nui,

I Tawhiti-roa,
I Tawhiti-pāmamao,
I te Hono-i-wairua.'

Welcome, son!
You have ventured forth from great Tawhiti,
From distant Tawhiti,
From a long way away,
From where departed souls meet.

The young chief's phrases linked his son with their various homelands and the original wayfinders who, fifteen generations earlier, so he had been taught, charted a deliberate course to make landfall on the eastern seaboard of Te Ika-a-Māui, the last-discovered great landmass of the Pacific Ocean.[7] These hardy and adventurous risk-takers survived a 20,000-nautical-mile voyage in double-hulled craft, and Tāwae implored the gods to infuse his son with these same qualities.

He had been told both mother and baby were well so the chief readied himself to visit. Above average height, slim but muscular, Tāwae was nineteen years old. About his waist he wore a flax kilt, a spatulate or greenstone mere tucked into his belt, and his brow, cheeks and lightly bearded-jaw were incised with moko — emblems of his superior rank. His kāwai or lineage was, without question, the most coveted in the district.

Of late, whenever the mountain Hikurangi was capped with snow, his people had started remarking, 'Ka rukuruku a Te Rangi-tāwaea i ōna pueru.' *Tāwae is gathering up his garments.* Rangi signified the sky and was a title given to chiefs. Tāwae had accepted the title when his elders made him chief in place of his deceased father. Often his people addressed him 'e Rangi' instead of 'e hoa' or 'e hika' — the terms for ordinary people. Tāwae knew of no one else whose mana or status had been likened to the mountain, and he was almost embarrassed whenever he heard the reference.

I have everything to be thankful for, he told himself, and for a moment his chest swelled with pride. But any sense of satisfaction he felt was always quickly replaced by a more familiar feeling: bitterness.

The dawn was looking set to blossom into yet another perfect summer's day as Tāwae made the steep descent from the pā. He breathed in the rich fragrance of the sweet-scented trees, ferns and other plants that flanked the path, while giving his daughter a beaming smile over his shoulder.

'You are about to see your new baby brother, little Manu.' She returned her father's smile with a dimpled grin of her own. She was the apple of her father's eye.

Tāwae walked swiftly as he reached the bottom of the pā hill and approached his village. At the stream he caught a whiff of pungent smoke coming from the site of the whare rauhi. After the warm air dissolved the morning dew, Kiri and her newborn had been moved to a whare kōhanga, where she could recover. The birthing hut, according to custom, was being burnt under the guidance of the tohunga, so that the area would be free of tapu.

A temporary lean-to with a nikau-leaf roof was set up nearby to serve as a cooking area, its palm leaves affording the cooks some shelter from the fierce rays of the sun. Kiri's meals would be placed at a distance from the kōhanga for her tapuhi to retrieve. The young woman, like Kiri's mother Arakura, was considered untouchable and had to stay away from her family and others until after the naming ceremony. Until then, only the couple's near relatives could visit.

As Tāwae approached the kōhanga, the tohunga suddenly appeared, carrying a wooden bowl. He was a big man, with bushy greying hair and stooped shoulders. Every Ngāi Haere village had at least one tohunga. Some were oracles, several were seers, diviners and necromancers, and others more like medicine-men.

Until their defeat at Te Maniaroa, Whānau-a-Mate had been feared by all in the surrounding country because of this particular tohunga. Other, less powerful, tohunga avoided him. He was strong in magic and potent in war-medicine so that the tribe never went into battle unless sanctioned by him. But these days he no longer claimed to be able to intervene in war matters, nor as a medium to conjure the spirits to appear. After Kiri became pregnant his demeanour became increasingly haggard and sombre.

'Kei te aha rāua?' Tāwae enquired. *How are they?*

The tohunga grunted, 'Kua pai.' *Fine.* He looked around as if he half expected someone else to be there.

'Have you completed the ritual?' Tāwae asked.

'Uh-huh,' the tohunga nodded. He now seemed very agitated and would not meet Tāwae's eyes. 'Kei a au nei te whenua.' *I have the placenta.* The old man seemed eager to continue on his way so Tāwae waved him up the hill.

'Whe-nu-a,' Tāwae rolled the word on his tongue as he reached the porch of the kōhanga. It not only meant placenta; it was also the word for land. The burial of the whenua was vital for it would forever connect his son to Ngāpō.

He crouched down at the entrance, his heart beating faster than a fisherman with several tāmure on his line. He pushed his daughter through the small opening into the warmth of the kōhanga, then crawled in after her. Intricately patterned mats were lying on fresh fern leaves to make it comfortable for the three women.

Kiri appeared as if in a trance, gazing at the bundle swaddled in her armpit, then nuzzling into him as if she was going to gobble him up. Manu-pōkai scurried over to her baby brother and gently patted his black patch of hair. The little girl's face glowed.

'Nohi-nohi,' the toddler said quietly. *Little one.* She looked up at her mother.

The chief gazed admiringly at his wife. The dark circles under her eyes were the only hint of what she had been through. She had such a perfect face. When Kiri glanced up at her husband he was reminded of the ocean — refreshing, exciting, humbling, mysterious, sometimes terrifying, but always beautiful. Not for the first time the young chief was struck by how lucky he was to call this beauty his wife. Tāwae gently touched his palm against Kiri's upper arm and turned her to him, pressing his nose against hers for several long moments in an intimate salute. 'Taku kare-ā-roto,' he whispered. *My soulmate.*

Tāwae did not even look at his baby son until he was satisfied that his wife was in good health. The first thing he noticed when he did finally look down were tiny toes peeking from the frayed ends of the shawl. Tears of relief and joy flowed down his cheeks.

'This is the answer to our prayers,' he said in a wavering voice. Taking up the bundle, the chief inhaled the newborn's sweetness, a kind of intoxicating purity. He then studied their son for several minutes. He was dark brown, nearly black, ample-chested and, like his mother, long of limb. Tāwae could not have been happier and his huge grin said it all.

'He often kicked in my womb, you know,' Kiri remarked.

'That augurs well for us,' Tāwae replied.

'Remember the tohunga's prophecy?' Kiri asked. Tāwae's expression turned momentarily thunderous as his eyes went from their son to his wife.

'I could not forget if I tried.' He clenched his jaw as the reality of his father's murder hit him like a dagger. For a moment he pictured himself back lying among the dead at Te Maniaroa. The pain nearly made him double over, as it had thousands of times before. He would never stop grieving.

Then he gazed down once more upon his son and his expression softened. He hugged the baby to his chest, confident in the tohunga's prediction that this child would be the one by whose hand the wrongs would be righted.

'E taku tama, tēnā rā koe,' he said. 'Me tāu mahi e rūnā te ihu ō tō tātou waka ki waho ā tōna wā.' *My son, greetings to you. In time you will steer the prow of our canoe towards the open sea.* The baby gave a small gurgle. Tāwae glanced through misty eyes at his mother-in-law and his wife's attendant in the hut and in a moment of unspoken recognition they acknowledged the importance of the birth to them all.

'Nohi-nohi,' Manu-pōkai said again, pointing at her brother while looking from one parent to the other.

'Yes, yes, we haven't forgotten you, little Manu,' Tāwae said as he passed his son back to Kiri and ruffled his daughter's hair.

Again Kiri fixed her gaze on their baby with a parent's unconditional love. Despite her joy, the tohunga's prophetic words in the back of her mind made her smile fade a little. She could never forget her son's life purpose and the risks that lay ahead of him.

She tried to shut out these thoughts but not before her mind filled with images of her mother and older female relatives cutting themselves and wailing with grief. She saw again the blood flowing freely down their arms, shoulders and breasts as the razor-sharp obsidian flakes, held tightly in their hands, lacerated their flesh. Her ears rang once more with the piercing sounds of their haunting wails and sobs. Never before had she seen her mother — usually so strong and so composed — in such despair. She would not forget.

The death of her father, Tūnoa, was still raw for Kiri, despite the six years that had passed. She too had cried copious tears after Te Maniaroa, and even now the grief could still engulf her. She just needed to hear a phrase he used or catch the scent of an oil he wore and she was undone.

But now she had something to work with at last — something to nurture in pursuit of her end-goal. The thought that her son would never know either of his grandfathers steeled her resolve. She knew what she had to do.

'Husband, like you, I am ready to commit our son to his destiny so that our people can finally taste the sweetness of revenge,' she reassured her mate. 'But for now, let me be besotted with him, as you were with Manu when she arrived.' Tāwae nodded as he drew Manu up onto his lap. Kiri turned and placed the little one's head to her breast to feed.

Arakura spoke next. 'In six or seven days my grandson's umbilical cord will fall away, and just before that he will be welcomed by the people at the maioha ceremony.' She turned to address her son-in-law specifically. 'Don't forget that they will be expecting you to announce his name.'

'When did you become chief of Ngāi Haere?' Tāwae replied sarcastically. His cold stare was enough to remind her that, despite his youth, he was their rangatira and needed no instruction in protocol, least of all from his mother-in-law. Kiri broke the uncomfortable silence. She knew her husband's caring heart and his tender embrace, but others found his sharp tongue hard to take at times.

'Thank you, Mother. Tāwae and I have discussed potential names, but he has not made his choice yet.' The name of one of their deceased fathers was the obvious pick, but she did not want to get her mother's hopes up. Kiri held out her hand to her husband and said, 'The final decision is Tāwae's.'

The young chief gave a curt nod before excusing himself. 'I must go and bury my son's whenua.' Tipping Manu gently from his lap, he rose to his knees, nuzzled his son and smiled at his wife.

'Kare-ā-roto, I shall be down again soon.'

+

The tohunga conducted the burial ceremony at Kō Pā. As Tāwae trampled down the last of the fresh soil, the old man seemed to be muttering something under his breath. He still seemed ill-at-ease, so Tāwae tried engaging him in conversation.

'Every month more and more babies are born, the majority of them boys. Every second woman of child-bearing years seems to be pregnant! It seems our strategy to rebuild Ngāi Haere is going to plan.'

'Why shouldn't it?' the tohunga grumbled. 'Your rūnanga encourages it.'

'Well, it's the most pressing matter that we leaders have to deal with,' said Tāwae, a little taken aback at the older man's brusqueness. 'Since Te Maniaroa our fighting force has been vulnerable. We all know we need to grow another generation of warriors.'

Deciding perhaps a word of gratitude was due, Tāwae praised the tohunga. 'Nā tōu karakia whakahapū tamariki i whiwhi ai a Kiri ki tētahi tama,' he said. *It is because of your prayer that Kiri has given birth to a son.* 'I offer you our thanks, and I offer our thanks to your god too. We are forever grateful.'

The old man said nothing, his eyes flitting about. Tāwae was about to give up trying to engage the tohunga when he finally responded in a venomous tone.

'Nā te aha koe i haramai ai ki au?' *Why did you come to me?*

Tāwae was taken aback. Surely the tohunga had heard what all the women were saying? That other tohunga may be able to help them conceive, but it was the atua of this one that gave them the best chance of having a boy.

'Kiri kept pestering me,' Tāwae replied, which was the better part of the truth. 'One day she said she wouldn't eat again until I fetched you. So I did.' The rest of the truth was that he needed a son and welcomed any help he could get.

'He aha koe i kore ai i haere atu ki tētahi atu tangata?' the tohunga snapped. *Why didn't you go to somebody else?*

The old man's stare was piercing, and Tāwae eyeballed him back. If anyone else in the village had spoken to him this way the chief would have every right to sentence them to death. But the tohunga was considered above such rules.

Then suddenly the tohunga dropped the belligerent tone completely. 'He aituā kei au.' *Misfortune is upon me.* The old man's huge frame started to tremble. He picked up the empty wooden bowl and offered a cryptic whakataukī. 'Ka pū te ruha, ka hao te rangatahi. Kia whakaritea ngā mea katoa.' *The old net withers, while another replaces it. Balance must be restored.*

He turned on his heel and left.

Proverbs, the old people said, were the kīnaki or relish with which the words of uncommon men were consumed. The more obscure the reference the more intriguing.

Tāwae watched the old man disappear down the track.

CHAPTER FOUR

Nāku te rourou nāhau te rourou, ka ora ai te iwi.
With your basket and my basket, we will feed the people.

Envoys on foot and in canoes delivered the report of the chief's newborn son to the four neighbouring Ngāi Haere pā and beyond.

'A healthy boy! Praise be to the gods!' one man exclaimed. 'There have been too many stillbirths lately. Another one and people would have been making accusations of witchcraft.' Others nodded in agreement.

Tāwae had visited his wife and their son at the whare kōhanga several times and all the while he had been giving a great deal of thought to the infant's name. He had chosen to call their daughter Manu-pōkai because of the declaration Taniwha had made at Te Maniaroa all those years before: 'Kātahi te manu āta pōkai.' *There you lie huddled like a bevy of birds.*

At the time Kiri had approved of the name 'Bevy of Birds', as it ensured their daughter would be party to the tribe's plan for revenge.

'We can't let Manu alone carry the burden for Te Maniaroa,' Kiri told her husband as she nursed the baby. 'You must give him a name that reminds everyone about the dark shadow that Te Maniaroa casts over us. It's our son's destiny.'

'Kare-ā-roto, I often think you are more warlike than me!' Tāwae cast a wry glance in her direction.

'Well, didn't you feel as if you too were dead when you brought us the devastating news of our defeat and the slaughter of our people?'

Generally, Tāwae felt aroused by the way his wife sizzled when her anger was brewing, but this time he was consumed by his own bitter rage, which made the hairs on his forearms bristle.

'The whole village felt that way,' he replied. 'No one expected a rout.'

'And do you recall the chant of the women rebuking the war party for its defeat?'

'I doubt that anyone who was there that day could ever forget it.'

'I can see them now as plain as day,' Kiri said, staring into nothingness. 'Those who'd lost their husbands, their eyelids swollen with crying. Worst was your tipuna, Old Ue, cutting herself while her pupils rolled back until only the whites of her eyes were visible.'

'I know. I felt just as guilty as the others.'

'Sometimes, during my sleep,' Kiri's tone softened, 'in the silence of the night the name Te Maniaroa rises up to meet me, again and again, and I keep imagining the violations inflicted on our fathers. It gives me no rest.'

Tāwae was looking at her intently. She searched his face for an acknowledgement of her pain, but he was obviously dealing with his own ghosts.

'I can't even watch the kai-rākau when they train without reliving the battle in my mind,' he said as he lowered his forehead to rest on his palms. 'In my dream I am charging headlong into the fray, searching in vain for my father. I hear him, and my uncles, groaning in pain, their hands severed. They call to me, "Son, will the monsters who did this to us be disfigured as we have been disfigured? Will they be defiled as we have been defiled? And will they be consumed as we have been consumed?" I yell to them from afar, "I'll get them, I'll hurt them, I'll make them pay!" When I wake up, I feel like an impostor for saying those things. For what have I done about it?'

Since Te Maniaroa, Tāwae had used fishing as his escape, spending long hours, sometimes well into the dark night, out on the ocean.

Occasionally he found himself battling wild waves, and more than once he had wished the god of the sea would devour him once and for all.

'It is not your fault that the leadership of Ngāi Haere was thrust on you so suddenly, and so young,' Kiri said in a consoling voice. 'Right after Te Maniaroa you had neither the experience nor the kai-rākau to avenge your father's death. And since then you have had to prioritise the responsibilities of chieftainship over warrior training.'

She removed the baby from her breast and sat him up. 'Remember, Ngāi Haere have a courageous tradition. Our people will spend years — our entire lives if need be — righting the wrongs that have been done to us. Our time will come.'

Tāwae ran the back of his fingers over their son's hair. 'Yes, but we must always work towards that goal. Right now, we don't even have an army,' he replied. 'We must commit the next generation to the cause or else the spirits of our fathers will never rest.'

Kiri let out a slow breath and closed her eyes, nodding.

'As much as I don't like it,' Tāwae continued, 'I have had to accept that vengeance will not come by my hand.' With his index finger he gently lifted his son's tiny hand. 'But for my son it will be different. No man in whose veins my blood flows,' he said, 'should ever rest until the vermin have been found and killed.'

'Ko tāua tahi tēnā,' Kiri added, unflinching. *That makes two of us.*

+

The arrival of relatives from the other four Ngāi Haere pā for the maioha ceremony was eagerly anticipated. Ngāpō was a hive of activity from dawn to dusk. Tāwae organised everything with aplomb and, with the backing of the rūnanga, set out to make the ceremony an occasion to remember. His instructions were conveyed to the people by his uncle, Wehe, commander of the kai-rākau at Kō Pā.

'Are there any pā that will not be represented at the ceremony?'

'No, of course not, e Rangi,' replied Wehe sternly. 'They know that

43

would be disrespectful and we would make the offenders pay.' Wehe ran his fingers along the flat, hard surface of his patu ōnewa while eyeing its edge. 'Our numbers may have decreased and Te Maniaroa was certainly a setback, but I assure you, we are still feared by all our neighbours. Everyone knows that if you want to pick a quarrel, Whānau-a-Mate are not the people to pick it with.' He slid the stone club back into his belt.

Tāwae envied his uncle's beefy frame because it exhibited a litany of injuries: a thick cut to his neck from a stab wound that was still healing; a visible bump over the part of his collarbone that had been broken at Te Maniaroa; and several scars across his stomach, chest and back — all proud battle wounds. Around his neck he wore a string of human teeth extracted from the dried skulls of butchered enemy. In comparison, all Tāwae had was light scarring across his right eyebrow and forehead, which Kiri thought made him more handsome.

'And what about our own people?' he asked Wehe. 'How are they progressing with preparations? We both know Whānau-a-Mate must offer the best hospitality toward its visitors.'

'The people have arranged themselves into the usual working groups to complete the various tasks under those with the most experience.'

'Good! No one can afford to be idle.'

'Do you want meat for the occasion?' Wehe asked.

'Of course! Our relatives will be expecting it.' Tāwae said without hesitation.

'I could go to the people at Rātahi and demand they give us a man to eat.'

'No, it will cause less trouble if you choose one from among our pononga.'

'Leave it with me,' Wehe nodded. 'What about you, e Rangi? Have you chosen a name for your son?'

'I've been discussing the matter with the elders. Do you have some advice to offer me? I know my father always valued your opinion.'

'Your father was a true warrior. We will not see his like again.'

Whether it was Wehe's intention or not, Tāwae felt the sting of his words.

'My only advice,' Wehe continued, 'is that you follow custom and name him after a significant event, or in memory of one of our ancestors. That way you will ensure the next generation retains an awareness of the past.'

'I am keenly conscious of that.'

'You must never forget that your child is special. His name has to be full of promise, not just for Whānau-a-Mate, but for all our relatives.'

+

The chief walked among his people regularly over the next few days, offering an encouraging word here and there. The fruits of their hard work could be seen all about Ngāpō. Temporary sleeping quarters had been erected; parties of older women were making floor mats, baskets and plates from harakeke; while young girls scraped the flax leaves with mussel shells and, along with their mothers, wove garments from the remaining fibre to offer as gifts for the baby. A shell was a clumsy tool in the hands of a novice, but marvellously efficient in the deft fingers of the more experienced. The boys were collecting rubbish while their fathers chopped wood.

Knowing that they would all have a small part in raising his son, the workers cheerfully addressed the young chief as he walked past.

'Tēnā koe i tā tātau tamaiti, e Rangi.' *Greetings on the birth of our child, oh Chief.*

Out of earshot they discussed the baby's name.

'I bet it will be something to do with Te Maniaroa,' one woman suggested.

'No, their daughter has that covered,' said another.

'It will be Kū, I'm sure,' a third woman postulated. 'You watch — he'll name him after his father.'

'What about Kiri's father?' another woman said. 'Surely she'll want his name on their child.'

'It's up to him. It will be his father's name for sure. It will be Kū.'

Tāwae was eager to examine the varieties of fish that were suspended from the trees to dry. He saw hāpuku, tāmure, tarakihi, kahawai and even shark carcasses. All had been caught by the men observing the rhythms of the moon and offering up the appropriate invocation to Tangaroa, the atua of the sea.

The chief cook was overseeing a group of pononga who were busily removing the backbones, heads and tails from eels and hanging them on mānuka railings to dry. Tāwae could almost taste the sweet, succulent meat.

'Over five nights,' the cook told him, 'we've caught almost four hundred tuna, with one large hīnaki still to be emptied.' Tāwae opened the lid of the wicker basket and salivated at the sight of dozens of slimy, black, silver-bellied eels, slithering over, under and around one another.

A couple of other pā had sent supplies of taro, a starchy foodstuff reserved for important people, while others sent kete of sweet kūmara. The only delicacies missing from the menu were kererū and kākā preserved in their own fat, as it was not the season for bird-fowling.

The kīnaki or relish was to be provided by an unsuspecting pononga, and this time Wehe did the honours himself. While some of the kai-rākau watched, he silently walked up behind a female slave who was crouched over a large smooth stone making dough patties from pounded fernroot. Taking his patu from his belt, Wehe struck her swiftly across the back of her skull, the blunt force he used ensuring a sharp, clean fracture. The woman slumped forward, her lank hair soon saturated with blood.

Turning to the pononga's companions, Wehe bellowed, 'If I catch anyone else stealing from the kūmara pits you can expect the same treatment. You two, pick her up and take her to the cooking area.' The servants scurried over and collected the body. Wehe then drew alongside the three remaining pononga. The men didn't look up but pounded their fernroot harder and harder.

'No good, eh?' One of the pononga said quietly to his companions, his shaggy hair hiding his eyes, which were fixed on Wehe's feet. Wehe stood motionless for a moment, still clenching his patu.

'Ehara te kupu i te papaki mō te pononga: ahakoa hoki ia mātau, e kore ia e rongo,' he said over his shoulder to the kai-rākau. *Sometimes slaves cannot be disciplined by mere words. Though they understand, they won't respond.*

The trembling pononga before him didn't know whether he was next for the earth oven or if his master was just admiring his work. Wehe slid his patu back into his belt and walked off, just as a trail of urine made its way out from under the pononga's flax kilt.

The chief cook, a ferocious-looking character, was waiting with his own group of workers and pononga for the tohunga's two apprentices to complete their invocation over the slain body. As soon as they finished their karakia, Wehe barked instructions to the cook.

'Make sure it's not overdone like last time.'

The cook glared back at him.

Wehe and the kai-rākau watched as the two pononga laid the body on a large rock slab. *Thwack! Thwack! Thwack!* The adze did its work and the head rolled away. The dogs, which had gathered instantly at the scent of blood, began licking the severed neck. The legs and arms were chopped off at the joints and two women skilfully boned the thighs before wrapping them in leaves and placing them in a basket, which was covered to stop flies getting at them.

'E tā! *For goodness' sake!*' the cook snarled as he threw the bones to the dogs. 'Just the one, Wehe? That won't be enough.'

'It's for the visiting chiefs, not us,' Wehe fired back. 'Why don't you slaughter a couple of those kurī and cook them in the umu too?'

'Ha! Then what will keep me warm when the cold nights arrive? I need my dogs,' the cook chortled.

'A warrior can survive on water and fernroot if need be,' one of the kai-rākau chipped in. 'We're not sure about you though, Cookie — seems like you eat all the time.'

As the pononga was about to put the last limb in the basket the cook grabbed it, poked out his tongue and pretended to lick it. Then he closed his eyes and smiled to indicate extreme pleasure. The kai-rākau couldn't contain their mirth, while the other pononga kept their eyes cast down.

'The main thing is hospitality,' Wehe said. 'Making sure we have a variety of food at the feast, and more than enough to send our relatives home satisfied.'

The cook could see his workers and the pononga were handling the torso with reluctance.

'Here, I'll do it,' he growled as he nudged them aside. Wehe's men observed with interest as the cook displayed his impressive butchering techniques using an obsidian knife and long-handled adze. The torso was quartered, the entrails removed and fed to the dogs, whose powerful jaws tore at them while their bushy tails wagged wildly.

'You have an easy job,' one of the kai-rākau teased. The cook wiped perspiration from his forehead.

'This is easy work? Here, you try it.' He offered the warrior the knife and stood aside, his muscular arms decorated with sweat, blood and visceral fat. The kai-rākau seemed reluctant to take up the challenge.

'Ah . . . no thanks. Really, you're doing fine.' His mates teased him, while the cook grinned.

'Back to work, men.' Wehe clapped and the kai-rākau departed, leaving the cook's helpers washing the body parts in a stream of fresh water.

CHAPTER FIVE

Ki te kore he māramatanga, ka ngaro te iwi.
Where there is no vision, the people perish.

On the day before the maioha ceremony a carnival of scents blew in the air around Ngāpō while threads of light came from the sky. Shouts from Kō Pā could be heard resounding right across the basin below as visitors from the various Ngāi Haere pā, all heavily laden with provisions, drew closer to Ngāpō. No sooner had one group of visitors wound its way down through the hills than another arrived by way of the beach. The population of the little village swelled quickly.

Each arrival party was greeted by a cacophonous yowling from the local dogs. The elders' commands were ineffective in stilling the clamour, so a group of boys had to be continually despatched to chase the pack of canines away. Even then, a few of them kept managing to steal back to nip at the visitors' heels before being herded off again, their bushy tails between their short legs.

As each group of visitors appeared, twenty or so sturdy men, all kai-rākau, lined up and sallied out as a formal greeting party, weapons in hand. The warriors were naked save for their penis cords. These strings, which were fastened to their harakeke-plaited belts, were tied in such a way as to keep the foreskin covering the glans of the penis, the only part of the body the warriors were assiduous about concealing.

The kai-rākau chanted and roared as loudly as their lungs would allow. Most of them were around six feet in stature, brawny, and altogether impressive specimens of fighting men. They followed their haka by rushing forward and saluting their guests with hongi.

At the village entrance a group of Whānau-a-Mate women were talking excitedly. When their turn came to greet the visitors they waved mats, branches of greenery and seaweed while issuing, again at deafening volume, the formal karanga.

'Haere mai! Haere mai!' *Welcome! Welcome!*

The kai-rākau formed a thoroughfare, channelling the visitors towards the front of the whare puni where Tāwae was waiting to receive them. His relatives sat around the young chief in such a way that Tāwae was immediately distinguishable as the highest-ranking person in the village.

After formal speeches, the visitors took turns, each bending towards Tāwae and pressing noses for a few seconds, repeating the phrase, 'Tēnā koe, e Rangi'. *Greetings, oh Chief.* Then they enjoyed a light meal before settling into their quarters for the night.

+

The next morning the village was astir as everyone began to prepare themselves for the great day. Men, women and youths alike fixed their hair, put on their neck and ear ornaments, clothes and feathers and plastered themselves with kōkōwai. This red-brown ochre was liberally pasted all over their heads and bodies. The fishy odour of whale and shark oil, with which they groomed their hair, pervaded every hut and house.

Outside the village the cooks and their pononga moved busily to and fro, carrying vast amounts of food to where the grand feast was to be held. Aromas from the umu and cooking shelters permeated the air.

When Kiri stepped outside the whare kōhanga with her baby she was confronted by a great throng of people, most seated on the ground, some crouching, others standing. For a moment she fought an impulse to retreat inside, but Tāwae took her elbow and gently motioned her to sit beside him. About three hundred had gathered outside the whare kōhanga. Tāwae and Kiri remained on the porch facing the crowd, their infant son asleep on Kiri's lap. Alongside were her mother Arakura and the tapuhi. Next to Tāwae on the other side sat his grey-haired grandmother, Old Ue, her face and arms, the only parts visible outside her kaitaka, a hideous spectacle of thick scars. She was cuddling little Manu-pōkai. Old Ue kept to herself these days, never the same, people thought, after losing her sons. The horror of that event for her remained unspoken, her anguish sealed behind her closed lips.

The maioha ceremony was a serious affair in which an infant was officially welcomed out of the womb and into the world. It began with both sets of relatives emerging from the crush of people and laying their gifts on the ground in front of the kōhanga.

A couple from Kauae-nui, the furthest pā, were particularly interested in the newborn because their own babies, born a year apart, were both girls. The husband, Tūterangi, son of Wera, had gone out of his way to gather tāwhara, the sweet-tasting flower bracts of the kiekie, from the bush below the mountains in order to make fermented juice to give to the parents of the newborn. It was a real treat. Too much of it gave even the most solid of men wobbly legs, and some couples sought it for intimate occasions.

They laid six calabashes before the kōhanga, and Tāwae acknowledged it by quoting an old saying, 'He whā tāwhara ki uta, he hiko tāmure ki tai.' *The tangy taste of the kiekie fruit on land, the salty flesh of the snapper at sea.* These words, uttered to acknowledge the quality of the gift, served also as a reminder to all those gathered that, despite his youth, the chief had been for many years educated in the traditional knowledge of the tribe.

'Destiny is an unexplained force that no one can fathom,' the visiting father replied.

Tāwae wondered what he meant, though he was careful not to

show this in his response. Kiri smiled at the young mother standing at Tūterangi's side, whom she recognised as her cousin Poka, then went back to looking at the son in her lap.

'Your cousin and her husband are up to something,' Tāwae whispered to Kiri. 'Any man who can make fermented tāwhara juice last this long after the fruiting season, only to give it away, either has the highest esteem for our son, or he has an ulterior motive.' Kiri raised her chin to get a better look at the six tahā on the ground before them.

Te Ūneke, son of Te Tau and Tāwae's cousin, stood and welcomed everyone. He was a pū kōrero, a powerful orator, and was always asked to speak at important occasions. The village was perfectly silent as he addressed Tāwae and Kiri, then directed a greeting to the infant.

'Nau mai, e tama! *Welcome, boy!* 'Kia mihi atu au. I haramai rā koe i te kunenga mai o te tangata i roto i te āhuru mōwai.' *I greet you! You have come from the origin of mankind, from the cosy haven.*

One of Kiri's grandfathers, Roro, stood up to respond on behalf of her relatives, some fifty of them, who had walked from their pā in the Waiapu Valley, a half-day's distance. He unfurled his cloak as he stood. Wearing only a rāpaki or kilt, with deeply etched moko on his face, lower torso and thighs, he was a wiry man who bore the scars of many battles. His eyes were red and fierce like the eyes of one who has stared into a fire all night long.

Roro was not interested in matching Te Ūneke's poetic oratory. Rather, he was intent on reminding the gathering of the significance of his great-grandson's birth. The grey-haired chief brandished a patu parāoa and pranced about with the agility of a man half his age, grimacing and gesticulating. After greeting his neighbours, he pointed the whale-bone club at his granddaughter.

'Kiri, it is only right that we congratulate you and Tāwae on the birth of your son. May your child be healthy, and may he grow up to be a great warrior.' He paused, his hand quivering while holding the patu outstretched, and he turned in a complete circle. The tone of his address then became somewhat melodramatic.

'Six winters have passed since Te Maniaroa. At that great battle with the dreaded Aitanga Nui I lost two sons, one being Kiri's father. I recall the day we brought the terrible news back to you all as if it was yesterday. Some of you wanted to assault us, so distraught were you. Others tried to hang themselves, but we stopped them.'

Each time Roro emphasised a point, he dropped into a low fighting stance and raised the patu parāoa above his head.

'There sits your cousin Kūharu, son of Pakupaku, whose brother never returned.' He shot out his hand towards a thickset young man who was sitting between two women while two children bobbed up and down behind him. All eyes fixed on the young man, whose face started to flush.

'He was one of those who were very angry, and rightly so. To his credit, he has taken to wife his brother's widow and is raising his nephews to avenge their father's death.' The elders nodded in agreement while the young man sat a little taller and puffed out his chest a fraction.

'And consider me, an old man upon whom the sun is setting. When I had to break the news to my daughters-in-law,' he said, indicating Arakura and then Rākai, the woman sitting next to his cloak with a sleeping baby in a harakeke sling on her back, 'I had no living son to offer either of them. They wept vehemently and Rākai, through her copious tears and fury, told me, "It is a fortunate thing that it should chance to be you who comes to tell me of my husband's death, for I now propose that you take me for yourself."' He looked around for encouragement and the elders murmured their approval.

'Tāwae, as you are aware, we also now have a son, Te Ika, and I expect that he, along with your son, will one day severely punish the Aitanga Nui so that our grieving may cease. Let none of us rest until this has been achieved, no matter how long it takes.'

A murmur washed through the crowd. Then, like a man possessed, Roro finished by thrusting his clenched fist into the air, gnashing his teeth and shouting four times, each time facing a different direction, 'Mā tātou te rā apōpō!' *Tomorrow will be ours!*

His challenge seemed to charge the atmosphere. Young men who had not yet tasted battle nudged one another and whispered their hopes for the part they would play in the tribe's future victory. Tāwae and Kiri signalled their approval as Roro resumed his place.

Then the great warrior chief Tū, Arakura's aged father, indicated he wished to speak. He and his people had come by sea from the mighty Ōkau Pā, the fortress to which Tāwae had fled after the battle at Te Maniaroa. In times of war the patriarch had held sway over the whole region from Ōkau to Ngāpō. Draped in a paepaeroa, one of the finest dress cloaks, the old man did not stand. He didn't need to. Age was respected, achievement was esteemed. Old Tū had them both in spades. He raised his hand and a hushed silence fell over the gathering.

'I have commanded three generations of our tribe in battle, including many of you,' he said as he stroked his white beard and stared at the ground in front of him. 'I have seen them all in my lifetime, from the incomparably brave whose expertise in weapon handling was unrivalled, to the arrogant, self-asserting braggarts whose recklessness led to their untimely deaths.'

The old chief looked war weary; rumour had it that he had given control of his fighting force to his surviving sons. He slowly raised his head and glowered at the gathering. 'I too had a son killed in the fighting and almost lost another.' Many young men dropped their eyes to avoid his stare. But when he began speaking again, the stern look had been replaced by a menacing smile.

In a clear, dispassionate voice he told the people: 'It was at my request that your fathers took part in the battle at Te Maniaroa. After his triumph, Ringa-mutu, chief of the Aitanga Nui, did not go directly home, but instead came to my pā at Ōkau bearing the corpse of my son. I was overcome with grief and asked him, "Why did you slay our youngest?" Perhaps to mollify a grieving father he apologised, and reasoned with me, "How can one avoid striking the bird that flies across the bow of a canoe?"'

'He could see I was not satisfied with his answer, so he said, "Well then, I'll see that someone is slain in return for the loss. After I return home you may follow me. On the way you will find one of my sons along the coast. He lives alone and is content to spend his time fishing. Him you may kill to comfort you for the loss of your son. Then I shall also mourn with you.'"

'In a further gesture of recompense, Ringa-mutu invited me to fight the warriors from his own pā. He promised he would order them out into the open and would absent himself from the fighting. Both of us knew that battles are won or lost depending on leadership, and without his involvement, victory would almost certainly be ours.'

'I took an armed contingent by sea. On the way we found his son fishing, just as he said. We killed him, cooked and ate him. When we reached Ringa-mutu's pā all his fighting men came outside as promised. Ringa-mutu stood in the gateway and raised his hands to signal to me that he was about to withdraw. We were victorious and the Aitanga Nui were left to mourn their losses. So, you see, I have had my revenge for the loss of my youngest son. Did we not also avenge your fathers then? Is my newest descendant to be burdened with our insatiable desire for retribution? That was my fate from birth and I can assure you it is a heavy yoke to place on anyone.'

Tū said nothing more and the gathering was silent.

One of the tohunga's apprentices, attending in his teacher's absence due to the old tohunga having taken ill, eventually broke the silence when he took centre stage and recited an incantation over the infant. This apprentice was known simply as Parakore because he always appeared immaculate in his dress. When he was full of his atua his speeches could hold the attention of everyone.

During his training, Parakore had learned the various tikanga or customs of the tribe; his role was to guide and protect the people from unwelcome spiritual forces. His companion, Kaiora, specialised in consulting the dead. It was said that Kaiora could conjure up the spirit of a deceased relative, who would speak through him. Both apprentices appeared normal until they were possessed by their atua. Of the two, Kaiora, like his teacher, was more greatly feared. He was athletic but his unattractive face conveyed cunning and ferocity.

Parakore finished with some stirring passage of address to the gathering, which he seemed proud to deliver. He paused before calling for the baby's name to be made public.

Then it was Tāwae's turn, and the crowd waited expectantly. One child cried but was hushed by its mother. Kiri leaned forward to ensure she missed nothing.

The young chief began with a riddle. 'E whānau rānei te iwi i te wā kōtahi?' *Can a tribe be born all at once?* The people mulled over his meaning.

'At Te Maniaroa, when I saw that my father and uncles were dead, I was so distraught that I no longer valued life. When I learned that their bodies had been eaten, I felt there was nothing left for me in this world and I was ready for the next. But you, our elders, counselled moderation. "No," you all said. "Let us live, that we might avenge these atrocities in time."'

He glanced at Kiri. 'We have deliberately bred for that purpose and now Kiri and I have our son.'

With a steely countenance Tāwae turned to face Old Tū. 'E Koro,' he said to him, 'kua ea te wāhanga ki a koe, ko te wāhanga kei a mātou kei te toe.' *O Elder, while your loss has been appeased, ours has not.*

Tāwae looked around the gathering, paused, then made the announcement everyone had been waiting to hear.

'Our son's name shall be a reminder to him, and to all his generation, that it will be by their hands that our tribe shall be avenged.' He reached down and Kiri passed the sleeping infant to him. Holding his son aloft, he declared the name aloud so that even the cooks and pononga in the village might hear:

Ka tapaia te ingoa ko te Kaitanga
i te rongonga atu i te kainga
e te Aitanga Nui
ngā kurī paakā a Ue.

His name is 'the eating'
to mark the day that we heard
the Aitanga Nui had consumed
the brown dogs of Ue.

Old Ue averted her eyes and frowned at the mention of her name.

'Kia whakairo rawatia te tikanga o tēnei ingoa ki tōna wairua mo ake tonu atu,' Tāwae declared. *Let the meaning of this name be seared deep into his soul forever.* At that moment the infant let out a squawk as he awoke.

The assembly responded, 'Āe, āe, āe!' *Yes, yes, yes!*

Tāwae glanced back at Kiri, whose body had slumped against the wall of the kōhanga. She was beaming.

Parakore resumed his incantation, invoking further goodwill upon the infant's physical and spiritual welfare, before extolling: 'May this name, Kaitanga, one day be feared among tribes!'

The people responded: 'Eke, eke pēnu, haumi e, hui e, tāiki e!' *Let us surmount the waves, clearing their crests, we command it be so!*

This was the signal to everyone that they were free to come forward, cast their eyes over Kaitanga and greet the parents.

Tāwae and Kiri exchanged a look of satisfaction. Kiri soon confirmed from her cousin Poka that the couple hoped one day that Kaitanga might be matched with one of their daughters. Of all the talk, though, it was what Parakore said to Tāwae that he later remembered most clearly.

'He aha oti tō tātou ora?' *What is our life?* 'We are like the snow,' he proffered, pointing to the mountains. 'Here one season and gone the next. We do not know what will happen tomorrow. The gods decide our fate. They have decided my teacher's, and they will decide your son's.'

CHAPTER SIX

Ka mate kāinga tahi, ka ora kāinga rua.
When one house dies, a second lives.

Winter in Ngāpō could be especially tough, but in the limestone caves on the hills above the village it was only tolerable so long as a healthy fire was maintained. The old tohunga had removed himself to one of the caves when his health had waned, wanting to be near the shaft where the bones of his teacher had been laid to rest.

Lying on his side on a thick bed of ferns, moss and mats, the tohunga seemed oblivious to the howling of the wind and the thrashing of the trees, despite the best efforts of each to permeate the silence of the cave. The old man's weary eyes were fixed on the dancing shadows and the thin trail of water that seeped down the cold stone wall before disappearing into the dirt. He had long ago stopped eating and the only sustenance that passed his lips was the bitter kawakawa juice, which his wife forced him to swallow.

In the fire's flickering light his two apprentices did their best to keep their master warm. At first, Parakore and Kaiora had assiduously visited to bring firewood to the cave, but in the past few days the tohunga and his wife had become so dependent on them that the two men had stayed there. They placed yet another woven garment around the old man's emaciated frame.

The three of them sat silently at the tohunga's side. It would not be long now.

Out of the night a figure appeared at the entrance to the cave. It was Tāwae, water dripping from his raincape. He was holding a fire torch, his hand cupped over it to shield it from the storm. All day the tohunga had been saying he wanted to see the young chief, so a message had been sent to Kō Pā.

'Kei te aha a ia?' Tāwae asked. *How is he?*

'Kei te ngāngā tonu,' replied Kaiora, observing the young chief out of the corner of his eye. *He's still alive.*

'Tāpara kē ahau i nāianei.' *I should hope so too.*

Tāwae removed his cape and shook off the water. The apprentices moved aside to allow him to greet the kuia who crouched at her husband's side.

Tāwae's fingers gave the tohunga's hand the faintest touch, which made the old man's head lurch sharply, like a dog that had suddenly sensed prey. Then, without any apparent effort he sat up, his eyes staring intently straight ahead, his teeth bared and his jaw locked.

'Nāhau i tono mai a ia i ngā atua. He utu kei te toe.' *You had him called forth from the gods. There will be a price to pay.* His voice was unearthly. 'When he sees Mahuru for the twelfth time . . .'

A startled Tāwae knew he was looking at a spirit in the tohunga's eyes and the chief felt a sudden powerlessness come over him. He silently pleaded with the tohunga's atua to allow no harm to come to his son.

'When he sees his twelfth Mahuru then shall his star begin to rise, and then will his parents' stars begin to wane.' Tāwae's blood ran cold. He was still mentally pleading for his son when the tohunga shrieked, 'Kia tūpato, Tāwae! *Be careful, Tawae.* Be wary of bartering with Whiro, the lord of darkness. Man should not voice his opinion in the presence of an atua.'

Then, as suddenly as he had roused, the tohunga lay down and lapsed back into sleep.

Tāwae left abruptly, rattled, and knowing that the tohunga was not human that night.

+

In the stillness of the night the tohunga laboured to breathe. The kuia rubbed his back with some oil concocted from kānuka leaves. The soothing effect brought some relief, though never for long.

'Kei te pōhiri mai ngā tīpuna,' he whispered. *The ancestors are beckoning me.* Then he began to call the names of relatives who had been dead for many years.

His time had come. The domain of the ancestors was thinly screened from those alive. From the time a man was born he was progressively moving closer and closer to his ancestors.

The tohunga's voice became so weak it was almost inaudible. With great effort he reached out to his wife and gripped her hand. 'That . . . that boy has killed me.'

His wife started sobbing, burying her face in his dogskin cloak. He reached up and touched her cheek softly and for a moment she managed to compose herself. Through glassy eyes she gazed into his, but soon enough he started nodding his head again and mumbling.

Just before the tohunga finally succumbed he said, 'Te reka o te kiko tangata.' *How sweet is the flesh of man.*

The apprentices, who were stoking the fire, heard it. They turned to see their teacher's eyes fixed on the roof of the cave; his mouth hung open.

The kuia disappeared into the night. Later, when they enquired down in the village, no one knew where she had gone.

+

Tāwae was reclining on the porch of their house against one of its carved slabs, watching storm clouds gather in the silver-black sky.

The mountains in the distance, which only moments earlier had stood majestic and white, now hid their heads.

'Kua hinga te tōtara o te wao nui a Tāne,' were the words the messenger had used to convey the news to Tāwae. *A great tōtara in the forest of Tāne has fallen.*

The chief exchanged a wide-eyed stare with Kiri before dismissing the runner.

The previous night Manu-pōkai had woken them both with a scream. They found her sitting bolt upright, staring into the darkness. When Tāwae asked the three-year-old what had frightened her, little Manu described what could only be explained as an apparition of the tohunga, seated in the corner of their house with a veil over his face. She said he was pointing at her little brother.

Tāwae kicked the wall of the porch and his foot almost went through the thatching.

'What is it?' Kiri asked.

'The old man has been lingering for many moons. He had convinced himself that he would die.'

'He whakamomori?' *A self-inflicted death?*

'Yes, it seems so, although he would say it was his atua.' The two gazed at Kaitanga on the mat in front of them. The baby held up his head briefly and began to push up with his arms before rolling himself onto his back.

Tāwae frowned. 'Do you recall how he said he would not see our second son?'

Kiri nodded. 'I wonder how he knew these things.'

'I once asked him that.'

'What did he say?'

Tāwae reached over and placed a hand on his wife's, giving it a light squeeze. 'That he was simply a medium, and that his ability to tell the future did not spring from him. "Man alone," he said, "has no power to see these things."'

'And what did he mean when he said Kaitanga would be both hero and rogue?'

'I don't know. Last night his atua told me our influence would wane once our son came into his destiny. I admit it did not please me to hear that. I suppose we'll have to wait and see.'

+

The next day some fishermen found the broken body of the tohunga's wife near Ahu Point, sprawled on the rocks. The woven rope and damaged shrubs on the high cliff face above were a sure sign that she had tried to hang herself but must have slipped on the muddy track during the storm. At the couple's joint funeral, Parakore explained that the kuia had honoured the promise she had made to her husband: 'Haere koe i tai o te ata, mō tai o te ahiahi au e whanatu ai.' *You go on the morning tide and I will follow on the evening tide.* In death, her spirit would accompany his into the next world.

+

Since the birth of Kaitanga, who became known affectionately as 'Kai', Kiri had been anxious that Tāwae might look for a second wife, as chiefs were often known to do. One afternoon, while sheltering from the rain at the foot of Kō Pā, Kiri raised the matter with her mother.

'Your father didn't wait long before he was seeking nuptial bliss again,' Arakura replied scornfully. 'You were only a month old when he first took my twin sister.'

'What? Did Aunty agree?'

'Ha!' Arakura sneered. 'It wouldn't have mattered — it wasn't up to her. But I think she had her eyes on your father from the time he and I were betrothed.'

'Really, Mother!' Kiri blushed.

Just then the rain became deafening, stalling the conversation. The nearby Ngāpō Stream was rushing so loudly the two women could only stand and watch as the huge raindrops exploded on the ground around them. When the downpour finally diminished, mother and daughter waded through the icy water towards the village.

'You shouldn't be surprised,' Arakura started up again. 'You know your grandfathers had three wives each. Best you get through nursing my grandson so you can make yourself available to your husband again.'

For the rest of that day Kiri was plagued with jealous thoughts of another woman joining their household. She needed a plan, so that night she said to Tāwae, 'You need to make a pakokori for our son.'

A playpen would help him learn to stand and walk, and his walking would mark the end of the nursing period.

On the next fine day Tāwae constructed the playpen in the courtyard outside their house. Kiri watched him cut four lengths of kareao or supplejack and ram the ends into the ground, bending each one over to form an arch. Then he curved a length of the tough but pliant akapirita creeper into a circle, which he suspended from the four arches at a height that would allow Kai's armpits to rest on when the infant stood. Finally, he padded this circular top piece with soft flax fibre.

Each day Kiri placed Kai inside the playpen and encouraged him to stand up, supported by the circular akapirita. If he cried, she sat next to the pakokori and fed him while he was standing.

'Don't cry, my son,' she told him. 'This playpen is going to help strengthen your legs and body.' Meantime, his grandmother, along with her twin sister Whakaata, massaged the infant's limbs and softened his skin with kawakawa oil.

'Kia miria ngā waewae o taku mokopuna hei whai i a Whiwhi-rangi,' she said. *I'm rubbing my grandchild's legs so that he may pursue Whiwhi-rangi*. And there it was, the name that would accompany Kai throughout his life, uttered for the first time in the presence of the infant. Although it would mean nothing to him for many years yet, he would soon enough learn to recognise the name of Taniwha's son.

While they were rubbing, Arakura and Whakaata began singing to little Kai. It was a song linking the little boy to the aristocratic lines of Ngāi Haere by naming various points along the coastline where noted members of the tribe had lived.

'Why are you singing that?' Kiri asked her mother. 'He won't understand all those names. He hasn't even uttered his first word yet.' But then Kiri found herself joining in, reciting some of the words, although she could not recall ever having learned this lullaby.

Her aunty smiled. 'Āe e Kiri, i waiatatia i a koe e pēpi tonu ana.' *Yes, Kiri, we sang it to you when you were a babe too.*

The power of memory, Kiri mused. She decided she would compose her own song to Kai about his grandfathers. She began walking him up to Kai-namu-namu every day, chanting it to him. At the summit she would point to the north and tell her son, 'I patua ō tīpuna ki reira. Nā Te Aitanga Nui i patu.' *That's where your grandfathers were killed. The Aitanga Nui killed them.*

She also sang when Kai lay in his pō-rakaraka. Attaching a piece of bush creeper to the cradle and tying the other end to her big toe, she gently swung her son while she wove a mat. Kiri soon found that the defiant lyrics of the kaioraora eased her own mind.

+

It was almost the end of Takurua, the cold season, when the weather was no longer so violent and changeable. Tāwae welcomed the warmer mornings.

He could hear Kiri singing outside so he went out and sat under the matai tree beside her. She had just brought up Kai's wind after feeding him, so Tāwae took him from her and laid him in his pō-rakaraka. As he rocked the cradle, the chief breathed in the aromatic scent of matai resin. Kai, who had been staring up at a solitary cloud in the sky, slowly closed his eyes. Kiri carried on quietly chanting her kaioraora as she leaned back against the trunk of the tree. Tāwae listened carefully to the words for the first time.

'That's an impressive composition,' he said as he shuffled closer to her.

'Thank you.' She stroked his arm with her fingers and smiled. 'When our son is older, I expect he will want to know what it means.'

'No doubt. When the student is ready, the teacher always appears.'

Kiri lay her head on her husband's shoulder. 'Do you want to know something mysterious?'

'What's that, Kare-ā-roto?' He continued to rock the pō-rakaraka.

'Every time I start chanting my kaioraora, our son always goes quiet.'

'Maybe he thinks it's a signal for sleep.'

'No, I feel sure he knows something of what it means.'

She gazed at the distant mountain. 'Have you noticed that Hikurangi has begun to shed its garments?' She took hold of Tāwae's hand and placed his palm against her stomach. 'Winter will soon be over and our babies will be with us for Mahuru, all three of them.'

Tāwae had glanced at the snow-capped peaks when he suddenly realised what she was telling him. He stared at her for confirmation.

'Yes, my darling.'

Tāwae sprang to his feet, shouting at the top of his lungs.

'Shush! You'll wake the baby!' Kiri scolded him, though she was grinning as broadly as he was. Surely Tāwae would not look for another wife now, not while he had such a fertile woman at his side who loved him as much as she did.

CHAPTER SEVEN

He waka eke noa.
We are all in this canoe together.

The day Kai's baby brother was born was a beautiful one. Scented flowers had sprung forth along the banks of Ngāpō Stream and among the trees, which had donned their best lush green hues. The sky glowed bright blue and the sun was a carnival of dazzling yellow. It was no wonder his parents called the baby boy Te Wī-o-te-rangi, after the heavens.

His brother's name proved too much of a mouthful for the toddler, so Kai simply called him Tui, and the name stuck. Two-year-old Kai and four-year-old Manu loved their baby brother from the moment they set eyes on him, touching his little fingers and toes and marvelling at the smallness of his eyes, mouth and ears. Kai was instinctively protective of his little brother, right from the start.

One day, Kiri took her three children down to the grass verge above the beach, where they played in the sun. As Tui lay in Kiri's lap, Kai watched his mother pressing on the baby's head. When Kiri began pinching Tui's wide nose and stretching his full lips he began to grizzle. Kai wobbled over to them, taking a few spills on the way. When Tui let out a shriek Kai slapped his mother in the face. It caught her off guard and although she knew he was too young to understand, she explained herself anyway.

'Māmā did the same thing to you when you were nursing, and now look at you! You are a handsome boy.' Tāwae, who was lying with Manu and had been watching the scene, appeared amused.

'He's a feisty one, that Kai,' he said to his wife. 'If his little brother shows half his aggression, they'll make a formidable team.'

At that moment two teenage girls from a neighbouring pā appeared walking along the foreshore, their heads down as they whispered to each other. They looked up as they passed and Kiri waved to them.

'Do you remember I told you about a young woman, the daughter of one of our fishermen, who strangled her newborn?' Kiri asked as she began pinching Tui's nose again.

'I do,' said Tāwae as he fell onto his back with the children crawling over him, squealing. 'What about it?'

'Well, that's her. The shorter one.' She nodded in the direction of the girls. 'Apparently she did it because she believed the rūnanga was only interested in male babies.'

'Really?' Tāwae craned his neck to see who she was talking about. 'What made her think that?'

'You know everyone wants boys. Every young woman is giving gifts to Parakore in the hope that he will influence the atua to give them a boy. We invoked the old tohunga to do the same.'

'It's true we need to rebuild the kai-rākau, but we'd be a bit stuck with no girls!' said Tāwae.

'I know,' said Kiri. 'I told her when I saw her, "We need females too, you know!" But then her friend said she wished her own mother had killed her when she was born. "Why should my baby end up a servant to her husband's wives?" she said. "To be beaten by them, and to be made to wallow in misery?" I should have had her punished for her insolence but I admit I felt sorry for her. I understand her position. And later I found out that that girl had drowned her own infant daughter too.'

Tāwae got up on his knees, with Manu at his hip and Kai clinging to his neck.

'How can a mother forget the baby at her breast?' he asked as he swung Kai around onto his back. His son yelped with delight.

'The mother who truly loves her child would never destroy it,' Kiri said as she looked adoringly at Tui, 'but there are others who value their own lives above all else.'

Tāwae stopped playing with the children, sat back on his heels and stared at his wife.

'I've heard it's very common among the pononga,' Kiri continued. 'Even those who have been taken to wife by some of our men. I heard of one who put her hand over her baby girl's mouth until life left her. She said the child could only expect a life of tilling ground, then as soon as she finished her first menstruation she would be given to an older man, become pregnant, and the cycle would begin again.'

'And what do you think?'

'Well, you can see her point. Hasn't this always been our practice?'

'What do you mean?'

'Many husbands have no respect for their pregnant wives. They continue to heap all the heavy work upon them — carrying firewood, preparing food and all the other burdens. Then when the baby is stillborn they blame it on the tohunga and his witchcraft.'

'Kare-ā-roto, you and I must do all we can to remind our men,' Tāwae replied. 'Women are as important as our land. What's the proverb? He wahine, he whenua, e ngaro ai te tangata. For these two things, men will give their lives.'

+

It was only one more lunar month before Kai could wander about the pā unassisted. Arakura and Whakaata shared the task of tending to the toddler during the day, just as they had done with Manu. Until this point, Tāwae and Kiri had denied their son nothing, so it was time for his grandmother and great-aunt to take him into their care, for he was becoming stubborn and a little spoiled.

For the rest of the summer the two sisters kept a close eye on the boy, who was inclined to ignore instructions and wander off. He was mischievous by nature, which often got him into trouble, especially when he was around fire. He had already been burnt on the legs, but thanks to a māhoe poultice his grandmother made he bore no scars.

The sisters allowed Kai to play naked, even in the cold. When Kiri expressed concern, her mother put her in her place.

'Don't you remember your own upbringing, girl? You and all the other young children in the village ran around naked, all year round. That's why you're so hardy — one of the qualities that made you so attractive to your husband.'

If Kai cried when he wanted to go outside and was told he could not, his great-aunt Whakaata smacked him on the bottom with a mānuka branch.

'You can't keep throwing tantrums just because you aren't getting your way,' she cautioned him. 'One day you will lead. Do you want others to follow your example?' Kai frowned and quietened his sobs, even though he didn't yet understand her words.

Tāwae took his son away sometimes to teach him some of the things his father had taught him. He often talked about the ocean, which was clearly visible from the pā.

'Beyond the horizon, my son, are Hawaiki Nui, Hawaiki Roa and Hawaiki Pāmamao, the various islands from where our tīpuna set sail for this land.' Then, with the boy swaddled in an aute shawl on his back, he would recite their kāwai rangatira, *chiefly lineage*, from the original wayfinders.

Tāwae hung Kai's greenstone pendant from the thatched roof. In the early mornings, as they lay under the warmth of blankets, the little boy's eyes would fix on it. His fingers explored it while Tāwae recited the names of the various insects that appeared out of the thatching. In time Kai began mimicking his father: 'Arā a pūngā-were, arā a pā-papa, arā kē a rō,' he said, waiting for his father's praise, which was always forthcoming. *There's spider, there's beetle, there's stick insect.*

Kai's early years and the times spent alone with his father were happy ones. He knew his father loved him dearly, which brought him deep contentment and security; he recalled this period distinctly until the end of his life. He remembered sleeping among his parents and siblings, listening to his father's stories, and falling asleep to his recitations. He even remembered his father's warnings about omens and he always took them seriously.

'Take note of spider, my boy. For if ever she comes down on her web line, it's a warning that this house will be either burned or deserted before long.'

+

As the children grew, their play area spread beyond the confines of the pā. Most of their days were spent down at the village, in the bush, along the stream or near the beach. They joined the other local children, swarming in and out of the raupō huts and along the paths that wound through the village.

By Kai's fifth autumn, when Tui was three and Manu-pōkai was seven, all three were a regular sight at the bushline, frolicking in the water, playing on the sand or climbing trees under the watchful eyes of Arakura and other kuia. The children brought delight and much comfort to Tāwae and Kiri. So much so that at times the chief and his wife almost forgot the purpose for which their children had been brought into the world.

It rained most mornings now — it always did in autumn — and the children stayed closer to home. Sometimes on wet days Arakura and the other grandmothers would usher them into the dimly lit whare tapere. This house of recreation was uncarved and looked like an ordinary house, except it was much larger with two central fires.

They would duck outside to play games between showers. String games, using flax fibres, were among their favourites. Kai and his sister often teamed up to play. Manu tied a cord together and placed it around Kai's hands as he stood with his arms upright. Standing opposite him she did the same, and by twisting and turning their fingers and wrists between them they created wonderful shapes that, in their minds, represented houses, canoes or people. Children from the village challenged one another to create increasingly complex shapes.

Tui wanted to play too, of course, but the older children ignored him because he was too young. Once, when some of the boys pushed him away, he fell on his bottom, crying. Manu was quick to confront the offenders, while Kai consoled his little brother.

Although outnumbered three to one, Manu settled her opponents with ease. She had always been the more easily riled of her siblings, although Kai wasn't far behind. From the day her brother was born, Manu had sensed she was now in second place in her parents' eyes, and it was as if she had been furious with the world ever since. She rebelled against domesticity, refusing to do particular tasks just because she was a girl.

After she had chased the other boys off, Manu turned to Tui. 'Stop being a tangi-weto *cry-baby*.' Tui stopped snivelling and wiped his tears.

'Leave him alone,' said Kai. 'He's all right.'

'And you're not much better,' Manu snapped. 'Lucky you have your tough sister around to save you both.'

Kai glared at his sister. Next time he would show her.

+

Old Ue was usually to be found in a corner of the whare tapere plaiting flax baskets. Since their deaths at Te Maniaroa she had never spoken of her husband, nor the sons she bore him. In fact she had never again uttered a word to anyone. Their deaths had transformed her into a mute and wizened old woman.

'There goes poor Old Ue,' people lamented when she passed by. 'Her life has lost all meaning and she is just waiting to die.' But Old

Ue never lost her love of children, and whenever rain forced the children into the whare tapere for shelter, her eyes lit up and she was transformed. The children always ran to her for hugs.

On one particularly wet day, the nannies ushered the children inside, issued each one with a small flax mat and settled them in front of the fire. The rain drummed against the roof so heavily that the sound blurred into one long whirring noise. As soon as it diminished, some of the children said eagerly, 'Meatia mai tāhau pūrākau, e Kui?' *Can you tell us one of your legends, Nanny?*

'All right then,' said Arakura. 'When you are all quiet, Nanny Ue and I will tell a story.'

Silence descended over the group. 'We will tell the story of your tipuna Māui and his great fish.' Old Ue waved to Kai and signalled him to come to her. She always had a big smile for Kai that exposed her four remaining teeth and he in turn always wanted to cuddle up to her during storytime, with Tui never far behind.

Arakura's raspy voice softened and her eyes widened as she fell into the rhythm of the story.

'One day Māui joined his elder brothers on a fishing expedition,' she said, and turned to look at Old Ue. The kuia's bent frame leaned forward between her two mokopuna and her bony, toil-worn hands mimicked a paddling action.

'When they reached the first fishing ground the brothers said, "Hei konei tātou." *We are here.* But Māui encouraged them to paddle further. When the water turned blue-black, he called out, "Tukua te punga." *Drop the anchor.* Then Māui took the jawbone of his tipuna and tied it on to his fishing line.'

The children all stared in awed silence.

'Māui then struck his nose, smeared blood on the jawbone, recited a charm and let his line down. Soon an enormous fish went for the bait. It was too strong to reel in and it spun the canoe around in the swirling water.' Old Ue was quite animated now, moving this way and that in the capsizing canoe. The children's mouths hung open.

'Māui's brothers cried out in fear!' Arakura raised her voice. '"Release it, Māui! Tukua atu tō ika, koi mate tātou katoa!"' *Let your fish go or we will all be killed!*

'Instead, Māui brought about another charm, compelling the fish to the surface. And as the great fish emerged,' Arakura declared, 'their waka came to rest upon it.'

Old Ue slumped forward as if she had fainted and all the children drew back to look at her in fright. There was a moment of silence before she sprang upright again. Even though they knew to expect it, having seen this trick before many times, the children all still jumped with fright before dissolving into relieved laughter.

'This land we live on, Te Ika-a-Māui, is the fish our ancestor caught,' Arakura concluded, before asking the question she always asked the children: 'And how do we know this story is true?' They all chimed in together: 'Kei runga o Hikurangi tōna waka!' *Because Māui's canoe is on Hikurangi!*

Kai had often heard adults talking about the canoe when he played about the pā. Some bird-fowlers even claimed to have seen the tip of its stern-post in the tarn on the mountain.

Arakura and the other grandmothers handed out bowls of hīnau berries to fill the children's empty bellies, followed by a strip of dried shark for each to chew on. When the rain stopped, the children all rushed outside again and frolicked naked in the puddles around the village.

'Tama tū, tama ora; tama noho, tama mate,' the women would chant to the children. *An active child remains healthy, while a lazy one becomes sick.*

'Tama tū, tama ora!' Kai, Tui and the other children mimicked as they chased Manu about the pā. Once Kai asked his sister, 'Why do we always have to be the ones who do the chasing?'

'Cause I'm Manu. Only birds can fly.'

'It's my turn,' he protested.

'No, I'm the oldest,' she replied, and that was that. She turned on her heel and was off again, the other children in hot pursuit. When

Kai eventually caught up with his sister he grabbed her by the hair, only to receive a cuff across the ear.

Sometimes Uenuku, the rainbow deity, appeared in the sky and the children ran about calling his name, trying to touch his colourful arcs. The kuia called out to remind them to use that name with caution.

'Uenuku is the warrior's atua,' Arakura said gravely. 'Some of you boys will learn about him soon enough.'

CHAPTER EIGHT

Tā te tamariki tāna mahi he wāwāhi tahā.
It is the job of the children to smash the calabash. (Boys will be boys.)

The waves subsided gently into white foam on the light-grey beach. Minute crystals in the sand sparkled in the sun's rays. Kiri leaned back and took a deep breath as she reached both hands behind her and dug them into the sand. Her belly was starting to show again. Tāwae sat down next to her and together they watched their children scampering along the sand with the other kids from the village.

'May the gods continue to look kindly upon us.' Kiri smiled affectionately at Tāwae and rubbed her palm over her puku.

'You know, I think it's time we took our children to meet their Hautanoa relatives,' said Tāwae. 'Now that things have settled down in that district.'

'Good idea,' Kiri replied. 'Our cousins have brought their children here to see us, but only Manu has been to their pā and that was quite a while ago.'

'It's important they get to know who they can rely on in times of trouble. Let's take them by waka rather than going overland. Tāwhiti Hill would be too strenuous a climb for you in your condition.'

+

The night before the trip the two boys lay awake, too excited to sleep. Tui snuggled close to his big brother.

'Kei whea a Hautanoa, e Kai?' *Where's Hautanoa, Kai?*

Kai only knew that Hautanoa was somewhere far beyond the southern end of their bay. Not wanting to disclose his ignorance to his greatest fan, however, he dismissed the question by nodding towards the south.

'Kei kō atu,' the nine-year-old replied. *On the other side.*

'Have you been there?'

'No. Go to sleep, Tui.'

Tui was silent for a few minutes but soon enough piped up again. 'You know, Kai, some of the kids were teasing me today.'

'I said "go to sleep".'

'They said Father ran away from a battle.'

'Who said that?' Kai sat up.

'Is it true?'

'Course it's not. Don't listen to them. Our father is a very brave man. Now close your eyes or you might sleep in and be left behind.'

Kai lay back down but his own eyes remained open, staring into the shadows of the thatched roof. He remembered as a little boy how he had suffered when an older playmate, Kōrihi, teased him that he was the son of a tangata hū-ngoingoi. If word had got back to the chief, Kōrihi would have been severely punished, or worse. But even then, young Kai was not one to let others settle his squabbles. He had first heard the expression used by other boys when they teased the more feminine among the boys. But it was through Kōrihi that he first came to know that hū-ngoingoi not only meant frail, it was also a name for a man who was faint-hearted or, even worse, a coward.

He had heard the rumour about his father before, but it didn't make any sense. He had caught it in snatches of small-talk when people thought him too young to understand, or in whispered discussions between elders. He had thought up all sorts of explanations for why his father might have run from the battle. Meanwhile, he had learned how to compensate for his doubts by creating his own persona. One who was the best and toughest of them all.

+

In the dawn light, Kai was the first to stir and he quickly woke his brother.

'C'mon, let's go.' Outside the house they found their parents and two pononga packing kete for the trip.

'Don't stay down there too long,' Kiri warned the boys as they headed down to the village.

They ran over to join their cousins, and the gang of boys ventured up the Ngāpō Stream, spreading out to look for trees to climb. The rich, green bush was their leafy paradise.

At one bend, as he splashed across the stream, Tui heard a screech high above him. Standing in mid-stream he looked up through the forest canopy just in time to see a karoro land on one of the uppermost branches of a giant tōtara tree. By this stage the seven-year-old had had it ingrained in him that nothing happened by chance. Perhaps this seagull could be a sign, Tui thought. Kai would know what it meant.

'It's a bad omen,' came his brother's stern response when he asked. 'Don't tell our parents, in case they call off the trip. Or go without us.' Kai himself had never seen a seabird deep in the bush.

After playing for a while the boys were famished so they began to forage for berries and fruit. They soon found some trees that were well laden with ripe fruit.

'Tirohia, me te whata raparapa tuna e iri ana.' *Look, the tutu berries are hanging as thick and black as eels on a drying stage,* said Kōrihi, licking his lips.

'But you know we have to strain the juice before we drink it,' another said. 'If we eat the berries straight from the tree we'll poison ourselves.'

'You guys can have tutu,' said Kai, turning to his little brother.

'There's plenty of other fruit in the forest that we can eat straight away. Let's keep looking.'

The two boys wandered upstream until they came to a grove of kahikatea, the tallest tree in that part of the bush. They spied a variety of smaller trees further into the grove and headed towards them. The dense bush became darker the further in they went.

'Kai, it looks like there's eyes in those trees,' said Tui nervously.

'Yeah, they look like huge birds, with their wings spread, ready to *pounce* on you!' Kai grabbed at Tui suddenly.

'*Don't*, Kai!'

Kai laughed and ran his fingers down the brindled bark of a tree before stepping over its buttress roots. Stopping at the base of one of the more mature kahikatea, he scooted up its trunk, swiftly reaching its lowest branches, some three metres above ground.

'Come on up, Tui,' he called, startling some forest birds who were chatting noisily above them. Tui clutched at the tree's twisted grey trunk, feeling for clefts, then clambered gingerly up towards his brother. Kai offered Tui his hand as he got near and pulled the smaller boy onto the thick branch where he was seated. They shuffled along the branch until they were deep in its greenery. Its splayed foliage was the perfect camouflage.

The boys were now surrounded by an abundance of koroī, the tree's tiny orange-red fruit. They sat for some time, sucking on the sweet berries and spitting out the purple-black seeds before they heard rustling on the forest floor below.

Kai parted the tree's leaves, expecting to see the other boys, only to reveal a woman from the village following the stream. She was loaded with calabashes and she moved with the confident gait of someone on a mission. He wondered why she had come so far upstream to fetch water.

'It's one of the pononga,' Kai whispered to his little brother. 'Don't let on that we are here. Let's see how well we can stay hidden.'

A perplexed Tui continued to pop berries into his mouth as they watched the slim, frizzy-haired young woman fill the first of her six tahā at the water's edge. Every so often she looked back over her shoulder in the direction she had come. It was suddenly deathly quiet, save for the cicada. The birds had flown.

The pononga was squatting on the bank, about to submerge another tahā in the water when the boys heard the crunch of twigs. One of the kai-rākau, Hara, suddenly appeared almost below them. He strode directly towards the woman, making Kai suspect he had been following her. The pononga heard the kai-rākau too but, seeing nothing, she turned quickly back to filling the tahā.

In an instant Hara was upon her, grabbing the petite young woman about her waist and forcing her onto her hands and knees. She shrieked as he positioned himself behind her and wrenched away the covering from her hips. Kai and Tui watched, dumbfounded, their berry feast abandoned.

The boys had to muffle their giggles when Hara removed his maro and stood there with his manhood revealed. They couldn't see what Hara was doing, but as he leaned over the naked woman, Kai heard her say, 'Stop it,' in a low, weak voice. 'Stop it,' she said again, sounding resigned.

Kai saw her elbows straighten and her knees spread as Hara gripped her shoulders. He figured Hara must have been hurting her because her fingers dug into the earth and she let out a yelp. Hara's hands slid back to her hips as he kept thumping into her.

Then, curiously, when Hara finished administering the pononga's punishment, he helped her gather up and fill the calabashes. As they departed, Kai noticed that they were both grinning.

Once Hara and the pononga had left the brothers climbed down and went off in search of more fruit. Kai soon found a tree with glossy green leaves and bright orange berries. He picked a handful to eat. When they caught up with their cousins they were sitting on the banks near the stream's mouth.

'Did you see Hara and one of the pononga come past?' Kai asked.

'Not long ago,' one of the boys nodded. Kai told them what he and Tui had witnessed.

'Oh, Aunty won't be happy about that,' one of the boys said.

Suddenly Kōrihi noticed Kai gnawing away at the kernel of one of the orange berries.

'Those are karaka berries,' he said with a frown.

Kai's mother had often cautioned him against eating the kernel of the karaka but Kai was too proud to show the fear he suddenly felt.

'E tā, mataku koutou?' *What, are you all frightened?*

'My nanny says never to eat the kernel raw,' Kōrihi warned. 'She always soaks the berry and then steams the kernels for ages before we can eat them.'

'My father bakes the nuts before we eat them,' another of the cousins said. 'Eating them raw is a no-no.'

'Not if you have a stomach like mine,' Kai said as he bit into the pulp of another karaka. None of his companions were keen to follow his lead so he wolfed down the entire handful, spitting out the nuts as he went.

On their way back to the village, Kai began to feel queasy. He held his stomach and started to stumble the way his father did after he'd been drinking fermented tāwhara juice. As they reached the outskirts of the village he fell to the ground in convulsions, his limbs rigid.

A wide-eyed Tui was petrified. He wanted to go for his father but he was afraid to leave Kai. Two of the other boys ran to get help.

Tāwae and Kiri arrived swiftly to find their son unconscious. Kiri wailed when she saw the muscles in Kai's face twitching and saliva dribbling from the side of his open mouth. Tāwae frantically picked up his son and rushed to place him in the stream.

Thankfully, the cold water brought him around. By then, the other boys' parents had started a fire and placed a dense mat of piripiri leaves over it. Tāwae held Kai near the fire so he could inhale the smoke. Little by little, the future chief began to cough and splutter, and after several minutes he started vomiting.

'Carry him up to the pā,' Tāwae said to Kiri and the others, and he strode off into the bush.

Back at their house, Kiri knelt by her delirious son, trying desperately to cool his burning brow with a wet cloth. She pleaded over and over again to the atua to restore him to health.

Tāwae soon returned from the bush carrying more piripiri and some bark from other medicinal trees. He sat down next to the fire and began feeding fuel into it. Kiri helped him.

'Is that enough?' she asked anxiously.

'It should be.' Tāwae's focus was as sharp as an adze. The smoke was stifling in the confined space. 'Bring a large mat,' Tāwae said as he carried his son closer to the fire. Kiri retrieved the mat and together she and Tāwae used it to form an inhalation chamber around Kai and the fire. Kai tried to pull away from the choking smoke but his father restrained him, keeping him inside the chamber until his breathing started to slow to a more natural rhythm.

They removed the mat and guided Kai to lie down again. Kiri stationed herself beside him, mopping the perspiration from his drenched brow, neck and shoulders.

Eventually, Kai seemed more lucid. Now that he was out of danger, his father rounded on him. 'You're lucky you didn't die, Son. You know you're not supposed to eat karaka berries raw. You've been taught that. Told time and again. What were you thinking?'

Kai held his tongue. He knew he was in the wrong.

For the rest of the day he slept. The trip to Hautanoa was postponed.

+

When Kai was sufficiently recovered, Tāwae decided it was time to put to sea. As he helped prepare provisions for the trip, Kai noticed there was a new resident in the pā. It was the young woman he had seen with Hara in the bush. She was seated near a fire alongside two other pononga, beating fernroot, roasting it, then throwing it to the wives of the kai-rākau. The wives, including Hara's, were seated in a semi-circle and seemed to be demolishing the kai as quickly as the pononga could deliver it.

Down on the beach Tāwae prepared to launch his family and all necessary provisions in two waka, each with a crew of twenty. Although there was a light breeze blowing from the south, suggesting wild weather might follow, he decided to proceed anyway, for the sea seemed placid enough. Hautanoa was only a few hours away, after all.

The two vessels passed Ahu Point before striking out for Waikawa. It was not long before the light breeze became a winnowing wind that moaned across the bay and rippled the surface of the sea. They had not yet reached Kotunui, the southern headland, when the swell began rising high before them, forcing the helmsmen of both waka to steer a course towards the rocky coast. Before they knew it, rain sliced the air and began pouring down from the heavens.

'Kia mau, tamariki mā!' Kiri shouted into the storm. *Hold on, children!* She forced herself to remain calm in the face of this clear danger, for nowhere along this part of the narrow coast would they be able to make landfall safely. She passed one of the broad-bladed hoewai to Manu-pōkai and, despite her swelling stomach, took up one herself to assist the paddlers. Kai and Tui found themselves paddles as well.

The whānau looked to Tāwae for reassurance. He was standing in the middle of their waka, his senses fully engaged for any imminent change in conditions. He held a short kōrero with Wehe, who commanded the other canoe, about whether to go on or try to return to Ngāpō. They decided not to go back because of the risk of overturning the waka while trying to turn them around in the growing swells.

As the mighty ocean billowed and crashed on the rocks before them, the kai-whakatere standing in the stern listened to Tāwae and Wehe's directions while watching for breaking whitecaps, steering their vessels carefully through the depressions between the rocks. For some time it was not clear that they would be able to round the headland but the crews rowed stoically in hope.

Tui stopped paddling momentarily and pointed towards the cliffs along the narrow shore. He called out to his brother.

'E Kai, rā kē he karoro!' *Kai — look, a seagull!* Kai's blood ran cold as he recalled the gull they had seen in the bush a few days before.

The boys had been raised to love the thrilling power of the sea and in fact they relished the days when the Tonga-huruhuru, the south-south-easter, lashed the bay into a wild ocean. Bad omens, however, were far more worrying, and Kai felt certain this storm must have been the event the karoro in the bush foretold. He realised with a sinking feeling that he should have reported the sighting to his parents. All he could do now was keep digging his paddle into the surf and pull as hard as he could. Ahead of him, Manu was working hard with her hoewai, keeping time with her mother's stroke.

If anyone felt fear, they didn't show it. Not for the first time, Kai marvelled at his father's remarkable skills in such testing conditions. Everyone hung on Tāwae's word. He and Wehe held their positions in the waka, never once sitting down or projecting concern.

They soon rounded Kotunui Point and finally Waimahuru came into view. The isolated cove was the only place they could shelter before reaching Hautanoa. Tāwae indicated to Wehe that they should put in and wait out the squall.

As the waka drew into the tiny cove, Kai muttered under his breath to Tui.

'See? Our father is a very brave man. If the angry sea can't scare him, no man will.' He gave his little brother a squeeze. The relief was written all over Tui's face.

CHAPTER NINE

Kuruki, whakataha!
Evil, pass by!

By the time Kai had seen his eleventh autumn, he and Tui, now nine, had become intrepid foragers. With the sea on their doorstep, they were often seen in the water at low tide gathering shellfish or diving for crayfish.

The family mostly ate fish and fernroot, but often supplemented their diet with smoked eels. Kai was an expert at catching these tuna in the stream during daylight hours, when they tended to be asleep. He ran his hands under the banks and flicked the sleeping eels up onto land, where Tui and his mates were waiting to retrieve them.

Some nights the boys accompanied their nannies, including Arakura and Whakaata, to hill ponds to bob for eels. Toitoi tuna was fun, they both agreed. First they had to dig up some earthworms, then they threaded fine flax string through them and tied them together to form the bob. Kai knew by name the various species of worm that could be found around Ngāpō: the light-coloured noke waiū and noke wharu, as well as the darker noke rākau and noke whiti. He liked the noke whiti best for bait because these were the biggest.

When Kai first lowered his bait into the murky water he was not expecting the eels to bite so quickly. He was so surprised that when he flicked the flax, which was attached to his mānuka rod, the eel smacked Tui right in the face instead of landing on the bank. Kai was not very popular with his little brother for the rest of that night.

Sometimes during the day they would tread around in the ponds to stir up the mud and wake up the sleeping eels. Kai found the feel of the slush squeezing between his toes a bit weird at first, but three or four of his mates were stomping around with him, which soon turned it into fun. As soon as they saw the tuna appear on the surface they flicked them onto the banks for their female cousins to stun and stash in pīkau bags.

Tāwae, who loved the ocean and the solace of fishing, had passed on this passion to his sons. From when the boys could scarcely walk he had taken them out in waka and they would paddle out to nearby Ahu Point. They would sometimes take along their white kurī, with a string around its middle. From a very young age, their relatives all noticed that Kai had great stamina in the sea; whether the stroke was quick, light or strong he kept up a remarkably good rhythm. The boys learned never to disrespect the ocean.

'Kei a Tangaroa, te atua o te moana, ōna piki, ōna heke,' their father would tell them. *The denizen of the sea, Tangaroa, has many moods.*

At eleven years of age Kai could steer a large waka when it was being propelled by a team of paddlers. This was quite an accomplishment, especially as some of the steering oars were around two metres long.

Sometimes the sea cut up rough, and father and sons had to make a run for the shore, taking great care to avoid being swamped by the waves behind them. Similarly, when heading out into heavy surf, Kai learned not to steer directly at the waves, or else the bow dived headlong into the wave and the waka would become swamped.

+

As he reached his teenage years Kai was still unaware of his purpose in life. His parents had never explained what his name meant; nor had he thought to ask. The first hint of what was meant for him came when Tāwae started taking his son along to rūnanga meetings. As the two huddled together to keep warm under the same kaitaka, Kai listened intently to the debates between the village leaders. He asked his father many questions during and after the meetings, and Tāwae was careful not to ignore any of them. In fact, he encouraged his son's queries.

It was after one rūnanga meeting that Tāwae told his son there was something special he wanted him to do. 'Something only warriors are usually asked to do.'

'Anything, Pāpā,' an eager Kai replied.

'But I can only tell you after I have spoken with your mother.'

The chief found his wife under the māhoe tree checking their younger daughter's hair for lice. As she wet and combed Haere's hair, Kiri sang to the two-year-old:

Ūpoko, ūpoko,
Whiti te rā!
Hei kai māu
Te kutu o taku ūpoko
Ūpoko, ūpoko,
Whiti te rā.

Head, head,
The sun shines!
You may eat
the lice of my head.
Head, head,
The sun shines.

Tāwae smiled, recognising the song from his childhood. It was supposed to cause the sun to shine, and he and his friends would sing it when they were going to bathe.

Kiri stopped singing when she saw her husband approach.

'I have something to discuss with you and it concerns Kai,' Tāwae declared in a formal tone. His words gave her a chill. 'News out of the rūnanga is that your Uncle Tūhoro is headed this way.'

'From Ōkau Pā?'

86

'Yes, he's sent envoys to all the Ngāi Haere pā to let them know. He wants us to commit some of our kai-rākau to assist him in an attack on Poko Pā.'

'Poko? Why, what have they done?'

'They haven't done anything, but Tūhoro has heard that the Aitanga Nui chief Kapua is at Ōtama visiting their pā. He is keen to get there before Kapua leaves — so much so that he's not even waiting for the hapū to respond before setting out. He thinks he can take the pā all by himself.'

'Uncle would give it a good go, you know that, eh?' Kiri laughed.

'Anyway,' Tāwae said abruptly, 'the rūnanga has agreed to send two waka made up of men from the four local Ngāi Haere pā to support him. Uncle Wehe will command our ope taua.'

'Uh-huh.'

Tāwae watched his wife keenly as he continued. 'Your uncle is taking his son Whai with him in the war party. I am going to let Uncle Wehe take Kai too.'

'What? No! He's just a boy!'

Tāwae had been expecting this. 'He's not much younger than Whai,' he said.

'But Whai has started warrior training. Kai hasn't!'

'I don't mean for him to fight, Kiri, but to observe. Let him witness his first battle.'

Kiri was quiet for a few minutes as she absent-mindedly flicked her fingers over Haere's hair. Her daughter let out a shriek when her mother pulled too hard.

'Sorry, darling. Off you go now.' When little Haere was out of earshot, Tāwae picked up the conversation again.

'Kiri, winter is coming and then, whether we like it or not, Mahuru. His twelfth Mahuru.'

'But Mahuru is not here yet,' Kiri said, looking up at her husband.

Tāwae felt a flicker of anger, which he tried to suppress.

'Rest assured, we . . . we won't tell him everything until then,' he stammered, 'but he *is* going with the ope taua to Poko Pā.'

'As long as Uncle Wehe promises he will keep our boy out of harm's way.'

'I will make sure of it,' said Kai. 'Then the matter is settled.'

Kai rarely put his foot down with his wife, but she knew to back off when he did.

+

When Kai learned that he was to accompany the kai-rākau to Poko Pā at Ōtama he was excited. In the village he strutted among his cousins with his chest out and nose in the air. They were not impressed.

'How come you get to go?' one of the boys asked.

''Cause they're getting me ready for warrior training.'

'I doubt it, you're too young. We're *all* too young.'

'Why would they want to train a coward?' Kōrihi piped up from behind.

Kai spun around. 'You got a problem, Te Kō?'

'You better make sure you don't run like your father,' Kōrihi spat back.

Kai's hands balled into fists. 'What do you mean?'

Kōrihi was a year older and taller than the others. He smirked when he realised he'd got Kai riled.

'Not everyone's got the stomach for battle, cousin,' he said with a malicious twinkle. 'You're about to find out if you've inherited your father's traits.'

Smack. Kai slammed Kōrihi so hard he knocked him over. Kōrihi got back up and lunged at Kai as the other boys started yelling and egging them on. The ground shot out from under Kai but he managed to twist himself so that he was on top of his opponent. Kōrihi's fist came up from the dirt and caught Kai in the face but Kai had him pinned down.

'Help me! Get the bugger off me!' Kōrihi yelled to the others. No one moved.

Suddenly everyone went quiet and Kai felt himself being wrenched away. It was Uncle Wehe. He pulled Kai and Kōrihi both to their feet, almost tearing their arms out of their sockets in the process. Both boys stood cowering.

'If I catch you two in the village again today,' Wehe snarled, 'I'll give you something to fight about. Now get outta here!'

They scattered.

When Kai turned up back home with a bloodied nose and blackening eye his mother frowned.

'Son, you're too quick to lose your temper.'

'I couldn't help it. Kōrihi wound me up.'

'Next time,' Kiri said, 'try using this phrase rather than your fists: "Kuruki, whakataha!"' *Evil, pass by!*

'Kuruki, whakataha,' Kai repeated.

'It's a simple and very useful karakia for averting anything unpleasant. In the meantime, stay away from those boys for a while.'

Kai stayed in the pā that afternoon, mostly playing with Tui. Every time he thought about what Kōrihi had said, he put that ghost to bed, saying, 'Kuruki, whakataha!'

While they were playing, the two boys spotted a column of kai-rākau down on the beach. To get a better view they climbed up onto one of the paerangi, a small platform attached to a palisade. They couldn't see over the top of the stockade so they peered as best they could through the narrow gaps in the saplings.

'They must be getting ready for Ōtama,' said Kai.

The kai-rākau were jogging along the sand armed with sticks. Wehe led them to the cordoned-off area that people called Kirikiri-tatangi. Wearing only war belts made from flax leaves, the warriors' muscular thighs and sinewy calves glistened as they pranced and leapt about, whacking and blocking one another's poles. The muscles on their arms and on their backs were well defined. With their tightly tied topknots they seemed larger than life to Kai. He was full of admiration for the warriors and couldn't believe he would be going with them to Poko Pā.

+

Three days later the pūtātara or conch shells sounded from the lookout at Kō Pā, warning the village that two waka taua were approaching. It was a warm autumn morning and the sea was unusually placid — not the kind of day one would expect killing to take place, but all the same, these were favourable conditions for a surprise attack. Tūhoro was in the lead vessel. His men paddled the waka in close but not all the way to shore. The chief yelled out to Wehe and his men, who were getting ready to launch their own waka to follow him. There were women in Tūhoro's canoe, which was his ruse to appear friendly to the occupants of Ūpoko Pā.

'Listen to your Uncle Wehe and do as he says and you'll be all right, son,' Kiri said as she handed Kai a warm cloak and a raincape in case the weather turned.

'Make sure to wrap your kaitaka around you tonight,' she said and gave him a final hug. Kai, his black eye now barely visible, simply nodded. He wished his mother wouldn't fuss around him so much, especially since the other children from the village had come down to the foreshore to see him off.

Still, nothing could extinguish the excitement he felt about going with the kai-rākau. Kai spotted his fourteen-year-old cousin Whai in the other waka and waved. Seeing him put Kai at ease, and he looked forward to catching up with him. They were the only boys on board.

As Tāwae watched the waka pull away he thought of the times his own father had taken him to witness battles and the impact those engagements had had on him. The first time was when he was Kai's age, when he had gone with his father to the great fight along the Matā River, which lasted several days. And he would never forget the fateful time at Te Maniaroa. How he missed his father.

Tāwae looked out at the waka, at the little frame of his boy among those men, warriors all, and he almost shouted to Wehe to bring his son back to shore. But he stopped himself. If his son was going to be the warrior he himself had never been, he had to let him go.

CHAPTER TEN

Tamarahi kei au te ika i te ati!
I have killed the first fish!

Leaning on the gunwale, Kai trailed his fingers in the water, brought them back up and tasted the salty flavour. It was good to be on the sea again. He leaned over the rauawa a second time, trying to see his own reflection. The silhouette of his plumed hair, adorned with the feathers of both the huia and the kōtuku or white heron, cast a shadow on the water. His parents had wanted there to be no mistaking his rank.

The man in front of him drew his hoewai back and out of the water, spraying Kai's face with droplets that would dry to a salty sparkle. He sat upright and allowed himself one last look back at the tiny figures on the beach. The morning's sun had not quite dispelled the mist sitting over the bush behind them. Kai wished his father was with him now.

Once the waka was beyond the breakers and away from the safety of the shore, the kai-rākau got down to work with their paddles and the vessel surged forward. Wehe called the pace until the kaihautū took over. Once the crew hit their straps, the waka virtually glided across the bay.

'Tūhoro's waka must already be at Hautanoa by now,' Wehe called to the fugleman. 'If we don't get a move on, there will be nothing left for us to do.' The kaihautū called to the kai-rākau and their pace picked up again.

Wehe's solid frame blocked out the glare of the sun for Kai momentarily as the warrior leader made his way back to where he was sitting. He sat down next to Kai and slapped him on the thigh.

'What do you think, boy? Good day for a fight?' Kai looked at the vein protruding from Wehe's strong arm. It was like sitting next to a kahikatea tree.

'Aua . . .' replied Kai, trying to appear nonchalant. *Dunno.*

'What do you mean "Dunno"?' Wehe raised an eyebrow at him. 'Mark my words, boy, any fight is better than no fight. Anyway, must be the season for it, eh?' He grabbed Kai's chin with his big hand and inspected his bruised face. 'What was that scuffle about, anyhow?'

'Nothing,' Kai said, pulling his chin away.

Whack! Wehe's open palm slapped him hard on the bruised side of his face.

'Don't muck me around, boy,' Wehe said angrily. 'You're lucky to be here. You might be the chief's son, but when it comes to warfare, you're under my command. Now, I asked you a question.'

Anger brewed in Kai. 'Kōrihi called my father a coward,' he blurted. 'I would have killed him if I could.'

'Don't get mad at me, boy. If you expect to be a leader of men one day, you need to start acting like one now.'

Kai unclenched his jaw, took a breath and muttered, 'Kuruki, whakataha.'

A mocking grin spread slowly over Wehe's face. 'You reckon you can kill a man, eh?' Kai didn't reply but eyeballed Wehe back. As the warrior leader got up to return to the middle of the waka, his tone changed.

'Maybe Kōrihi was just confused about why your father sent you and did not come himself.' Kai stared at the water for some time. Why hadn't his father come? It was a good question.

+

The midday sun beat down from a cloudless sky as the Ngāi Haere waka rounded the last headland and entered the bay of Wawe-ki-uta. It had been met by two more war canoes at Hautanoa, bringing Tūhoro's force to over three hundred fighting men and some thirty women.

Tūhoro was disembarking in the cove at Ōtama; Poko Pā was just off the beach on flat ground. Its encircling palisade was all that stood between its two hundred and fifty inhabitants and Tūhoro's attacking force. Its occupants were rallying to the pūtātara that sounded across the bay.

Tūhoro strode up the beach to exchange formal greetings with the local chief and demand his pā's submission.

'My arm is tired of dispatching victims for the ovens,' Tūhoro said. 'I only want Kapua.' Tūhoro was nearly fifty and big-boned. His full-face moko accentuated his natural grimace.

'I will not let harm come to him,' the chief replied. 'He and his people are our guests.'

'If you resist us, then you will suffer with them,' said Tūhoro.

'We will not endure the indignity of giving up our guests without first offering resistance to your attack,' said the chief of Poko Pā.

The sound of fire-hardened weapons and the clash of stone patu and people shouting soon echoed in the cove. The combat was frantic at first, spilling out onto the sand and into the water, but as soon as they spotted the other three waka approaching, the defenders fell back into the pā.

The waka Kai was in had rounded the cliffs and was fast approaching the mouth of the cove. He felt a rush of energy and a tingling in his fingers and hands as he observed the defenders retreating. Tūhoro, who was about the same size as Wehe, was leading the advance with taiaha in hand. Warriors were almost always naked, clothing being a hindrance to movement. The chief was wearing nothing but an apron-like maro huka between his beefy thighs — the warrior's preferred garment. A stone patu was tucked into his belt.

Shouts and screams from within and without the palisades rang out across the cove. Tūhoro's two waka were drawn up on the beach, while several smaller vessels, belonging to the defenders, sat above the high-tide mark. The first of the kai-rākau from Kai's waka spilled into the water just as the bows of the other waka kissed the sand. Warriors poured up the rise of the beach towards the pā. As he leapt over the rauawa, Wehe yelled to two of the kai-rākau.

'You two grab one of those canoes and stay out on the water with Kai.' Then he led the rest of his men around to the far side of the pā.

'Hop in front, little chief,' one of the kai-rākau called to Kai. His mate stabilised the stern next to the bigger vessel. Kai sat down, still clinging to the garments his mother had given him. His palms were sweating. One of the kai-rākau pushed the canoe out then jumped in. Another waka was also leaving the cove, with Tūhoro's son and the women aboard. Safely out in deeper water, the two canoes pulled alongside each other and watched the battle from their safe distance.

The last time the two boys had seen each other was when Whai had been to visit Ngāpō two years earlier. Whai was now fourteen. They briefly greeted each other, then turned back to watch the action. Kai fidgeted with the tassels on the kaitaka in his lap. The battle was in full swing and while he knew there was always the chance that their side might have to make a speedy withdrawal by sea, it looked increasingly unlikely.

When the fighting stopped, the men paddled their waka back towards the beach. Kai's muscles tightened and his heart was in his mouth as the two boys were led up the beach. Bruised and bloodied warriors were sitting on the sand while their wounds were attended to by the women who had accompanied Tūhoro. Dead bodies lay scattered.

Kai kept his arms wrapped around him as he walked, his mouth open as he gazed around the battle scene. He saw one of the kai-rākau, who had been seated ahead of him in the waka, raise his patu above a writhing body and strike the man forcefully on the head. The victim moved no more.

The scene inside the pā was like nothing Kai had ever seen in his eleven years in this world. It was carnage; bodies everywhere. The sky had begun to cloud over and the air was full of a sickening stench. The sound of shrieking, weeping and groaning filled the air.

Bloodied captives were lined up along the inner palisade, wrists and ankles bound with flax ties. Some looked dazed or dejected, while others had murderous hatred stamped all over their tattooed faces. Several kai-rākau stood guard over the prisoners.

A group of women huddled in one section of the pā clutching their children to them, while others wailed as the lifeless forms of their loved ones were dragged away. One young girl, no older than Kai, sat back on her heels, rocking back and forth. Her eyes were glazed over as she sang to herself. She was hauled off, as were several other young women. Kai never saw them again.

'Bring Kapua down to the beach,' Tūhoro yelled. Yanked onto his feet and prodded with a tao to get him moving, the Aitanga Nui chief kept tripping over because of the rope binding his ankles. Eventually Wehe grabbed one armpit and a kai-rākau the other and they dragged him across the sand. Wehe called for the two boys to follow.

'That's the chief, Kapua,' Whai whispered to Kai. 'He's gonna get it from my father.'

'Why?' Kai asked.

'My mother told me that not long before I was born, Kapua took my father prisoner and tortured him.'

'What did he do?'

'Cut his balls and staked him out on the ground. He lay there all day in the hot sun, blood smeared all over his body.'

Kai grimaced.

'But Kapua's father came along and ordered his son to release my father. Since then, Pāpā has been waiting for a chance for utu. So this is payback.'

When they reached the beach the two boys sat down on the sand to watch. First, Tūhoro asked his young wife, Hīraia, to mash some dried kūmara with water and feed it to him. While he was eating,

Tūhoro asked Wehe to organise some men to dig a deep hole in the sand. Kapua, whose wrists and ankles were still bound, was forced into the hole.

Kai chewed his lips, anxious about what might happen next. But no one on his side was showing any sympathy for Kapua, so he tried to look staunch too.

As Tūhoro ate, he watched Kapua being buried up to his shoulders.

'How rude of me,' Tūhoro remarked, 'eating in front of our guest. My dear, fix some more kōpura kao, only this time mix it with mimi.' Kapua glowered at Tūhoro as Hīraia squatted and placed the bowl of dried kūmara under her garment. Her urine audibly filled the bowl and she slowly and deliberately mixed it into the kūmara. Kai held his breath.

'Now, feed our guest,' Tūhoro said. Kapua opened his quivering mouth to receive a spoonful while Tūhoro spoke to him.

'I kō ngā riri, i reira koe; i kōnei ngā riri, i kōnei hoki koe.' *When the fighting was elsewhere you were there; now that the fighting is here you are here too.*

Kapua began chewing as if he was enjoying the morsel. He swallowed before replying.

'E! Nā wai te koko ka uru he tāwiri ke!' *Ah! But who in a corner cannot but tremble?* Then he asked for another mouthful. Kapua clearly feared a coward's death more than any other kind.

Tūhoro could not contain his fury any longer. He drew his patu and rushed at Kapua, his wife springing out of the way just in time. Kapua's head whipped around so fast with the blow that Kai heard his neck pop. But even as the kūmara spilled from Kapua's open mouth, the Aitanga Nui chief managed one more provocation: 'E Tū! E Tū! Te rangona hoki te reka o tō kai?' *Oh Tū! Oh Tū! How am I to taste the sweetness of your food?* Tūhoro then landed an even heavier blow across Kapua's temple, the blade dashing open his skull.

Kai had watched the scene unfold reluctantly. It was true that he had seen men and women killed before, and he felt that Kapua had got what he deserved, but Kai still found killing confronting.

When it was over, the tohunga demanded the heart of the first enemy killed in battle. It was duly cut out and presented to him. Once he had completed the sacred ceremony, accompanied by ritual chants and prayers, he cut off pieces and presented them to Whai and Kai to eat raw.

It was not the first time Whai had eaten part of a heart, but it was Kai's. The younger boy tried to remain expressionless, following his cousin's lead, but when he went to swallow, his stomach resisted and he vomited up the contents. Wehe looked disdainfully down at the lad, whose face had turned pale.

'Try again,' he said. Kai bit off a small piece and swallowed without chewing.

Wehe gave a sardonic smile. 'Is this the man who will one day lead Whānau-a-Mate? Who will wreak havoc among our enemies? Eat up, boy! Learn to enjoy it!'

+

When the waka put to sea that afternoon, the clouds that had been threatening rain released a light shower. Wehe had deliberately placed one of the bound Aitanga Nui prisoners on the thwart behind Kai and Whai and then instructed the boys to sit facing the prisoner. The man was shaking in fear. Wehe punched him in the stomach and the man dropped to his knees in front of the two boys. He pleaded for his life.

'E tā, tō waha! Koi kainga oratia koe!' Wehe shouted at him. *Shut your mouth lest we eat you alive!* The kai-rākau were all laughing. Wehe looked over at Tūhoro in the other waka, who nodded his approval. Kai swallowed, feeling a cold dread raise the hairs on his neck.

'Stand up, Kai,' Wehe said to his nephew, but the boy didn't move — he couldn't. He didn't think his legs would carry his weight. All around him people in the several waka were laughing, all except the prisoner, who looked as terrified as Kai felt.

'Get up!' Wehe ordered. Kai got to his feet as the kai-rākau steadied the vessel. Whai stood up too.

'This morning I asked you if you could kill a man. Now's your chance.' He withdrew the patu from his belt, handed it to Kai and said, 'Kill him.'

Kai started shaking uncontrollably as tears welled up in his eyes. *No, no!* he wanted to shout, but nothing came out of his mouth. He could only stare at the man, who glared back at him.

The kai-rākau were urging Kai on. 'Do it, Kai,' they cried.

Even Whai encouraged his young cousin. 'First time is hardest, Kai, but once you've done it, you'll feel better.'

'These are the people who murdered your grandfathers. They don't deserve to live,' said Wehe.

A red-eyed tohunga behind Kai started some half-crazed chant Kai did not understand, waving a branch over him. Then suddenly he roared at Kai. 'Kia kōtahi te pō! Kia kōtahi te ao!' *Be as one with the dark! Be as one with the light!*

Paralysed with fear, Kai stared at everyone around him, tears streaming down his face.

When the prisoner urinated, Wehe struck him again. A kai-rākau grabbed the prisoner by his hair and hauled him back to his knees.

'See, Kai, he's no better than a dog,' Wehe said as he grabbed his nephew's arm.

Kai was unaware that warriors often disabled prisoners, then drove boys to kill them. The aim was to promote an aggressive impulse in the boys — a spirit of violence that would eclipse any appeal to compassion during or after battle.

Wehe placed the patu in Kai's small palm and cupped his nephew's hand within his own, wrapping the boy's fingers around the handle. Kai felt the smooth, cold stone in his sweaty hand.

'Just bring it up and strike here at the side of his head. That will open his skull.' Wehe's forefinger pressed the prisoner's temple. 'It's just like stunning an eel.' Then he leaned towards Kai and whispered in his ear, 'They killed your mother's father, they killed your father's father. Kill him.'

Kai's head was spinning.

'If you raise your weapon to slay,' the tohunga added, 'do not keep it suspended; it is extremely unlucky to do so.'

'These people are beasts,' Wehe whispered. 'Kill him.'

Kai raised his arm as if he was in a trance.

'Be quick,' the prisoner implored him. There was growing courage in the prisoner's eyes — an apparent acceptance that his death was imminent.

With tears blurring his vision, Kai pressed his lips together and hardened his heart. Then he brought the patu down as hard as he could.

'*Aaeeii!*' the man screamed, his bound hands flying up to his head as he fell sideways.

'Too low,' called Whai. He grabbed the patu from Kai and struck the man's temple again, so powerfully that he cracked his skull. Blood splattered Kai's legs and mingled with the rain.

Kai looked up at Wehe, who was smiling.

PART TWO

CHAPTER ELEVEN

Waiho kia oroia, he whati toki nui.
Just leave (him) the big stone axe to be re-sharpened,
his edge is merely chipped a bit.

Kiri was keen to know what had happened, so when Tūhoro's waka stopped in on their way back to Ōkau Pā she sought out her uncle's wife. Hīraia, who was also Tūhoro's niece and half his age, was overjoyed to see her cousin. After the formal welcome the two mothers hurried off together, chatting away, just as they had so often when they were children, leaving their attendants to follow in their wake.

'Tell me, cousin, how did it go at Ōtama? My son has said nothing about it.'

'I'm surprised you let him go.'

'It's the beginning of his education — it had to start sometime,' Kiri said firmly. 'The sooner he becomes hard-hearted and pitiless, the better for his future. So what happened?'

'Well, when we reached the cove,' Hīraia explained, 'Tūhoro got ahead of himself. He was the first to breach the pa's palisade, and my husband soon found himself surrounded. But he was undeterred and started fighting off every warrior as they came at him. Talk about audacity! None of them could match him!'

'Ka mau te wehi, he tini toa.' *Wow, what a champion*, said Kiri, thinking of her own husband's inexperience in the art of war.

'He got really thirsty so he stopped and asked the enemy warriors, "Ko wai rawa o te ope hei hoake wai mōku?"' *Who among your force will bring me water?*

Kiri shook her head, smiling. 'Who but our uncle would try such a thing?'

'One of the Aitanga Nui men offered him a water-gourd. He drank from it, then tossed it aside and bid the next warrior to come at him. Soon Wehe and the others arrived in the pā and we overpowered our foe.'

'They arrived not a moment too soon, by the sounds of it,' said Kiri.

'Yeah, our enemy's ranks thinned pretty quickly after that,' Hīraia said, grinning. 'When the fighting was over the kai-rākau brought Whai and Kai ashore and they were taken over to the battle site to watch the wounded being despatched.'

'And how did Kai react?'

'The kai-rākau took him and Whai into the pā so they could see the enemy close up. They both stayed quiet and just stared. Then Wehe fed Kai a slice of the heart of the first enemy killed. It seemed to shock Kai, which is hardly surprising. But Wehe made him try again and eventually he managed to get some down. He was invited to kill his first prisoner, too, although he only wounded him — his cousin finished him off.'

'Ā, ka tika,' said Kiri, more relaxed now. *That was the right thing to do.* 'A rite of passage, eh?'

That night Tūhoro and Hīraia joined Tāwae and Kiri in the chief's house. Tāwae also asked Tūhoro to provide an account of the attack. His version was matter of fact, though he did reveal one startling additional detail about his motivation, which Hīraia had not spoken of.

'The people hosting Kapua had earlier raided a neighbouring pā at Hautanoa,' Tūhoro explained. 'During that raid one of my female relatives was captured and assaulted on the beach. Her captors held her naked against a large rock, and while each one had their way with her she cursed them with threats of revenge.' Kiri noticed Tūhoro clenching and unclenching his hand.

'They stood around her, jeering at my cousin as the abuse continued. In a last desperate attempt to stop them, she shouted, "You keep on opening the legs of Te Rangataua's cousin!" You know I was called Te Rangataua when I was a child. I was told the men stood back, wondering who she was referring to, and while they were discussing it their chief came along and said, "You fools, she means Tūhoro!" With that, they killed her.'

+

Kai said very little to anyone back in Kō Pā, about what he had experienced, least of all his parents. In fact, he was quite changed from the boy he had been before he left. When his mates told him they were going diving, he stayed back and watched them from shore. Not even his younger brother could penetrate the wall he had put up.

Kai felt uneasy whenever he saw his father and Wehe talking. On one occasion, late at night, he came across them arguing but they stopped when he appeared.

When he returned to his bed, he couldn't sleep. He awoke one night out of a dream in which he was drowning in a sea of blood, screaming soundlessly for his father to help. When he came to his senses he was breathless, clutching his neck, his skin cold and clammy. The nightmare visited him again and again.

To avoid lapsing into deep sleep he slapped himself as soon as he felt heaviness on his eyelids. Panting and shivering in the darkness, he would turn onto his back, desperately trying to keep his eyes open. He longed for sunrise the way children long to swim on scorching hot days.

Sometimes, when he was alone in the bush, Kai imagined that the spirits of those slain at Poko were watching him. The aged trees looked like sleeping giants, their creaking boughs awakened by his presence. He would break into a cold sweat, and when he saw his reflection in the stream he thought he could see the prisoner looking back at him. He couldn't believe Wehe had made him kill a man and eat a heart. The thought now made him gag. Why had his uncle done something so terrible?

Kai knew every child, adult and dog in the village by name. He conversed with them almost every day. Why, then, did he now feel like such an outsider?

He managed to keep his nightmares to himself for some time. He didn't want to tell his parents because he knew Wehe had taken him to the battle with their permission. He felt shame. *What is the matter with me?* he thought. *Why am I going to pieces like this?*

One morning, after a particularly bad night in which he woke in a cold sweat after seeing an apparition disappearing from the entrance to their house, he reluctantly told his father what was happening.

'He atua e ngau ana i roto i a koe.' Tāwae nodded. *A spirit eats away at you.* He seemed to know immediately what to do. 'We need to see the tohunga.'

'Can they help me?' Kai asked.

'They treat any form of disease, physical or spiritual,' Tāwae told his son. 'The signs of recovery will be seen immediately, their position as tohunga depend on it.'

Later that day, Tāwae took his son to see Parakore and Kaiora. Kai answered their questions cautiously. He closed his eyes as he described his dreams to the tohunga. Then his dark eyes flew wide open. His look was wild and crazy.

'There is more going on here than the after-effects of what he experienced at Poko Pā,' said Parakore gravely. 'The black arts are at play.' He looked at Kaiora.

'Let him be,' said Kaiora in a quiet but confident voice. 'I know how to deal with them.'

'Tell me, boy,' he asked Kai, 'what do the spirits say to you?'

'That I am weak. That I am bad. That I am worthless.'

'Someone has caused an attacking spirit to attach itself to the boy,' Kaiora told Tāwae. 'We must destroy its power by giving Kai the protection of a stronger atua.'

That evening Kaiora led the chief and his son to the ahi-tautai, the special spot by Ngāpō Stream, where they lit a ritual fire. Kaiora and Kai removed their clothing, save for the girdle around their waists, and stepped into the sacred waters. The tohunga dipped the leafy end of a karamū branch in the stream and sprinkled water over Kai as he called on his god, using a multitude of names: Tū the angry face, Tū the fierce fighter, destroyer of armies and eater of mankind.

When he had finished the incantation they returned to the bank and Kaiora offered Kai a cooked kūmara. 'Take a bite of this and swallow. Keep the rest of it in your belt and carry it with you.' Kai did as he was told. 'This will lift the heaviness in your soul by stopping the evil influence that is at work on you,' Kaiora explained. 'But it cannot return you to who you were. Your childhood has ended.' Those last words rang in Kai's ears.

Once they were back at Kō Pā, Kaiora said, 'After you have seen more men slain, that feeling of inadequacy inside you will begin to dissipate. You will no longer feel fear or disgust when your enemies are killed. Instead you will feel joy and elation, and eventually you will long for the taste of their hearts and flesh.'

After that evening, Kai sensed something significant shift inside him. It was indeed as if the old Kai had died and a new, more resilient one had been born in his place. He had acquired something. It was a feeling he both welcomed and feared.

+

Before Tūhoro left Ngāpō, the warrior chief told Tāwae he was keen to arrange a marriage between his son Whai and Manu.

'Your uncle intends it as a political alliance,' Tāwae explained to Kiri, 'to ensure our two pā continue to commit our military support to each other. And no doubt so that our lands are retained within the same family.'

Kiri reacted positively. 'We should accept the proposal. My uncle is a skilled fighter — everyone knows he is fearless. If his son grows up to have half his traits and abilities, then this marriage would be a useful alliance, not just for our daughter, but also our son.'

'My thoughts exactly.' Tāwae grinned.

+

The taumau ceremony took place two months later. This ritual allowed the parents to publicly pledge their children in marriage. Such promises could be made from the time the children were scarcely able to walk, but the agreements would not usually be fulfilled until the younger partner had at least reached puberty.

When Tūhoro returned to Kō Pā, the villagers greeted their relatives as if they had not seen them for years. As his people came forward to lay gifts of fine cloaks, Tūhoro spoke in a loud voice.

'I wish to offer our son Whai as a husband for Manu-pōkai, daughter of Tāwae. If you are willing, I shall seal the betrothal by leaving you the vessel *Te Rūrū-a-Tarapīkau*.' The people were stunned at the generous gift of the seventy-seater war canoe, which indicated how serious Tūhoro was about the marriage. It would be a huge affront if the girl's parents declined the proposal, but there was no fear of that happening this time.

Tāwae responded by quoting a proverb: 'He taura taonga e motu, he taura tangata e kore e motu.' *A link through a gift may be severed, but not so a human link.*

His relatives stood with him to recite the karakia hono. From this binding entreaty Tūhoro and his people understood that the matter was satisfactorily arranged. Everyone was happy, knowing the future marriage would strengthen the bonds between the two families and the two pā — Kō and Ōkau.

Tāwae thought back to his own arranged marriage. As soon as Kiri had become fertile, their marriage had to be consummated. She had no choice but to acquiesce regardless of how repulsive she might have found her mate. Tāwae, however, as the son of a chief, was not constrained in the same way and he could have broken the betrothal if he didn't like his new wife. At least they had been of an age where they understood the seriousness of the commitment. Some partners were committed as babies. Whai was one year older than Manu so, just as Tāwae and Kiri had, both understood exactly what was at stake.

CHAPTER TWELVE

He toa mau rākau he toka piringa,
he toa mahi kai he rākau whakamarumaru.
The man who holds a weapon is a rock in a defence,
but one who is expert at food production is a sheltering tree.

'E Kai, me piki ake tāua ki Kai-namu-namu.' *Kai, let's go up to Kai-namu-namu.*

It was just on dusk and the birds were singing goodnight to the daylight when Kiri invited her eldest son to accompany her to the highest point in Kō Pā. As they trod the well-worn track, the blue of the sky had almost gone and the first of the brilliant pearls of the star god, Uru-te-nga-ngana, began appearing in the sky.

'Mahuru was seen last evening,' Kiri panted. 'Everyone will be getting ready to plant.' Kiri suspected Kai knew they were not going to Kai-namu-namu for a chat about planting.

'Rest here on the summit with me,' she said as she slapped a mosquito off her ankle. The twelve-year-old sat below his mother with his back to her and tapped his fingers on his thighs. She pointed over his shoulder at different stars and he tried to say their names before she did. They laughed. It was a game they had played often when he was younger.

Kiri wrapped her arms around her son's chest and rocked him from side to side as she sang a few lines of the kai-oraora she had composed for him when he was a baby. Kai joined in.

'You remember!' she said with surprise.

'I should. You sang it to me enough times when I was young!'

Kiri wished she could keep him in this moment forever so that harm would never come to him. But he had had his first initiation, at Ōtama, and she and Tāwae had agreed on what would happen next. She had accepted the impending change. He was given by the gods, she told herself, and for his sake I have to show strength too. I need to act like the mother of a warrior chief.

'You were born during Mahuru,' Kiri said. 'Since the day you could walk, I have been bringing you up here. I have done that for one reason and one reason only.'

'To point out to me where the people who killed your father live?' Kai answered.

'And your father's father.'

'Yes, both my grandfathers.'

'At your maioha ceremony,' she said, 'your father explained to everyone the meaning of your name.'

She felt her son's body stiffen. At that moment they heard movement below them. Tāwae was climbing the track to join them.

'Have you told him?' Tāwae asked as he sat down next to Kiri. She shook her head, withdrawing her arms from her son. Tāwae paused for a long moment, then cleared his throat.

'Son, your name has to do with Te Maniaroa. You know about Te Maniaroa . . .'

'Of course. It was a famous battle.'

'Many of our relatives were killed there. The chief you saw at Poko Pā . . .'

'Kapua?'

'Yes, Kapua. What was done to him settles the score for your great-uncle, Tūhoro. Your grandfathers' killers, however, still live.'

Kai turned to look at his father, his eyes wide with alarm. 'Kaitanga, your name is a memorial to the day our people heard the news of the slaughter and the eating of our people.'

Kai dropped his head to his hands.

'Taniwha is dead, but his son Whiwhi-rangi lives on. He is *our* Kapua.'

Tāwae and Kiri exchanged a long look, clearly gratified at the effect that the chief's words were having on their son.

'If my uncle, Tūhoro, treated Kapua as he did,' Kiri asked Kai, 'what do you think should be done to your grandfathers' killers?'

Though Kiri didn't actually expect a reply, the weight of the question lay heavily in the air around them.

'Son, tonight will be your last night in our house.' Tāwae placed his hand on Kai's shoulder. 'In the morning you will take your sleeping mat to your Uncle Wehe's wharau. I have arranged it with him. You will live there with him and my uncle will ensure that you are ready for warrior training school when the time comes.'

Kai sat with his head in his hands. He didn't say a word.

+

That night, his last under his parents' roof, Kai felt a huge mix of emotions. There were so many questions he had wanted to ask when they were up at Kai-namu-namu, but he knew better. Sons do not question the decisions of their chiefly fathers. He knew he should feel excited that his life now had a purpose, and that he was about to take the first step towards warrior training, but he felt more apprehension than fear. He felt sure Uncle Wehe disliked him.

Kai had no doubt that his life from this point was going to be tough.

Wehe had temporarily relocated to Ahu Point for the warm season, along with some of the kai-rākau and their wives. They had erected a group of huts on the long stretch of flat ground that ran out from the point.

Upon arrival, Kai looked around Uncle Wehe's new wharau. Its roof was gabled like his own family's dwelling. It was built from timber, raupō, ponga and bark, but much smaller than Kai was used to. Earth was banked up against the walls, and the dirt floor was the usual dug-out covered in ferns and mats. It smelt musty, the smell of a single man's quarters. There was an oblong hearth, with sleeping places set out either side of a central passage. Straight away Kai noticed the human skull lashed to the rushes in the back corner of the wharau. The contusions on one side of the cranium told him that it had been subjected to many violent blows. The bone above the eye had been chipped off.

He reluctantly laid out his sleeping mat. Outside he could hear Uncle Wehe and his father talking and he strained his ears to catch what they were saying.

'You know he can be stubborn, eh?' Tāwae reminded his uncle.

'Yeah, I've seen it, e Rangi. He acts from his emotions — like your father did.' Wehe's throaty guffaw scared Kai more than the thought of being left here.

'He's still at that age where his character can be shaped though,' said Tāwae.

'He is. This is when the power of self-control is best learned. You know I won't go easy on him.'

'As we agreed, you have my permission to do what's required.'

Kai sneaked a peek out the door, hoping to see some evidence of guilt or remorse written on his father's face, but Tāwae had already turned to go back down the beach.

He was on his own now.

Uncle Wehe, who was sitting on a block of wood, called to him to come and eat but Kai said he wasn't hungry. Instead he asked, 'How long will it be before I can return home?' The kai-rākau and their wives, who were seated in a circle eating, froze, waiting for Wehe's reaction.

Without hesitating, Wehe gave Kai a backhander and the boy fell back on the grass, more shocked than hurt. The warrior leader glared at him and said, 'Eat!' It was an order.

The logical response was obvious, but Kai slowly got to his feet, looked his uncle in the eye, and said, 'No.'

Fuming, Wehe punched his nephew in the face. Kai dropped to the dirt, dazed, and Wehe set to stomping him. As Kai tried to protect himself from Wehe's feet, he could see that the kai-rākau and their wives were all watching, but clearly no one was going to intervene.

'Your parents gave you to me, so you do as I say or you'll be sorry. Now, *eat!*' Wehe sat down and resumed his meal.

Bruised and bloodied, Kai definitely had no appetite now, but he stretched out his hand from where he was lying and slowly took a piece of crayfish out of a kono basket. As he did he looked at Wehe, who had his face buried in his kono. I'm going to kill him when I get older, he vowed silently.

Kai struggled to put the meat to his lips and, when he did, he watched the blood from his mouth stain the white flesh red. Then he fell back unconscious.

When he awoke, Hara, one of the kai-rākau, was treating his bruises. As Hara helped Kai into Wehe's hut he told him that his uncle had gone to Ngāpō. Kai curled up on his sleeping mat facing the wall.

'For your own good, boy, do as you're told.' Hara lit the fire and then left Kai alone.

When Wehe returned later, he told the twelve-year-old he was never to make the two-kilometre walk back down the beach to Ngāpō without his permission. Kai, who was still curled up, closed his eyes and said nothing. He thought of his mother and his siblings, especially his brother Tui, and he wept silently.

+

The next morning, Kai was stiff and sore, his face and body bruised and swollen. After they had eaten, Uncle Wehe spoke to him.

'It was not my idea for you to come here. Nor was it my decision for you to join us at Poka Pā. But I have heard that some think you are no longer a child, because you have been committed to Tū-kā-riri, the angry-faced war god. Apparently, so they say, in you lies a ferocious fighter, a conqueror of armies and a devourer of mankind. Ha!' He didn't even try to conceal his contempt.

'Well, I don't see any of that, but while you live under my roof you will do as I say. You will not challenge or question me. In return I will train your character. I have my doubts that you will ever be the fearsome warrior some predict, but if anyone can mould you into that person, it will be me.'

Kai looked at his uncle in silence.

'Every day you will have a range of chores — working in the gardens, digging fernroot, gathering firewood and cleaning in and around our hut. Building a fire will be your final task at the end of each day.'

Kai worked hard during that first day, something he was not used to. By the time he had got the fire going that evening, he was simply too exhausted to eat.

Long after Kai fell asleep, Wehe rose, making his way on all fours to the low doorway. As he passed the boy, he slapped Kai on the side of the face. Kai sat bolt upright. Bewildered, he listened to Wehe urinating at the latrine, but when he returned to his sleeping mat Wehe said nothing.

The next day brought another long day's labour in the gardens, but this time Kai made sure to eat with the others before he turned in for the night. He lit the fire, then drifted off to sleep, allowing it to smoulder on through the night. Once again, as he departed the wharau for the latrine, Wehe slapped Kai's face as he passed. Why was he doing this?

On the third night, as soon as Kai heard the slightest rustling, he squinted into the darkness and listened for Wehe's approach. The warrior drew near and just as he lifted his hand, Kai swiftly moved his head away, evading the blow. Wehe struck the mat instead.

'Hmmph,' he mumbled as he continued on his way.

The next morning, as before, Uncle Wehe did not acknowledge the incident.

Each night after that Kai slept lightly, conscious of every movement in the wharau. Even when he did fall asleep, he found himself waking at the slightest sound. The slapping didn't happen again. His uncle had made his point.

For Kai, most of Mahuru was spent above Ahu planting kūmara and taro. The tribe's gardens were numerous, wide and open, sloping gently down to the beach to maximise exposure to the sun's rays. A thicket of mānuka, which provided shelter, flanked the fields on one side, while a copse of miro trees stood guard on another. The gardens were tightly fenced with reeds so that not even the smallest of rats could creep through.

For some time Kai's daily task, along with two kai-rākau, was to move gravel and sand from the beach up to the hill slopes. Then he had to dig shallow pits and line them with the material. Once the others from his camp had placed kūmara tubers in the pits Kai had to add another thin layer of sand on top and then erect a mānuka brush fence to shelter the pit against the wind. The earthy scent that clung to his hands was a constant reminder of the drudgery of such work. He could work faster, but he was angry that the chief's son was being forced into such menial labour. Several weeks later, after endless days of turning soil for the gardens, the tipu or shoots were picked from the kūmara tubers, laid in furrows, covered over with soil and gently moistened with water. Soon mounds of soil in straight lines could be seen all over the gardens.

One day, as Kai leaned over a furrow, the early morning sun warming his back, he carelessly dropped a bunch of shoots beside Hara.

'Kūmara is the mainstay of life, so you should give this vegetable the utmost respect,' Hara snapped at Kai. The boy was regretful but he was not one to apologise. Hara retrieved the tipu and pushed one into the soil, about half an arm's length from the previous one he had planted.

With the exception of Hara, Kai never spoke to the adults unless he was asked a question. Hara and his wife Rōpā were the only ones who had shown him any kindness since he arrived at Ahu.

'Face the roots towards the east, where the sun rises,' Hara instructed, 'and not too close together, or they won't get enough sun.'

'How do you know when it is the right time to plant?' Kai asked.

'The signs, of course,' said Hara.

'What signs?'

Hara made a mound and heaped sand around it.

'When the yellow tufted blossom of the kūmara-hou plant begins to appear, we know the time is approaching. And for two days now the sky has been speckled. I kiia ai e tātou he rangi kō-tingo-tingo.' *We call it a mackerel sky.*

Kai looked up at the rippling pattern of clouds, which did indeed resemble scales on a fish.

'The clouds tell us that the atua are busy planting above and we ought to be doing the same down here.'

After a last pat around the top of the mound, Hara added quietly, 'Wehe is watching you. You'd better be off to get more sand.'

When the signal was given to stop work for the day, Kai piled up his kete and headed down to the beach to bathe. As soon as he had washed away the dust and grime he headed back to camp. He found his sleeping mat lying outside Uncle Wehe's hut.

'I will not have someone who does not do a hard day's work sleep in my wharau,' his uncle said. Kai frowned but said nothing. Shortly afterwards, when he lined up for the food Rōpā had prepared for the workers, Wehe called out to him.

'Nothing for you tonight, boy! If you don't work hard, don't expect to eat. And if you keep staring at me like that I'll give you something worse than hunger to worry about.'

One night in the cold without food was all it took. Kai was never idle after that. When he worked, he *really* worked. It got so that he embraced the hours of arduous toil, for they kept him so occupied and made him so weary that he had little time or energy to think of anything else.

That was the only night Kai slept outside Uncle Wehe's wharau. Even when Wehe brought a female companion back to their hut, he did not ask the boy to leave. When Kai opened his eyes in the morning the women were never there.

+

From the time Tāwae sent him away, Kai's bitterness towards his father grew. Somehow, he lost sight of all the instances of his father's bravery and the tenderness he had experienced when he was younger. He focused on the rumours he had heard about Tāwae's cowardice, and Uncle Wehe's aspersions about his timidity, and combined these with his sense of his own abandonment. He vowed he would never end up like him.

One day, when Tāwae visited his son at work in the gardens, Kai decided he would say something. As his father approached, Kai asked, 'Why is it that you allow the chief's son to break his back alongside the commoners and the pononga?'

His father crouched down beside him. First, he complimented Kai on the neat and tidy gardens. 'I have not seen better tillage anywhere,' he said. He patted the soil around the kūmara plant and added, 'E Tama, e tupu ana te kūmara, e ohu ana te anuhe.' *Son, as the kūmara grows, the caterpillars gather round it.*

Typical, thought Kai. An obscure answer to a straightforward question.

But Tāwae had not finished. 'A good leader should not be afraid to get down in the dirt alongside the lowest of the tribe. That way he will always have their loyalty.'

Kai thought of their uncle, Tūhoro. It had been his fighting prowess that made others follow him to the battle, not his gardening skills.

'Moea he tangata ringa raupā,' Tāwae continued. *Marry a man with calloused hands.* 'That's what the women of Whānau-a-Mate are advised by their elders.'

Kai glanced at his father's palms and saw that they were indeed covered with hard patches of skin.

'Every person needs to know how to fend for themselves. The day may come when even a chief has only himself to rely on for survival.' Tāwae smiled at his son.

Kai could see the sense in his father's words, though he was not about to say so.

+

The only excitement that occurred during these monotonous toil-filled days took place at the end of one afternoon when a tired and famished Kai was following Hara through the trees back to their camp. Hara, he had learned, was the most superstitious of all the kai-rākau in their camp, always consulting the tohunga for karakia to repel perceived witchcraft or bad omens.

Hara suddenly recoiled, startled by something ahead of him. 'Be careful,' he said, the colour draining from his face. Kai watched nervously as Hara edged his way along the side of the track, his eyes fixed on a tree opposite them. Kai almost missed the tiny reptile, it was so well camouflaged. It scurried down the trunk and into the grass.

'What's the matter?' Kai asked.

'It's mokomoko.[8] He brings news.'

'What news?' the boy asked.

'Whiro, the atua who lives in the underworld, has sent him to tell us that someone close to us is not long for this world.'

'Who?'

'We must wait and see,' Hara said mysteriously as he regained his composure. 'If you're ever in a war party that's on the march, Kai, and a green lizard crosses your path, be warned: that party must turn back. And so it is with us — let's go back the way we came.'

Kai thought about the omens his father had taught him when he was younger.

Perhaps it's something to do with Hara, not me, he told himself.

CHAPTER THIRTEEN

He ora te whakapiri, he mate te whakatakariri.
There is strength in unity and defeat in anger.

Kai squeezed his eyes shut then opened them wide in an effort to stay awake. He was lying on the embankment, listening to the steady pulse of the waves breaking on the beach, his feet idly kicking the sand. The last few afternoons he had been constantly tired from all the early mornings and pulling weeds all day in the hot sun.

Every moment of his life at Ahu was filled, leaving no time to dwell on how things used to be. The only thing Kai sometimes longed for was the company of his cousins and his younger brother. He really missed Tui.

Living with his uncle was tough. Wehe would punish him for the slightest mistake or oversight. When they were out fishing and Wehe had his back to him, Kai imagined himself striking the warrior leader with his paddle and leaving him to drown.

'When you finish your work today, wait down at the beach,' Wehe had told him that morning. Kai was to have his first formal wrestling lesson.

Kai flared his nostrils, trying to separate the odours on the light sea breeze into seaweed, fish, salt, water and shellfish. Every now and then he glanced down the beach, unsure what he was expecting to see. He knew by now that there was no limit to what his uncle might have him do.

It wasn't long before he spotted Wehe coming from Ngāpō. Kai sat up and squinted at the two figures following behind him. There was a boy walking not far behind, and about two hundred metres further back was someone else. As they came closer, Kai realised the third person was his older sister, Manu, sneaking along with them, probably unbeknown to Wehe.

'Come over here,' Wehe commanded the two boys as he marked out a large circle in the sand with his foot. The other boy was about the same size as Kai, although perhaps a little older. 'Boy,' Wehe said to Kai, 'this is Te Ika, son of Roro. Te Ika, this is Kai, son of Tāwae.'

That was the niceties out of the way.

'Stand each side of me,' Wehe instructed. 'You're here to learn to fight.' He recited a wrestling incantation while the two boys stood on opposite sides of the circle, heads bowed.

Tipua te mamau, tahito te mamau.
Hei konā koe noho mai ai
Noho ki tipua, noho ki tahito.
Noho ki Maru-ā-nuku
Te hongi, te kata, te tangi, te ūmere.

Let me be vested in the art of wrestling, an expert at grappling.
And may you be forced to the ground
Where you will remain under [me], an experienced fighter and
 expert.
Remain at Maru-ā-nuku
Where I will greet you, laugh, cry and shout in applause
 [after winning].[9]

When Kai looked up, he saw his sister had sat down on the embankment a short distance away to watch them. Some of the kai-rākau, having cleaned themselves up, had come to watch too. Kai spotted Hara amongst them.

'Mamau requires endurance, speed and strength,' Wehe said as he began the lesson. He told the boys how to position their feet and showed them the basic moves of wrestling, making them practise until he felt both boys had a firm grasp of them. Then he set them to try the moves on each other.

Kai was eager to engage with Te Ika and test these grappling techniques. He moved cautiously. His plan was to seize Te Ika's neck and throw him across his hip, like he and his mates used to do when they wrestled back in the village. But somehow Te Ika slipped out of his grasp like an ascending vapour. It was clear to Kai right away that his opponent was much more capable than he was, as if he had had previous training.

Like the spikes of a kina, which rise at the slightest touch, anger grew in Kai's belly as Te Ika continually managed to put him in a choke hold — and laughed as he did so. It was only a matter of time before Kai's anger erupted. Powered by fury, he manoeuvred his chin down so that his jaws were near the fleshy part of Te Ika's forearm. As he clamped on, he tasted the mix of brine and sweat on Te Ika's skin. When Te Ika could no longer stand the pain he broke his hold and Kai let fly with his fists. Wehe waded in and grabbed Kai, throwing him on the sand as easily as he would a calabash of water.

'Control your aggression!' Wehe bellowed at his nephew. 'Or I'll get in there — and you know you won't like that. Now stay outside the circle until you've cooled down.'

Kai sat on the sand, hugging his knees to his chest. His heart was beating wildly and his hands were shaking.

'E kore te pātiki e hoki ki tōna puehu,' said Wehe. *The flounder does not return to his dust.*

He was telling Kai not to make the same mistake twice.

'If you use your speed you can outmanoeuvre him, but you haven't realised that because you're letting your rage scorch you from the inside out. You need to channel that anger to your advantage. Until you learn to do that, you are useless to your people.'

'Tika tēnā, e Kai,' Hara added from the sidelines. *That's right, Kai.*

While Kai was cooling off, Manu approached Wehe. 'Uncle, I want to learn mamau too. Can you teach me?'

'So that's why you followed us?' Wehe said with surprise. Te Ika gave a contemptuous bark of laughter.

'What are you sniggering at?' Manu glowered at him. 'I'll beat you in a fight any day.' Te Ika gave her a smirk then looked away.

'Now, now, young lady,' Wehe started. 'You know your husband-to-be is expecting you in two moons.'

'What does that matter?'

'Imagine if your parents presented you at Ōkau Pā all battered and bruised. Mamau doesn't come without sprains, bruises, dislocations and sometimes concussions. If Whai's parents see you in such a state, they might change their minds.'

'I can beat this boy or my brother, or any of the other boys my age for that matter. As for Uncle Tūhoro and Aunty Hīraia, they would probably prefer a warrior wife for Whai.' Her penetrating look reminded Wehe of her mother and he grinned.

'I'm sorry, my dear, I cannot. Not without your father's permission, and I already know what he would say.'

After the session ended, Wehe told Kai that Te Ika would be moving into their wharau and that Wehe was shifting to a hut alongside.

'Show your relation where he will be sleeping, boy.'

Kai was pleasantly surprised that someone his age was joining their camp and any anger he had felt towards his rival instantly disappeared.

In the wharau Te Ika asked Kai, 'So, we're related, eh?' They worked out that Te Ika's father, Roro, who had passed away a few years earlier, was Kai's great-grandfather. And yet the difference in their age was no more than a half-dozen moons.

Despite their rocky beginning, Kai and Te Ika soon became friends. Kai had grown accustomed to being on his own but he found Te Ika easy to be around because he was outgoing and never took anything too seriously. He also had an endless supply of folk stories, which he shared each night. He had gleaned these from the people in his pā in the Waiapu Valley. Even the stories Kai knew already, Te Ika told with a freshness and a humour that never failed to entertain.

Te Ika, for his part, was a little wary of his mate. He liked and respected him, but he also knew not to mess with him.

Kai had slowly begun to feel more accepted at Ahu. Te Ika was there, and Hara had become almost a friend to them both. Hara had taken to allowing the boys to ask him one question each night before they retired, which he vowed to answer if he could. This was how Kai learned that the skull that had been in their wharau (and which, thankfully, Uncle Wehe had taken with him to his new wharau) was the first of half a dozen trophies the warrior leader had taken over a lifetime of battles. If Hara could be believed, the skull was particularly special to Wehe because 'it used to sit on the shoulders of the man who killed his wife'. Kai had often seen Wehe talking to the skull, or, more accurately, taunting it with remarks like, 'You're not so fearsome now, are you?'

Hara also told them that the only thing Wehe feared, if he feared anything at all, was a surprise attack. Hara said he had never known Wehe to sleep more than a few nights in the same place, and if he received an ill-omen he would not sleep in a whare at all. This explained why his uncle so often disappeared at dusk.

+

One day Kiri came to the camp, bringing word that Kai's great-grandmother, Old Ue, was suffering more than usual from the weather. Kai was beside himself with joy to see his mother. She immediately noticed the welts and bruises all over her son's face and body but said nothing. He now wore his hair shaggy, rather than groomed in a topknot, which is how she used to keep it.

Fighting the urge to run to her son and wrap him in her arms, Kiri stood at a respectful distance. Wehe and the kai-rākau were watching. 'Come with me, my son,' she said to him instead, then she turned and began walking back up the beach. 'We must visit Nanny.'

Kai was quietly thrilled at the chance to spend time with his mother and pay a visit to his great-grandmother. It would also be a chance for him to catch up with his siblings. He still missed them often, but he kept uttering the words his mother had given him — 'Kuruki, whakataha' — and the feeling seemed to dissipate.

Kiri explained to her son that Old Ue had been moved to a temporary hut outside Ngāpō village.

'Hara told me our people never occupy a house in which anyone dies; that we burn it instead,' Kai said to his mother as they left the beach and strolled up the Ngāpō Stream together. 'Is that why Nanny has been removed from the village? Is she going to die?'

'Sickness carries a stigma of being unclean. That's why her hut is away from the village,' Kiri replied. 'Nā ngā atua ngā māuiui katoa.' *All sickness is the work of the gods.*

They walked in silence for a while.

'What else has Hara told you?' Kiri asked.

'A few things. I ask him questions and we discuss stuff.' Kiri felt a twinge of jealousy. Kai was no longer hers. He may only have been two kilometres along the beach, but they were as far apart now as two islands.

+

When they reached the open-air hut, Kaiora and Parakore were just leaving, chanting karakia as they did so. Tāwae and Tui were seated at Old Ue's side while Manu tried to feed her, but their tipuna wasn't interested in food. Manu gave her father a look of despair.

'He kiore, nāna te tono,' she told him. *It's rat — she requested it.* The air was smoky because the fire had to be kept stoked. Old Ue, propped up against a wall, smiled feebly, displaying her now toothless gums, and beckoned Kai and Tui closer.

She's nothing but skin and bone, Kai thought, trying to smile back at his great-grandmother. She ran her scrawny fingers down their cheeks.

'She thinks you're her sons,' their father explained.

'She'll be all right, won't she, Pāpā?' Tui asked.

'Toitū te whenua, whatu ngarongaro te tangata,' Tāwae said softly. *The land remains, but people pass on.*

Overcome with sadness, Kai spent the rest of the day in solitude, walking along the beach, dragging a stick behind him. He had promised to return to Ahu by nightfall. He only wished he could outwit Hine-nui-te-pō, the goddess of death, so that his great-grandmother would remain with them a little longer and his family's sorrow might be lifted.

+

'Aiee! Aiee!' The whole village heard the plaintive cries coming from the kuia's hut a few nights later.

The pahū in Kō Pā was used to relay the message to the closest Ngāi Haere pā. The carved block of mataī, in an inverted canoe-shape, hung from a tree in the pā and one of the kai-rākau drummed incessantly on it. Everyone knew the different rhythms and what they signalled. First the drummer identified the tribe and repeated it again and again. Next, he named the pā: Kō of Ngāpō. Repeatedly the name Kō was drummed out, and then Old Ue was named.

Kai was lying on his bed mat at Ahu when he heard it. He leapt up and ran out of his hut, onto the sand and down the beach to be with his beloved tipuna. As he neared Ngāpō Stream he stopped briefly to catch his breath. He could hear the loud sobs of the women. Fire torches had been set on wooden poles to light up the area outside the hut.

Many of his relatives had already congregated at the entrance to the hut. The crowd parted and ushered him forward. Kai surveyed the pathetic scene. His father had laid his head on the kuia's bony frame and was singing a lament, while Kiri and Manu, wearing mournful looks, each held one of her hands. Kai dropped to his knees and laid his cheek on Old Ue's thin, scarred arms. He tried to hold back, but tears gushed forth.

The following morning more distant pā were notified by means of smoke signals.

Two men and two women, led by Kaiora, had carried Old Ue's corpse to an ancient kahikatea tree, quite a distance from the village. There they prepared the tūpāpaku for the funeral ceremony.

Kai told his father he wanted to go along to observe. Tāwae advised him against it — the family of the deceased were under the tapu of death and were restricted in what they could do — but Kai was insistent.

'I need to understand death, Father. And what better time than with one who was always affectionate towards me?' Tāwae was unconvinced, but Kiri touched his arm and said, 'Let him go. He needs to do this. He's not a boy any more; he's a young man.' Kai looked at his mother, his eyes shining with gratitude.

Although it was unusual for children to observe the ritual, the funeral party dared not order the chief's son away. They had been at their work for some time. The corpse had been hung by its feet from the tree, washed, dried and now the two women were rubbing the skin with some oil that gave off a strong scent. Kai thought the women looked close to death themselves, they seemed so old and frail. All the time Kaiora was waving leaves and chanting words of encouragement to Old Ue's spirit to transition to the next world.

As the two men unfastened Old Ue's thin frame from the tree, Kai recognised the kahikatea. It was the one they had been told as children never to play near, nor gather kindling from beneath it.

'Sit her up,' the tohunga instructed the men.

'She's so small,' one of the men remarked, 'this won't be difficult.'

Kai watched as they tucked his tipuna's knees up under her chin, then wrapped her arms tightly around her legs and tied them in place with flax cord. Next they sat the corpse on a litter and wrapped mats and cloaks around it up to the chin.

Then it was the women's turn. 'Turn up her hair,' one of them directed, and they pulled Old Ue's thin locks into a tie before they combed and oiled them. They placed snow-white toroa or albatross feathers in her hair, and set a garland of pungent-smelling kawakawa leaves encircling her forehead. Kawakawa was also inserted in her orifices.

Tufts of toroa down were used as ear ornaments and a jade pendant was suspended from her neck. Next, they took the kōkōwai they had brought with them, smeared the red ochre over Old Ue's body and slathered it with shark oil. Finally the tūpāpaku was carried to a mat laid out on the marae in front of the main whare puni.

Up until this point, Kai had observed the procedure with fearful fascination, but showed no emotion. As he followed along, watching people scatter as if his party were infected with a plague, he finally broke down and began weeping.

'E tangi, e tangi ki tōu tipuna,' one of the old ladies encouraged him. *Weep, weep for your nanny.*

The rest of his whānau joined him in sitting at the feet of their nanny's corpse. Those who had handled the body or conveyed it onto the marae were, like the immediate family, under the strictest tapu. They could not enter a house or come into contact with anyone or touch food with their hands without spreading contamination until the tangihanga was over. Food had to be placed in baskets in front of them, and they would have to kneel or sit, with their hands held behind their backs, and nibble at it the best they could. The immediate family had their own personal feeder.

Parakore arrived with some preserved heads and bones belonging to Old Ue's tīpuna and placed them on a platform behind the tūpāpaku. These human heads looked eerily alive. After death they had been steamed to soften the insides for removal. The brain had been drawn out, the tongue cut away, the eyes plucked out and the eyelids sewn down before the head was smoke-dried and oiled. Displayed to one side was an array of weapons that had belonged to Old Ue's sons and husband.

The tangihanga lasted for days as a steady stream of mourners from villages and pā throughout the district continued to arrive from morning till just before nightfall to pay their respects. Each group filed onto the marae to where a row of women waved sprigs of kawakawa and called them forward.

The manuhiri stood in front of the tūpāpaku and poured out their grief for all the recent dead. Some of the kuia, who had known Old Ue well, were swaying, a quivering hand held up as they spoke directly to her in short phrases that recalled times shared. Mournful wailing drew more welcoming calls from the reception party.

Kai and Tui, their bodies rubbed all over with kōkōwai, sat impassively alongside their father to greet each new group. Tāwae held a small lump of dry ochre, which he used to reapply colour to his own and to his sons' bodies whenever required.

Kai felt numb, barely noticing the hugs and hongi, which the visitors intended to be comforting. His mother had to remind him to eat in order to sustain himself for the duration of the tangihanga.

During one lull in proceedings Tui asked Kai what it was like living with their Uncle Wehe.

'At first I was really scared, but now it's not as bad as you might think. Things are getting better.' He spoke with conviction and Tui looked satisfied with his reply. 'Our cousin Te Ika and I share a hut,' he told him. 'It's not like our house, but we get to look after ourselves.' Kai noticed his father listening in.

Kai was mesmerised by the drama that played out on the marae as different speakers held court. One sour-looking, hefty man, adorned by moko that covered his face, arms, thighs and lower back, castigated his Whānau-a-Mate relatives for letting Old Ue die without witnessing vengeance for her sons. He pranced across the marae, gesturing wildly and flourishing his greenstone mere. He would take about fifteen steps in one direction while making a point (Kai was counting), then turn and run back fifteen steps, giving voice to another vital point. Kai thought it quite possible he might keep going forever.

'That man looked like he was really angry,' Tui said to Kai later.

'I thought that too, at first, but I realised he was acting angrier than he really was. It's all part of the drama, little brother.'

Another speaker paced to and fro, a magnificent feather cloak across his shoulders and a whalebone club — his family's cherished heirloom — in his hand.

'Ko wai tēnei tangata, a Aituā?' he taunted. *Who is this person, Death?* He leapt from the ground, slapped his thigh, shouted and waved his mere. Kai and Tui sat up. 'Had he but taken the form of a man,' the speaker cried, 'I could fight him with this wahaika of mine! But he is elusive — he cannot be conquered!'

'Boy, I'd sure like to be able to speak like that when I grow up,' Tui whispered.

'Hmm,' Kai replied distractedly. He was focused not on the quality of the man's oratory but rather the deeper meaning of the words. One day I, too, must face death, Kai thought to himself. I hope, when that day comes, that I will not shame myself, nor my family, like my father has done.

Kai soaked it all up, knowing that as the oldest male among his siblings, he would be expected to perform in this way one day.

Many of the speeches were directed at his father and sometimes even himself. Although they often used euphemisms and allegories, Kai now understood that the speakers were referring to Te Maniaroa and the fate of Old Ue's sons. When the ceremony finally ended, the burden of expectation that had been bequeathed to Kai had finally been bestowed in its entirety.

CHAPTER FOURTEEN

Ka moe whārōrō tangata i te whata pakapaka,
ka moe koromeke tangata kāre āna whata pakapaka.
The man whose storehouse is filled stretches out his legs and sleeps in comfort,
but he who has no such storehouse sleeps huddled up.

Kai straightened his back and looked up admiringly at the canopies of the trees seeking the sun. The days now were full of bright sunshine and blue skies that sang of the coming summer.

He and Te Ika had joined some of the kai-rākau and their wives in the bush-fernland near Puia, a morning's walk south of Ahu. Although the whole country abounded with the bracken fern, not all fern was edible. The best roots flourished in loose, rich soil. Certain areas were prized and carefully preserved because of their superior fernlands. Kaupeka-a-Haumia was one such, Haumia being the atua of fernroot. It had been placed under rāhui or embargo by Tāwae — no trespassing was allowed and no one could take aruhe *fernroot* from it out of season, except on pain of death. This is where they had come, an authorised foraging party, to dig aruhe.

Kai had laboured day after day digging, until time lost all meaning for him. He had thought planting kūmara and taro was hard work but he'd gladly be back in the gardens now.

'Let's go again,' said Hara, and the line of men gripped the handles of their kō or digging sticks and planted their feet down on the foot treads. Kai felt the soil loosening as his kō dug in. Then the group all heaved together, and the long mass of earth tore away. The women were soon on their knees breaking up the clods of earth with their timo or grubbers, then plucking out the bracken roots and throwing them into a heap. The first three pieces of root they had laid aside as an offering on the first day at Kaupeka-a-Haumia. At the same time, they had examined the aruhe by breaking it. They were pleased to find it dry internally because that meant it would grow a superior crop.

'How many more days of this, Hara?' Kai asked.

'The more we collect the better,' Hara replied. 'We don't want to run out in the days when food is scarce. And we need a good supply for your sister's wedding.'

At the end of each day the roots were gathered into bundles and packed in pīkau kete to carry back to Ahu.

Kai was the only one who had to carry his load in front of him rather than on his back, which was more challenging.

'A chief's back is not made for carrying anything but his children,' Hara told him. 'Any provisions you carry on your back are rendered tapu and useless to anyone but yourself.'

As they plodded along the beach, Hara said to Kai and Te Ika, 'A man who is diligent in providing fernroot is looked up to and has no difficulty finding a wife.'

'I'm not after a wife,' Kai responded quickly.

'Nor am I,' said Te Ika.

'Not yet, but you will be,' Hara laughed.

At Ahu the fernroot was laid out on elevated platforms. Kai and Te Ika were tasked with placing fronds of tree-ferns over them to protect them from the sun.

'When they're dry,' said Hara, 'we'll sort them by quality — some for the chiefs, some for the kai-rākau, some for the wedding, some for visitors, some for daily use, and some for the pononga. Then we'll pack the roots in kete and put them in the storage pits.'

+

The rātā trees were blossoming when arrangements were finalised for Tāwae and Kiri to visit Ōkau Pā to deliver Manu to Whai and his people.

It had been two months since Wehe had started training Kai and in that time Manu had not been allowed to participate, although she often sat up on the embankment and watched. One day after he had finished mamau training Kai sat down next to his sister.

'You've got a lot better at that, brother,' Manu said.

'I'm sorry you weren't allowed to join us.'

'It's all right,' she shrugged. 'I've got to focus on my wedding anyway. You seem to have the better of Te Ika now.' She smiled.

'Yeah, I've learned how to wrestle with skill instead of rage,' Kai said solemnly. 'I've realised speed and technique can overcome muscle, as long as I remember to keep calm.'

'I've heard our parents say you have Grandfather Kū's temper.'

They both chuckled.

Kai asked Manu how she felt about leaving the pā and living away from the family.

'To be honest, I thought I'd be here until after Te Maniaroa was avenged,' she told him. 'I've heard about it all my life, and I often overheard Nanny Arakura and Nanny Whakaata talking about my name and how it was connected to the battle. I assumed there was always a chance that I'd be part of the war party. But when you were sent to live with Uncle Wehe I realised our parents were investing everything in you.'

'It does look that way. Are you nervous about getting married?'

'At first I was terrified at the thought. I'm less afraid now, but still nervous. I asked Mother, "Me mea kāre māua e pīrangi i a māua anō, me aha?" *What if my cousin doesn't like me, or I find I don't like him?*

'She said, "When your parents commit you, the matter is settled." Just like you, brother. They committed you to the task of avenging our grandfathers, and you have no option but to follow through.'

'Believe me, I know.'

'But I do have one thing to ask of you . . .'

133

'Anything.'

'Not now, but when the time comes for you to fulfil your destiny, you must first visit me at Ōkau Pā.'

'You have my word.' Kai hugged his big sister. 'I'll miss you, Sis. So much has changed. Sometimes I wish we could go back to when we were small.'

Manu looked her brother in the eyes. 'Time only moves forward, Brother. We must always look to the future and be ready for whatever it brings.'

+

All the wedding provisions and a great dowry were placed in two large waka. Then, nearly one hundred relatives of all ages — men, women and children — were assisted into the vessels, which were decorated with kōkōwai. The carved prow was festooned with bunches of toroa feathers. Haere, now almost four, managed to escape Kiri's grip and race into the water, reaching up on tiptoes to the rauawa, eyes wide, hoping to be allowed to sit next to her sister.

There was much chatter and an unmistakable aura of excitement.

Once the vessels were ready to depart, Kai turned to Tui. 'What beautiful weather to go to sea,' he said.

He welcomed these breaks from the routine at Ahu, mainly as it meant he got to see his family again. He enjoyed the visits while they lasted, for they were few. He treated them as a holiday from the long hours of work — and beatings — he had grown accustomed to.

The ever-so-slight breeze, if there was one at all, carried a scent of something faint, hardly noticeable. Kai tried to put his finger on what it was. It was fresh, but not like the freshness of the sea. It was coming from the north and in an odd way he felt drawn to it.

'I love visiting our whanaunga,' Tui said to him.

'Without our relatives where would we be?' Kai replied.

'How long do you think we'll stay this time?'

'Until the next new moon, I hope.' That's what Wehe had told

Kai. 'Grab your paddle,' he said to Tui, quickly taking up his own hoewai and joining in the paddling in case his younger brother asked him something he did not know the answer to. He often did, and sometimes Kai took the questions to Hara, so that he was ready when he next saw his little brother. Now that Kai no longer lived with Tui, he wanted to give the impression that he was already a warrior in training. 'Nothing is unknown to the warrior,' he would say to Tui, and his brother would gaze at him in awe.

The ceremony at Ōkau Pā was to be a grand affair. Manu looked stunning. Red ochre adorned the soft skin of her face, shoulders and arms; shark oil enhanced her chin tattoo and long black hair; and a fine kiwi-feather cloak, dyed in many colours, reached down to her knees. All of this was complemented by a tuft of sweet-smelling leaves, which hung from her waist.

When the waka delivered them ashore, Manu followed a procession of her people who had formed into four lines on the warm sand. All were dressed in their best attire. Kiri, Haere and two teenage cousins, their hair sleek black and all wearing pounamu, escorted Manu to the front of the group. The bride, just turned fourteen, was the spitting image of her mother at that age, who was once Ōkau's beauty. Leading the party up the long path to the first tier of the huge pā was one of Manu's uncles, performing a haka.

They advanced towards the marae, seeing the bright flowers and tree ferns that decorated the inside perimeter of the palisaded pā. Kete of kūmara were piled up well over two metres high against one of the palisades. For Kai they brought to mind his endless efforts in the gardens at Ahu. The kete that held the kūmara had been freshly woven by the women of the pā. Beyond these dangled a long line of dried shark hanging from mānuka poles.

The local people were congregated beside the house that had been built as a wedding gift to Manu. Whai's relatives, some seeing Manu for the first time, scrutinised her to confirm for themselves that she was as others had said, beautiful and ready for marriage. The manuhiri walked slowly towards the large, decorated whare puni, their expressions focused and seemingly oblivious to the cacophony of the welcome. Some of the local women, standing singly out on the marae or mounted on a palisade, were wailing loudly and dolefully. Each was waving a small piece of tapa cloth to encourage the visitors forward.

The manuhiri finally stopped about thirty metres from their hosts. The Whānau-a-Mate visitors wept for Old Ue and other relatives who had lately passed. Salutes took place between the groups of relatives. Kai and Tui greeted Whai, their cousin, who was soon to become their brother-in-law.

'Ah, my cousins, I hope I can rely on you both in the future,' Whai said solemnly.

'We would do anything for our sister,' Kai replied.

Whai, now fifteen, was stocky like his father. Kai and Tui, in contrast, had inherited their mother's lean genes and it was clear they would outstrip Whai in height before long.

Tāwae's tohunga were invited to lift the tapu from the new house. Until that ritual was complete, no one was allowed to enter it. Parakore, wearing a white kaitaka, escorted Manu to the porch, while Kaiora climbed on the roof and stood over the ridgepole. Kaiora recited the necessary kawa whare to free the house from tapu. When he had finished the incantation, Parakore turned to Manu.

'Me piki i te paepae poto, e Manu.' *Step over the doorstep, Manu.*

Kiri had explained to Manu that custom required that a virgin bride-to-be must be the first to enter the house. As Manu approached the door she looked up at the carved lintel and paused. Then, just as she had been taught, she reached into her cloak and placed her hand under her waist covering. She smeared her fingers with the fluid of her vulva, then reached up and wiped it along the under-surface of the lintel before walking through the door.

The tohunga followed her into the house reciting karakia. Manu's parents and close relatives trailed behind and they all took seats in the house. Then, one after another, the leaders of both pā made speeches outside.

Tūhoro began. He walked back and forth in front of the whare as he delivered his words of welcome: 'May our hapū continue to be bound in friendship.'

The people responded, 'Āe!' *Yes!*

'We know each other well, for you are a tribe of warriors just as we are.'

'Āe!'

'Indeed, we are branches of the same stream.'

'Āe!'

'For that reason, our son will be a good husband for your daughter. Good health to us all.'

'Āe!'

And to Manu he called, 'Haere mai, taku taonga.' *Welcome, my treasure.*

Tūhoro's oratory was followed by others offering their warmest greetings to Manu.

When they finished, Tāwae's cousin, Te Ūneke, began the series of replies on behalf of their people.

He spoke to Whai. 'We are entrusting you with our daughter. Not for the first time, for her mother was also one of yours. And like her mother she will bear you many sons and daughters. She will be a good wife to you.'

Finally, Manu was led out of the house by her family and, amidst everyone's tears of joy and approval, Whai placed his cloak around hers. Tūhoro's tohunga recited invocations over the couple to preserve them in health and prosperity and to ward off all evil.

Manu was visibly nervous so the tohunga repeated his incantation over her, encouraging her to cleave to Whai, or for them to be whakapiri — fastened together. Whai turned and pressed his nose to Manu's. Nervous he might have been but he was also deliriously happy. Whai had always been keen on his younger cousin, although Manu did not know it. Their eyes closed, foreheads slightly touching in a prolonged embrace. The ceremony ended when the couple's siblings rushed up to congratulate them.

'Our girl is coy in his company,' Kiri remarked to Tāwae as they threaded their way through the crowd.

'So is he,' Tāwae replied. 'Just as we were.' His eyes were teary at losing his firstborn.

'We couldn't be prouder of you, Manu,' Kiri said as she wrapped her arms around her daughter.

'Remember this, my girl,' Tāwae choked, 'living with a man is not something to be endured, but savoured.'

Manu smiled, struggling to hold back her own anxious tears.

A procession of people from the pā, each bearing a basket of cooked food, and all singing, slowly advanced towards the house. They placed the baskets in a row on flax mats and drew back. Tāwae and his whānau seated themselves before the food and began eating.

Tui turned to Kai.

'It's great to be away from home.'

'It sure beats weeding gardens,' Kai agreed.

'Oh yeah, I'm sick of that too,' Tui said.

Kai, often entertained by his brother's comments, smiled. 'Has Pāpā got you working in the gardens?'

'Hardly,' their mother chimed in.

'"Marry a hard-working man." That's what the women say, Tui,' said Tāwae.

'It should be "Marry a warrior,"' Kai muttered under his breath.

Tāwae raised his eyebrows but said nothing.

'Anyway, who needs a wife?' Tui responded, and everyone erupted with laughter.

'Why is the marriage feast called kai kōtore if kōtore means buttocks?' Kai asked his father.

'Ehara i te mea i moe ko tōna māhunga i te tāne. Kātahi rā! I moe ko tōna kōtore kē,' said Tāwae with a twinkle in his eye. *It's not as if the man cohabits with her head. No, he does so with her lower half!*

'What does that mean?' asked Tui, clearly perplexed.

Kai laughed and prodded his brother. 'You'll find out when you're a man, little brother.'

'Fact is, Tui,' Kiri chimed in, 'Your brother is just as confused as you are, but he's not letting on!'

Kai stuffed his mouth full of crayfish meat to hide the fact that he was blushing.

The food for their family had been cooked in a separate umu, it being the very best that Tūhoro's people had procured over the past months. Only Manu's immediate relatives were offered the delicacies drawn from the umu kōtore, with some exceptions. The newlyweds themselves were not invited to partake. Nor did Kiri allow Haere or little Kura, the latest addition to their family, to sample those dishes, the superstition being that it might cause her daughters to become barren.

The rest of the party were fed from other ovens and they took their meals at a distance from Manu's family.

That night, Whai and Manu were expected to consummate their marriage on their specially made takapau-wharanui in the chief's house.

The next morning the newlyweds emerged smiling. Whai was holding the flax mat, intent on retaining it for their own whare, as custom required. As people cheered the happy couple, Kai over-heard Tāwae talking to Wehe.

'Though Kai doesn't see it yet,' Tāwae said, 'this alliance will be of the utmost importance to him in the future.'

Wehe said nothing.

Kai wondered what his father meant.

CHAPTER FIFTEEN

He puta taua ki te tāne, he whānau tama ki te wahine.
Fighting with men, and childbirth with women.

The cool atmosphere around Ahu numbed the boys' faces, giving them red noses and cheeks that felt rubbed raw. Though the sun still shone often enough, it did little to penetrate the chill winter air. The sea was cold; when Kai and Te Ika went diving for shellfish off the point they didn't stay in the water long.

The seals hauled themselves ashore more often to laze in the weak sun, while the birds started readying themselves for their winter migration. When the biting winds did arrive, they were accompanied by a blanket of white across the mountains and an unpredictability in the weather.

When Wehe didn't have work for Kai and Te Ika, which was more often now, they were allowed to visit Ngāpō, where they spent their free time mucking about with Tui and their cousins. Kai seemed to get into fights almost on a daily basis, often because he felt Tui was being bullied.

Morning frosts tended to keep the adults at home, where they sat huddled over their fires for such long periods that their faces were garnished with a semi-permanent veil of soot. With their flax cloaks pulled over their mouths, and their eyes reddened and inflamed by the smoke, they reminded Kai of the ghosts he had seen in his nightmares.

Though their huts were the warmest places in the village, the smoky confinement made some of the older ones short of breath, and there was a lot of coughing. The younger family members ventured outside whenever they could.

One day as Kai and Te Ika were leaving the village, heading down the beach back to Ahu Point, they spotted someone sitting half-obscured under a tree beyond the mouth of the Ngāpō Stream. Kai stared and worked out it was Hauā, who was named so because she was paralysed in one leg below the knee, Hauā meaning *crippled*. She was the poor soul tasked with feeding the kiri mate or bereaved family during funerals. She had fed Kai and his whānau at Old Ue's tangihanga. It was her only practical role in the village. Dragging her foot behind her, and a basket of kai in her hand, Hauā would sit herself in front of each family member and, using a stick to skewer the food, stretch out her arm so as not to touch any of them because her hands were considered permanently tapu. Morning and night, maramara kai or scraps of food were thrown to her and she, without using her hands, would gnaw at them with her teeth.

People with deformities, either through birth or from being wounded in battle, were an uncommon sight at Ngāpō and received little sympathy. A severely deformed child was sometimes killed at birth. Poorly clothed and often daubed in kōkōwai, the funeral paint, Hauā spent most of her time on the outskirts of the village, some way off the thoroughfare, gazing at the happenings on the beach or in the village that she was barely a part of.

'E . . . e . . . e . . . Kai!' she called.

'Ignore her,' said Te Ika.

'She does no harm,' Kai replied, turning to walk towards her.

He pulled away a few branches so he could see her face in her lair of sticks and leaves. She was not an old woman, but, haggard and miserable, she looked beyond her years. Her eyes were like slits, barely open. Kai knew she was taunted by the children as half mad. He had never indulged in this behaviour himself, but then he had never stopped his mates from doing so either.

'Many things for you to overcome, Kai,' she said in a weak voice. 'Many, many things.'

'What things?' asked Kai, slightly taken aback.

'Men . . . spirits . . . fear,' she said slowly.

'I'm not afraid,' Kai hit back.

Again, Hauā said slowly, 'Men . . . spirits . . . fear.'

Clearly she was not going to elaborate, so Kai flicked his hand at her, turned and walked back to Te Ika.

'Tuahangata! Nauhea!' she called out. 'Tuahangata! Nauhea!' She kept repeating the words, her voice getting louder and louder.

'Do you understand what she's saying?' Te Ika asked.

'No idea. Sounds like rubbish. She's crazy.'

'No, they're real words. I used to hear my father say that, and some of the old people.'

'What's it mean?'

'Hero. Rogue.'

'Huh.' Kai kicked the sand. 'Like I said, she's crazy.'

'Yeah, she's crazy.'

+

The kai-rākau had been erecting more huts at the foot of Tūtata Hill adjacent to Ahu, but no one seemed to be using them. Kai knew better than to ask Uncle Wehe about them.

Then one day Wehe told the two boys to move their gear back to their homes in the village until the end of winter. A few days later, outside the village, the kai-rākau gathered together thirty local boys, all aged between thirteen and sixteen. Kai and Te Ika were among them and assumed it was a planning meeting about the forthcoming planting season.

'You boys have been selected as the next group for warrior training,' Wehe announced, to thirty audible gasps. The boys gave each other wide-eyed looks. Kai was elated. *At last.*

'Would you look at that?' Te Ika said, grinning himself. 'I didn't think you ever smiled!' Kai gave him a shove but could barely conceal his delight. Part of the joy, he acknowledged to himself, was because for him there would be no more long days in the cultivations.

'Ahu is now off limits to you all,' Wehe continued. 'Don't let us catch you going down that part of the beach any more. On the night before the new moon you are to take your mats to the whare puni in the village, where you'll all sleep under the same roof.'

The meeting broke up and the excited huddle of boys wound their way back to the village.

'I reckon you and I are about the youngest in the group, Kai,' said Te Ika, looking around him. 'We should stick together. Watch each other's backs.'

'Yep,' Kai responded vaguely. He was remembering back to three harvests earlier, when the last school was convened. He had been terrified witnessing his older cousins being struck, kicked and jeered at by armed kai-rākau who ushered them out of the whare puni and down the frosty path to a bitterly cold Ngāpō Stream to begin their training. Yet, when he saw them pass out of warrior training school three years later, fully tattooed and with splendid physiques and festooned with weapons, he longed to be one of them.

Over the next few days the boys carried on with their lives as if nothing had changed, but in fact each of them thought of little but the impending training. They watched for the slightest sign from any kai-rākau that things were being readied, and they tried to eavesdrop on the conversations of their elders. When Tāwae returned from a rūnanga meeting not saying a word about what had been discussed, Kai assumed it must have had something to do with the training.

The kai-rākau were definitely coming and going from Ahu more often than usual.

'I've heard that the huts at Tūtata are some sort of compound,' Te Ika confided one day to his friend. They looked at the moon every night, their excitement growing as the moon waned.

The night before the new moon, the group of thirty boys filed into the whare puni. The door was closed behind them and manned by two kai-rākau.

143

Wehe stood before them. 'Welcome to your first night on the path to becoming a warrior,' he bellowed. 'Forget your parents and siblings. We are your whānau now.'

That was it. The boys were left to get to know one another until they were told to get some sleep.

Before dawn Kai awoke to Kaiora reciting a lengthy karakia. He knew the words and found himself mouthing along with the tohunga. In the quietness of the still morning the drone of the tohunga's voice had a haunting resonance. Kai sensed that all the boys were awake, but they all just lay there listening.

As soon as the tohunga finished there was a sudden commotion as kai-rākau swarmed into the whare puni and began laying into the boys with reeds. There were almost as many kai-rākau as there were boys, and Kai thought the warriors seemed to be enjoying themselves. He felt for his mates, who were not as conditioned as he now was to physical punishment.

'Get up, leave your clothes! Hurry up!' they shouted as they whacked the boys' thighs and backsides, herding them outside. Two kai-rākau waiting in the porch area ushered them onto the path that led out of the village. Dogs started howling at the commotion, adding to the drama and confusion.

As he stood shivering in the faint light, Kai could make out some of the boys' parents watching from their huts and the odd child peeping out a doorway. The frightened boys were shepherded out of the village and into the bush below Kō Pā. Naked and nervous, they were made to stand in a line beside the stream while one of the kai-rākau counted them off. Kai shifted his weight from one foot to the other as he listened to the count. It was dark in the bush so the kai-rākau placed his hand on the boys' backs as he walked along behind them to make sure he missed no one.

'They're all here,' he called to Wehe.

The kai-rākau led them along the bank of the stream, jeering at them and striking anyone who stumbled in the dark. Deep in the bush, they turned up a stream tributary that led to a natural pool. Fighting his fear, Kai told himself this must be how the warrior training was conducted. Hundreds had survived it before him, and so would he.

Both tohunga were waiting at the pool, which was nestled below ancient trees that stretched endlessly into the sky. Flames from a small fire flickered near the bank. The boys huddled together in groups near it for warmth, their teeth chattering. They barely noticed the delicate floral scents of the trees and the first rays of dawn.

Kaiora addressed them again. 'That fire was not lit for your benefit. We are here to conduct the serious matter of your dedication to Tū-mata-riri, the angry-faced war god,' he said in a measured tone. 'All of you must now form a line facing the pool.' The boys spread out. They looked stiff and uncomfortable; some were swaying.

They were then told to immerse themselves, one at a time, in the water so that Kaiora could recite an invocation over them.

Kai's skin tingled as the water flowed over his body. He mumbled under his breath the phrases the tohunga uttered:

Korikori, tama, ki tūā
Ka riri ki tūā
Mau huata ki tūā
Kia niwha, tama, ki tūā
Mau patu tama ki tūā
Mau taiaha tama ki tūā

Move gracefully, lad, beyond
Quick to anger beyond
Wield the spear beyond
May you be resolute, lad, beyond
Cleave the short club beyond
Grip the long-bladed taiaha beyond

The ritual completed, each boy was given a war girdle or maro huka to put on. The belt was about fifteen centimetres wide, made of fine muka or strips of yellow and black dyed flax fibre. It was worn folded over and fastened with attached strings so as to serve as a bag for small articles. A small apron-like garment hung from the belt. When they had all fastened the maro huka about their waists, Wehe told them to get back into line and follow him.

Kai was excited now. Wearing the maro huka made it feel real. When they spilled out of the bush onto the sunlit beach, he saw a pile of mānuka poles and a line in the sand running down to the water.

'Stand on this line facing in the direction of Ahu,' yelled Wehe.

'Line up! Line up!' the kai-rākau shouted as their reeds added more welts to the boys' backs. As Kai stood, trying to anticipate what was coming next, the kai-rākau distributed a mānuka pole to each of the trainees. The poles were padded at both ends, presumably to prevent serious wounds. Two of the kai-rākau stood in front of the group and the rest lined up behind the boys. Older youths from the previous season's intake of trainees arrived from Kō Pā and took up positions behind the group. They had moved up to the pā when Kai went to live with Uncle Wehe.

'The mānuka you are holding is yours,' said Wehe. 'It is to be taken with you everywhere — to meals, to the latrines, even to bed. Do *not* leave it unattended. Understood?' The boys nodded. 'From here you will follow these two runners to Ahu,' shouted Wehe. 'Make sure you keep up. Go!'

The two kai-rākau in front set a rapid pace.

'This is better than digging fernroot!' Kai said to Te Ika as they raced over the hard sand. Kai nodded in agreement. He felt invigorated by the unpredictability of this new adventure. The two kept pace with the front group of boys, slowing only when they hit stony patches in the sand revealed by the low tide. Up ahead, at about the halfway point, Kai and Te Ika could see two more kai-rākau waiting. They were ushering the boys to run towards them.

As they drew near, the two warriors who had been setting the pace, dropped back and the two new men took the lead just as swiftly. With another kilometre still to go, this was a dirty trick, Kai thought. Te Ika immediately dropped off the pace, as did most of the rest of the boys, but Kai was desperate to keep up. He transferred his pole to his other sweaty hand but it was getting heavier. In the end he accepted he couldn't keep up and soon he started slowing too, his lungs and calves burning. The older boys who had started behind them, the ones from the last intake, were gaining on him. They had overtaken all the other new recruits, who had now slowed to a jog, keeping apace in one solid group. The older boys were soon alongside Kai.

'Not far now,' he huffed. But despite his best efforts to keep up they soon passed him and reached Ahu just after the two leaders.

'They left together, arrived together, and their pace just got faster and faster,' said Te Ika as he wiped perspiration from his brow.

'And now look at them,' Kai added. 'Standing staunch, not even puffing, and looking down their noses at us.'

Wehe brought up the rear with the stragglers. Soon all the younger boys were doubled over or crouching, trying to catch their breath. Kai saw Wehe look to his kai-rākau and raise his head ever so slightly, and all of a sudden they launched into another onslaught with their reeds, laying crimson welts anywhere the boys' flesh was exposed.

'Stand up straight!' the kai-rākau shouted at the cowering group. Some fell to the sand and were set upon, even worse when they dropped their poles. Others tried to use the poles to block the striking reeds.

'Enough!' bellowed Wehe. 'Get up!' The boys staggered to their feet as the kai-rākau backed off. 'Let this be a lesson to you,' he pronounced as he walked among the group, many of whom were breathless and terrified. 'That was *far* from good enough,' he snarled. 'You need to learn how to pace yourselves, and to work as a team.'

'From now on, you will all be accommodated in this compound.' Wehe pointed to the new huts, which had proliferated in Kai's absence. 'The kai-rākau will be responsible for seeing that you complete the duties assigned to you at Tūtata and that you are always on time for training.'

Kai stood in the late spring sun, staring at what would be his home for the foreseeable future. He felt the warm salt breeze rustle through the trees and ripple over the rush thatchings on the roofs of the wharau. The scarped camp was three times as large as it had been before he and Te Ika had been sent to live in the village. Thirty huts now ran from the edge of the sand all the way up Tūtata Hill, which had been cleared and terraced. The site was surrounded by lush green bush that rose steeply for at least fifty metres. It had been chosen for its proximity to Tūtata Creek, which gouged its way down one side of the camp, ensuring the boys had easy access to fresh water.

Until the next moon the trainees, under the guidance of the kai-rākau, transformed the camp into their own little village. They built several amenities: a makeshift whare puni on the flat where everyone could gather together, a covered lean-to where weapons could be made, and three whata kai platforms elevated on poles, with little dovecote-like houses on top to protect food from birds and rats.

Five wharau stood on the plateau at the foot of the incline. The rest of the huts were tiered up the hill, some on ledges cut into the slope. Midway were the wharau set aside for the previous intake of youths, now aged between seventeen and nineteen. At the top were houses for the kai-rākau, whose job it was to manage the camp. Each group of huts shared a latrine and a waste dump for food scraps. Kai's wharau sat on a low embankment a stone's throw away from the sand. Two boys were assigned to each hut.

And so it was, on the first new moon in Kai's thirteenth Mahuru, that he and his cousins prepared themselves for the most important phase of their lives.

CHAPTER SIXTEEN

Mehemea ka uru koutou ki roto o ngā pakanga a muri ake nei,
kaua e wareware i a koutou a Uenuku, te atua o ō tātou
tīpuna i kauria mai ai te Moana-nui-a-Kiwa nei.
Should you participate in the battles of the future, do not forget Uenuku,
the god of our ancestors when they crossed the Great Ocean of Kiwa.

Kai had hoped he and Te Ika would be accommodated together, but instead he was paired with an older boy. His name was Kere, son of Wehiwehi, who was from the inland Kauae-nui Pā. Te Ika was also quartered with an older boy — Pona, his half-brother, in the next hut. Pona brought his kōauau with him. The flute was made from the arm bone of an enemy killed by his grandfather and whenever he played it, which was usually at night, its ethereal sound penetrated every hut in the compound.

Kai was three years younger than Kere but he liked his companion, who seemed to know something about everything. Kere's voice was deeper than the other boys', which added to his air of maturity. Kai quietly admired the way Kere treated others, taking the time to walk around the huts comforting the younger boys, often giving away his last piece of food.

Tūtata was a hive of industry. Thirty boys and a similar number of kai-rākau had begun their first group task, erecting a palisaded fence around the seaward side of the camp. Some were in the bush hewing out posts, others were gathering flax for ties, while a third group was digging holes to sink the posts. The compound rang with laughter and the cracking of jokes, which seemed to shorten the long hours of work.

Kai had readily taken to the life of a trainee warrior, and he was especially keen to start learning the art of weapon handling. He was relieved to be among his own age group and he even willingly accepted Wehe's discipline, which had been so repellent to him when he first moved to Ahu. 'It's a necessary part of the great game of war,' he crowed when other boys complained to one another.

Kai and Kere were working on the outer side of the picket fence. Kere arranged strips of tōtara and mānuka bark along the fenceline, while Kai lashed each pole to its neighbours to keep it in position, then passed the lashing through to Kere to wrap it around his side and back to Kai to tie; in this way each palisade post was strengthened. The mānuka poles they had been issued were always within an arm's length of them.

Kere sang as he worked — a song Kai didn't know:

Tēnei te tūwatawata;
Tēnei te aka te houhia nei
Tēnei te mounu ko au kai roto
E . . . e . . . e . . . i . . . a . . . e!

Here is the stockade;
Here is the lashing being bound
Here am I, the bait, within
E . . . e . . . e . . . i . . . a . . . e!

'Where did you learn that?' Kai asked.

'That's one of the songs our watchmen sing at night.'

'What's it like at Kauae-nui Pā?'

'It's along the Matā River, below Aorangi Mountain. There's bush everywhere. Thousands of birds, too, just a stone's throw from our whare. We're never short of food.' He paused, looked at the sea and inhaled deeply. 'But you guys are lucky — you have the ocean at your doorstep. It's a long way for us to come to get kaimoana.'

'Yeah, there's no shortage of it here,' said Kai. 'You roll out of bed and there's a crayfish waiting for you.' Kere beamed at the thought of fresh kōura so easily caught.

Their conversation was interrupted by the beat of the pahū at the top of the camp. They dropped what they were doing, grabbed their poles and hurried down onto the sand. The other boys were making their way down to join them. They reminded Kai of ants rushing around when their nest was disturbed.

'Where's your pole, boy?' Wehe asked Te Ika. Te Ika had that 'oh no' look as he turned back and saw his pole leaning against a tree where he had been working. Wehe slapped him. 'Go and grab it, then up you run to the top of Tūtata, strike the pahū once, and get back down here. Go!' Off Te Ika raced.

'From now on, mornings will be spent in combat training,' Wehe bellowed as a dozen kai-rākau cobbled the rest of the boys together. 'Then, afternoons will be given over to improving your camp.' He was holding a stick, which he used to mark out a straight line in the sand. When he reached the water's edge he yelled back to the boys.

'Each day will start with a run to Ngāpō. Spread out along this line to start, and remember, pace yourselves! When you get to Ngāpō, look for the cordoned-off area — you'll see a group of elders standing beside it.' As soon as Te Ika rejoined them, panting heavily, Wehe gave the command: 'Go!'

This time the boys kept together and ran as a unit all the way, including Te Ika, who kept telling the others he would *never* leave his pole behind again.

The group of koroua they found on the beach at Ngāpō were all dressed in fighting kit.

'These Ika-a-Whiro have seen many battles,' said Wehe, gesturing towards the seven lithe old men. 'Their task will be to monitor your development and decide who progresses to the next stage.'

One of the veterans, with a heavy hardwood taiaha in hand, slipped under the cordon and stood opposite two thick poles that had been bound together with flax and sunk firmly in the sand.

'This is Tukua, master of arms.' Kai recognised him — he was Wehe's father. A relative he might have been, but neither Tukua nor any of the men behind him looked particularly friendly. In fact, they glared at each of the boys in turn as if they were the offspring of an enemy tribe.

Tāwae had once told his son that Tukua was among the oldest men in the village; in all the Ngāi Haere pā there were only five men who were older. Kai had never heard the koroua say much; he tended to listen more than he spoke. However, when he did speak at rūnanga meetings his opinion carried great weight, apparently. He always leaned heavily on a spear, so Kai had thought of him as a bit doddery, but now in front of them, stripped to the waist, he looked anything but. His firm body belied its age. The koroua was of average height and balding, which made the moko across his wide forehead stand out. He stood with his feet shoulder-width apart, one foot in front of the other.

Kai gazed at his chest, which was covered with scars, undoubtedly spear wounds. He also had two impressive scars across his head, which Wehe had told Kai were the result of three men attacking him at once.

'Though he appears aged, this man has never lost a one-on-one fight and he is still a match for anyone here,' Wehe said proudly. Tukua stood erect, his hands gripping the taiaha. The weapon's long blade cast a shadow down his face and body; its decorated point was in line with his knees. He recited a karakia, then turned the taiaha horizontally and brought it almost to his lips before returning it to its original position.

The boys held their collective breath as the koroua began a choreographed pattern of strong, graceful movements with the taiaha, his fleet-footedness holding the youths spellbound. Like his son, he was quick on his feet and had a good, long reach.

'It looks like his feet aren't even touching the ground!' Te Ika whispered to Kai.

'Yeah,' replied Kai. 'The only way you can tell is the sand flicking up behind him.'

One of the kai-rākau was staring at them. 'Better be quiet,' Kai mumbled under his breath.

The boys' eyes were still glued to Tukua as he brought his taiaha back to its starting position. He advanced slowly towards the bound poles in the sand, poking his tongue out and throwing ferocious looks at them as if they were enemy warriors. Then, in a flurry of lightning-fast moves, he ran his taiaha between the poles, and subsequently drew his stone patu from his belt and set about laying brutal, unrelenting blows across the front of the poles, any one of which would probably have split a man's head open. The message was clear — give your foe no quarter.

Tukua got up and resumed the rest position, catching his breath.

'You see?' Wehe bellowed at his trainees. 'Don't be fooled by age. Ka mau ake tana ika, he ika ngutunui. *Whenever he pulls up a fish, it has a large mouth.* By that, I mean, if Tukua speaks, he will say something worth listening to. The information he imparts to you on this training ground will stimulate your thinking. Ki te pai koutou ki aua kōrero, mauria, whakaarohia ki te ngākau. Ki te kore, whiua atu ki tahora.' *If it interests you, receive it and reflect upon it. If not, cast it back into the sea.*

Wehe then invited his father to speak.

'I was born a long time before anyone else here, so I know more about the world than you. If that is not true and one of you knows more, let him speak now.' It was an awkward moment, but no one said a thing. 'The roped-off area is our para whakawai, our parade ground,' the old man continued, still breathing heavily. The area contained hard, flat sand between the high- and low-tide marks. 'Its name is Kirikiri-tatangi, *the Singing Sands.* It's one of three small-arms training grounds along this coast. For five generations our warriors have learned their fighting skills here at Kirikiri-tatangi.'

The old man looked at them intently. 'What takes place here is tapu.' He prowled along the line of boys, staring each in turn in the eyes. 'Tapu,' he continued, 'because what you learn on this ground, if you become skilled at it, will more than likely one day save your life, the lives of your whānau — even the lives of our iwi. If you cannot protect yourself and your whānau, our enemies have a fate worse than death awaiting you.'

He stepped back with a flourish. 'Kirikiri-tatangi is now open for training.'

Wehe lifted the flax rope and moved inside the cordoned area. 'You are no longer boys,' he addressed them. 'You have now entered the world of men, where you will be required to dedicate your mind, body and soul to Uenuku, atua of all things associated with warriors.'

The boys were hanging on every word. As Wehe ran through the rules of the para whakawai, the boys noticed two pononga passing with their hands raised above their heads, their fists clenched and eyes averted. Then a group of women walked by doing the same until they were past the training ground.

'You see what they're doing?' Wehe said. 'They're showing respect. Men, whenever you are bearing arms on this ground, passers-by must show respect by raising their arms and closing their fists like those women. If they don't, you are free to strike them with your weapon.' Some of the boys smirked at each other. Wehe's move to calling them men had inspired a newfound pride.

Soon the older youths from the previous intake, who had now graduated into the kai-rākau, arrived carrying reeds. They had a swagger about them that the younger boys envied and Kai found himself straightening his posture in order to stand a fraction taller. The kai-rākau heaped up the reeds on the sand before falling into formation on the opposite side of the para whakawai.

The Ika-a-Whiro *veterans* laid an assortment of short- and long-handled weapons out on the sand. The boys were told to place their mānuka poles there too, and file through to the roped-off area. The kai-rākau sat them in rows where they could see the weapons.

Then Tukua looked to the younger kai-rākau, selected six of them and asked each to choose a weapon and explain its use to the group.

'There's not much they don't know about these weapons,' Te Ika whispered to Kai as the last of the six delivered his spiel. 'And they give the impression they're pretty good at using them, too.'

Feeling cocky and keen to prove himself after being outrun by the older boys, Kai replied, 'Let me have a crack at one of them and then we'll see how good they are.'

'This isn't like wrestling, cousin,' Te Ika muttered under his breath.

'Can't be that hard,' Kai shrugged.

Suddenly Wehe turned and pointed straight at him.

'Kai, stand up,' he called.

'Oh no, not again,' Kai sighed. His private bravado fast evaporating, he reluctantly got to his feet and brushed off his knees with his hands.

'Throw him a stick,' Wehe called out. From the outside of the cordon a kai-rākau tossed Kai a mānuka pole. Wehe then instructed one of the older boys, Iriao, son of Te Rangi-tike-tike, who was killed at Te Maniaroa, to fetch a second stick.

'Make some room,' Wehe ordered as the Ika-a-Whiro collected up the weapons on the sand. 'Now, men, watch how effective a weapon can be when it is in the hands of someone proficient in its use.' Kai figured Wehe didn't mean him.

Wehe showed Kai how to stand wielding the stick, then bellowed: 'Begin!'

The two boys circled each other.

Iriao was about seventeen, four years older than Kai, and he had nine or ten kilograms on him. He appeared composed and confident, though Kai was unfazed. Iriao circled twice, swatting aside the first of Kai's clumsy strokes, then made his move. Surprising everyone, Kai blocked his opponent's first blow. But it was intended as a feint and *whack* — before he could recover his stance, Kai felt the padded end of Iriao's stick strike the side of his mouth. He stopped, taken aback for a second. He could taste the blood on his lips. Angry, he lunged.

Iriao moved aside quickly and *boom*, he let Kai have it in the ribs. Pain spread quickly down Kai's side, his scowl replaced by a grimace. Off guard again, he immediately received a sharp prod to the gut, prompting him to let go of his stick, turn away and drop to one knee, one hand clutching his ribs, the other raised to shield any further strike. It was all over.

'What the hell was that?!' Wehe thundered at Kai. 'You turned your back on your opponent! You might get away with that during training, but if you ever do it in sight of your enemy, may your warrior grandfathers forever haunt you. Now sit down and shut up!'

Kai hung his head in shame. As he limped back to join the other boys he noticed the Ika-a-Whiro all staring at him, their expressions unreadable. Whatever they felt, it didn't appear to be sympathy.

'Men, the life of a kai-rakāu can be short and treacherous,' Wehe said. 'Not everyone is cut out for it, so don't try to run before you can walk.' He turned and stared at Kai. 'It would have hurt a lot more if the stick wasn't padded. So from now on, I don't want to hear you talking unless spoken to by one of us.'

'You all right?' Pona asked under his breath as he gave his cousin a concerned look. Kai wisely said nothing.

'We'll start training with mānuka poles until you have learned the basic grips and moves.' Wehe was talking to the whole group again. 'Once the Ika-a-Whiro think you are familiar with the block, the thrust, the feint, the guard and the strike, you'll be allowed to use weapons like these.' He took up a taiaha in his huge fist and heaved it at a kai-rakāu, who caught it, swung it about his body, then dropped into a fighting stance.

'Lastly, you need to learn to tolerate pain. In battle you may be required to fight for long periods, so during training you will come to consider pain as weakness that needs to leave the body.'

Each boy was paired off with a kai-rakāu to begin learning the fundamental moves. Kai was told to stay seated until he recovered. He sat next to the Ika-a-Whiro and was surprised when the veterans sparked into life. Their eyes shone and their hands were animated as they watched the boys drilling. They swapped opinions on which moves a boy should learn first, not afraid to criticise one another's views. Kai watched them draw in the sand the layout of battles they had known, then he listened to them describe and analyse the attackers' battle plans. In that moment Kai realised that the art of war had been brought to near perfection by his forebears, and that if he were going to lead warriors he needed to not only master weaponry, but also understand tactics.

Before Kai rejoined the training session, Tukua offered him some advice. 'Ko tā te mamae e whānau ai he manawanui, e tama.' *Out of suffering is born endurance, boy.* 'Only through pain and deprivation does a heart become as strong as akeake, the hardest wood in the forest. We are not atua. We are but mortals, fragile and foolish. But with knowledge of how to wield a weapon, a man can rise above his station. At all times be wary of it, no matter in whose hands you find it. Always treat it with respect.'

Throughout his training Kai always remembered the words spoken by Tukua on his first day. Over time, he understood more and more of the message the old man was trying to impart to him. But it would be several years before this wisdom became wholly his.

+

Back at camp that evening a pononga roasted fernroot for Kere and Kai on their fire. Te Ika and Pona joined them. The boys sat in silence for a while, watching their meal of fresh fish and aruhe cooking. The pononga then removed some of the charred fernroot from the embers and tossed it to the boys. Another pononga meanwhile was beating further roots with a wooden pato over a stone to remove their tough outer layers. These he soaked in a bowl of sweet tutu berry juice.

Eventually Kere spoke. 'What about the koroua, old Tukua, eh? Boy, can he move for an old fulla.'

'You know why he always carries a tao?' Te Ika said. 'So he's ready to defend himself. My father told me Tukua has always been wary that some young warrior, keen to make himself a reputation, might suddenly rush him, hoping to have his head.'

'How are your ribs?' Kere asked Kai.

'Okay. Pretty much back to normal.'

'Why do you think Wehe singled you out?' Kere asked his mate as the pononga tossed him another charred morsel.

'I was talking and not paying attention,' Kai replied truthfully.

'You weren't the only one,' said Te Ika, a little shamefaced also.

'If you ask me, Uncle Wehe's got a mean streak,' said Pona.

'For sure. But it seems to me he is always picking on Kai,' said Kere.

'Seems like it, doesn't it? Someday I'm gonna make him pay,' Kai muttered darkly.

'My mother reckons too many battles can turn a man funny,' Te Ika said as he chewed on a piece of root.

Pona cast a look around at the other boys huddled over fires, then turned back to his companions and spoke in a low voice. 'I heard that when Wehe was about our age, old Tukua cut the jugular vein of a bound captive, sucked a mouthful of blood from the neck, then ordered his son to do likewise. They say Wehe drank half a gourd of blood.'

'Whoa,' said Te Ika. They all looked at one another in silence.

'You need to keep on the right side of Wehe, Kai,' said Pona. 'For whatever reason, he's got it in for you.'

'He's driven by our fear,' Kai replied, sucking the soft meal out of the fernroot fibre and enjoying its sweet clamminess. 'But I think his problem lies with my father more than me.'

'Why do you say that?' Te Ika asked.

'Well, they say my father ran away from the battle at Te Maniaroa.'

'And did he?'

'Actually, I don't know. I've never asked him about it and he's never mentioned it. But I wonder if Uncle Wehe thinks I might do the same.'

Kere, having swallowed the juice of the fernroot, spat the fibres into a basket. 'And what do you say?' he asked.

'Hell, no. I belong here, but I feel like I'll have to work twice as hard to prove myself.'

'Then that's all that matters, Kai. Don't listen to what anyone else says. They're not you. You'll do just fine.'

The friends grew silent until Pona pulled out his flute and soon produced a haunting melody. A melancholy silence fell over the camp as the boys all gazed at the flames, pondering their future as warriors.

CHAPTER SEVENTEEN

Whakatiria te hī o Rua, kia hīhiri, whakapoua te hao o Rua, kia rarama.
Embed the knowledge in your long-term memory, so that it
springs up exactly when needed and informs your actions.

Kirikiri-tatangi was a serious place. If the young men had not absorbed that fact on day one of training, they certainly had by the end of the first month. The kai-rākau acted quite differently towards them when they were on the parade ground compared to how they were at Tūtata. Each session in the early stages of weapons training, involving mamau and mekemeke — a form of bare-fist boxing — was nerve-wracking and this tension sometimes spilled over into a real fight.

All sported bruises and cuts but they wore them like badges of honour. Because the young men came to experience beatings regularly, usually inflicted by the kai-rākau on one of their mates, the impulse towards violence became accepted as normal. The kai-rākau, who had experienced the same rough treatment when they were trainees, had no intention of dropping the standard of the para whakawai. And who could blame them, given that the new intake would one day fight alongside them in battle?

At Tūtata the boys all got on well most of the time. It was a happy group — everywhere you looked the boys were smiling. They derived great satisfaction from their rapid mastery of the complex moves associated with long-handled weapons, which was down to the long hours of practice they put in with their mānuka poles in their spare time at the camp. Kai always dedicated more time to it than his mates. When he had no one to practice with, he'd place a post in the sand and imagine it was an opponent. In this way he added real speed to his developing technique.

One of Kai's chores was to shift soil to make way for a new building near the top of Tūtata Hill. He and his companions jibed and joked as they levelled the huge rectangular area. To identify any uneven spots they would wait for a shower of rain and then take note of where the puddles lay. Then they dug or filled as necessary until the ground was almost perfectly level.

Inevitably, however, sometimes personalities clashed or tempers frayed. One day the kai-rākau had to stop a fight between Kai and Kōrihi. When it was reported to Wehe he was not impressed.

'You will sort this out at Kirikiri-tatangi,' he ordered.

The fight started like this. There was a rule that the area in front of the huts had to be swept clean every day with a mānuka brush. The boys took turns at this chore. When it came to be Kōrihi's turn, he strapped the brush to his mānuka pole and used it like a broom. While he was sweeping the rubbish past Kai and Kere's hut, Kai remarked, 'Is that all you think of your weapon? Only good for sweeping rubbish?'

That led to a war of words about who had best mastered the latest weapon techniques. Kai felt his fists clench and when Kōrihi called him a coward; he grabbed his pole and a fight ensued. Kere, Pona and Te Ika broke it up, but not before the kai-rākau had spotted them.

When the boys were next at Kirikiri-tatangi, Kōrihi and Kai were called out. Kai was told to go to the centre of the para whakawai. A young man brandishing a pole stood at each corner of the rectangular area. Kai had been expecting to face Kōrihi, whom he was itching to fight, but instead it seemed he was to go one-on-one with each of these four in turn. He knew he had neither the skill nor the size to beat his opponents, but he wasn't about to back down.

He glared at each of the young warriors with slowly rising indignation, until Wehe called for the fight to begin.

Kai gave his all. The fight was intense, made more so by sixty or so kai-rākau and boys silently watching. Kai's opponents sparred with him until he had nearly collapsed from exhaustion. Then Wehe ordered him to the outside of the cordon and called on Kōrihi to enter to undergo the same treatment. Again, everyone could feel the energy as Kōrihi tried to best his opponents. When his time was up, Kōrihi was told to remain in the cordon and an exhausted Kai was called back to face him.

'Commence!' called Wehe.

The two started attacking each other, but the wind had already gone out of their sails. In their fatigued state their strikes and blocks were a lot less effective and they soon fought themselves to a standstill. Wehe ordered them to stop. Shattered, the two boys rejoined their mates.

'Let that be a lesson to all,' bellowed Wehe. 'You want to fight, you fight here. Nowhere else. Got that?'

Then he said to Kōrihi, 'Your stick is your weapon. Treat it with respect. You all have weapons in your homes tied to the wall near the door. Why? So that on exiting the home in a rush it's the first thing your father grabs. One day you will hang up your own taiaha and patu. And, like your father, you'll name them after your ancestors. Treat your stick as you would your tīpuna.'

Yet for all the difficult times and the hard work — not to mention the sobering fact that they were being trained to kill — there were contrasting moments of wonder for the boys. On one occasion Kere came running to the hut and called to Kai, Pona and Te Ika to come outside quickly and see the spectacular sunrise. They stood and watched the horizon turn to gold, then the whole sky came alive with clouds of ever-changing shapes and colours. Streams of pulsing light curtained the surface of the sun with a beautiful haze.

+

The training camp disbanded briefly in early autumn to release everyone for the harvest festival. The three-moon period between the challenging but enjoyable harvest month of Ngahuru and the arduous and demanding planting season, which began in the month of Mahuru, was to consist of a weapons drill in the mornings, and special indoor lessons at night.

This was how it began for Kai and his cousins. One evening, as twilight became darkness, the kai-rākau gathered the young men outside their huts and told them they were going up to the newly erected house at the top of Tūtata Hill. No explanation was given.

'What do you think is happening?' Pona whispered to Kai.

'Don't know,' Kai yawned.

'I heard we're going to be inducted into something top secret,' said Te Ika.

'What's the point of wondering?' Kai shrugged. 'We'll find out soon enough.'

Kai could see his own breath in front of him as he followed the other boys up the path in the diffused light. The cold air stung his cheeks, so he wrapped the edges of his kaitaka tightly around his face. Wind whipped through nearby trees, creaking and groaning, while the roaring waves of a high tide crashed on the beach.

'Watch where you step,' said someone.

'Who said that?'

'I can't see.'

'Put your hand on my shoulder.'

'Ouch! You stepped on my foot!'

'Quiet!' barked a kai-rākau.

The glint of light from the crescent moon was just enough for them to pick a route between the huts. By the time he reached the top of the hill, Kai was constantly rubbing his hands together and blowing on his fingers. His toes felt like they were burning, having almost frozen walking over the frosted ground. He jogged on the spot and Te Ika did likewise before they were led towards the newly erected whare wānanga. They passed piles of firewood and Kai realised why he and several others had been sent to the beach to collect kindling the previous day.

'Strip and leave your clothes out here!' one of the kai-rākau ordered the boys.

Really? Kai thought with dismay, but said nothing. He dutifully placed his kaitaka and rāpaki on the porch and followed the others through the opening to the house. As they entered the hallowed abode for the first time, their eyes ran everywhere to familiarise themselves with this new space. It smelled of freshly cut ponga and mānuka blended with the smoke coming from the two fires in the centre of the building. Apart from the fires, the only light came from some bird-fat candles.

The Ika-a-Whiro and the two tohunga, already in the whare, stood silently, watching each boy file in and, standing stark naked, warm himself at the crackling flames.

When the last boy was through the door, Parakore instructed them all to clothe themselves in a garment befitting the sacred rituals of learning. A pile of garments sat near the hearth. Appropriately attired, they were to sit against the far wall where mats had been laid out for them. Kai and Kere propped their backs against one of the short, carved slabs that leaned inwards from the walls. Te Ika and Pona rested against the dry toitoi cane that was laced with flax between the slabs. Behind these, the upright stems of ponga ferns formed the outer walls, which gave off the heady aroma that Kai had inhaled on first entering. Wehe and a handful of the kai-rākau crouched where they could observe all thirty of the trainees. Kai felt a lot warmer now.

Tukua spoke first, reminding the kai-rākau, 'The salvation of our people lies in the training that we provide these boys over the coming years.'

Kai straightened up as Parakore related the rules of this house of learning. 'And no food shall be brought into this house,' he concluded. He walked over to a pile of small pebbles, bent down and picked one up.

'You will be taught old-time lore unchanged,' he said in his low, eloquent voice. 'Any deviation from the old teachings would be an insult to Tāne, the atua from whom this sacred lore was derived. When this house was being erected, a lizard was placed in the earth immediately behind these stones. It is the abiding place of the atua under whose protection this whare has been built.' Kai thought of the little green mokomoko that had startled Hara.

'A lizard, I say — so when you are in here, stay away from this area. It preserves the welfare of the house and all connected with it.' Parakore then recited a karakia to placate the atua and to have it awaken the boys' minds and quicken their thought processes: 'Whakatiria te hī o Rua, kia hīhiri, whakapoua te hao o Rua kia rarama.' *Embed the knowledge in your long-term memory, so that it springs up exactly when needed and informs your actions.*

Observing that Kai seemed impressed with the tohunga, Kōrihi whispered to him, 'Watch out for him.'

'What do you mean?'

'Don't sit in front of him in a canoe,' Kōrihi chortled.

Kai gave him a perplexed look. Wehe's eyes narrowed when he saw the boys whispering.

'None of you are permitted to talk,' Wehe said. 'You are here to listen, not to waste the teachers' time. Kai, I'm looking at you.' The glares of the kai-rākau reinforced Wehe's words. Kai glowered at Kōrihi, who made out he was listening attentively to Wehe, but Kai caught his slight smirk.

'You will be tested on what you are taught,' Wehe continued. 'You will memorise everything, together with hundreds of charms, incantations, rituals and whakapapa, some containing hundreds of names. The best among you will go on to specialise in celestial lore.'

'What if we can't recall all of it, Uncle?' Te Ika piped up.

'How many times must you be told? Only speak when you are asked a question, boy,' Wehe snarled.

Kai wondered how he could possibly learn and memorise all that over a single winter.

Parakore then distributed a small stone to each of them. Kai held the smooth, round pebble between his forefinger and thumb and studied it. His was shiny brown with streaks of white through it.

'To help you,' Parakore declared, 'I shall recite an ancient incantation that will invest your pebble with power, assisting you in retaining what you are taught. Place the pebble in your mouth.'

Kai was still gazing at the stone when Wehe prodded him. 'Get it in there, boy!'

Kai quickly popped it on his tongue and closed his lips. He rolled it around his mouth. It had no flavour.

'Be careful not to chew or swallow it,' said Parakore.

'That little pebble will prevent you from chattering!' Kaiora laughed, but then his expression turned serious. 'You will keep it in your mouth the whole time we are in session. It will cause you to salivate, and the extra moisture in your mouth will eliminate any feelings of thirst. This will make it easier for you to focus on what is being recited.'

The lessons began right away, with the genealogies that connected the boys with one another.

Kaiora explained: 'These kāwai rangatira have long been performed orally by those before us. Let us not be the ones to forget them.'

With each group of names Kaiora recited, Parakore gave a little history about the tīpuna. Sometimes he mentioned a battle that Ngāi Haere had won, at other times it was an account of a fight lost. Tukua, seated with the group of Ika-a-Whiro, warned the boys against the dangers of pride, and the fleeting nature of fame and power that came with victory in battle.

'Remember,' he said, 'just as we await our chance to get revenge against another iwi, so are others looking to even the score with us.'

Kai looked across the room at the newest kai-rākau, young men as yet unproven in battle, hanging on Tukua's every word. For they knew the old man was once a young warrior like them, without the great reputation he had now, and that he too once had to prove himself. Kai had heard that it was Tukua, with the support of the other Ika-a-Whiro, who had assigned Wehe the responsibility of training the boys.

Kai was fascinated by the veteran warrior and studied him whenever he could. A whole life given over to battle, to single combat and murder in some cases, involving the most daring actions, great courage and constant self-sacrifice— the effects of this existence were plainly evident in the way Tukua carried himself, especially at Kirikiri-tatangi. He had lost none of his power or single-minded purpose over time. He would yell at boys who were felled by a blow from an opponent: 'E koe! Nōhou te hē!' *Serves you right! You were at fault!*

As far as Kai could see, Tukua was utterly devoid of compassion — not unlike his son. He had absolutely no compunction about inflicting death, pain or torture; seemingly no feelings whatsoever.

When Tukua sat down, the tohunga resumed the genealogies.

'The object of this exercise,' Parakore explained to the boys, 'is to make you aware of how closely you are all related so you feel confident that you can depend on the cousin either side of you, no matter how desperate the situation.'

The kai-rākau fed the fires with more sticks and driftwood so that the room became uncomfortably hot. The lessons continued late into the night, until eventually the kai-rākau stopped feeding the fires and they slowly died away to a low glow. The boys were sleepy, some of them having trouble keeping their eyes open.

While the tohunga continued talking, the Ika-a-Whiro quietly picked up blades of flax that had been spread on the floor. They stripped away the dry spine, then, by cutting the tough ends at an angle, fashioned themselves small darts. They began firing them at boys who had fallen asleep, with the desired effect. As more and more darts flew, Kai used his hands to parry any that were tossed in his direction, though his reflexes often let him down.

Little did he realise — little did any of them realise — their every movement was being scrutinised and analysed.

In this way, three years of winter and summer training passed.

CHAPTER EIGHTEEN

He whare tū ki te pā tūwatawata he tohu nō te rangatira.
He whare tū ki te paenga he kai nā te ahi.
A house standing within a stockade pā is the mark of a chief,
while one standing beyond its perimeter is food for the fire.

In the month immediately before his last winter training camp, Kai
was to join a bird-snaring party on its annual trip to Kauae-nui Pā.
The fifteen-year-old, who had gained height, strength and condition
through almost three years of warrior training, asked his friend Kere,
who was from Kauae-nui, what he should expect. Kere, now eighteen,
had been part of the bird-fowling group for the past two seasons.

'Have you spotted Kaipō yet?' Kere asked Kai as they gazed up at
the night sky.

'Yep, there it is.'

'Ever since that star appeared, our keen-eyed old bird fowlers have
been out in the bush. They say the fruit of the miro and the flowers
of the kōwhai are especially bountiful this year. You know what that
means, eh?'

'Plenty of food?'

'Plenty of birds! The bush will be teeming with kererū, kākā and
tūī this season.'

'Do we get to snare the birds or are we just there to do the grunt
work?' Kai asked.

'Sure, you'll have a chance to snare them, but there's a lot involved before you get to that stage. The bush people will show the sea people a thing or two!'

'We'll see,' Kai winked at him.

Wehe and the party of youths he selected left early in the morning. An escort of kai-rākau, several pononga and a handful of kurī tagging along with their owners accompanied the boys. Most of the group were heavily laden with crayfish and dried pāua for their inland relatives. Tāwae joined the party, bringing along his six-year-old daughter Haere and Tui, who was now thirteen. Kai was pleasantly surprised to see his siblings, although he no longer pined for them as he once had. Being the youngest in the party, Haere had her own personal pononga to carry her whenever she felt tired. She also took along her puppy, Ihumātao, a name she had given him because of his cold nose.

It was a tough journey — a full day through dense bush, over streams, across rivers, up and down hills. In some places they followed the corridor of tracks formed by the constant traffic of relatives going to or from the coast. These were narrow and generally kept to ridges and stream beds. They all had names, and were kept passable by their users breaking off any branch that impinged upon the trail.

The earthy scent of the bush was quite different from the salt air they were used to at Ngāpō. As Haere clung with one hand to the back of her pononga, and to Ihumātao's furry frame with the other, her eyes ran up from the ferns to the forest canopy. She gazed in awe at the huge trees that grew so straight and tall.

'Tahi, rua, toru . . .' Haere counted at least twenty different varieties of tree. She imagined they were guarding the way to the Kauae-nui fortress.

'How are you getting on, my daughter?' Tāwae called to her.

'Kei te ngangahau tonu, Pāpā!' she yelled back. *I'm full of life, Father!* Haere was always happy to be the centre of her father's attention. Now that she had a baby sister, it happened less and less.

Coming down a hill as the afternoon wore on, the party finally spotted Kauae-nui Pā in the distance. The terraced rise was covered from top to bottom with clusters of thatched houses built from raupō rushes.

'Wow,' Kai said to Kere, 'some of your houses are so close together it would only take a spark on the wind to torch the whole place.'

'No fear of that,' replied Kere. 'It's quite damp below the mountain most of the time and with all the green foliage it would be hard for a fire to take hold.'

The hill they were on was denuded of trees — possibly for planting, or to allow greater visibility of the approach to the pā — and this afforded the party a grand view of the Matā River and the forested basin below.

Back in the bush they became aware of a huge variety of birds. A screeching pākura, startled by the kiore or scout at the front of the party, darted away. The dogs with their terrier-like snouts gave chase. Little Ihumātao leapt from Haere's loose grip and joined in. Two pīwaiwaka flitted cheekily just ahead of him.

'Uncle, it must be difficult for warriors to approach a pā undetected,' Te Ika said to Tāwae.

'I'd say so,' replied the chief.

'Virtually impossible in daytime,' Wehe grunted.

'Tell him, Hara,' Wehe called behind him.

'Once you startle the birds,' Hara yelled back, 'they'll spring up above the canopy and make a racket.' The sound of the men's voices had just that effect on the birds now.

'You'd have to approach at night,' Wehe said, 'remembering that the watchmen of the fortress are always on the lookout.'

'How would you do it, Uncle?' asked Kai. Wehe snapped his head around sharply and glared at Kai.

'Keeping my attacking force concealed,' he explained grudgingly, 'I'd send my kiore forward under cover of darkness. It would be up to them to discover the fort's weakness. On a cold night the watchman might have gone to warm himself by a fire in his hut or, worse for him, fallen asleep. Then I'd move my force forward silently. We'd throw our makeshift ladders against the palisade and we'd be in.'

Kai was thoughtful.

'You'll all learn such strategies in time, men,' Wehe said. 'Well, the smart ones among you will. Those not ruled by their emotions.'

The party crossed the river above the Mākarika Stream junction with the Matā River, the adults using poles to feel the depth and to help stay upright, and assisting the younger members of the party across. On the other side they sat down to rest. Tāwae had caught the skin at the back of Ihumātao's neck and restrained him. He was panting heavily. While patting the dog, the chief drew his sons' attention to the rock face.

'Do you see where the two rivers meet? That place is known as Waipuna-a-roto. Now look for the grove of tītoki trees to the side of the rock face . . .' The boys scanned the bush, looking for the change in foliage from the evergreen māhoe to the shiny-leafed tītoki.

'I see it,' Tui piped up first.

'That area is Pā-pōhatu. You mustn't go in there — it's tapu. It is a toma, a shrine, where we place the bones of our chiefs who die at Kauae-nui or in the mountains.' His expression was serious. 'Kāre hoki tātou e whakaatu ana i te wāhi i tanumia ai ō tātou rangatira, koi mōhiotia e ō tātou hoariri ka hahua, ka meatia ngā iwi hei matau ika.' *We never reveal to anyone where our chiefs' bones are buried, in case our enemies steal them and make them into fishhooks.* They stared at Pā-pōhatu and Kai felt a sense of foreboding.

'My father's eldest brother, Te Tau,' Tāwae continued, 'was the last chief whose bones were placed there. Kauae-nui was his pā.'

'What happens when someone dies, Pāpā?' Haere asked, still gazing at the tītoki trees.

'My Uncle Te Tau died when I was still a boy. We held his tangi at Ngāpō and it lasted a full three months because he was a chief. Afterwards his corpse was wrapped and brought here to Pā-pōhatu and placed in a tree. A year later the hahunga ritual took place, where his bones were scraped for internment. They placed his bones behind that big toka at the foot of the hill.' The boys looked at the large rock embedded in the embankment.

'Why bring his bones all this way when they could have buried them at Ngāpō?' asked Tui.

Kai sensed the adults bridling at his brother's question. The pononga, especially, seemed uncomfortable with the conversation.

'Because he specifically requested it,' Tāwae replied. 'He told his brothers: "Ki te mate au, me kawe rawa au ki Waipuna-a-roto."' *Should I die, carry me to Waipuna-a-roto.*

'It's getting hot,' said Wehe, changing the subject and standing up.

What none of Tāwae's children knew was that a pononga, acting on the orders of Te Tau's brothers, had killed the chief.

At that moment came the sound of the wooden gong at Kauae-nui Pā.

'It's the watchman letting us know that the pā is on the alert,' Tāwae informed them. 'They know we're coming, but they're also warning anyone unexpected who might be approaching. We must be on our way.'

A short while later the party emerged from the bush near the foot of the pā. Haere managed the last kilometre on foot, doubling her steps to keep pace with her brothers' strides.

'Your pononga can carry you if you like,' her father said to her.

'No, I can walk,' Haere said proudly. A moment later she asked Kai, 'He aha te pononga, e Kai?' *What is a pononga, Kai?* Her brother, who didn't really know how to answer her properly, mumbled something about her keeping up, evading the question. He felt self-conscious at how little he knew about anything.

'Someone captured in war,' Tāwae stepped in. 'Once they were our enemies, but now they are as much a part of our village as we are.'

'Why don't they eat with us, then?' Haere asked innocently.

'They are not equal to us. Their jobs are to cut wood, fetch water, prepare the ground for crops, cook for us, and carry you when you get tired,' Tāwae explained. Tui laughed. Haere turned back and tried to hit his leg but she missed, making her brother laugh even more.

Kai surveyed the pā. Smoke rose from cooking ovens. The sounds of song and laughter filled the air; the lilt of rehearsing poi girls and general chatter hummed across the valley. People started coming down to formally welcome them as soon as they noticed their relatives' arrival.

The height of the pā's palisades was breathtaking — much more intimidating than at Kō Pā. While the visitors waited to be welcomed in, Kai's eyes were drawn to the disdainful face of the carved figure that kept guard high above the gateway. Every three or four metres around the stockade stood similar huge sculpted wooden figures with painted or pāua-shell eyes. Some of the effigies' enormous heads were cocked to one side, featuring an exaggerated expression of pain, while others, rigid and upright, glared straight ahead, their faces imprinted with moko and their lower parts covered with the same tattoo pattern that the kai-rākau wore on their buttocks. Their hands gripped taiaha or toki-pou-tangata.

'Inā rawa,' Kai gasped. *Amazing.* 'These posts are three times higher than a man! The stockades must have taken forever to build.' The palisades ran right to the top of the hill, some two hundred metres away.

'And if that's not enough to deter the enemy, what about those heads?' Te Ika chimed in. He was pointing to some stakes on which were impaled human skulls bleached white from years in the sun.

'The pā is called Kauae-nui because the ridge it sits on is in the shape of a jawbone,' Kere told his mates. 'The smaller area, where the skulls are, is no longer in use. That's Kai-pūtahi. My relatives, the Ngāti Ira people, lived there, but they have long gone.'

Kai sensed from Kere's tone and body language that there was more to know about the circumstances under which Ngāti Ira left.

CHAPTER NINETEEN

Hei te pō, ka timata ngā mahi ngahau, kātahi anō koe ka kite i a ia.
Tonight, when the entertainment begins, then you will see her.

After the welcome, the gathering formed a big circle to allow the two parties to bring forward their wrestling champions. Two local kai-rākau, carrying kākaho fronds and reeds, jogged around the circle, pressing the crowd back by whacking the ground with the reeds and waving the fronds in front of them.

The local youths started chanting, 'Mamau! Mamau!' and one of them was soon elbowing his way through the crowd to challenge the visitors' best young wrestler. The crowd roared. The young man looked about eighteen and had a strapping physique. While he stood waiting in the centre of the ring the pahū started up and his people called his name to the beat of the drum: 'Tāmō! Tāmō! Tāmō!'

Wehe looked around the eager faces of the youths under his watch. His first thought was that Pona would make an even match for the local boy, yet before he had a chance to name him, Kai stepped up.

'I'll do it.'

Wehe snorted.

Kai began disrobing but Kere grabbed his arm. 'This guy is good.'

Kai shrugged off his hand and took a second step forward. 'I can take him.'

'Shut your mouth, boy,' Wehe snapped. 'Put your cape back on.'

Kai's recent growth spurt had increased his brazenness and he stood his ground, looking defiantly at Wehe. E tā, I'm ready to take your hiding, he said to himself. Come on, let's show these people what a bully you are.

With the eyes of the roaring crowd on him, Wehe demurred. To Kai's surprise he motioned him to the middle of the ring and the crowd erupted again, momentarily drowning out the drumbeat.

Tāwae was watching the scene unfold when a heavy-set man in a handsome knee-length flax kilt secured by a tātua or belt greeted him with a hongi. It was Tūterangi, son of Wera, whose wife Poka was Kiri's cousin.

'Your son will be fighting my boy Tāmō, it seems,' Tūterangi said as they watched the two youths limbering up. 'I have been wanting to talk with you on the subject of our children, Tāwae. We ought to strengthen the ties between our families.'

'What do you suggest?' Tāwae asked.

'You have two boys. Poka and I have several girls.' Tāwae nodded at Poka, who was sitting regally on a dais, her belly large with child. She nodded back, her head held high. 'Surely one of yours and one of ours would be compatible?' Tāwae's thoughts went back to Kai's maioha ceremony; he remembered the special gift of tāwhara the couple had brought.

'That sounds logical and we should talk more about it,' Tāwae said. 'Perhaps when you next visit Ngāpō?'

The crowd kept surging forward and the two kai-rākau were kept busy racing around the circle striking the dirt and waving their fronds. Tui managed to get a front-row seat and Haere scuttled between people's legs to sit next to him just as the fight began.

Tāmō stretched out his hand and as soon as Kai locked his fingers with it, the action was underway. Wehe and a local kai-rākau moved around the fighters, watching closely. After two or three lunges, Tāmō hooked his foot behind Kai's ankle and sent him sprawling. Kai sprang back to his feet snarling, and advanced more cautiously. He managed to lock Tāmō's neck in the crook of his elbow. Too easy, Kai thought

175

in his overconfident way. He never saw Tāmō's next move coming: the young wrestler threw himself backwards, lifting Kai into the air at the same time and slamming him into the dirt.

The noise from the onlookers was deafening. His opponent clearly knew the sport well; Kai realised he would have to rely on his wits rather than his strength to get the upper hand.

'Kia tūpato, he tipua a ia!' Pona and Te Ika called to Kai from the sideline. *Be careful, he's not human!*

Kai's strengths were speed and agility. Several times he escaped his opponent's hold by ducking out of the way just in time, but the bigger boy had remarkable stamina. He simply did not seem to tire. Observing Kai's knees beginning to quiver, Tāmō barrelled forward. Using a complicated twisting manoeuvre, he lifted his younger opponent into the air and brought him crashing onto the dirt directly opposite where Tui and Haere were sitting.

'Auē! Kua taka i te taniwha a Kai!' Haere wailed. *Oh no! The monster has beaten Kai!*

Before Kai could get to his feet, Tāmō had him in a deadly stranglehold. It was surely just a matter of time before Kai passed out. But anyone who knew Kai's character would likely guess that there was more fight left in him yet.

'Come on, you bugger,' Tāmō muttered. 'Concede!'

'Never,' Kai gurgled. His eyes streaming, he could just make out Tui willing him to submit. His little sister's eyes were wide and she had both hands over her mouth in shock. Then he saw Wehe. Was that a smile?

A sudden slap from the adjudicator on Tāmō's bicep caused him to release his grip and Kai collapsed, finally able to breathe again. Cheering exploded from the Kauae-nui people who mobbed the victorious youth, patting him on the back.

Pona, Kere and Kai's other mates and whānau hung their heads despondently.

Tāmō broke away from his well-wishers and extended a hand to Kai, who took it and allowed himself to be pulled to his feet. They pressed noses before dusting themselves off. Kai knew it was forbidden to harbour bitterness towards an opponent after a wrestling match. Wehe clamped a hand on Kai's shoulder.

'Just like the sky today, boy, your sunlight has been obscured by the clouds of defeat.' Wehe knew exactly how to kick a man when he was down. 'Let this be a lesson to you,' he said. 'Don't volunteer yourself unless you are sure you can win.' He went to walk away, then turned back with a final word. 'If you dare defy me again, I'll give you a thrashing you'll never forget.'

Kai said nothing but his cheeks burned. He watched as Wehe made his way over to Kai's father. No doubt to tell him what a disappointment I am, the boy thought. Well, I'll show him. I'll show them both. I'll die before I lose another fight.

When Wehe came up to him, Tāwae said nothing to him about the wrestling match. Instead, he spoke about Tūterangi's suggestion.

'Tūterangi's father was not from here,' Wehe said gruffly.

'I know that, but such an alliance would guarantee we have the support of Kauae-nui when we need it,' Tāwae replied. 'I don't mean imminently — Kai needs to stay focused for now — but in time. And Poka is of high birth.'

'Tūterangi's father came as a mercenary to assist your father and his brothers in the fighting against Ngāti Ira.' Clearly Wehe was going to take some convincing.

'His father was a chief. What's more, he fought courageously,' Tāwae was starting to raise his voice, 'and in gratitude my father offered him a wife and an allotment of land to encourage him to remain among us. Tūterangi and Poka's clan numbers fewer than seventy, many of them children, so it's very much in his interests too.' With that, the chief turned and walked away.

Later that evening, the young people gathered in the whare tapere to play games and socialise. As the fires crackled the Kauae-nui women rose to perform a haka. The younger participants included Tūterangi's three daughters, all of whom were olive-skinned and strikingly attractive — and they knew it. One of them, sixteen-year-old Wairere, had had her eye on Kai since the welcoming ceremony. She had noticed his impressive bone structure and the fact that he was half a head taller than most of the boys his age. Then she had watched him wrestle her brother. He may have lost, but his truculence made her even more keen.

'Who's that?' asked Tui, who had been the first to notice the pretty girl gazing in their direction. Kai had been distracted by a group of older boys but turned to look where Tui was indicating. Tui pointed out the girl who had been paying them close attention. When Kai's eyes met hers, she gave him a pūkana. Her dilated eyes looked stunning, he thought, and she backed this up with an enchanting smile. Kai's legs turned to jelly, though he feigned nonchalance to Tui.

'The oil and red ochre that her mother has plastered on her face and arms don't do her any favours.'

'True. I bet she doesn't even know how to dive. They're strangers to the sea, our cousins.'

Kai's eyes kept flitting back to the charming performer. Several of the kai-rākau were leering at the attractive young women, knowing that the keen sexual desire of girls was rarely suppressed by their parents unless they were of chiefly stock.

'You boys won't always be impervious to the allure of beautiful young ladies,' Hara leaned over and said to Kai and Tui. 'It won't be long, you'll see.'

As the haka party advanced towards their guests, the girl began to unleash her artillery of charms in the direction of Kai. He crossed his arms, unfolded them, then folded them again as he watched the swinging threads of her piupiu skirt accentuate the movement of her hips. He tried to deflect her gaze by shifting his attention to her sisters, but his eyes kept being drawn back to hers; something was stirring within him that rendered her irresistible.

His pulse raced to the alluring beat of the haka. Her green tattooed lips curled upwards again, permitting a gleam of white teeth. At one point she danced right up to him, her unbound black ringlets swaying

178

below her elbows. She uncrossed his arms, her touch sending a shiver through him. He inhaled the sensual smell of perfumed oil mixed with sweat across her small-breasted chest. As soon as he allowed his gaze to lock on her big black eyes at close range, he was snared in her noose.

Wairere knew that such a bold and public action was perfectly acceptable, especially during such festivities; she had wanted to claim ownership of the new boy before her older sister beat her to it. Even as her body continued the actions of the haka, she held on to Kai's hand, her index finger purposely stroking his palm as if to say, 'You're mine'.

She whispered in his ear as she withdrew. 'Wairere.'

Her warm breath on his earlobe sent a shiver down his spine.

'He autaia te kōhine nā. Wepua e tama!' *She's quite a girl. Go for it, lad!* one of the kai-rākau teased him. As Wairere twirled her piupiu and danced back to join the group, another prodded Kai.

'Kua whaitohungia koe, kia kitea ai te hunga māna koe.' *You've been marked out; she's letting everyone know she's claiming you.*

'Oh, I'm not really interested,' a flush-faced Kai mumbled as he tried to regain his composure and quell any further attention. Tui giggled at his brother's discomfort.

'She wants you, you know that, eh?' Hara nudged Kai.

Kai shrugged his shoulders with seeming indifference. But deep down he desperately hoped Hara was right.

If Wairere was worried about her sisters getting a look-in, she needn't have been. Kai had been won over by her beauty and boldness and didn't even notice the others. He was well and truly smitten.

Tāwae and Wehe had watched the whole thing.

'How can a girl so young be such an expert at seduction?' asked Tāwae.

'Perhaps her parents have put her up to it. Perhaps they don't want to wait till you have spoken with Kiri,' Wehe responded.

'Or maybe a tohunga's magic is at play?' said Tāwae anxiously. 'Make sure your men keep an eye on my boy.'

'I don't think it's the girl you have to worry about. It's your son who's the problem. He's like your father — walks to the beat of his own drum. Pretty soon neither of us will be able to stop him.'

+

That night, Kai lay on his mat wide awake thinking about Wairere. Since the haka he had repeatedly replayed in his mind the moment of her touch. He had tried a thousand times to rekindle the feeling of her warm breath in his ear. When he finally fell asleep, she walked through his dream, leaving him paralysed by the smell of her perfume and sweat.

This time, not only did she whisper her name in his ear, but her warm breath said, 'Meet me at Kai-pūtahi.' Then she made her way swiftly out the door; moments later he excused himself from the company of the kai-rākau.

'I'm just going to relieve myself.'

'I bet you are!' someone cracked.

Within a few minutes he was below the fence groping in the darkness for her. She waited a moment in the shadows, watching his desperate search. Then she grabbed him by the waist and pulled him to her, her cheek touching his. She loosened his girdle and reached down between his thighs. The eyeless skulls on the fenceposts felt like a warning but every part of him craved this moment. As her warm hand moved upward he grabbed it in a feeble attempt to stop her but he was powerless to resist. Just as she stroked his pouch, he jolted awake.

Disoriented in the darkness, Kai took a moment to remember where he was. The sounds of snoring and the dying embers of the fire reminded him that he was in the guest house at Kauae-nui Pā with other members of their birding party. He lay motionless for a moment, then found his hand moving to his groin and felt a warm, viscous wetness on his belly. Alarmed, he fumbled for a cloth and wiped himself.

Kai turned on his side, overcome with embarrassment, but as he lay there pondering, his indignity was soon replaced by a pleasurable feeling of having attained a rite of passage. He instinctively knew he had reached a pivotal point in his life and felt an urge to share the news with someone — but who?

He was not inclined to tell his father, and certainly not Wehe. Tui was too young. Maybe Pona or Te Ika? No, they'd just tease him. Kere? Perhaps. For now, he concluded the best plan was to keep it to himself. Fatigued but elated, he stretched out on his mat and sank into a deep, satisfying sleep.

CHAPTER TWENTY

He kākā tāwari ki Hikurangi, he moki ki te moana.
The tāwari trees filled with forest parrots at Hikurangi,
fat like the blue fish moki at sea.[10]

The wet grass flattened under the feet of the forty-strong fowling party as they trod a long, damp trail down to the Matā River. The wide stretch of green grass, which had replaced the bush long since burnt off immediately outside the pā, reminded Kai in some ways of the sea with its white-foam crests reaching towards the sunlight.

The party had risen early that morning and eaten quickly, then they had thrown on raincapes and set off out of the gates of the pā. Twenty of the warrior trainees from Ngāpō were among the group. Each carried four calabashes and a flax-woven pīkau pack. Tāwae left Haere and Ihumātao with relatives, but took Tui along for the experience.

Kai strode into the chilly river without hesitation, impervious to the bite of rocks against his half-frozen feet.

Tui was unconvinced. 'Aren't your toes freezing?'

'Don't think about your feet,' replied Kai. It was something he had learned from Wehe. 'Instead, focus on the sun's rays warming your face.' Kai went back to daydreaming of the girl with eyes like polished obsidian. His encounter with her had more than made up for the embarrassment of his wrestling defeat. He was walking behind his father and when he felt the moment was right, he asked Tāwae how he had met his mother.

Tāwae seemed surprised by his son's question. 'I never laid eyes on her until the day she was brought to Ngāpō to live with me. I had no say in the matter. It was all arranged by our parents.'

'Did you like her? Did you want her?'

'We were strangers fulfilling our parents' wishes. But luckily we found ourselves immediately attracted to each other, so there you are. Parents know best!'

Kai cleared his throat. 'Do you think Tūterangi's daughter Wairere might make a good wife for me?'

'Now, hold on, son,' said Tāwae, turning around and putting up his hand in front of Kai's face. 'It's not for you to ask such a question.'

'Why not? I know that Wairere wants me and I want her.'

'When establishing a union, there are certain preliminaries to be settled between the parents first. Your wishes don't come into it.'

'Like what?'

'The parents are the ones to decide if the match is the right one. There are wider ramifications, like establishing a tighter union between hapū. Let's say I did approve of a match between you and Wairere. Remember, your mother hasn't been consulted yet. She knows nothing of this. But even if she were to give her approval, the people have a say too.'

They continued wading through the icy water in heavy silence for a while but Kai couldn't let it go.

'It may not be correct for me to speak up about this, but I feel certain about Wairere.'

'I'll tell you what,' replied Tāwae, 'let me seek an omen. The atua will show us. If it's favourable, I will speak to your mother and the council of elders when we return to Ngāpō. But for now, nothing must pass between you and that girl, either in daylight or by darkness. Do you understand?'

'I understand.'

Tāwae cut a blade from a flax bush and tore a thin strip from it.

He tied the strip in an ordinary loose knot, then turned around and walked back to one of the young men from Kauae-nui. He muttered something to him and the young man took the flax and ran back the way they had come.

Tāwae rejoined Kai and they walked quickly to catch up with the others. 'I told him to take the flax knot back to Tūterangi and to tell him I wish to have a reply,' Tāwae explained to his son. Kai was puzzled. His father continued, 'If Tūterangi draws the knot tight, it will be a sign that a marriage is to be tied.'

The fowling party followed the river upstream for about seven kilometres, crossing many times. It started to drizzle and the temperature began to drop, but as long as they kept moving the trekkers were warm. As they came out of one crossing, Kai found Kere alongside him.

'About yesterday — I'm curious, why did you volunteer to wrestle?' Kere asked.

'Because I know mamau.'

'No more than the rest of us. There were older boys among us who could have beaten Tāmō though.'

'Yeah, but they didn't step up, did they?'

'They were waiting for Wehe's word, which is what we've been taught. To wait for the command.' Kere's voice was strained.

'Well . . . I thought I could win.'

'But you didn't, and it wasn't just you who lost. Now my cousins are taunting me — "What are they teaching you guys in that warrior school?"'

'You wait. We'll show them. We get our taiaha when we return to camp. Then they'll see how good we are.'

Kere sighed. 'That's your problem, Kai. You're too quick to put yourself forward.'

'That's right, Kere. Fearlessness is what makes a warrior.'

'I'm not talking about courage. You worry me; you worry all of us. In a real fight to the death, you'd have been killed.'

'Hah! I'm not afraid to die.'

'We're all willing to give our lives, but for the right cause. Not because of someone's selfish arrogance. You might not like some of us, Kai, and some of us might not particularly like you, but we all need to know we can rely on one another.'

Kai saw the seriousness on Kere's face and let his words sink in. Perhaps he had been driven by his burning need to prove himself — to Wehe, to his father, to them all. His face grew hot as he realised his friend spoke the truth. He still had much to learn.

They reached another bend in the river and without thinking, Kai went straight for the shortcut, rushing into a stretch of low rapids, knowing the rest of the party would likely take the easier route above. Suddenly he tripped and lost his grip on his calabashes. They floated downstream and when he looked up he saw Wehe and Hara, who were bringing up the rear, retrieving them. Damn! Damn! Damn!

As they passed the junction with the Makomako Stream the river flattened out and Tāwae called for a rest. The runner who had been despatched to Kauae-nui Pā was soon seen hastening towards them. He stopped and caught his breath before he spoke. Kai ran over.

'I waited in silence as Tūterangi puzzled over the knot, turning it about in his hands,' the messenger told the chief. 'When he couldn't work out its meaning, he unloosened the tie and handed it back to me.' He opened his hand and he and Kai looked at the piece of unknotted flax.

'He roa te wā ki a koe, e Kai,' said Tāwae. *It shall be a long time yet for you, Kai.* While no whakataukī bore its full significance in its apparent meaning, Kai understood this one. The marriage was not to be tied. He was crestfallen but knew better than to challenge the omen.

'You should focus on completing your warrior training and let nothing detract from that,' Tāwae added.

I will wait, Kai told himself. But one day I will have my Wairere.

+

185

The river was much shallower past the Makomako junction and while the boys were wading across, they heard the *whop-whop-whop* wingbeats of a slow-moving flock of birds.

'He pōkai kererū,' Tāwae called to the party. *A flock of pigeons.* They watched the well-fed birds land heavily in the trees halfway up a densely forested hill. Kai studied the varying shades of green and soon spotted the birds among the darker leaves of a miro grove.

Tāwae said a karakia was needed to break the rāhui that had been put on the pua manu the previous season. Pua-o-te-Roku was known far and wide as the most bounteous bird reserve in the district, he said. The name was one their ancestors had brought from Hawaiki. The rāhui was placed in order to prevent outsiders from poaching birds.

'You may find it hard to believe, but even though the birds feed in these groves, none will be caught if we don't say the right prayer,' Tāwae said.

They moved off to locate the three makeshift huts that were erected and left there last winter. Tāwae, Wehe and Hara stayed at the huts with the boys, an experienced bird-fowler and two women from Kauae-nui. A smaller group headed further upriver towards two other pua manu, Pāraeroa and Pouturu, searching for kākā feeding in the kōwhai trees that grew profusely along the river. Another lot climbed to Te Whākoau bush, high above the river, while a fourth group crossed the Makomako Stream to the forest known as Te Ngaere. There were old camps at each of these pua manu.

In the three huts, Tāwae's group set up space in which to prepare their snares. The main hut was reserved for the men to work in. Women were not permitted to enter in case they passed over the snare-making materials. That would defile them, meaning no birds would be caught.

The two women set about preparing the other two huts as accommodation. Wehe sent Kai to the main hut to light a fire while he, Hara and Tāwae went into the bush to check out the groves. The old bird-fowler took the other boys — Tui, Kere, Pona and Te Ika — to a stand of kāuka and showed them how to strip the leaves. 'The fibre of these cabbage tree leaves is stronger than flax,' he explained. 'We use them to make nooses for the snares. They stay rigid and keep their shape longer. We will hang them in the hut overnight and the smoke will blacken them and make them more durable.'

As they worked, the boys listened to the koroua talk of the endless hours he had spent studying the stars over the past month, the different types of frost and dew that carpeted the area, and the richness of the bush flowers and fruit he observed.

'These signs speak to us of a tau kai,' the old man said. 'A bounteous supply of plump birds.' Te Ika involuntarily licked his lips.

'Do not have any food on you tomorrow while we are setting or clearing the snares,' the koroua cautioned the boys. 'Don't leave any feathers behind in the bush when you retrieve the birds. Don't even speak badly of the birds.'

Back at the hut, where Kai had the fire going, the old man continued his long list of do-nots while fixing as many as six or seven nooses onto each horizontal rod.

Te Ika whispered to Kai, 'There are so many rules! How is it possible to catch anything?'

'You're like a poorly woven old kete, Te Ika,' Pona chortled. 'The words go in, but they fall straight through the gaps.'

'Ssh, you two,' Kere frowned at them. 'That kind of talk might be the very thing that keeps the birds away.'

The group spent all that evening and the next morning in the main hut making hundreds of running nooses.

+

It was damp and shaded in the miro grove. Kai and Kere looked up through the dark green needle-like leaves and saw several plump-breasted kererū feeding on the berries, sometimes four to a branch. The boys crept so close that they were directly below the trees. Kai marvelled at the birds' small heads, massive bodies and crimson eyes, beaks and feet.

187

'They look majestic,' Kere spoke softly. 'Proud, and completely unaware of the danger the snares present.'

Earlier that morning the men had split the boys up to go and set their snares. Pona, Te Ika and Tui went with Tāwae and Hara, while Kai and Kere carried snares behind Wehe and the older bird-fowler.

At Wai-kirikiri, where the pebbles in the water were reddish in colour, Wehe's group tied several perches between upright stakes just above the water's edge, and placed the rods with their running nooses about twenty centimetres above these.

'The kererū mistake the pebbles for miro berries,' Wehe explained. Then they went off to fix more snares in the miro grove.

The boys were surprised to learn that some of the trees had names. The old man pointed out one called Kārearea-nui.

'Many of the spectacular, dark-feathered bush falcons have been caught here. They rest in the tree before taking to the skies again to spot rats, lizards and smaller birds.'

'It is something to see,' said Wehe, nodding. 'From the sky the kārearea make a swift direct attack and either strike or grasp their prey with their sharp talons. You could learn a lot from the kārearea and apply it to your training.'

Once they finished fixing snares in the miro trees the group returned to Wai-kirikiri and sat at the edge of the bush. There were already some kererū ensnared, but Wehe wanted the youths to see how the running nooses worked. They didn't have to wait long. More kererū, their breasts bloated, glided in and settled on the perches at the water's edge. Kai watched intently as one placed its head through a noose. Its neck, a metallic green flecked with bronze and a purple sheen, stretched out from its magnificent white breast only to feel the noose tightening. When it tried to withdraw, the bird was caught by its feathers. As it struggled, it drew the noose tighter and was ensnared.

Another kererū put its neck through the very next noose and tried to grasp a pebble. It met the same fate. After watching for an hour, the party retrieved twenty-four kererū and reset the nooses. Wehe and the older man put the birds in their packs and quietly faded into the bush.

'Keep watch,' Wehe said. 'We're going to check the miro grove.'

'Wow, that is so clever!' Kai remarked to Kere.

There was not much for the two youths to do but lie and wait for more birds to arrive. During one of these spells, Kai said to Kere, 'You were right, you know.'

'About what?'

'What you said at the river the other day. About how arrogance and courage are not the same thing.'

'Ah . . . is this you apologising?'

'No,' Kai said quickly.

'Look, I know it's tough for you, being the chief's son. But, from what I've seen since we were paired up, you're a real risk taker. It makes me nervous that one day, in a real situation, your bravado will cost us.'

'There is just so much expected of me, and no matter how hard I try, Wehe just slaps me back down. I don't feel good enough. He doesn't think I'm good enough. Even my father thinks I'm not good enough.'

'Have they told you that?' Kere asked.

'They don't have to. I can tell. I can see it in their eyes.'

'When did you become a mind reader? You should ask them straight out. At least then you'll know for sure.'

They went back to watching the hapless birds in silence. Kai's thoughts drifted back to Wairere. Then he recalled the dream . . . He plucked up the courage to tell Kere about it and ask the older boy if he had ever had such an experience.

'Of course,' Kere replied.

'And?'

'It means you're becoming a man,' he laughed. 'So what are you going to do about it?'

'What do you mean?'

'Well, Wairere is clearly set on you. It was pretty obvious in the whare tapere the other night. You ought to give her what she wants. Make a man of you!' Kere dug his elbow into Kai's side.

'I can't. My father received an omen, so I must wait.'

'How long?'

189

Kai shrugged. 'I'm not sure. Perhaps until after we graduate. Maybe longer.'

'Don't worry, Kai, she'll wait for you.'

Just then another kererū landed. At first it curiously observed the other asphyxiated birds, then hesitantly put its head through a noose to drink.

'Poor Kai,' Kere laughed. 'You're just like that kererū. Even though you know you are headed for trouble, you still want to quench your thirst. Watch out, Wairere's going to ensnare you . . .' They put their hands over their mouths to muffle their laughter so as not to scare the birds.

+

When the two groups met back at the whare kākā that evening Hara brought in forty birds. Pona and Te Ika followed him, with a cheerful smile and a load of fifteen each, which was as many as they could lug in their packs. Tui dragged a further ten birds in two kete behind them.

The first pigeon caught (the koroua knew which one it was) was rolled, feathers and all, in moist clay. The clay was patted around it to completely encase the bird so none of the fat could escape, then it was placed in the fire to cook. Meanwhile, the older man recited a karakia to placate the atua Tāne. Once the clay parcel was red hot, Tāwae withdrew it and opened it.

'See how the plumage comes away?' he said. The feathers were all stuck to the clay. He placed the baked bird into a flax kono for the women to eat. The boys, who had had nothing to eat all day, sat drooling as they watched the women enjoying the succulent meat.

'The sweetest seafood could not compare,' the women told them as they licked the fat from their fingers and sucked the bones clean.

'Now our women can join us in our tasks,' Tāwae explained, 'without fear of reprisals from the atua.'

'Tomorrow,' the koroua said, 'some of you will stay back with our women and cook all the birds on a spit over the fire. Make sure you collect all the dripping fat in bowls so that after you have boned each bird and potted them in your calabashes you can pour the fat over the top. Remember, too, to tie some tail feathers to the neck of the calabash to serve as a label. That way we will know what type of bird is in each tahā.'

'But now it's time to eat,' said Tāwae. They wrapped more kererū, their stomachs full of sweet berries, in clay, and placed them in the hot embers.

PART THREE

CHAPTER TWENTY-ONE

Inā te mahi, he rangatira.
See how he does, a leader indeed.

Three Ika-a-Whiro huddled around one of the fires in the whare wānanga, warming themselves against the chill winter night. The flames cast dancing shadows upon their faces as they sat sharpening the small mānuka sticks they had cut that morning.

The Ika-a-Whiro laid the ends of the sticks on the embers until the points glowed red while they kept a hawk-like eye on their charges, watching out for the heavy-eyed or somnolent. The first time Kai nearly nodded off he received a short, sharp shock as a mānuka stick scalded him. Anger stirred in his gut. 'Kuruki, whakataha,' he whispered to himself. Clearly they had graduated from flax darts.

The second time a burning stick hit him he fired it back twice as hard. Before he knew it, two kai-rākau were dragging him to the door and he was tossed outside onto the ground.

With the bird-fowling season over, Kai had returned to Ngāpō and to his education in the whare wānanga. He was not so interested in the lessons now, especially as they had been joined by a group of younger boys, including Tui.

Kai knew he was changing. At fifteen his body had enough muscular development to liberate him from boyhood. Where being kicked out of the house into the biting cold would once have been an effective measure to ensure he paid attention, it no longer had the same power over him. Consequently, the kai-rākau could often be heard berating him outside.

Kai was pleased to have his brother with him at Tūtata at last. Kere was still back at Kauae-nui so Kai was now quartered with Pona, while Tui was partnered with Te Ika. On inspection days, Kai often overheard Te Ika telling Tui to tidy up around their wharau before the kai-rākau arrived, while Te Ika himself lay resting inside the hut. At first Tui seemed eager to win the admiration of his older cousins, but once he realised he was doing all the work, his keenness soon evaporated. On one occasion Kai heard Tui castigating Te Ika for not helping, and a mānuka stick suddenly burst through the thatched wall. When Te Ika crawled out of the opening of the wharau sporting a bruised thigh, Kai and Pona burst out laughing.

'I see my younger brother is fully capable of looking after himself,' said Kai.

When Kere returned, Tui was moved, happy to no longer be Te Ika's general dogsbody.

+

By the end of winter Kai and his contemporaries were inured to hardship — sleeping in the bush and going hungry for long periods had been part of their training. The young chief had learned how to trust his intuition and instinct, essential skills for a warrior.

During his sixteenth Mahuru, Kai's intake undertook their final exercise before graduation. Before dawn, the kai-rākau formed the young men up on the sand. Travelling light, each with nothing but a portion of dried kūmara and a wooden patu in their flax belts, they jogged in single file down the beach, up the Ngāpō Stream and along the inland path. They moved all morning, resting only briefly to eat or drink or to relieve themselves. When they reached Atua-rere, the place where kōkōwai was procured near the Tōtaranui Stream, they saw some twenty small calabashes on the ground. A kai-rākau called a halt and the young men quickly scooped fresh, cold water into their mouths.

'Enough!' the kai-rākau shouted and ordered them away from the stream. The kai-rākau then each collected a tahā and filled it with lumps of the red ochre, then strapped the tahā over their shoulders. The youths were curious but knew not to ask what the kōkōwai was for.

They jogged on, and by midday the party passed Kauae-nui Pā. Kai couldn't believe how quickly they had come this far. Various people were standing at the palisades of the pā waving to them as they passed and Kai looked eagerly for Wairere but couldn't see her.

'Eyes forward, men!' the kai-rākau yelled.

Soon they were crossing the fast-flowing Matā River. The level was down and the pace set by the kai-rākau gave the boys little time to think about the stones under their feet. Then one slipped and cried out in pain. It seemed he had twisted his ankle.

'You'll have to take him back to Kauae-nui!' Wehe barked at one of the kai-rākau. 'The rest of you — watch where you step in future.'

At the junction with the Waitahaia Stream they turned off and followed the waterway a fair distance until they hit the mouth of the Waingata. Halfway along this stream they turned inland and began climbing up a long, high ridge from where they had a great view of the back of Mt Hikurangi.

Pointing to the lightly snow-capped mountain-top, Te Ika called out to Kai, 'Ka rukuruku tōu matua i ōna pueru!' *Your father is gathering up his garments!*

Kai gave a half-hearted smirk.

The ridge climb sapped whatever energy the young men had left after the long river run. Halfway up Wehe stopped the group, much to Kai's relief as his calf muscles and thighs were burning. He could tell this part of the bush was ancient. The huge trees seemed to stare at them like silent sentries. The boys were all breathing heavily, exhaustion written all over their faces.

'We stop here for two reasons, men,' Wehe declared. 'Tonight you will sleep here, and tomorrow you will find your own way back to

Ngāpō. In the morning we will let you go individually at intervals, and your mission will be to make it back to Kō without being caught by the kai-rākau. If a kai-rākau marks you with kōkōwai, consider yourself caught. For you, the mission will be over.'

A hush fell over the group.

'If you meet any of your mates along the way you may travel together, but at your own peril.' Kai could feel his heart racing.

'It's easier to track a group than it is to follow an individual,' Hara explained.

With that, Wehe ordered the kai-rākau to head back and station themselves at various points along the streams. He kept Hara back with him to watch over the group for the night.

'Tāhoratia ngā kōtukutuku me ngā mako,' Wehe said. *Gather up some kōtukutuku and mako berries.* They went foraging and soon returned with handfuls of dark purple, red and black berries. They then crouched around Wehe.

'E kai,' Wehe instructed them. *Eat up.* They gobbled up the berries and ate some dried kūmara. No one felt full enough, especially after their long physical day.

'No fire is to be lit tonight,' said Wehe.

No one said anything but it was obvious how they felt.

'This is clearly another test,' Kere whispered to Kai.

'Just don't think of your stomach and you'll be fine,' replied Kai, sounding more confident than he felt.

'This ridge is known as Kōrau-whakamae,' Wehe went on. 'The other reason we're here is because you men need to understand why this place is important.' They looked around them.

'He wehewehenga tō tātou i mua i nga tīpuna,' Wehe said, leaning against the trunk of a huge tōtara, its thick bark peeling off in strips. 'Otiia nā ngā pakanga nāna i wehewehe.' *As a people, we have been divided from the time of our tīpuna. Fighting has separated us.*

'Well before most of you were born, during the month of Pipiri, a party of our bird-fowlers spotted strangers passing along the stream below. It was drizzling. Runners from the fowling party took the news to the chiefs Kū, Kō and Takē at Kauae-nui Pā. "These strangers," they reported, "seem to know the area.'"

The sun set early in the mountain forests and, as the shadows fell around the party, Wehe's silhouette seemed to blend into the trunk behind him, the whites of his eyes glowing even brighter.

'The brothers needed little encouragement to go on the attack,' Wehe continued. 'Early the next morning they grabbed their weapons, rallied their men and set out along the Matā River. At the bottom of this ridge our chiefs found the fires of the strangers still smouldering. They followed their tracks, which led up here, where they came upon the strangers setting bird snares.'

Kai looked around at the remote environment. It struck him as an unlikely destination for poachers, being so far from any pā other than Kauae-nui.

'It turned out these men were remnants of Ngāti Ira,' Wehe's voice had quietened. 'A people who had once shared Kauae-nui Pā, and who were now living on the other side of the ranges at the mouth of the Tūmo River, alongside the Aitanga Nui.'

Some of the boys shifted about in their crouching positions. They all knew of that tribe.

Wehe spat out a berry seed before continuing.

'That's how they knew this area. Their leader was a man named Taniwha.' Kai's blood ran cold at the mention of his notorious enemy.

Kere bowed his head. Of all the boys he was the one who was most closely related to Ngāti Ira.

'I was no older than you at the time,' said Wehe, 'but I was there with the chiefs. I can still see Taniwha, standing right where you are all sitting. He was a thickset, stout man, his eyes bloodshot. When interrogated, Taniwha said that they were taking birds for their chieftainess.

'"You have crossed our boundary and you are poaching on the lands that belong to Whānau-a-Mate." Kū virtually spat out the words, daring Taniwha to challenge him. Outnumbered, there was little Taniwha and his party could do. Our kai-rākau cut the straps of their pīkau packs and they dropped to the ground. All their hard work from the last several days was lost.

'Kō taunted them — "Why has your face fallen?" — and they just stood there, jaws clenched, while our men cast more insults at them. Then Kū said: "Return immediately to the Tūmo and never set foot in these ranges again if you know what's good for you."

'Going back to their people empty-handed was a humiliation for them and Taniwha took the insult to heart. He brooded over it. The next time the two parties saw each other was the battle at Te Maniaroa.'

There it was again. The name that was etched on Kai's heart. He felt his blood run cold.

Blackness had engulfed the bush by the time Wehe finished his story. The murmuring of night birds increased and somehow intensified the feeling of remoteness. The boys, wearing only maro huka and raincapes, lay down and huddled together in groups for warmth, plotting strategies for the following day.

'We've got to make the best of the daylight hours,' Pona whispered to Kere, Te Ika and Kai. 'At night we could follow the streams, but that's most likely where the kai-rakau will be patrolling.'

'Pona, let's travel together, at least until we get past Kauae-nui,' said Te Ika.

'Okay, but we'll need to stay under bush cover. He looked at Kere and Kai. 'Will you two join us?'

'Maybe we should until we're out of this mountainous terrain,' said Kere.

Kai wasn't so sure. He knew he would have more chance of avoiding capture on his own. But then Kere's words from when they were bird snaring came back to him: *You might not like some of us, Kai, and some of us might not particularly like you, but we all need to know we can rely on one another.*

'We stick together and if any kai-rākau gets on our trail, we smash him,' Kai said.

'Whoa, that's a bit extreme, isn't it?'

'You wanna get back to Ngāpō without getting caught, cousin, then you need to do whatever it takes.'

The boys tried to sleep, but the temperature was plummeting. The night held a vague dread for the fertile imaginations of the young men. Even the bravest of the kai-rākau feared evil spirits lurking in the trees. Throughout their childhood they had been warned of mythical creatures — tūrehu, patupaiarehe and pake-pakehā — fair-skinned people who some believed were the original inhabitants of the island. These spirits materialised in deep bush or rugged mountain terrain, they were told, to prey on women and children and sometimes carry them off. On wet or misty days their spirit voices were often heard on the hills, singing, talking and playing flutes.

Wehe and Hara sat quietly at the base of the tōtara tree, awake and listening. Every now and then Wehe stood up, leaves susurrating underfoot, placed both his hands on the trunk of the tree and sidled around it to warm himself up. When he sat down Hara stood up and took a turn. They kept this up throughout the coldest part of the night.

Kai observed what they were doing and shook his mates.

'C'mon,' he whispered. 'Let's do as they're doing.'

'It's too cold and dark,' Te Ika replied grumpily.

'Don't let the elements get the better of you,' Kai said as he felt around in the pitch dark for the nearest tree. 'C'mon, get up.'

Slowly, one by one, they dragged themselves up and began circling trees.

Kai's initiative did not go unnoticed by Wehe and Hara.

+

In the early morning, as the first boy was sent off, a light drizzle began to fall. As soon as he was out of sight, the next one was despatched. Most headed back down the ridge a bit before dropping over the side into dense bush. Kai was one of the last. As he was departing, Wehe called out to him.

'I thought you'd be at the front of the line trying to get ahead of everyone.'

'Tēnā rā, he maha ngā ara a Tara,' Kai responded. *Well, Tara has many ways to go.* Like their tipuna, Tara, he wasn't worried, for he believed he would be the most difficult to catch.

'Wasn't Tara cornered and killed in the end?' Wehe smiled.

Kai ignored him and headed down the slope, plunging into the dense bush as the others had done. He clung to trees as he slipped and slid. The ground was wet with dew and the bush felt damp and claustrophobic. He looked up to see fog over the lower reaches of the bush, with birds scattering above the mist ahead of him, no doubt because a couple of dozen boys were rushing through.

He had arranged with Kere, Te Ika and Pona to climb towards Mt Hikurangi, aiming for Te Tone-o-Houku, *The Clitoris of Houku*, a small, sharp rock point that could only be seen from the Kōrau-whakamae side of the mountain.

Before he left, Kere had whispered to his friends, 'We need to get as far away as we can from the others.' That was why they had decided to climb up the mountain before skirting around its shoulder.

Kai crossed the stream and came to the foot of the only track leading up the mountain, which the other three must have taken. He thought about taking an easier route, following the waterway downstream, but just as he started he spotted a tiny lizard scampering over the smooth stones ahead of him. He quickly turned back.

It was a long, wearying hike to the mountain's shoulder. He veered around the patches of denser bush, which were full of shadows. As he reached the sub-alpine foliage he finally found himself looking straight up at Te Tone-o-Houku.

'Hoi,' came a faint call. He turned and smiled to see his three mates sitting together on a boulder. It seemed unlikely that anyone would be on their tails up here so they chatted a bit as they picked their way around the side of the mountain, careful to avoid the sharp stones and the spike-tipped taramea. The view, once the fog had lifted, was sublime.

'Can you imagine the sunrise from the summit?' asked Te Ika.

'You couldn't get any closer to the gods,' said Pona.

'It's a tapu place. The old people say we should never go up there,' Kere said in a low voice.

'What did you think of Wehe's story last night?' Te Ika asked.

'Fate is a strange thing,' Kai replied. 'Had Taniwha and his people not been there that day, my grandfather would not have insulted them and later been killed for it. Now we're all tied into a blood feud three generations old.'

'What does Old Man Tukua always say?' Te Ika said. '"E mau ai te rongo-mau nā te noho takatū o te tangata ki te haere ki te whawhai."' *Peace is preserved by man's constant preparation for war.* He mimicked the droll monotone of the old man's voice, which made them all smile. 'Or what about Uncle Wehe,' he added, trying to sound like him too, '"Ki te toa, he pai ake te whawhai i te kore whawhai."' *For the warrior, any fight is better than no fight.* They burst out laughing.

'Ssshh!' said Kere, looking anxiously around him for any sign of the kai-rākau.

They set off in silence until the narrow track ran into a tarn.

'Water all the way up here!' Pona half-whispered.

'This must be Taka-whiti, where Māui's canoe is submerged,' said Kai. 'I remember the story my nanny used to tell us when we were kids. I thought it would be much bigger than that.'

'It's big enough to hold a waka,' said Pona. While they were studying the tarn, Kai turned sharply, thinking he might have seen something move in the bush back down the track.

'We'd better get moving,' he urged the others.

They hadn't gone far when they heard the distinct crack of twigs. Turning back, they saw Hara, Wehe and another kai-rākau spilling out of the bush onto the track.

'Split up!' Te Ika yelled. 'Every man for himself!'

'Hey, what happened to us smashing them?!' Kai yelled.

Then in a flash he was sprinting too.

CHAPTER TWENTY-TWO

He urunga tangata, he urunga pānekeneke.
A human pillow is a slippery pillow.
(Do not depend too much on others, but rely on yourself.)

The four boys ran in different directions but their pursuers were swift. Pona and Kere headed for a scree slope, while the two younger boys, Te Ika and Kai, dropped back down into the bush. Wehe sent a kai-rākau named Kakama after Pona and Kere, and told Hara to go after the other two.

When they hit the scree, Pona and Kere kept losing their footing and Kakama was soon abreast of them. He tagged them both with his hand, leaving splotches of kōkōwai on their lower backs. For them, the mission was over all too soon.

As Kakama led the two young men back down the track, Wehe called out to them. 'Most of the group have been caught down at the stream already. Let's see if we can corner your friends quickly so they can join you.'

With that, he walked back into the bush to see how Hara was faring. A kākā squawked and rose above the canopy just ahead, and Wehe did not miss the sign.

Te Ika had raced ahead of Kai down a track through thick scrub before hiding in a copse of trees. He had cut his foot and had been pulling himself up into a tāwari tree when he frightened the bird.

Next he'd climbed to a perch at the top of the tree before spotting Wehe walking below. Wehe hadn't gone far when Hara came back up the narrow track towards him.

'I lost them,' Hara said. Te Ika couldn't see the two men but he knew they were close to the base of his tree.

'Let's wait up top,' Wehe said. 'They're bound to come back this way — it'll be too tough for them heading down.' At that moment a droplet of blood from Te Ika's cut foot dripped onto Wehe's shoulder. Wehe slowly tipped his head back and ran his eyes up the trunk. Te Ika held his breath but Wehe caught sight of the boy's brown legs sticking out of the canopy.

'Kua mau koe i a māua,' he said smugly. *We've caught you.*

'Kāre anō kōrua kia pā ki a au. Anā, kei kōnei au e noho ana,' Te Ika replied. *You haven't tagged me yet, so here I sit.*

'E tama, heke iho āianei tonu!' *Boy, come down right now!*

Te Ika shrugged. 'I see no kōkōwai on me.'

Hara started climbing the tree as Wehe called out, 'Koi mekea ō taringa, e tama!' *I'll box your ears, boy!*

Hara had almost reached Te Ika when Kai appeared on the track below them, yelling, 'Hey! Here I am.'

Wehe turned sharply, a look of surprise on his face. Quickly, the surprise turned to anger.

'Too late, Kai,' Hara yelled. 'We've got Te Ika!' He dabbed Te Ika with kōkōwai.

Slowly Wehe moved his hand down to his tahā and scooped up a handful of kōkōwai. Quick as a flash, he raced down the hill towards Kai.

The young chief waited until Wehe had almost reached him before dropping in front of him and clipping Wehe's legs. Wehe went head over heels into the scrub below.

'Take that, you old bugger!' Kai shouted.

'Arrgh!' Wehe tried to mask the pain of the sharp branches that had dug into his back.

Taking out his patu, Kai yelled, 'Come on! I'm not scared of you!'

'You should be, boy. Just you wait until I get hold of you!' Wehe struggled to free himself from the briar patch but it was no use, he was stuck fast.

Kai hesitated, unsure for a moment what to do, then his conscience got the better of him and he started walking towards his uncle to offer him his hand, despite fully expecting a beating as thanks. By this stage Hara was out of the tree and rushing towards them.

'Leave him!' Wehe shouted at Hara. 'Get going, Kai!'

'Eh?' said Kai, visibly perplexed.

'If you hadn't come back to help Te Ika, we wouldn't have caught you. There's no kōkōwai on you, so go. The other kai-rākau will be on your tail soon enough.'

Kai could hardly believe it but he didn't need to be told twice. He thrashed his way swiftly through the tangled mass of brushwood, avoiding any hint of a track, until he was almost back in the gully above the stream he had crossed that morning. His eyes darted unceasingly back and forth, and often up as well, into the branches above him.

After a while he rested up a bit, staying hidden while he thought about his next move. He decided to stay under scrub cover until nightfall, in the hope that the majority of the party would have moved from the stream area by then.

Kai took his kōpura kao from his belt and ate most of what was left. He then foraged in a rotting log for huhu grubs and gulped them down. To pass the time, he cut blades of mountain flax, stripped them and made some crude sandals. They were little more than toe-caps, fastened with a cord from the heel and passed around his ankle, but they were better than nothing. He also plaited an arm-length line, which he threaded onto his flax belt.

As dusk descended, Kai set off cautiously down to the stream, on the alert for any sign of kai-rākau either out in the open or in hiding. He neither saw nor heard anyone, only the whisper of leaves and the trill of myriad insects.

When he reached the stream Kai thought he heard faint cries in the direction of the Matā River, but they were so distant he wasn't sure.

He sat under some bush cover for some time just in case. He took a drink from the stream while he waited, careful to only take enough to quench his thirst.

He lit a small fire and warmed himself. Then, attaching a piece of kūmara to the flax line he had plaited, Kai had a go at catching himself an eel. It wasn't long before he felt a nibble on the line. As soon as the next peck came he flicked the line, causing the eel's teeth to get caught on the flax fibre. He swung the line ashore, catch and all, and a long, plump eel landed on the stones. Before it could slither back to the water, Kai scurried across and hit its head with a heavy rock.

If there's anyone out there, they'll know I'm here now, he thought. But he still saw and heard no one. After cleaning as much of the slime as he could from the eel, Kai gutted it, cut the flesh open and roasted it on the hot stones. He was starving, and the taste was too wonderful for words.

The young chief threw more wood on the fire and fell asleep. He was awoken by raindrops splashing on his arms and face. The fire had died down and it was a lot colder. He set about gathering more dead wood. Just as he stooped to pick up a splintered branch he was startled by an eerie laugh.

'Hahaha!'

Kai whirled about, clutching the branch in one hand. Squinting into the darkness, he couldn't see anyone. The dark bush from which the laugh had come appeared lifeless. Thinking it must have been a bird, he tucked the branch under his arm and went back to poking about for firewood.

Again, it rang out. 'Hahaha!'

The laugh was high-pitched, unnatural, and sent shivers down Kai's spine. He froze, resigning himself to the fact that he was about to be set upon by one of the kai-rākau.

Instead he suddenly saw a bright, bodyless head hovering in the air on the other side of the stream. It was grinning at him. Kai's knees trembled. Whatever this was, it was no human. In terror, he plunged off blindly downstream.

He tried to recall any lessons he had learned about countering spirits, but his mind remained frustratingly blank now that he needed the information. He whispered to the spirits of his tīpuna and recited what he could remember of a spell for protecting a person against witchcraft.

The ghostly visage remained across the water, moving downstream as he did, continually cackling. Kai was determined not to be frightened by the sun-like face. What could it do to him? It wasn't real.

By now the rain had turned into a steady downpour and the narrow stream appeared to be filling out. Large boulders began shifting with the force of the water and the cackling of the apparition was momentarily drowned out. The stream was almost in flood, Kai realised, then noticed with relief that he had almost reached the junction with the Waingata.

He clambered onto the bank and slumped down, exhausted. Realising that the laughing had stopped, he looked back and saw the head racing back upstream. If he had not come downstream when he did, he would have been caught in a flash flood and likely drowned.

The young chief walked through the rest of the night, until he reached the Matā River, which he could not cross because it was too high. At first light the rain stopped, and Kai retreated into the bush to rest for the day. At one point he heard two kai-rākau happen by, but he had concealed himself well so wasn't discovered.

That night he passed Kauae-nui Pā. He was so hungry he even thought about building a rope ladder and climbing over the pā's palisades to steal food. But he pressed on and by dawn he had reached the hills above Ngāpō. He spent the day resting and feeding on berries. At dusk he stole down to the head of the Ngāpō Stream, taking his time to ensure he was not spotted.

He found out later that he must have passed right by one of the kai-rākau patrols but neither had seen the other. At another point, near the ahi-tautai, he heard kai-rākau talking, so he backtracked and cut a wide berth around them.

Finally, Kai reached the foot of Kō Pā, where he hid in a copse of kānuka. Before dawn he crossed the stream and nonchalantly walked into the village. He put his patu down before calling the night watchman.

Everyone was delighted at Kai's arrival, especially his friends.

'By day two everyone else had been caught,' Kere told him. 'After three days they had given you up for lost.'

'You would not have been the first to go missing in the bush below Hikurangi,' said Te Ika.

+

That night Wehe announced to Kai's group that their training cycle had now ended.

'Between now and the next moon, the graduates will receive their tattoos and their own weapons to indicate that they have become warriors.'

Wehe and the kai-rākau celebrated the occasion by drinking tāwhara juice, while the boys feasted around their fires. Realising he had had a little too much drink, Wehe decided to go down onto the sand and walk it off.

Kai was sitting with his mates listening to Pona playing his kōauau when Wehe gestured to him to join him. They walked for some time without talking, until Pona's flute became so faint they could barely hear it.

Suddenly Wehe stopped and turned to Kai. 'Boy, I want you to know something,' he said as he looked up at the crescent moon.

Kai kept his head down. He had no idea what was coming.

'I was dedicated to Tū-kā-riri early on in my life,' his uncle continued. 'I was beaten for the slightest slip-up. Eventually I became hardened to displays of emotion. I am grateful for this because it made me the best warrior I could be.'

Kai was surprised. It wasn't like Wehe to volunteer information about himself. He wondered if the fermented tāwhara juice had loosened his tongue.

'I treated you the same way, for the day is coming when the lives of your tribe will be entrusted to you,' Wehe continued. 'You have proved yourself to be a warrior of the highest order, but you have not yet learned to keep your anger in check. This is something you must work on.'

Kai couldn't believe it. Had his uncle really just called him 'a warrior of the highest order'?

'I . . . I always assumed you didn't think I was good enough. That you thought I would prove to be a coward . . . like my father.'

Wehe gripped him by the shoulders. 'What are you talking about? Tāwae became chief at a very young age, and no finer chief has there ever been. He is no coward.'

'But what about Te Maniaroa? Didn't he run from the fight?'

Wehe shook his head vigorously. 'No, no, no. Your father was only a boy when he joined us at Te Maniaroa — the same age you were when you started your warrior training. He was under strict instructions to stay back and observe the battle, the same way you did out on the waka at Wawe-ki-uta. But when he saw his father being attacked, he grabbed my tao and raced in to join the fight.'

'What? You were there?'

'Of course I was there. His father had told me to stay with him. When he took off I tried to stop him but he was too quick. I saw him struck and he went down. I thought he was dead — almost everyone around him was. I can tell you this much, Kai — your father was absolutely no coward.'

Kai closed his eyes and tried to process what he was hearing. All this time he had believed something so different.

'So why didn't he come with me to Wawe-ki-uta?'

'You must remember, Tāwae returned from Te Maniaroa and instantly became chief of a broken tribe. He had no warrior training; instead, he had to devote himself selflessly to rebuilding the pride, dignity and hope of our people through strong leadership. His presence at Wawe-ki-uta would have been inappropriate, not because he is a coward, but because that was not his place.'

Kai could hardly believe it. If what Wehe said was true, Kai had been wrong about his father for years. Why hadn't someone told him all this ages ago?

'When your grandfather and his two brothers were killed at Te Maniaroa, we began withdrawing to Ōkau Pā. The most fleet-footed Aitanga Nui warrior set out after one group of our men. When he caught up with them he struck each man with a single blow, crippling them and leaving them for those behind to finish off.'

He paused. 'I was lucky. I was carried into the bush badly wounded and managed to escape and get home. How your father wasn't clubbed by those barbarians despatching the wounded was just sheer luck. And how he got away after that is nothing short of a miracle.'

CHAPTER TWENTY-THREE

Kōrerotia ki runga i te takapau wharanui.
Let the discussion be on the nuptial mat.

'It's like the whare wānanga at Tūtata — there's an uneven number of spaces between the rafters,' Kai said to his father while gazing up at the ceiling in the warm interior of the whare puni. He lay on a large mat, and his father and younger brother sat at his feet. His mother, sisters and some of the women from the village, all of whom had trudged up to Kō Pā, were gathered at the far end of the house.

'All our houses are built this way; there's never any deviation. You should know that by now,' said Tāwae.

'I should take more notice,' Kai grinned nervously. This small-talk was his way of avoiding focusing on what was about to happen. He ran his hand over his freshly trimmed chin while studying the black, red and white hand-painted motifs on the kōwhaiwhai boards attached to the rafters.

'It won't take long to grow back,' Tāwae reassured the seventeen-year-old. Kai grinned again. Since Wehe had told him the truth of what happened at Te Maniaroa, Kai felt quite differently about his father. If he ever again heard Kōrihi or any of the others cast aspersions about Tāwae's cowardice they'd know all about it. He looked at his father's moko, which covered nearly all of his face. Ever since he was a child Kai had admired the elegance of the figures and spirals that marked Tāwae's cheeks and forehead. He hoped his own would be just as impressive.

Anganui, the tohunga tāmoko, and his apprentice organised their utensils. Throughout all the Ngāi Haere villages Anganui was considered the expert in this extremely skilled art.

When they were ready to begin he took up the charcoal and water to mark Kai's face on either side with a pattern held only in the artist's mind. Each line was drawn freehand, with remarkable precision, the designs on either side in perfect symmetry.

Tui, who was watching closely, appeared awestruck at the steadiness of the tattooist's hand. Anganui next selected one of several albatross bone tools, each fitted with an ornately carved haft resembling a tiny adze.

'What kind of wood are they made out of?' Tui asked. The tattooist, completely absorbed in the task at hand, did not reply.

'Tōtara,' said his apprentice. 'It's the easiest wood to work with.'

Anganui ran his fingers over the handles, looking for the right one. The uhi were of varying widths. Some had flat edges; others had serrated ends, like miniature combs.

The apprentice stirred the pigment before pouring it into a small carved pumice container.

'What's the pigment made from?' the ever-inquisitive Tui piped up again.

'That awe māpara is almost as old as you, Tui,' the apprentice replied. 'It's a combination of kahikatea soot, water and oil. This same batch adorns the faces of several Ngāi Haere chiefs, though no two chiefs have moko exactly alike.'

The tattooist chose a flat-edge chisel and began tapping the adze with a light wooden hammer made from māhoe. The first incision of the bone chisel into Kai's lip drew blood, yet the young warrior did not flinch. To take his mind off the pain — and it was at times almost unbearable pain — he went back to counting the spaces between the rafters.

His father began singing to him and was immediately joined by the women in the house. Kai closed his eyes and focused on the lyrics. He soon realised it was a waiata about women admiring a warrior's moko. His thoughts drifted to Wairere and for long moments he disappeared with her into the recesses of his mind. He hoped that when next she saw him she would be impressed with his new look.

Blood flowed profusely at every incision Anganui made. He continually wiped away the blood with dressed flax tow wrapped around his finger. He gave an extra tap if the flesh was not cut deeply enough. Kai had to summon all his strength of mind to appear calm before his audience, though the quivering of his body revealed the pain he was suffering. Once Kai's lips were both stained blue, the apprentice placed the funnel end of a kōrere to his mouth and the young chief sipped water from the vessel.

The tattooist next started on the side of Kai's face. He spent quite some time perfecting the design — the spirals on the high cheek bones required the greatest concentration. The tattooist's apprentice stretched each section of skin being worked on so that the chisel pierced a taut surface.

Tui sat transfixed as each incision opened the skin, allowing the artist to use the serrated chisel to penetrate the flesh and insert the pigment. He winced as some of the deeper incisions produced a small river of blood.

After five hours or so, with the nose, cheeks and jaw completed, Anganui stood back and inclined his head from side to side to admire his handiwork.

Then it was time for the forehead. Hardened to the pain by now, Kai chatted with his father and brother while Anganui worked. The operation continued all morning and well into the afternoon and so did the singing.

When Kai's facial moko was completed, the apprentice turned to Tāwae.

'Karaka leaves are best for the healing process.'

Anganui studied his human canvas a final time, then gave Kai some instructions.

'Until you are fully healed, you must have no intimate contact with another, nor should you go to a pool to look at your reflection.'

'When will you mark my body?' Kai asked.

'E kore e tārai te waka i te rā kōtahi. *A canoe is not fashioned in a day.* Your thighs and buttocks can be done in time, but first your face markings must heal.'

Kai thanked the tattooist and his apprentice.

'I will see that a gift is delivered to your house,' Tāwae told Anganui. As they departed, Pona entered the whare for his turn.

A feast celebrated the end of the tattooing process and a pononga was killed for the feast to mark the fact that some of those who received their tāmoko were the sons of chiefs.

+

When it healed, Kai's face was a work of art, each excoriated line now hardened and firm. Eventually the rest of his body was done, and Kai was pleased with the result. Even better, he noticed the unmarried women in the village gazing at him admiringly; while the men seemed to take him more seriously.

The young chief had grown into a tall, dark-skinned and good-looking young man. He was lean yet muscular, and he could now beat most of the other kai-rākau in a race to Ahu. Put a weapon in his hands, either spear or club, and Kai would soon demonstrate how quick and effective he was at sparring.

One morning at Tūtata, while Kai was practising his weapons drills, he was interrupted by Pona, Te Ika and Kere. Kere, now twenty, had returned to Kauae-nui for his tattooing, and now that he had healed he was back with the kai-rākau. Kai was happy to see his friend again.

'Have you heard Kere's news?' Pona asked Kai mischievously. 'He's betrothed to Tūterangi and Poka's daughter. The one with the beautiful hair.'

Kai froze. 'Which one? They've all got beautiful hair.'

His hostility was palpable and Kere quickly put an end to Pona's game. 'Ūkaipō,' he said. 'The eldest. Now that I have been tattooed our parents have matched us.'

Kai was visibly relieved. 'That's great news,' he said, slapping Kere on the back. 'Congratulations.'

Pona and Te Ika flashed each other a wide grin.

When Kai lay on his bed that night he couldn't stop thinking about Wairere. Kere's news made him worry that she too might have been promised to someone else. The thought was unbearable and he tossed and turned all night, imagining the worst. Just before dawn he hatched a plan. *I must procure a love charm*, he decided.

Later that morning he waited on the beach for Parakore. Everyone knew the tohunga often went into the surf at the break of dawn to practise levitation. Kai crouched on the sand and stared out at the ocean for a long time before the sage called to him from behind.

'For whom do you seek an ātahu?'

Kai turned and stood up, momentarily taken aback that Parakore already knew the purpose of his visit.

'I want my whaiāipo to come to me,' he replied carefully.

'That's not so difficult a request,' the tohunga said. 'It requires only a potion, a spell to be recited over it, and a little miromiro bird to fly it to your sweetheart. But for the latter there is no need as she is already here.'

'What do you mean?' said Kai, alarmed.

'Have you spoken with your father recently?' Parakore said as he continued walking down to the shoreline.

Kai hurried back up to Kō Pā, not sure whether to be worried or excited. He found his father in the porch of his house soaking up the morning sun. Before he could ask anything, Tāwae addressed him.

'Ah, Kai. Your arrival is timely, my son. Have you seen your mate Kere?'

'Yes, he came back yesterday.'

'And did he tell you who accompanied him from Kauae-nui?'

216

'No . . .' Kai replied, his heart beating wildly.

'Last night your mother and I concluded a lengthy discussion with Tūterangi and Poka and also your own elders. It was decided that you and Wairere are to be joined in marriage.'

Kai stared wide-eyed at his father. His eyes filled with tears and he looked to the sky as if to acknowledge the influence of the gods. Then he smiled at his father and asked, 'Are they here?'

'Yes, Tūterangi and Poka were among the group who escorted Kere.'

'No, I meant . . . is . . . is Wairere here?' He held his breath for the answer but Tāwae continued talking as if he hadn't heard the question.

'Tribal opinion decided the matter. The debate was focused on whether such a union would be suitably advantageous to both families.'

'Pāpā, please. I need . . . is she *here*?' Kai looked imploringly at his father. The proud young warrior vanished like a column of smoke, and it was as if he were a child again, a boy begging his father to take him fishing.

Tāwae laughed heartily. 'Son, there are times when I marvel at the fearsome warrior you have become, and there are other moments when I fear you'll throw it all away. Yes, she is here and yes, you will see her soon enough.'

Kai was virtually delirious with anticipation. 'When, Pāpā?' he asked in a whisper.

'This afternoon. Wairere and her parents are staying down in the village,' Tāwae said. 'So what are you waiting for, son? You need to get yourself ready. Your mother will be along soon to dress your hair. Wairere will be asked before an assembly if she consents to the betrothal. Assuming she does, she will become your wife — after Te Maniaroa has been avenged.'

Kai was so happy he scarcely heard the caveat.

'The two of you are not common people. As the saying goes, "Kōrerotia ki runga i te takapau wharanui."' *Let the discussion be on the nuptial mat.*

'Meaning?'

'Like Manu's, your marriage will be marked by proper ritual and ceremony. Unlike the common people, whose consent is given by going to the other's bedside at night.'

Kai nodded gravely. 'What if she says no?' he asked suddenly. 'It's been a long while. Perhaps she has changed her mind . . .'

'Then we will seize her for you,' Tāwae laughed. 'I have seen that done before. No, in truth, I believe she will consent. Her parents say their daughter has been consumed with desire for you since she first set her eyes upon you at Kauae-nui.'

+

The meeting that afternoon was held in front of one of the whare puni in the village. Kai and Tui stood alongside their parents and elders, awaiting the arrival of Wairere and her people. Tāwae and his sons were easily distinguished among the locals by their dogskin cloaks. Kiri and her daughters, with feathers on their heads, were dressed in handsome kaitaka of silken white or glossy jet. The effect was very becoming.

When Wairere finally appeared, Kai was far from disappointed — she was even more lovely than he remembered. She was flanked either side by her sisters. Ūkaipō, now nineteen, and Hinewehi, who at fifteen was about two years younger than Wairere.

Poka was swaddling a baby girl while Tūterangi and his son Tāmō, the wrestler, escorted them. Kai could tell from the way she carried herself that Poka was the one in charge of this brood. Kere was also with them. He threw Kai a wide grin. He had known all along.

The beautiful sisters all had hair cascading down their backs and wore stunning pounamu ornaments in their ears. They wore belts made from the braided strands of kāretu grass, which quivered as they moved. Daubs of red ochre covered their bare skin and shark oil had been liberally applied to their legs and arms.

As they approached, Tui spoke in a low voice to his brother. 'Look at them showing off. Are you sure you want her, brother?'

'That's not showing off,' Kai told Tui. 'It's confidence. Their mother is high born. Daughters of such women are in a class of their own and they know it.' His eyes were fixed on Wairere's every movement. Where she had been not much more than a girl when she had performed in front of him two years earlier, now she had blossomed into a curvaceous young woman. Kai was mesmerised.

'I was smitten that night at Kauae-nui and nothing has changed, little brother.'

When Hinewehi gave Tui a flirtatious glance, the younger brother blushed and looked away.

As the visitors lined up to greet their Ngāpō relatives, Kai nervously awaited Wairere's approach. When he offered his nose to greet her she flashed her beautiful smile, grabbed his hand and gently scratched his palm, just as she had done at Kauae-nui.

'Tēnā koe, Kai,' she said as she looked up at him.

'Tēnā koe, Wairere,' replied Kai, his voice deep. She smiled as she withdrew and saw the red mark her kōkōwai had left on his nose. He did not smile — his eyes remained locked on hers in an intense gaze for what felt like an eternity. Eventually Tui stepped up to greet her also, breaking the spell.

When all were seated, Wairere was asked to stand and give her consent to the betrothal. She rose to her feet and spoke without hesitation.

'Hai a kōrua taku kōrero, e Rangi, me tō hoa rangatira. He tono nāku mō tā kōrua tama mō Kai, hai tāne māku. Ka mutu tonu taku kōrero. E whakaae ana kōrua?' *What I have to say I address directly to you, oh Chief, and your wife. My request is simply that you allow your son, Kaitanga, to be my husband. Do you agree?*

There were murmurs of approval all round, and admiration for the direct way the young woman had addressed Tāwae and Kiri.

'Nā wai tō whakaaro? Nāhau ake, nā te tangata rānei?' replied Tāwae. *Where does your request spring from? From you or from some other person?*

'Nāku ake taku whakaaro. I tipu taua take i roto i au.' *It is mine alone. My request springs from within me.*

'Ka pai tonu koe ki te tekoteko nei?' *Will you be all right with this carved figurehead?* Tāwae motioned towards the tattoos adorning his son.

'He ātaahua ake a ia. Ka pai tonu au.' *He's even more attractive. Fine with me.* Wairere smiled as she looked at Kai. 'Kia kī atu anō au, nāku tonu hoki i whakaaro.' *As I have said, there is no doubt in my mind.*

After glancing at Kiri to confer, Tāwae responded to Wairere.

'We welcome your bold request, befitting of the wife of a future chief. Your man is presently living with us. You must stay with Kiri and me for the next few days so we can all get to know you better.'

Tūterangi, clearly overcome with delight, instructed his people to come forward with their dowry. 'We hereby offer you these three greenstone heitiki, three fine flax cloaks, three whalebone clubs, two dogskin cloaks, three ōnewa clubs, a whalebone club and one taiaha.' Tāwae knew these gifts would have been a significant portion of the family's assets.

'It is not as if a woman is a thing of small worth,' Tūterangi continued. 'While food comes from the ground, fish from the net, it is a woman who brings forth a man.'

Wairere was invited to take her place next to Kai. She sat close enough that her upper arm touched his and he could inhale her fragrance. His heart pounded furiously but he dared not look at her as the speeches continued. The rest of the ceremony was a blur as he became increasingly intoxicated with the scent and nearness of his beloved.

After a celebratory meal, Wairere was invited up to Kō Pā. At last Kai could speak to her in private, although his mother was never far away.

'Come with me,' he said, and he took Wairere by the hand and led her up to Kai-namu-namu. Seated on the rise Kai was silent, his head spinning as he gazed at her. The moment he had dreamed about was suddenly upon him. He wanted nothing to break the spell. Eventually, Wairere, after surveying the ocean view, turned to look at her future husband and spoke.

'Warrior training has given you good shoulders,' she remarked. Kai grinned. 'And your eyes,' she added. Kai waited for her to continue. 'Your eyes. They are mesmerising when you stare. I can feel your power.'

A silence descended momentarily. Eventually Kai responded.

'I don't mean to stare,' he said as he brought one knee up and rested his chin upon it. 'It's just that I have waited so long to look at you again, to talk to you.'

'Drink me in,' Wairere said as she leaned back on her elbows. She allowed her own eyes to travel down Kai's body, eventually resting on the pūhoro on his thigh. 'I see you wear the marks that represent speed. Are you in a hurry?'

'From the time I first saw you I've been in a hurry,' he murmured.

'I knew it was not by chance that you came to our pā,' Wairere said. 'You know, I would have killed myself if they had not let me be with you.'

'I felt the same way,' Kai said. 'Although I would never do that.'

'Why not? Don't you want me?' Wairere feigned offence.

Kai placed his hand on her shoulder.

'If you only knew how much. But you must understand my life's purpose. I was born for such a time as this. I must live. Just as you must be mine.' Wairere looked into his eyes and smiled.

'Soon I'll be going away,' Kai continued, 'and you'll be going back to Kauae-nui. You are tapu now. No other man can touch you. I want to remember the sweetness of this moment so I can hold this image of you in my mind until we are together again.'

Wairere lay back on the ground and stretched her arm out above her head. Kai ran his eyes over the full length of her body as she basked in the sunshine of his attention. In time he leaned over her, letting his arms take his weight as he positioned himself directly above her.

She was about to reach out and touch his chest when he murmured, 'Wait for me . . .'

'Hey, you two!' It was Kai's little sister, Haere.

'What is it?' Kai asked sharply as he twisted his head towards her, while Wairere wriggled out from under him.

'Our parents want you both to come.' Haere, now seven, glared suspiciously at Wairere.

'And, I guess that's about as much privacy as we're going to get until we're married,' Kai muttered as he helped Wairere up.

That night Wairere lay down in the whare puni with Kai and his family, Kai having been granted permission by the kai-rākau to stay with them. Kiri positioned herself between the betrothed.

'This is the way it will be until you leave for Kauae-nui,' she told Wairere firmly. 'You must be pure on your wedding day.'

Over the following five days Wairere spent a great deal of time with her future mother-in-law, who instructed her in the art of weaving. The cloak they started on was to be a wedding gift for Kai.

The brief moments that Kai and Wairere stole to be alone together were few, but they were precious.

CHAPTER TWENTY-FOUR

E whai mahi hira ana i te moana waipū.
Great works are done in deep waters.

All of the kai-rākau had been called to a special meeting at Kirikiri-tatangi. Another winter had passed, during which Kai and his mates had been busy assisting Wehe to train Tui's intake. There was a buzz among those who were present as they waited to hear why they had been summoned.

'Our Ika-a-Whiro have decided the time is right for Ngāi Haere to once again taste battle,' Wehe told them. 'I shall let Tukua explain.'

Wehe's father, who was sitting inside the para whakawai, slowly got to his feet.

'He tohu tēnei hei tirohanga mā koutou aku tamariki, hei whiriwhiringa, a hei āta whakaarotanga,' he began. *This sign is for your scrutiny, my children. Search it and consider its meaning.*

The kai-rākau were apprehensive, for they knew the old man was about to tell them of some omen, which could be good or bad, there was no telling which.

'I was sitting right here on Kai-namu-namu talking with one of the Ika-a-Whiro when my leg began to twitch. Before long my calf muscle started quivering. "Friend," I asked. "What portent can this be?" He asked me, "From which direction has it come?" I replied, "From the north-east, beyond the mountain." My friend said: "Our enemy is at that place." We waited and the twitch came again, but more gently. "'Tis a good omen," said he. "Our adversary is talking about us."'

The old man sat down and Wehe rose again.

'Men, such things do not appear randomly. For those of you who have studied the various tākiri, what are we to take from this?'

Pona responded, 'Isn't it our rainbow gods Uenuku and Kahukura that trigger such omens?' Some of the other young men nodded in agreement. 'And beyond the mountains to the north-west is home to the Aitanga Nui.'

'You are correct, Pona,' Wehe replied. He paused. 'Your generation has reached adulthood now.' He looked around the faces of the youngest kai-rākau in the front row of the group that crouched in a wide arc on the hard sand. 'On this training ground,' he said, 'each one of you has been taught to handle weapons. You have mastered the thrust, the feint, the guard and block. Coordination of hand and eye, the aptitude to anticipate a rival's attack or to spy out his weaknesses — these things come naturally to you now. Even your deportment and the way you approach things, all that you learned here.'

He paused again. Kai sensed that something big was coming.

'Our Ika-a-Whiro feel we are sufficiently strong to make an incursion into Aitanga Nui territory,' said Wehe. 'With the help of our relatives at Ōkau Pā we intend to mount a formidable assault at a time when Aitanga Nui least expects it.' Turning to Tāwae, who had joined the meeting, he explained further.

'We will travel aboard Manu-pōkai's betrothal gift, *Te Rūrū-a-Tarapīkau*, because Manu is personally linked to the purpose of our venture. Once the planting season has ended, the rest of spring and all summer will be spent preparing for the battle.'

+

No matter which Ngāi Haere pā Kai visited over the start of the long hot summer, the only topic of conversation was the proposed attack on Aitanga Nui.

Te Rūrū could seat only seventy warriors. With some of the seats being reserved for Whai and other young men from Ōkau, it was clear that not all the kai-rākau would be going.

Competition for a place was fierce. Each kai-rākau was prepared to do anything to be chosen. Even one of the Ika-a-Whiro vied for the chance to join the ope taua. 'Give me one last fight,' he pleaded with his fellow veterans. 'The younger warriors will need an elder to guide them.'

'This is a young man's venture,' Tukua told him. 'Let the grey-haired men stay at home, while the black-haired men venture out.'

In midsummer Whai and a group of twenty warriors arrived from Ōkau Pā to join the training. Four joined from Kauae-nui Pā, including Tāmō, the wrestler and Wairere's brother. For the rest of the summer the combined group were put through their paces, and gradually the seventy selected themselves. Kai, Pona, Te Ika and Kere all made the cut.

When he knew he had been selected, the first thing that Kai wanted was his own taiaha. He now knew the exact weight, length, thickness and balance that suited his fighting style and he asked his uncle Kākahu, a master carver, to create it for him.

The pole shed where Kākahu worked, at the edge of the bush, was enclosed to waist height and smelt of resinous wood and dye. When Kai went to pick up his new weapon at the appointed time he found Kākahu oiling it. The taiaha had been placed in a nearby swamp for some days, then for two nights and days it had hung over a fire to thoroughly dry it and let the smoke seep through. Now, when he tapped it, it almost rang like iron.

'Akeake is the hardest wood in the bush,' the carver explained. 'Very difficult to work with, but it's the best.' Kai was keen to see how the taiaha felt in his hands but Kākahu was not going to be rushed.

As he waited, Kai looked around the workshop. A pile of wood chips had been swept to one corner of the palm-roofed structure; otherwise it was spotless. He looked out to sea. The sun had not been in the sky long but the temperature was climbing quickly. By way of conversation, and knowing his uncle was a great seafarer, he asked, 'E koro, our ancestors must have been amazing navigators to traverse the open seas from Hawaiki?'

'Indeed, but seamanship and navigation are only half the skill. Persistence, determination and knowing the right karakia to control the elements are also important. And, you must always trust your whatu manawa — your intuition,' Kākahu explained. He had stopped oiling to fine-tune a haehae line on the tongue of the weapon. His head and back were bent over the pointed end of the long-handled fighting staff as if he were speaking to it rather than to Kai. He tapped the wooden handle of his stone chisel rhythmically with his mallet, never once faltering.

'That's how Pāhi was able to return to Hawaiki,' he added as he brushed away tiny wood chips.

'Who is Pāhi?' Kai asked.

'You don't know who Pāhi is?' Kākahu stopped and looked at him. 'You have much to learn. He's the most recent one from here to return to our island homeland.'

'So there were others who went back?'

'Oh, most certainly,' Kākahu said as he laid his chisel and mallet down on a nearby log. 'Someone in almost every generation has arrived from or returned to Hawaiki. Pāhi lived just north of here at Reporua. One of his relatives offended a neighbouring chief when he declined to supply a particular type of food the rangatira wanted. The chief, Toka, vowed to take revenge on the man and his relatives. At the time the Reporua people were planting and Pāhi reassured them, "Toka will wait until our kūmara are almost ready to harvest before he strikes out for our pā." Pāhi reckoned the chief would want their crops to provision his ope taua.'

Kākahu went back to oiling the intricate rape pattern on the tongue of the weapon.

'Pāhi told his people early autumn was the most likely time for an attack, because the kūmara would be near maturity. Pāhi knew Toka had a far superior force so he advised his people to convert two of their waka into ocean-going vessels. "When the time comes," he said, "we will retrace the ocean pathways of our ancestors back to Hawaiki."

'At the beginning of autumn they hastily dug up the kūmara tubers, steamed and dried them, and packed them for the voyage,' Kākahu said.

'That would be a risky expedition, wouldn't it?' Kai asked, wondering why he had not heard this story before.

'No riskier than doing battle against Toka, who seemed to his neighbours to be an undefeatable tyrant. Pāhi thought they had more chance on the open ocean. If they fought and lost they would more than likely end up being cooked and eaten, or serving out their lives as pononga to Toka's people.'

'I suppose so,' Kai murmured.

'I *know* so,' his uncle replied. A glint of a smile spread across Kai's face.

Kākahu tapped the chisel ever so gently as he incised a final curved haehae line into the wood. Then he held it at arm's length to look it over.

'While some of the people prepared the waka and food supplies,' he continued, 'others busied themselves at their usual activities, in order to conceal their departure. The two vessels stole away under cover of darkness.'

'You can't be too careful with your words, can you, uncle?' Kai suggested.

'That's right, Kai. Many a tribe has been wiped out because someone said something that caused offence. It might have been an innocent remark but others imagine you meant something harmful by it. So always guard your tongue.'

'And what became of the two vessels?' Kai asked.

'I have heard that Pāhi and his people made it across the great expanse of Te Moana-nui-a-Kiwa and are now back in Hawaiki. I believe it because Pāhi's people were some of the best seafarers on this coast. No one knew more about the flight paths of the birds or how to read the stars than their navigators.'

He stopped for a moment and looked at his nephew. 'You too must become expert in these things, Kai. The moon, the stars and nature's signs are the way we manage our lives. But the really important lesson is this: E whai mahi hira ana i te moana waipū. *Great works are done in deep waters.* Those who stay close to the shore discover only that they are safe — safe from drowning, safe from disaster.

'Your destiny was determined before you were formed in your mother's womb. That destiny lies in deep waters where the tempest awaits. The deep for you is the Aitanga Nui. The time is coming when you will have to leave this shore, launch out into the deep and do business there. When you do, remember the story of Pāhi and take courage from it.'

Kākahu picked up the heavy long-handled taiaha and handed it to Kai.

'Now, see how that feels.'

Kai weighed the taiaha in his hands. He had gone into the bush with the old man to select the tree from which it would be made. He had helped him start a fire at the base of the tree to burn into the trunk some way, then knocked out the embers with their adzes and lit another fire, again and again around the trunk until the tree fell. Then Kākahu had shaved it down to form the haft of the taiaha. And now, here it was in his hands, completed.

Tears of pride welled up in Kai's eyes. 'I am truly grateful, uncle.'

'Old men like me,' said Kākahu, 'past fighting and hard work, pass our time manufacturing weapons. I'm just glad this one will see action.'

Kai slid his hands along the taiaha's slender neck. It felt remarkably light yet so steely and strong.

'I shall call it Te Atua-pūhohe,' said Kai. *The mocking laugh of the deity.*

'Why that name?'

'After the headless face I once saw below Hikurangi.' Kai looked down the blade of the weapon. 'May Te Atua-pūhohe strike fear in the souls of all those who challenge it.'

He thanked the master carver then said with a grin, 'I'm going to head over to Kirikiri-tatangi right now and try it out!'

+

Unbeknown to Kai, Wehe had met with the Ika-a-Whiro to inform them that he wished to place his seventeen-year-old nephew in charge of *Te Rūrū*. Tukua disagreed but would not explain why, and it was decided to take the issue to the rūnanga. Tāwae adjudicated at the evening meeting. The old men were sitting around a fire in the whare puni.

'Your silence implies either dissent or that you need to be convinced further. Which is it?' Wehe asked Tukua.

'He is simply too young,' Tukua replied.

'He may be young, but we've all seen how good he is with the taiaha. He already has the respect of kai-rākau much older than him and he has spent countless hours discussing tactics with the Ika-a-Whiro.'

'You yourself should be leading this ope taua, son,' Tukua said.

Wehe was having none of it. 'No one kai-rākau has more invested in this attack than Kai. It is his birthright. His whole life has been moving towards this moment and he'll die before he returns a failure.'

'That's my worry exactly — that they might all die if his leadership is reckless.'

'Prove to us that he is capable of leading his cousins,' one of the other Ika-a-Whiro cut in. 'So we can tell their parents with a clear conscience that it is safe to entrust their young men to the leadership of this youth because he is smart and unflappable, and that he will return with as many of them as he can.'

After further discussion Tāwae could see that resolution would not be forthcoming and he was going to have to rule. He unfurled his paepaeroa and slowly rose to his feet.

'I always knew that one day my son would fulfil his destiny by being part of the force that avenges our fathers' slaughter. In fact, I've longed for this day. But I did not realise the day would come so soon. My son is still young, and untried in this role. So I, too, remain to be persuaded.' He sat down again.

Wehe turned to the chief. 'His peers naturally follow him, not because he tells them to, but because they are reassured by him. I have taught many gifted warriors over my lifetime, but none of them compare to your son, e Rangi. The atua have bestowed supreme warrior skills upon Kai. My father and the Ika-a-Whiro know that. All we have done is refine those gifts through years of training. What's more, was he not prophesied as the tribe's redeemer, even before he entered this world?'

Tāwae sat looking down for some time, then raised his head and spoke.

'It is abundantly clear that none of you doubt my son's ability as a warrior, but it seems to me it's in the areas of tactics and leadership that some of us need reassurance. Let's test this further. Ask him to come up with a plan for how he would use *Te Rūrū* and the seventy warriors to assault Aitanga Nui. If his plan meets with the approval of the Ika-a-Whiro, then we have our answer. If not, Wehe will be in command.'

+

Kai was more than a little surprised when Wehe and the Ika-a-Whiro asked him to come up with a plan of attack for entering Aitanga Nui waters.

'Well, our strategy will require careful planning,' Kai replied, 'and must allow plenty of time for the ope taua to practise it.'

He spent the next few days discussing the matter with some of the more senior kai-rākau, who between them had seen many battles and skirmishes. Then he began to formulate a battle plan, which he ran by his friends. His approach relied on stealth and surprise.

'If we're going in with only one waka,' Kai told them, 'we're sure to be outnumbered, so we need a way to gain an advantage from the outset. Given the midday temperatures from now until the next moon, I suggest an early-morning assault when it's cooler. If the enemy can be drawn into the water, then we can first fight them from the waka,' Kai said. 'That way we'd have the upper hand at the start.'

With his friends' approval, and after adding one or two of their suggestions to the plan, Kai took it to the Ika-a-Whiro.

They listened carefully and raised no objections.

'You should put *Te Rūrū* to sea and test this tactic,' Tukua advised.

That afternoon Kai sent some of his mates to pluck leaves from a stand of kāuka trees, which they dried then steeped in water overnight. The next day, with the leaves more pliable, they split them into strands and, using five strands, plaited two ropes, each thirty metres long.

Te Rūrū was parked in its shelter with its prow facing the sea ready for water entry. The kai-rākau got to work replacing the ropes attached to its anchors. The two punga each consisted of a large water-worn stone with a natural hole through which the rope was threaded. The punga kārewa at the bow end was smaller than the punga whakawhenua in the stern.

Then Wehe gathered together the ope taua and told them they were going to trial Kai's strategy. Kai, holding a paddle, stood in the centre of the seated group onshore and explained.

'We lure the enemy into the water. How? By using these new, longer ropes attached to the anchor stones. Once we drop both anchors, we can haul on either one of the lengthened ropes, making the waka move back and forth as we please. During the clash, we move the vessel in and out of the shallows, giving us a chance to recover before unleashing ourselves on them again.'

Kai then detailed what each group of kai-rākau were to do. Kōrihi and two of his mates were muttering to each other constantly and Kai was becoming annoyed. Without breaking his momentum, or even looking in their direction, he swung the hoewai and caught one of them across the side of the face with the blade.

'If you don't want to be here, go!' It was done so quickly and with such authority that he immediately had everyone's full attention.

The injured man put a hand over where he had been cut. His mouth was upturned, as if he was smiling, but his eyes suggested otherwise. Kōrihi scowled, but none of them made a move to leave.

With help from others, they dragged the waka taua into knee-high water. As they steadied it, the great canoe swayed resplendent in the sun-warmed surf. Made from a single tōtara log, Manu-pōkai's betrothal gift was twenty-one metres long, with a width of one-and-a-half metres, and one metre deep. The men scrambled aboard and arrange themselves two abreast on each thwart. Te Ika was told to sit in the stern; he was the youngest, and would be the last to engage the enemy.

'Pona, you're the kai-whakatere,' Kai called to his cousin from where he was standing midway in the waka.

Pona shifted to a small seat in the stern, not knowing whether to feel honoured or disappointed that he had been chosen to steer the vessel, as it would mean he would be furthest from the fight.

It was a warm morning and the sea was placid — ideal conditions. Once they were a couple of hundred metres offshore, they tested the plan a few times — dropping the anchors, hauling the waka to and fro. They were out on the water for most of the day until Kai was confident the strategy would work.

'Hūtia ngā punga,' he commanded. *Pull up the anchors.* 'Turn the stern to face the beach, Pona!' Te Ika leapt up to help. Once the prow was fully facing out to sea, they paddled the magnificent vessel back to shore. In no time their feet were in the surf and they were hauling the vessel across the skids, which were laden with seaweed, and up above the high-water mark.

Wehe and Tukua were standing on the beach watching. Kai felt pretty happy with how it had gone, but he had no idea what his elders thought.

Wehe took Kai aside and said to him, 'It has been decided. You are to be given command of the ope taua.'

'What?' Kai was incredulous. 'I assumed you would be.'

'No, I won't be joining you. This is your time.'

'But . . .' Kai's head was spinning. 'What if the others don't accept me as their leader? I'm younger than most of them.'

Wehe knew what sorts of men the kai-rākau were, both the mature and the freshly graduated. Over the years he had trained them all.

'It's true that to your cousins you are a firebrand, the kind of warrior most enemy fighters will try to avoid, and even some of our own are fearful of getting on your wrong side. But that aggressive temperament of yours, coupled with your force of character, your determination and your never-say-die attitude, has won their respect and it is those qualities that will guarantee their loyalty.'

Kai was speechless.

'Do not doubt yourself,' said his uncle, looking him in the eye. 'Do not prove me wrong. Fulfil your destiny. For such a time as this.'

CHAPTER TWENTY-FIVE

Tini te whetu, iti te pokeao.
A multitude of stars may be obscured by a small dark cloud.
(A small, resolute party accomplish much in war.)

The seventy had some days to wait until the next new moon. Relatives from the surrounding pā, including inland Kauae-nui, arrived to farewell their sons and husbands. Fathers came with their wives and children, in groups as big as twenty, proud to watch their sons rehearsing. Wairere and her sisters accompanied their parents. They camped in the village and paid the kai-rākau almost daily visits.

Kai had at first felt incredibly nervous about having responsibility for all kai-rākau, but the role had been assigned by Wehe and the Ika-a-Whiro, and he had faith in their judgement, so he put nerves aside and assumed the mantle. His self-doubt only came to the fore when Kōrihi and a couple of his henchmen ribbed him again, asking him whether he believed he had earned the right to command them. Kai decided this had to stop. He ordered the ope taua to Kirikiri-tatangi and invited the Ika-a-Whiro to join them.

When all had gathered in the scorching midday sun, Kai prepared to address them. He loosened his dogskin cloak from his oiled shoulders and handed it to Kere. He then stepped inside the cordon where Wehe was waiting. Wairere joined a group of women who observed from Kō Pā.

The young chief coolly surveyed the perspiring kai-rākau — some seasoned campaigners, others fresh-faced warriors itching to make a name for themselves in their first battle. His hands curled into fists around the shaft of his taiaha, Te Atua-pūhohe.

He came straight to the point. 'If any of you think me unworthy of leading you,' he said archly, 'I urge you to take up your weapon and enter the cordon now.' For a moment no one moved and Kirikiri-tatangi grew deathly quiet. Then, as Kai had anticipated, Kōrihi lifted the rope and he and his friends Whakapiki and Ātea, the latter still smarting from Kai's backhander with the paddle, entered the square. Whakapiki took a further step forward but Kōrihi laid a calloused hand on his arm.

'Let me,' he hissed.

'No,' said Kai. 'Let's see how good all three of you are together.'

'At your own peril,' Kōrihi sneered.

'Popotahi!' Wehe called out, and the four men took up the vertical guard position with their taiaha. Just as Wehe slipped under the rope and out of the cordoned area, Kai set his jaw and brought his quivering taiaha before his body, the tongue end down, while the three others slowly began to circle him.

Sweat beaded Kai's skin and trickled from his brow as he slowly swivelled on his heels, waiting for the first of his opponents to make their move. As he expected, it was Kōrihi. The clang of fire-hardened wood rang out as their taiaha clashed, Kai blocking several times before leaping back. Then, in a sudden flurry of moves that sent Ātea reeling, Kai brought his taiaha crashing down on Kōrihi's shoulder. Tremors from the impact reverberated down his own arms.

There was a gasp of incredulity among the onlookers at the young chief's swiftness and agility. Even Kōrihi was clearly surprised. Kai and Kōrihi matched blows until the pain rising from his shoulder rendered Kōrihi's left arm ineffective. He dropped his taiaha and reached for his short-handled patu with his uninjured hand. But before he could wield it to defend himself, Kai struck at the other shoulder. Bone cracked and pain flared up Kōrihi's neck. His right arm now hung like the limb of a corpse and the stone club fell from his inert fingers. Stunned and struggling, he was finished.

Kai moved straight on and with another flurry he brought Whakapiki to his knees, leaving him doubled over in pain and clutching a badly bruised thigh. With renewed determination the young chief gave Ātea an icy stare. Throwing down his taiaha, he clasped his patu and beckoned the young man forward. As Ātea swung his taiaha, Kai turned side on in a flash and stopped it with the edge of his patu, before restraining it with his free hand. Clutching the shaft of the taiaha, he planted the butt end of his patu in front of Ātea's face and shoved it into the bridge of his nose. The whole affair had not lasted more than a few minutes.

'Anyone else got a problem with my leadership?' Kai challenged as he scanned the faces in the crowd. No one replied. Any niggling doubts about his right to lead had been well and truly quashed.

Tukua surveyed the scene. 'None of those three will be any good against the Aitanga Nui,' he said to his son.

'I'm fine!' said Kōrihi as Wehe approached him. 'I've been bruised before.' Wehe touched his shoulder and he winced.

'The collarbone is broken,' said Wehe. 'You won't be taking your place in *Te Rūrū*. You'll give your seat up to another.' Kōrihi's lips drew back in a snarl of pure hatred as he glared at Kai.

Wehe issued instructions to the members of the war party. 'Tonight you are to shift your bed mats to the whare puni in Kō Pā. For those of you who are married, this will ensure you do not give yourselves to your wives before your departure. You must conserve your energy.'

That afternoon Kai met Wairere at Kō Pā and told her about the plan.

'Well, if that's the case you should take me to your bed and soothe me now,' she said with a smile.

'We will have our whole future together for that,' Kai said in a low voice as he took her in his arms.

'I hope so,' Wairere said, looking momentarily worried.

'In all sincerity, do not fear for me. I will return to you.'

236

'I know that,' Wairere replied, smiling again. 'I've seen you sparring, and you're very good.'

'When did you see me?'

'I watched you from up here.' She blushed. 'I saw you give those three a lesson. Look, I know you have to do this. All I ask is that you return safely to me.' She nuzzled her face into his neck. 'And make sure you bring your brother back unharmed too.'

Kai stepped back, his strong hands on her shoulders, and looked down at her with a quizzical look. 'My brother?'

'Yes, your brother,' she said without looking at him. 'I heard you asked for him to accompany the seventy. My sister Hinewehi will never forgive you if anything happens to Tui.'

It was true — after the fight with Kōrihi and his companions, Kai had suggested to Wehe, Tukua and his father that Tui be allowed, despite his youth and inexperience, to replace the injured Kōrihi. It was quite a debate, but it was the old tohunga's prophecy that the two brothers would be redeemers that carried the day.

'Does Tui know that Hinewehi feels that way about him?'

'Ha!' she hooted as she looked up at him. 'They've been meeting in secret since our betrothal feast. Why do you think she stayed on with me when my parents returned to Kauae-nui?'

'Well, I never,' Kai exclaimed, shaking his head in disbelief.

+

That night Kai and Tui were asked by their parents to join them on Kai-namu-namu. Sitting together on the crest, Kiri pointed towards the north.

'Ka kite atu kōrua i ngā kapua e rere mai rā?' *Do you see the clouds in the distance?*

'Yes,' said Kai. He knew what was coming. He had been through this routine with his mother many times when he was younger. Yet having the discussion again on the eve of their departure seemed like a kind of omen.

'You will not have heard the stories about the abuses of the slain after Te Maniaroa,' said Tāwae. 'Taniwha was livid that he had missed the opportunity to deliver the death blow to my father, Kū. Unable to satiate his desire for retribution in life, he played it out in death. When he and his people returned to their home at Tūmo, they took with them several limbs they had severed from our dead warriors.'

The boys were silent; Tui's mouth hung open as he stared at his father.

'They fastened the hands, wrists upwards, to wooden crossbars and attached them to the outer palisade of their pā. When the hands dried in the sun they bent the fingers towards the palms as hooks. Then Taniwha ordered baskets containing the remains of their meal to be hung from the fingers.' Kai turned away from his father and stared out into the darkness. Tui closed his eyes.

'The bones of our other relatives were made into fishhooks and now our enemy catches fish with them.' Tāwae spoke matter-of-factly, though his hands gripped his mere as if his life depended on it.

'Kai, Tui, look at me,' Kiri broke in, unable to contain herself. 'Taniwha is long dead but his son Whiwhi-rangi lives on. Ko te tikanga kia whakahokia mai e kōrua tōna māhunga. Mā te pēnā anake ka whakamauru noa i te mamae e kai kino nei.' *You will bring us back his head — only that will ease this intense pain.*

She reached out a hand to Kai and stroked his cheek. 'When you return, your men will look to you as their chief.'

Their father stood and faced the two boys. As they looked up at him, he repeated Kiri's instruction, then held out a closed fist to them.

'I want one of you to take this with you.'

'What is it?' Tui asked. Tāwae opened his hand and the two squinted at what looked like a small piece of whalebone. The shape made Kai think of the crossbars to which his grandfathers' hands had been attached . . . but this cross was no bigger than his finger.

'My father gave me this before we went to Te Maniaroa. He said it had been passed down to him and that it was a good omen. I believe it saved my life. It originally belonged to the pake-pakehā who visited

238

our shores many generations ago. Place it in *Te Rūrū* so that you have something of your grandfather's spirit travelling with you.' He put it in Kai's hand.

'Whoatu. Mauria mai tōna ūpoko, hei whakaao māramatanga mō aua matenga i Te Maniaroa. Mō te wā pēnei i tae mai ai kōrua.' *Now go. Bring his head to us and lighten our hearts for those deaths at Te Maniaroa. You are both here for such a time as this.*

The couple walked away, leaving their sons to contemplate what they had heard.

'E Kai,' Tui confided, 'kāre au e pīrangi ki te hoki ngere mai.' *I don't want to come home a disappointment.*

'That won't happen. Trust me,' his older brother reassured him. He placed a hand on Tui's shoulder. 'You heard Father — this is our time to shine.'

+

A festive atmosphere prevailed in the village on the morning of their departure.

Everyone was chattering and laughing, children played, dogs barked excitedly and the birds all seemed to be out in force too. In contrast, the sky was overcast and it was threatening to rain, but the air remained warm.

The ope taua assembled at the ahi-tautai with a tohunga at the ready. Wehe said, 'Every kai-rākau is to immerse himself in the water and the tohunga will bless your weapon.'

Kaiora watched intently as each young man submerged himself. Some believed that the tohunga could tell which of them would not return from battle by the way they emerged from the water. Kaiora invited them to enquire about their fate, but none dared.

'Hei te rā i whakatika atu ai koutou i Ngāpō, kia mau ki ngā take e whai ake nei,' he explained. *On the day that you set out from Ngāpō, keep firmly to the following practices.* 'Make sure whatever food you are taking has been thoroughly cooked. Undercooked food will bring you bad luck. Mind your behaviour. You can't afford to be grumpy or irritable today. Don't talk about others, nor interfere with what they are doing, and never speak harshly to them. Lastly, do not involve yourself in any act you know is wrong, for this will bring you bad luck when the fighting starts.'

He invited Kai to enter the water last, then stand at his side. 'Follow all of your chief's instructions. Make sure you remain obedient to him, for he has been granted authority from Uenuku and Kahukura, the rainbow atua. Go now! Tū-mata-riri, the angry-faced war god, is also with you.'

War paint adorning their bodies, short-handled clubs tucked in their belts, and most wearing only the maro tūhou apron over their genitals, the ope taua walked back to the village and assembled in front of the main whare puni. The people stood waiting to farewell their heroes.

Wehe addressed the warriors: 'Whakaaturia te waewae ki ō wāhine, ki ō tamariki, ki ō koroheke.' *Reveal your legs before your women, young folk and old men.* This was his way of calling for the party to perform the tūtū ngārahu. Kai responded by organising the taua into four rows. Tāwae observed with quiet pride that his son appeared poised and powerful.

'I guess it's not until we face a real situation that we suddenly harness the power that has already been given us,' the chief said to Wehe.

'It's in the big moments,' Wehe replied, 'that a man will rise to his power and dominion.'

Meanwhile, Tukua, who was also watching the men limber up, muttered to the other Ika-a-Whiro, 'Ki te atatū, he rā kei tua; ki te whati, he hē.' *If rendered correctly, then the sun is shining beyond the clouds of war; if not, it's a bad omen.*

Once they were spaced about a metre apart, the warriors placed their taiaha on the ground and Kai led them in a rousing haka. Their relatives, who had seated themselves in a semi-circle, carefully observed the war party's hand actions and footwork, scrutinising their timing and unity. Eventually some of the women got to their feet and advanced on the war party, their faces distorted and their eyes bulging.

'A good sign,' Tukua said, nodding. He knew that if the women had spotted some error in the men's haka, either in deportment or action, they would have remained seated.

At the end of the tūtū ngārahu the two tohunga, Parakore and Kaiora, began a final incantation over the warriors and their weapons. Then it was time for the farewells — speeches, hongi, hugs and tears.

Kai and Tui saluted their parents.

'It seems like only yesterday that we were carrying them on our backs,' Kiri said to Tāwae. 'Now look at them — fine young warriors.'

CHAPTER TWENTY-SIX

Patu whakairi.
If you start in to fight, do it properly.

The whole of Whānau-a-Mate went down to the foreshore to see off the ope taua. There was an air of anticipation as Kai started the canoe-hauling chant and the men took up the ropes attached to the vessel. In no time they had dragged the now highly tapu waka onto the skids at the water's edge. Two by two, the kai-rākau leapt up onto the gunwales of *Te Rūrū*. The plumes in their topknots resembled terns on a sandbank. Most were bare-skinned apart from Kai, who wore a black and white dogskin shoulder cape, and the two tohunga, who wore kaitaka.

The fully manned vessel was an impressive sight once its triangular sails were set up. The ornate tau-ihu of the waka, which projected about a metre before the bow, was dressed in loose fringes of black feathers. Similarly, the beautifully carved tau-rapa standing some five metres high over the stern was also adorned with black feathers, which fluttered gracefully in the gentle breeze. The carved gunwale-boards were ornamented with bunches of white kanae and toroa feathers placed at equal intervals along the rauawa.

Kai, Wehe and the two tohunga were the last to climb aboard. Wehe and Kaiora were travelling only as far as Ōkau Pā, where Whai and another of his men were to replace them.

As the waka pulled away, a light drizzle fell and the mood on shore turned sombre. Kai would remember this scene until the end of his life — weeping relatives, wives and lovers wading into the water in the wake of the vessel; the wailing voices of the people who sang to them from the beach. On board someone started up a song in reply and the young men all quickly joined in. Kai cast his eyes around the youthful faces of his party and wondered how many of them would return in a few days' time.

As the waka rounded Waikahawai Point he got a final glimpse of Kai-namu-namu. I will see that sight again, he told himself.

Wairere and her sisters were among a group of young women who followed the vessel until the rocks prevented them from going any further. Every one of them was crying as they watched the vessel gradually round the point and disappear.

Kere, who was the kaihautū, called the stroke and the waka glided through the water. Whenever the breeze was light or turned contrary, Kere started up a canoe song.

'Monotonous though it is,' Te Ika said to Tui, 'we sound quite pleasant, don't you think?'

Tui wore a smile from ear to ear. He was so proud to be among the war party. He fixed his eyes beyond Te Ika at Kere and Kai and paddled for all he was worth. The crew joined in the chorus, keeping perfect time with their paddles by striking them on the thwarts, then plunging them into the water and pulling. Kai looked back and saw a rainbow breaking over the sea trail from the direction they had come. He pointed it out to Wehe.

'This rainbow behind us is a good omen,' said his uncle to the whole party. 'Uenuku is urging us on, telling us our enemy will be delivered into our hands by the god of war. Had it been ahead of us, fortune would favour Aitanga Nui.'

The young men dug deeper with their paddles.

The waka taua looked impressive when at full speed. Whenever they passed a coastal pā an alarm would sound indicating that a war canoe was on the sea, and the occupants would rush to watch as

Te Rūrū glided by. The vessel travelled north on a flat sea, then west along the coast until mid-afternoon. They made landfall near the Tere River, a short distance from Ōkau Pā.

The greying chief Tūhoro, his son Whai and all their people were waiting under a huge pōhutukawa tree named Te Waha — the very place from where Tūhoro's own army had advanced to Te Maniaroa two decades earlier.

Manu-pōkai was excited to see her brothers. She was no longer the anxious girl that her family had delivered to her wedding ceremony five years earlier. Tall and athletic looking, she held herself with mature confidence.

The ope taua tied the ropes of *Te Rūrū* to the pōhutukawa. Then they were formally welcomed. Tūhoro urged them to be aggressive throughout the assault.

'Hit them hard and they will soon falter,' he said. To Kai he cautioned: 'Be on your guard. Whiwhi-rangi has lived a life of fighting, murder and slaughter of the worst variety, with little respite. In single combat he has triumphed over all comers. When he falls, his death will be a victory for many.'

They walked down the beach to Te Maniaroa to see the site of the battle that had taken place all those years ago. Meanwhile, Parakore and Kaiora worked with Tūhoro's tohunga on charms to keep the sea calm for the next part of the voyage, and to ensure the ope taua caught the enemy by surprise.

As they walked over the ground at Te Maniaroa, Whai asked Kai, 'Are you ready for this, cousin?'

'I've thought of nothing else since I became a kai-rākau.'

'What about Manu?' Whai asked.

'What about her?'

'Your sister wants to travel with the ope taua.'

'No way.'

'She's been training here on our para whakawai.'

'Since when?' Kai's eyes were wide.

'She has kept it from you and your parents, but I assure you she is proficient with taiaha and patu. She said she would spar with any of your kai-rākau to prove she can look after herself.'

'No, I cannot agree. I already have enough responsibility, let alone having to look after my sister.'

'She would need no looking after, I can tell you that much. What's more, I'll be at her side. You can't deny her this chance. She's carried this burden her whole life, as you have.'

The two young chiefs trod the old battleground in silence before heading back to Ōkau Pā.

The kai-rākau were in a field going through their paces in preparation for the battle. The Ika-a-Whiro and kai-rākau from Ōkau Pā gathered to watch. Manu was there too, taiaha in hand, looking hopeful. Kai gave his sister a nod of acknowledgement but did not invite her to participate. However, as he watched the kai-rākau sparring, he realised he could not ignore Manu's presence any longer, as his men were distracted by the fact that she was bearing arms.

He approached Wehe. 'What do you think about Manu joining the ope taua? Whai swears she is up to the task.'

Wehe turned to look at Manu, who returned his stare with a fierce expression.

'If looks could kill,' Wehe grinned. 'You know . . . it could be a useful thing to have Manu along. He taonga nui te waha karanga i roto o te whawhai.' *The war cry is an important factor in warfare.* 'The higher pitch of a woman's voice can rally a war party where the male voice struggles to do so. I have seen warriors respond fiercely to a woman's battle cry, especially if she appeals to them by their tribal name. They throw every sinew of their body into the group's cause, no matter how challenging the situation.'

Kai walked over to his sister and saluted her.

'You recall our conversation before I left Ngāpō, my brother,' she said as he approached.

'I do. You said you had something to ask of me, but you would wait until this moment.'

'Let me go with the ope taua. That is my request.'

Kai said nothing for a good while as he mulled over his options. But in the end he knew he had only one. 'E tū tāua, me hanatū te haere.' *Let you and I go forth together on our journey.*

Then he walked out into the field and rehearsed his taiaha moves. As he was doing this, a pākau-roha-roha flew across his path. In a flash of movement, he shifted sideways, brought the taiaha up and sliced the grasshopper in half.

'A deft piece of footwork,' remarked Tūhoro.

'I told you he was quick,' Whai said to his father. Kai crouched down near the pōhutukawa tree and began making a hole in which to bury the grasshopper. As he did so, he spoke to the onlookers.

'Nā Whiwhi-rangi te rākau tuatahi ki a au. I kitea e au i te pākau-roha-roha, kotahi atu tāku, ko ia.' *I will allow Whiwhi-rangi to attack me first. As I detected the grasshopper's weakness, I will need only one strike and then he will be mine.*

In truth, Kai had rehearsed these moves in his mind over and over again. He had repeatedly practised them at Kirikiri-tatangi until they were near perfect. 'You can never do a thing you have not first seen yourself doing in your mind,' Kai added.

Whai was impressed and turned to his men. 'Ka tāpaitia tēnei wāhi ko te whakaumu o te tangata pākau-roha-roha a Kai.' *Henceforth this place shall be named 'The spot dug by the winged grasshopper man, Kai'.*

+

Late that afternoon Kai and his men boarded their waka and they were on their way once more. Just before sunset they came across four Aitanga Nui men who were line-fishing on one of their tāmure grounds. The surprised fishermen pulled up their lines and tried desperately to paddle away, but they could not generate the speed needed to escape the larger vessel.

'Don't kill them all,' Kai called. 'I want one taken alive.'

As the waka taua pulled alongside the fishing vessel the warriors boarded and killed three of the occupants. The bodies were tossed into the sea and the prisoner was taken aboard *Te Rūrū*. The terrified fisherman was bound and made to lie below the thwarts, where Kai could keep an eye on him. Meanwhile, a rope was attached to the fishing vessel and it was towed along behind *Te Rūrū*. Its prow consisted of a carved head with an enormous tongue sticking out.

'E hia te tawhiti ki te pā o Pātete?' Kai asked his prisoner. *How far is Pātete Pā?*

'Kia huri tātau ki tua o tērā kūrae, ka kitea atu te pā.' *When we round that headland, you will see it.*

As night fell and the tide ebbed, *Te Rūrū* drew past the headland. Pulling into a rocky outcrop they found tāruke kōura set in the water.

'We'll rest here for the night,' Kai told his men. 'These are their crayfish pots, so it can't be much further to the pā.' At Parakore's insistence they turned their vessel broadside to the coastline and rocked it violently from side to side. An old belief, the tohunga told them, said that this would help when an ope taua lacked the numbers to avenge an earlier defeat by force of arms alone.

The men had raw fish and kōpura kao for their evening meal. Te Ika was still hungry and muttered something to Tui.

'Don't worry,' Manu reassured them. 'After tomorrow you will have plenty of fresh meat.'

In the early morning light, when the horizon was barely discernible and the brighter stars were still visible in the night sky, the sentries on board *Te Rūrū* heard voices near the shore. Each man silently nudged his companion until all seventy men were awake. They listened intently as the distant splash of paddles seemed to be coming closer. As the voices drew nearer they realised it was a group of fishermen come to lift their cray pots.

Kai looked down at the prisoner and said, 'Make a sound and you're dead.'

As the fishermen began pulling their pots they had no idea a waka taua was stealing towards them in the dark. When they finally realised, they dropped their pots and reached for their paddles. *Te Rūrū* easily caught up with the smaller vessel and Kai called upon its occupants to bring it alongside. Instead the fishermen immediately took up their paddles or whatever they had to hand to defend themselves. Pona and Kere were among the kai-rākau who leapt aboard and killed the three occupants.

The sun was just below the horizon so there was enough light now for Kai to make out Pātete Pā in the distance. Like Kō Pā, it stood atop a terraced hill overlooking the beach. Its outer palisades were festooned with skulls and other bones.

Kai directed his men to paddle slowly and silently towards the landing place but to stop the vessel out from shore. And there *Te Rūrū* sat patiently on a shadowy, smooth sea, which almost seemed to hold its breath in anticipation.

CHAPTER TWENTY-SEVEN

———

Ko tēnei taonga ko te mate he tīno kākahu nō tēnei hanga nō te toa.
This prized treasure death is ever the garment of the warrior.

'Kia hiwa rā! Kia hiwa rā! He waka taua e whakatata mai ana!' *Be alert!*
Be watchful! A war vessel is approaching!

Dawn revealed the waka taua to the sentries in the pā and they sounded the alarm. When they realised the waka was just sitting there and no one was coming ashore, the Aitanga Nui warriors left their palisaded pā and headed down to the beach to challenge the strangers.

'Excellent — here they come,' Whai remarked to Kai. 'If the enemy had remained in his pā, it would have been a long-drawn-out business.'

'As for us,' said Kai, by way of rousing his men, 'they will lick the sand at our feet, our hands will ache with the slaughter, and it will be our turn to make fishhooks from their bones.'

The waves rolled in almost in slow motion — long, low and white-fringed. The beach had such a shallow incline that the Aitanga Nui could wade out almost fifty metres and the water would only be at their waists.

'Let's move further out,' Kai called to his men. 'Cut away their fishing canoe. Ready the anchors as we practised.'

Kai wrenched the prisoner up and spoke to him.

'Kua kite atu koe i a Whiwhi-rangi?' *Do you see Whiwhi-rangi?*

'Not that one, not that one . . .' The startled fisherman was searching feverishly despite barely being able to see over the side of the waka.

The paddlers dug their hoewai into the water and started paddling backwards while Tui and Te Ika at the bow threw the punga kārewa overboard. When the warriors on the beach realised the waka was not coming ashore, they raced into the water and began wading out to the anchor rope, which was becoming taut. By this time, on instruction from Kere, Tui and Te Ika had thrown the punga whakawhenua over the stern and were quickly letting out their rope.

Pona, Kere and the kai-rākau at the bow hauled the waka forward. The vessel moved rapidly back into the shallow water and the kai-rākau met the surprised warriors in the water with vicious strikes from their hoewai or weapons.

'Kei au te mātaika!' *I have killed the first fish.* Kere yelled as he struck with his hoewai at the head of one of the hapless victims who had ventured too far out. Tui, Te Ika and Whai pulled on the stern anchor rope and the waka retreated into deeper water where the warriors could not follow.

Once the front rope was taut, the others hauled the waka forward again. The kai-rākau aboard the charging craft again lashed out at those in the water, killing and wounding many. They repeated the process until they saw reinforcements spilling out of the pā to assist those on the beach.

When Kai asked his prisoner again if he could see Whiwhi-rangi, this time he responded positively.

'Arā! E haramai rā, te urukehu rā.' *There! Coming this way, that red-haired, fair-skinned man.*

Kai peered at the tall man the prisoner pointed to. He was an urukehu indeed, his hair and complexion amplified by the red rāpaki he wore from his waist to just above his knees. Whiwhi-rangi strode across the sand, taiaha in hand, clearly frustrated at the trouble his warriors were having. What was their problem? He looked determined to deal death to these strangers.

Kai struck his prisoner on the side of the head with the edge of his patu and the fisherman slumped back onto the floor of the waka.

Whai, Tui and Te Ika hauled on the stern anchor, sending the vessel back to deeper water. Tui watched his companions' forearms straining as his own calloused palms coiled the excess rope into the hull. Once away from the immediate threat of the warriors Kai, his heart pounding, made his way to the bow and sat next to Kere.

Whiwhi-rangi, who stood at the water's edge, was glaring at Kai, whom he recognised as the commander of the waka by the feathers in his headdress. The Aitanga Nui chief had a commanding presence, his countenance more distinguished-looking than savage.

'Na, kai te pātaritari rātou kia kau atu mātou i te pōhutu,' he said. *So, they're enticing us out into the surf.*

He looks to have about fifteen kilograms on me, Kai thought as he licked the sweat off his lips, and must be about twice my age.

'Let them come right in to us,' Whiwhi-rangi yelled to his men in the water, who turned and began to make for the shore.

Kai bellowed to Te Ika, 'Tapahia te punga whakawhenua!' *Slash the stern anchor rope!*

Tui and Te Ika cut the rope and the waka surged forward again, for some of the kai-rākau had taken up their hoewai. As they had practised at Ngāpō, they paddled furiously towards shore while others got ready with their weapons.

At last I have come face to face with my nemesis, Kai told himself as he stepped onto the bow, holding on to the tau-ihu while his other hand grasped his taiaha, Te Atua-pūhohe.

As the waka headed for the shore the warriors still in the surf were forced aside by the swiftness with which it passed them. *Te Rūrū* stopped abruptly when it reached the sand.

At the impact, Kai, who was crouched at the side of the prow, was thrown forward and lost his footing. He rolled onto the beach just as Whiwhi-rangi made his move. In a sweeping motion the Aitanga Nui chief brought his taiaha down to strike Kai, but the latter's reflexes were too quick. In an instant Kai's own taiaha blocked the savage strike at his head. Whiwhi-rangi swung again, but the flat blade of

Te Atua-pūhohe stopped the movement before he could complete the full motion of his strike. Kai leapt to his feet, leaving his foe cursing and baring his teeth.

Fighting broke out all around them, with shouts and screams, water splashing and the sound of weapons striking wood and stone filling the air.

The two chiefs, however, were aware of nothing but their own personal duel. Whiwhi-rangi had the more powerful strikes, but Kai's agility and speed saw him ward off every move the Aitanga Nui chief made. Then, as quick as a pīwaiwaka, he slammed a side stroke into Whiwhi-rangi's ribs and was repaid with a stifled snort of pain. Stunned and struggling for breath, Whiwhi-rangi drew up his splendid body, raised his taiaha and swung with all his might. Kai batted aside the blow and, with eyes ablaze, delivered the coup de grace.

Whiwhi-rangi fell to the same combination of movements that Kai had used to kill the grasshopper near the pōhutukawa tree. Kai's nemesis dropped to the ground and the incoming surf rushed around his crumpled frame.

Meanwhile, the battle raged all around. The water on either side of the waka was dark with blood as men from both sides fell victim to the blows of their adversaries' weapons.

Manu-pōkai, standing in the stern of the waka, called to the men to reignite their efforts, for the Aitanga Nui chief was dead. Then, catching sight of her husband Whai being challenged by two opponents simultaneously, she leapt from the waka onto the back of one of the men. Taken by surprise, her foe managed to escape from her headlock, throwing her to the ground. As he did, Whai came up behind him and, drawing his patu high, brought it crashing against the back of his skull. He pulled Manu back to her feet.

Tui, who had fought his way onto the sand, found himself faced with a much older man. The fifteen-year-old stood his ground, as he had been taught, while his opponent approached. From the way the old warrior held his long and heavy taiaha, Tui anticipated that his first move would be to strike with the oar-shaped end of it. But suddenly, and with unexpected vigour, the old warrior stretched out his arm and slid the pointed end straight at Tui's diaphragm.

Whack! At that precise moment Te Ika appeared and intercepted the blow. He danced about and tapped the old warrior on the breast and limbs before finally despatching him by swinging the taiaha like a baseball bat at the side of the older man's temple.

'Come on, Tui. Your brother's having it all to himself,' Te Ika said as they headed over to support their leader.

Kai had often faced two or three fighters at once at Kirikiri-tatangi, but never five. He was bracing himself for the assault when suddenly Kere was alongside him.

'Two against five offers much better odds,' said Kere as he drew his patu from his belt. He had always been the best of his peers with the short-handled club. Before anyone had made a move Te Ika and Tui jumped in.

Kai advanced first. His opponent had barely raised his taiaha when Kai struck. Kere slid under his opponent's guard, knocked him down with his patu and stove in his skull. Tui and Te Ika were having a harder time of it, but when Kai and Kere provided backup it was over almost immediately.

When the remaining Aitanga Nui saw Whiwhi-rangi lying motionless at the water's edge, their resistance abruptly ended. Some made a fighting withdrawal, while others simply turned and fled to the safety of the pā.

Kai ordered his men to remain on the beach and not give chase. The pā gates shut behind them, the Aitanga Nui warriors watched from the ramparts, awaiting the inevitable assault on their fortress.

Instead Kai gathered his warriors on the beach in front of Pātete Pā and together they delivered a rousing haka, taunting the occupants and gesticulating contemptuously.

Then they surveyed the beach. Both his siblings were safe, but Kai had lost a dozen of his kin in the fighting. Twice as many of the enemy had fallen, and half a dozen wounded were taken prisoner.

The kai-rākau began piling up the bodies of their own slain on the sand before lifting them one by one into the waka.

Kai stood over Whiwhi-rangi's body and called out, 'Taku tangata pākau-roha-roha i te whakaumu i Te Waha ka whakaheia, ko Whiwhi-rangi.' *My winged grasshopper buried at Te Waha has been satisfied; 'tis Whiwhi-rangi.* He ordered his men to lay the corpse with its neck across a log. Kai grabbed the chief's hair in one hand and, gripping an adze in the other, decapitated the Aitanga Nui chief with several swift blows. Holding it by the hair, he thrust the bearded head in the air and taunted the people watching from the pā.

'From your chief's bones,' he yelled, 'I will make needles that my mother will use to sew my dogskin cloaks.'

The kai-rākau roared. Te Ika, rolling his eyes and poking out his tongue, called to the men in the pā, 'Call yourselves warriors? Come out and fight!'

'Calm down, Te Ika,' said Kai. 'We've got what we came for.'

He ordered two of the kai-rākau to light a fire. When it was ablaze, Parakore cut out the heart of the chief and began to roast it over the flames. As they did, they chanted, and Kai and his men stretched out their hands towards the blackening heart. When the chanting ended, the warriors broke out into another haka and Parakore cut off a piece of the heart. While the haka was still in full swing, the tohunga walked up to the gates of the pā and threw the portion over the palisade in a symbolic action to weaken the enemy.

Kai ordered his men to take the wounded prisoners aboard *Te Rūrū*. Te Ika carried the headless, disembowelled body of Whiwhi-rangi on his back. He held the arms around his neck and the bloodied corpse smeared his back red.

It was midday when Kai finally climbed aboard and called to the men, 'Hūtia te punga o tō tātou waka, hanatu haere.' *Pull up the anchor of our waka and let's go.*

In an instant *Te Rūrū* was racing towards the headland. The men, women and children in the pā watched in silence, not giving their foe the satisfaction of a single scream of anguish.

'You should bleed out the bodies you intend giving to your hosts at Ōkau by hanging them over the bow,' Parakore advised Kai. 'It also allows the people to see your trophies and your prowess.' Kai nodded and told Kere and Pona to tie two of the corpses to the waka by their feet, slit their throats and hang them out to bleed into the water.

'Blood is a good lubricant when hauling waka on skids.' Parakore winked at Kai.

Near Ōkau Pā, *Te Rūrū* was driven ashore with the two bodies dangling over the sides, their heads, and that of Whiwhi-rangi, hoisted high above the paddlers on spears. Hundreds of people came down to the pōhutukawa tree to welcome them back.

They set up camp near the beach for one night. The kai-rākau gathered around a bonfire and regaled their relatives with descriptions of the fight. Kere was highly praised for the mātāika, making the first kill. The half-dozen bound prisoners cowered under guard in the night air.

It was as if a weight had been lifted off everyone's shoulders, and it was made even more triumphant by the fact that none of *Te Rūrū*'s casualties had been from Ōkau. Kai was of course the hero of the hour. As custom dictated, a woman was later sent to warm the young chief's bed, but he declined her. There was only one woman for him.

Instead he went to watch the bodies of the slain being cooked and shared out among the people. Some of the meat was potted into calabashes and stored in *Te Rūrū* to be distributed among the several Ngāi Haere pā. One of the heads remaining at Ōkau Pā was to be preserved, so the local tohunga began the process of drying and cleaning. After removing the brain, he placed the head on a pole over heated stones. A mat was wrapped funnel-like around it to direct the searing heat at the impaled head and very slowly it was smoked. From time to time the head was removed to allow the humidity to evaporate, then the tohunga would grease it with rendered-down human fat and place it back over the stones. All the while, the tohunga spoke mockingly to the head as if it were a living thing.

At first light Kai and his crew pushed *Te Rūrū* back into the surf, and before long they were out on the water again. The sea was calm. Wehe, who had rejoined the crew at Ōkau, called Kai to sit with him.

'Destiny chose you to lead these hard-bitten and sometimes unruly warriors,' said Wehe. 'You may have doubted yourself at first, but victory has secured your right to lead them. They will follow you anywhere. And for me? Well, when your eyes have seen your teachers, your teachers disappear.'

Kai said nothing, his gaze fixed on the horizon. Eventually he made his way back to the middle of the waka and stood looking at the coastline. Something in him had changed. Kere, Pona, Te Ika and Tui could all see it.

As the waka taua came around Waikahawai Point, the warriors saw their hillside pā and their people gathering along the shoreline. The bronzed warriors heaved harder on their oars. Kai wiped the sweat from his brow and called for two of the prisoners to be executed. This time the bodies would be hung over the gunwales near the stern.

Seagulls, having caught the scent of open flesh, began to hover above the vessel as it powered through the tide, adding their screeches to the wailing cries emanating from the crowd on the beach. Pona, sitting in the rear of the waka, struck up another chant to increase the stroke and spur the crew on as fifty hoewai dug in unison into the dark blue water. So unified was their timing that it was as if all the paddles on each side were being managed by a single hand.

Kai called to Pona to turn the vessel so that they could approach the shore stern first. Kai reached down between two blood-stained thwarts and removed the flax mats that were screening the heads piled in the hull. These were intended to assuage the grief of the relatives of those slain. He fanned away the flies, then took hold of his prize: the long-haired and bearded head he had severed from Whiwhi-rangi's torso the previous day.

Twisting the long hair round and round his calloused hand, he felt a surge of rage. As if possessed, he leapt to his feet and shouted to the people on the beach, his grip on the head so tight that he could have swung it like a patu.

Tēnei rā e te iwi o te hoe, ka āta rehua e, ahaha!
E tata te kaikapea atu te roa o te moana e!
E tata te kaikapea atu te roa o te whenua e!

This day, o' people of the paddle, drenched are we by the sea's spray!
Having almost run the length of the ocean!
And nearly outstripped the span of the land!

The kai-rākau, inspired by Kai's passion, yelled in response, 'Hi! Ha! Hi!' as they drove the canoe forward. Throwing off his dogskin cloak, Kai shouted at the top of his lungs:

E, kei tūtuki te ihu-o-waka paea noa tia e!
E, ka pupū te waha o te tangata whakatinatina ki te riri e! Hi, ha!
Pae ana te aroaro ka whiwhi e!

Take care lest we be capsized!
And let your voices burn with passion! Hi, ha!
For you have earned your rest!

The waka slowed in the shallow water and the warriors turned their paddles skyward.

On shore, women waved seaweed girdles and sang out the call of welcome to the returning war party. Kai leapt from the vessel into the receding surf and, still clutching Whiwhi-rangi's severed head, launched into the victory haka once more. His spittal flew and each time he rolled his pupils back, his eyes stared vivid white. The straining sinews of his impressive physique, stained with blood and gore, added to the intimidating sight of the decapitated head in his grip.

257

The others jumped out of the waka to join in the haka, some still holding their paddles. Others drew their patu, stamping their feet, their fists clenched, muscles rippling.

Some of the older men and younger boys who were on shore laying down seaweed on the skids could not refrain from responding with a haka of their own. The women, still clinging to their seaweed, advanced at the sides of the vessel, distorting their faces grotesquely. The effect was electric.

All the while, those ashore were scanning the kai-rākau to see who had returned — and who had not. One woman, realising her husband was not among them, was beside herself with grief. Spotting the four prisoners in the waka, she grabbed a patu from the belt of a relative and ran toward them, calling for utu. Two warriors at the prow of the vessel restrained her. Their hands tied, the prisoners cowered.

Kai signalled to Pona, who pulled one of the prisoners out of the vessel and stood holding him in the shallows.

Kai called to the woman, 'Anei, rapua te utu mo tōu tāne!' *Here, avenge your husband!*

The two warriors released the woman and she charged at the hapless prisoner, inflicting a solid blow to his temple. He crumpled to the sand, a motionless heap. In a torrent of rage she struck again and again, shattering her victim's skull and reddening the water around her. Then she turned and headed for the other prisoners, but the kai-rākau restrained her again, knowing Kai intended for other newly widowed relatives to share in the reprisals.

The wailing of the grief-stricken was heart-wrenching. Tears rolled down tattooed faces, young children sobbed, and women lacerated their arms and faces with sharpened stones. Some of the women cut their faces with mussel shells until blood and tears mingled.

Kai, still holding his macabre prize, spotted his father and mother up at Kai-namu-namu, scrutinising the scene below. From the womb Tāwae and Kiri had laid out the purpose and meaning of Kai's life. Now he was about to present his bloodied trophy to them at last.

'Don't forget the tapu has to be removed from you and your men before you are reunited with your kin,' Kaiora reminded Kai. 'For you have shed other men's blood.'

The returning warriors followed Parakore and Kaiora to the ahi-tautai but Kai stopped below the path to Kō Pā. As the rest of the kai-rākau continued up the stream, Kai said to Kaiora, 'We'll join you shortly.' The tohunga knew where Kai was headed and that none of his rules would stop the young chief. Kai then called out to his brother.

'E Tui, me haere ake tāua ki Kō.' *Tui, let's go up to Kō.*

At the top of Kai-namu-namu Kai placed the head of his enemy at his parents' feet.

'Kua ea te wāhanga ki a tātou,' he said. *Our people have been appeased.*

CHAPTER TWENTY-EIGHT

———————

Ka rite te tauira, ka puta te kai-whakaako.
When the student is ready, the teacher appears.

Nūpe Pā, December 1980

'Ka nui pea tēnā.' *That's probably enough.*

The koroua came to an abrupt halt at this point in the story. He slapped his thighs and sprang up with the energy of a man half his age, although the creak of old bones was discernible. He headed out the back door and disappeared.

I sat there stunned. For hours I had been utterly immersed in a world I had previously known nothing about. I stood up and felt my ancestors glaring down at me from the panelled walls. I made my way out to the veranda, my head full of the people I had just learned about. I turned and looked up at the name above the doorway.

KAI-TA-NGA.

This name is forever changed for me, I told myself.

The shadow across the porch told me that the koroua had talked right through into mid-afternoon. As I stood there he came around the side of the whare puni, shaking water from his hands and wiping them on his trousers.

'What a story, Koroua,' I said. 'Thank you for telling it to me.'

He smiled.

'Where did you learn all that?'

'Much of it my grandmother told me,' he said, stepping onto the veranda. 'Some I heard from her brothers when we went pig hunting or pigeon shooting in the bush. There's not much else to do when you're sitting around the campfire at night.'

'When were you born?'

'Nineteen-hundred-and-three, nineteen-hundred-and-four — don't know for sure,' he said with a shrug. 'Māori didn't need birth certificates until the Great War.'

'And when was that?'

'E tama! You don't know that? The First World War, nineteen-fourteen to nineteen-eighteen. What are they teaching you at school?'

'Wow,' I said, wide-eyed. 'That's a long time ago.' A quick calculation in my head and I reckoned the koroua had to be seventy-six or thereabouts, so his grandmother would have been born around the eighteen-fifties.

'So, how exactly am I related to Kai?' I asked.

'He's your tipuna eight generations removed,' the koroua smirked.

'So he's my great-great eight times grandfather?'

His smile widened as he pointed proudly to the pare above the door.

'There's his mother, Kiri.' The figure in the middle of the carved lintel held up its hands like in the pictures I had seen of Atlas holding up the world. While I studied it, the koroua walked over to the other window.

'Here's Tāwae.' His forefinger tapped the central figure. Then he turned almost a half-circle and looked up at the kōruru attached to the apex of the meeting house.

'And there's the warrior himself, Kai.'

I stepped down onto the grass, turned and looked up. The distorted face with a protruding tongue was huge — it must have measured almost half my height. I hadn't given it a second look when I arrived yesterday but now I was captivated by the huge pāua-shell eyes glaring at me.

'This whare puni is like a memory aide,' the old man explained.

'The carvings are full of visual language. They capture the traits and characteristics of our tīpuna.' He ran his fingers down the carved figures of the door jamb and said, as if he were speaking directly to them, 'The extension of human memory through time is not just the contemplative luxury of advanced civilisations.'

Was that a quote? I wondered. It sounded very much like a line I once had to learn for a school play.

'There are more things in heaven and earth, Horatio, than are dreamt of in your philosophy,' I murmured.

'Chow lega, e tama,' *Neat all right, boy!* [11]

We smiled at each other.

'Your lineage goes like this,' the old man continued. And he recited a whole string of names with the words 'ka puta ko' between them all, like the 'begats' in the Bible. He finished with, 'And Rāmari begat you.' It was nice to hear my mother's name again. After all, she was the reason I was here.

'So I really am a direct descendant then, eh?'

'Don't think you're the only one. And remember, everyone has ancestors whose stories are just as captivating; it's just that they're not always fortunate enough to hear them.'

That made sense, I thought.

'You hungry?'

Was I ever. I nodded enthusiastically.

'Let's have something to eat.'

We didn't go to the kāuta as I expected but instead went back inside. Somewhere among the muddle was an electric frying pan and some lard, which the koroua used to fry eggs and lamb chops, while I buttered parāoa rēwena and boiled the kettle.

As my companion chewed on a piece of bread, his false teeth clicking away, he pointed to a photo of his own mother. The large framed image was of a woman in her twenties wearing a Victorian-style, high-necked halter dress, complemented by elegant jewellery. She sat with a straight back, her head held high. She could have passed for a Pākehā, I thought, except that her chin was handsomely tattooed.

The koroua then pointed to a hand-coloured portrait of his mother's brother. 'That's your great-grandfather.'

He told me some stories about the bushman that made us both laugh. The rugged-looking Māori-Portuguese man seemed uncomfortable in his jacket and tie; I figured he had probably pulled on his Sunday best for the sitting. The faces in the frames were ghosts no more. It was an amazing feeling.

'So where's this place Ngāpō?' The question had been on my mind all morning. The koroua seemed surprised. 'Beyond those hills.' He motioned with his head towards one side of the house as he cut the meat from his lamb chop.

'How far away?'

'About ten miles.' There was a long period of silence as I pondered and he chewed. 'Takes about fifteen minutes by car. If you like, we can go there tomorrow.'

He smiled when my eyes lit up.

'Do you have a driver's licence, Koroua?' It occurred to me that he might not be the greatest driver.

'E tā!' the old man chuckled. 'You got a car?'

+

It was approaching twilight as I strolled out of the gate, across the one-lane bridge, and in the direction of my uncle's house. The cicadas had fallen silent and the mosquitoes were starting out on the night shift. I ambled along, kicking stones and slapping my neck and arms every now and then.

I knew the koroua had not censored his story. As I walked across the broken white lines in the middle of the deserted road I thought about his cautionary note — that there were some things about our ancestors that I might not want to hear. My own brash response — 'I can take it' — still rang in my ears.

Some of it had been tough to hear, for sure. Did I really want to know more? Of course I did. The old man was breathing life into history in a way I had never experienced before, certainly not during my formal education. And why did I feel so compelled to listen? That was easy: because this was *my* history. As I turned into my uncle's driveway, I told myself that the next few days might be the best investment of time I would ever make.

This story was a gift.

+

Under a bright, cloudless sky I arrived back at Nūpe Pā the next morning. I had a small backpack and I was holding a kete of food, including a warm cartwheel bread, as my aunty called it. She had baked it that morning and wrapped it in a damp tea-towel to keep it fresh.

I found the old man on the veranda basking in the morning sun, a mug of tea in his hand.

'Mōrena, e tama! Did you have a good night?' he asked cheerfully. It seemed he had.

'Kia ora Koroua! Yes, I did. Aunty made us some bread and plum jam to go with it.'

'That's nice. Put it in the car.' The back window of the old Vauxhall was wound down so I reached in and placed the kete on the worn vinyl seat next to a cardboard box containing a cold leg of lamb in a plastic bag, a butcher's knife, a jar of salt and a thermal flask.

'I also brought a change of clothes,' I said. 'I thought I'd take you up on your offer and stay with you tonight, if that's okay.'

'Mmm,' the old man nodded. 'He tī māhau?' *Cup of tea?*

I took the freshly brewed mug from him, pulled up a wicker chair and let the sun's rays warm my face. The brew was strong, the odd tealeaf settling on the surface. I gazed out across the marae, the scent of freshly cut grass wafting in the air. The morning was very warm, quiet, and heavy with languor.

'Whose is that memorial?' I nodded towards the obelisk next to the car.

'My nephew Parekura's. Got killed in Libya during the war. The Old Lady had it put up for him. She raised him virtually from birth.'

'How old was he?'

'Just a boy. Some of those young fullas with us were only kids.' The koroua's eyes glazed over and he shook his head gently.

'I used to carry his rifle — you know, when he got tired. In the desert. Moumou tērā tama.' *What a waste.*

The koroua gazed at the memorial stone.

'Parekura is the word for battle. You know that, eh boy?'

'Yeah.'

He sat forward, put his mug down on the veranda and leaned towards me.

'When we get to Ngāpō I'll show you where Kai trained for battle. It's still there, that place. Kirikiri-tatangi — the Singing Sands.'

+

He drove out of the pā hunched over the steering wheel, squinting his eyes as he strained his head forward. State Highway 35 wasn't a busy road but I thought I might keep him apprised of any potential obstacles well in advance.

We wouldn't be killed by speed, anyway — we were going about thirty kilometres an hour.

'Kia mau, e tama,' the old man said.' *Hold on, boy.* 'We're going like the wind!'

We passed the local school and a neighbouring pā. A few kilometres further on we turned onto a gravel road. There were three or four houses on the first straight, then nothing for about twenty kilometres. Mānuka trees crept almost to the edge of the road.

The koroua navigated the winding, undulating beach road as if piloting a ship on the high seas. We must have run into every one of its potholes, despite him giving his full attention to avoiding them. In fact he hit them so often that I gave up forewarning him. The few bridges were all single lane and in many places the road was not much wider. Not that it mattered; we encountered no one.

I had so many questions to ask, after a night of thinking about what I'd heard.

'So, we're from Ngāpō?'

'Not just Ngāpō, but Kauae-nui and other places. In the old days our people moved with the seasons, but Ngāpō was our base because the sea was the highway. When I was a child they put the main inland road through, which is why most people shifted away.'

'What about the Aitanga Nui — weren't they our relations?'

'Yes, of course Aitanga Nui are our whanaunga. My own father comes from there. But, just like today, relatives squabbled back then too. The difference of course is that arguments in those days were more likely to end in bloodshed.'

A huge pothole momentarily diverted his attention. I pitied his tyres.

'You must remember, this was before the Gospel, Te Rongopai, was introduced. It was like the days of the Old Testament — when jealousy was often the cause of killing, just like the story of Cain and Abel. A simple slight might see a whole tribe wiped out, as Gideon did to the men of Penuel. Those were times when "an eye for an eye" was the only justice our people knew.'

'Who was Gideon?'

'You're like an eel,' the koroua retorted, without taking his eyes off the road. He chuckled. 'I put my foot on its head and up comes its tail! I stamp on its tail and up pops the head!'

I laughed defensively. I didn't interrupt after that.

'Some say our ancestors were cruel in warfare, but I don't think so,' the koroua continued. 'Yes, our tīpuna did some things we would call bloodthirsty, but I know full well that if they could read the history of the world wars they would be shocked. I cannot see that they did anything worse in war than what we did to the Germans and they to us.'

That was interesting. I hadn't thought of that.

'Nor can I imagine our tīpuna bombing civilians in the great cities, had they been able to,' he went on. 'There are many things done today that our forebears would never have done.'

The car meandered up a high hill before dropping almost to sea level on the other side, into what seemed like complete isolation, not far from the coast. As we neared the bottom I caught a glimpse of the sheltered setting of Ngāpō. The original bush had been replaced, mostly by poplar and mānuka regrowth, but it wasn't difficult to imagine what the place would have been like in the seventeen-hundreds.

We passed a disused building — Ngāpō Native School, which the koroua said had closed in the fifties. Then we drove past two or three houses, a cemetery and church. Like the families of Nūpe, most had left for better employment opportunities.

The dirt road ran close to the Ngāpō Stream, which, although very shallow at this time of year, was much wider than I had imagined. Erosion in the hills had filled it with shingle and widened its mouth. The car crossed the stream twice, then lumbered over stones and up onto a grass verge, where we were greeted by the most serene scene of gentle waves lapping at the shoreline.

Suddenly I realised I'd been here before. 'Hey, I know this place, Koroua!' I recognised the short dazzling beach. I couldn't have been more than about seven the last time I was there. My brothers and I used to come to this place with our parents to collect shellfish — kina mainly.

The koroua shuffled off through the grass and down onto the deserted beach, where he made a beeline for a huge log on the sand. The sea had long since stripped the bark and months of wind and rain had worn its sapwood smooth. After he sat down the old man pointed out Kō Pā, an unmistakable feature rising out of the trees on the other side of the stream. He told me we had just driven right through the place where the village would have been in Kai's time.

'And this is Kirikiri-tatangi.' The old man looked intently at the area directly in front of us.

'We all came here in nineteen-forty to farewell the first of the local volunteers who went overseas with the Māori Battalion. The beach wasn't covered with driftwood then, or stones; just sand. One of our

267

officers had brought his taiaha with him. He stripped to his shorts and as we watched him go through his drill, we were all listening carefully to see if his fleet-footedness made the sand sing. That's where the name came from.'

I wanted to ask whether the officer had been successful, but the analogy of the eel came to mind so I bit my tongue.

'You told me you heard a voice outside the house the other day, e tama?'

'Yes, I did.' I sat up straight, glad to hear he was not dismissing it as my imagination.

'When Tāwae's Uncle Te Tau was mortally wounded, he said to his brothers, "Ki te mate au, me kawe rawe au ki Waipuna-a-roto."' *Should I die, carry me to Waipuna-a-roto.*

'Te Tau is not the only one to have used the phrase "Ki te mate au". Remember what Tāwae said at Te Maniaroa? Down through the generations several others have used those words too, including Kai. My nephew, Parekura, said it to me when he lay dying on the desert sands of Libya. "Should I die, give my love to Mother."'

A gentle breeze from the sea cooled our faces.

'If my mother was alive, she would tell you that your visitor was a kēhua, a ghost or spirit, and that it appeared for a reason. Trust me, it's not by chance that you are asking about our past. As the saying goes, "When the student is ready, the teacher appears."'

I wasn't convinced that this was fate, but what the koroua said did send a brief shiver up my spine.

'Kai's story is not the only important story,' the koroua continued. 'His story is his parents' story and his grandparents' story. It's the story of so many others too. They have no stone memorials like my generation, even though the reasons they gave their lives are just as worthy. They are remembered only in our whare puni or in our kōrero tuku iho, our oral traditions.'

All this time the koroua had been speaking as if to the sea, but now he turned and spoke to me.

'I told you that my grandmother told me much of this history.

She, in turn, heard it from her grandmother, Hineaute, who was Kai's granddaughter. So, e tama, my question to you now is, do you wish to hear the rest of the story as Hineaute told it to my grandmother?'

I looked up again at Kai-namu-namu, easily distinguishable on the cleared summit of Kō. The koroua spotted the direction of my gaze.

'Kai was banished from Kō Pā, you know; in fact from the whole of Ngāpō.'

I gasped. 'Really? But he was a hero!'

That carrot served its purpose.

'Yes — yes please tell me more of the story. I really want to know what happened next.'

The old man closed his eyes, mumbled what sounded like a prayer in Māori, took a deep breath, then began again.

CHAPTER TWENTY-NINE

Kōrerotia ki runga ki te takapau wharenui.
Let the tribe marry you according to proper rules and custom.

At the pākūwhā ceremony, Wairere's Kauaenui relatives would formally present her to her husband's family. After the victory at Pātete, Kai was recognised as a hero for finally exacting the revenge that their people had long sought, and his wedding was greatly anticipated by all.

In the three moons since Kai had returned, Tāwae had ordered posts and raupō brought in from the bush in order to erect a temporary whare puni in the village for the occasion. When it was finished, Kai stood with the builders and admired it.

'This should do perfectly for Wairere's people,' he said, and thanked them.

Eventually the visitors arrived bearing generous gifts from the inland bush. The Ngāpō people gave them a powerful welcome, with much wailing and singing. The visitors positioned themselves opposite Tāwae's people.

Kai looked across at Wairere, all made up for their special day. He thought how beautiful and voluptuous she looked, and his heart began to pound. She flashed a smile at him. It seemed incredible to Kai that despite the many hours he had spent with Wairere he had yet barely touched her. He felt delirious with the anticipation of what was to come.

In the whare puni Tāwae's spokesman began the speeches from their side of the house. Much of the talk was about their recent victory over the Aitanga Nui. One speaker likened them to people who had, for years, been smothered by the toxic fumes of a bushfire but who now, at last, had oxygen to breathe once again.

Then it was Tāwae's turn. He addressed the groom. 'After marriage a son lives with his people; not so a daughter.' Kai threw a glance at his sister Manu who had come with Whai specially for the wedding. 'Because you reside with us,' he said to his son, 'we live with the advantage of your mana, strength and knowledge.'

The celebration feast was held outside the house, where the dense throng of Kauae-nui visitors had laid their wedding presents.

The Ngāpō people had spent a full fortnight procuring and preparing the food. They approached the house singing and set down baskets of dried fish, tuna, kōura, kūmara and kererū on the food mats. The visitors filed out of the house and seated themselves before the food.

That night, back in the house, speeches continued and both sides provided entertainment in the form of singing and haka. Lamps burning bird fat helped light up the inside of the building.

Wairere joined her relatives in their haka. Kai was eager to see her perform again. His gaze followed her full figure, long black hair and dark eyes as she moved between the rows of young and older women. As always, she had eyes only for him and seemed to revel in his gaze.

'This takes me back to the first time I saw my wife,' Kai said, nudging Tui. 'You remember.' Tui didn't reply and Kai realised something else had caught his brother's attention — he was openly ogling Wairere's younger sister. When Kai looked to Hinewehi, he realised she was flirting with Tui just as Wairere had with him.

'Hey,' he said, elbowing his little brother. 'Wairere told me you and Hinewehi were meeting in secret before we went to Pātete. Is that still happening?'

'No,' Tui sighed. 'Mother said it wasn't proper for a chief's son to behave like that.'

'Ahh,' said Kai. 'It's tough when you long for something but can't have it.'

As Kai and Wairere left the whare puni for Kō Pā, Kiri presented them with a marriage mat that she had spent the past month weaving.

'May this takapau wharanui provide you many nights of pleasure and bring us many mokopuna.'

Kai laughed self-consciously and received the gift with gratitude.

It was a fresh evening and Wairere was grateful Kai remembered to collect her cloak on the way out, despite the fact that he himself was wearing only a flax kilt.

The moon peeped out from behind a cloud, enabling the couple to see the path to the stream. Kai wrapped Wairere's cloak around her and lifted her into his arms as he felt his way carefully across the stepping-stones through the stream, his eyes never leaving hers. She placed her hand on Kai's chest and felt his heart pounding. He set her down on the opposite bank and as he stood up she grabbed the back of his rāpaki.

'Lead the way, my husband,' she said sweetly, following him up the steep track through the trees.

Once inside the palisaded pā, Kai winked at her. 'Can I have my rāpaki back now?' Wairere smiled and released him. He directed her to the hut that the kai-rākau had built for them. They crawled through the opening and noticed a sweet aroma inside.

'Aah, karo flowers; how thoughtful,' Wairere remarked.

'Did you know that they save their sweetness for the evening hours,' Kai said, 'to tempt their lovers, the moths?'

Wairere smiled. 'And someone set the fire for us!' She kindled the flame, which produced a little more light. Kai, still on his knees, laid the takapau wharanui over the other mats that partially covered the fern and moss floor. Then he began to undo his topknot. It was the first chance in many months that Wairere had had to study his face.

His black eyes shimmered in the firelight; his expression serious. She reached up and slowly unbraided his long sleek hair. Then he loosened his rāpaki and tossed it aside. He stood before his new wife, unembarrassed by his own nakedness. He put out his hands for her cloak and she turned and shrugged it off into his hands. Next she slowly removed her flax skirt, while her new husband looked on adoringly.

'Did you enjoy the festivities?' she asked as she lay down.

'Mmm,' he replied, not really interested in a discussion at this point. He lay down beside her.

Wairere bit her lip. 'I for one am glad it's finally over. I couldn't wait to be alone with you.'

Again Kai said nothing. He had not taken his eyes off hers.

Wairere smiled bashfully and nestled her head against his muscled chest.

'You're not much of a talker, are you?' she chattered on nervously.

'I wasn't planning on doing much talking,' he said.

'I need to ask you something,' Wairere said, suddenly raising herself to rest on one elbow. 'Have you ever been with anyone else?'

'No!' Kai was clearly affronted, though Wairere wasn't sure why he would be. She had been told that chiefs' sons often had their first sexual experience before they were married.

'Then where did you learn what to do?'

'I have seen it enough times and I've been told. Same as you.'

Wairere rolled onto her back. There was an awkward silence, broken only by the occasional crackle of the fire and the distant sound of people enjoying themselves in the village below them.

Kai sighed. As they lay naked beside each other, staring up at the thatched roof, his desire became overwhelming. He uttered the first line from the tribe's phallic haka.

'Ko Rūaumoko e ngunguru nei.' *The earthquake god is rumbling.*

Wairere grinned. She waited, and when he eventually lifted himself and turned to her, his stiffening penis touched her thigh.

'I'm glad I can barely see you in this dim light,' she whispered.

'Why's that?' he said as he ran his index finger lightly from her tattooed chin down her neck and between her full breasts.

'Your eyes, they can be unnerving.'

Kai's finger circled her belly-button several times before he found the courage to venture lower. He leaned over her, the tips of his hair brushing one of her nipples as he inhaled the scent of her body. When his finger reached the top of her pelvis he felt a definite warmth emitting from her pubic region. She murmured and began arching her neck back. She could feel the strength in his hand as his fingers splayed outwards.

Consumed now by her own arousal, Wairere rose up and pushed back against him. Once he touched the wetness of her lips, his primal urges were unleashed. He put one hand on her shoulder and gently but firmly pushed her back onto the mat.

Kai's mouth touched her throat and she groaned as his fingers found their way inside her. Her fingertips pressed into his back and she urged him onto her.

Though he was young Kai did not rush. Nor did Wairere cry out when he entered her, though Kai could feel her passion rising up to meet his.

Kai thought of the haka line: 'Ka whakatētē mai ō rei, he kurī au au!' *Your teeth clench, as if it were a dog.* It seemed to perfectly sum up the feeling of being deep inside his wife's silken paradise. He remembered Kere's caution when they were bird-fowling: 'Watch out, Wairere's going to ensnare you.' I am like the kererū, he said to himself. There is no way out now, so I must drink as much as I can.

When they both lay still again he whispered to Wairere, 'You are everything I hoped for.'

'This changes everything,' Wairere said as she parted Kai's hair and looked into his face. He raised his eyebrows a fraction. 'It was nothing like they told me it would be!' she said, and they both laughed. Kai ran his hand freely through his wife's hair until it was tangled in knots. Yet again, he admired the confidence of the young beauty.

They clung to each other, talking about their future, until their desire was renewed. Wairere did not hold her breath when he entered her the second time, nor the third. She appeared as willing as Kai was to open herself up to all the pleasures of love.

No one bothered them through the night, and in the morning they found food laid out on the porch — a calabash of kākā meat, cooked kūmara, a basket filled with a variety of berries, and a container of the intoxicating tāwhara juice. They devoured every morsel like voracious dogs.

The couple spent the day talking, trading stories, napping and coupling. It wasn't until late afternoon that they ventured hand in hand down to the sea to bathe. Eventually they made their way into the village, where they were showered with greetings and cheers by everyone they happened upon, before eventually retiring to their wharau for another night of passionate intimacy.

They were together for three days, making love again and again. In between, they shared their most intimate thoughts and feelings, stories about their families and their hopes for the children they would have together. All Kai cared about in those heady days was discovering every inch of his lover's body. Wairere slept and awakened in his arms. She became familiar with his blemishes, tasted the flavour of his skin, and learned to recognise the smell of his sex before and after lovemaking.

Tāwae and Kiri arranged that the young couple should not be disturbed, sending them choice morsels at all hours of the day and night, instructing the pononga to leave the kono kai outside the door. Kai, who always slept lightly, knew whenever the pononga had been.

When they finally left their marriage mat and emerged permanently from the wharau, Kai and Wairere knew without a doubt that they delighted in each other, lusted for each other, and hoped to be together forever.

CHAPTER THIRTY

Kaua e mate wheke, me mate ururoa.
Don't die like an octopus, die like a shark.

In the decade that followed their marriage, Wairere bore Kai one son. He named him Ngāheru.

In that time Kai lost both his parents and consequently became chief of the Whānau-a-Mate hapū. Tāwae and Kiri drowned at sea when their canoe overturned off the headland near Reporua. Accompanied by Wehe and a handful of kai-rākau, they had been taking a supply of fernroot to Manu at Ōkau Pā when they ran into one of those terrible squalls so dangerous on that part of the coast. There were no survivors.

Despite their years of experience on the sea, the atua had not been with Tāwae or Wehe on that occasion. The people believed such spirits influenced all deaths, especially sudden deaths. When Kai asked the tohunga for an explanation of which atua had caused it, Kaiora and Parakore told him it was the fulfilment of their teacher's prophecy made on his deathbed — that Tāwae and Kiri's stars would wane when Kai's rose.

Kai's response to the crushing loss of both his parents was to harden himself. He put away fear and despair; they were kahu he swore never to don again. His reign as chief of Whānau-a-Mate was one underpinned by contempt for anyone who crossed him or his family.

One day when Kai, Tui, Pona and Te Ika, all now in their mid to late twenties, were seated on Kai-namu-namu planning a trip to sea, they heard a woman crying while a male voice consoled her. The voices appeared to be making their way up Kai-namu-namu. When the couple drew near, Kai realised the woman was his younger sister, Haere. Her husband, Tūhoro Paku, had his arm around his pregnant wife and he was leading her to the group of friends, who each got to their feet to greet them.

Kai tried to calm Haere.

'He aha te raru, tuahine?' *What's the matter, sister?*

'Kua kōhurutia a Ihumātao,' Tūhoro Paku answered on behalf of his inconsolable wife. *Ihumātao has been murdered.*

'Who?' Te Ika whispered to Tui.

'Ko tana kurī a te Ihumātao.' *Her dog, Cold Nose.*

'Ko wai te nanakia?' Kai asked. *Who has done this treacherous thing?*

'Ko te Kōrihi,' Haere answered between sobs. 'Kua kainga e ia.' *Kōrihi. He has eaten him.*

'That's the same as killing a family member,' said Pona.

'Tō tātou huānga! Tana hiahia pai!' Tui said. *Our own relation! How dare he!*

'As you see, my wife is devastated,' said Tūhoro Paku. 'Ihumātao went everywhere with her.'

Kai thought of how his sister had let the new puppy sleep with her, and even now she was married Tūhoro Paku had been struggling to oust the dog from their marriage bed.

'Kaua e āwangawanga, tuahine. Mā māua ko Tui e arataki atu te taua hei takitaki i te mate o tāu kuri,' said Kai. *Don't worry, sister. Tui and I will lead a war party to avenge the death of your dog.*

'You can depend on us, too,' said Pona, placing a hand on the shoulder of Tūhoro Paku, who was his sister's son.

After the couple had left, Te Ika observed to his friends, 'I've noticed in recent years that there are not so many kurī around. Remember the problems we used to have with packs of dogs roaming around the village when we were kids?'

'Yes, I think we are over-hunting them,' said Tui. 'It used to be only chiefs who wore the māhiti; now any second-rate leader thinks his shoulders should be adorned with dogskin.'

'We'll be in big trouble if the dog is wiped out,' Kai said. 'We need to make sure that doesn't happen. I will make an example of Kōrihi.'

In fact it would be his pleasure to do so. There was no love lost between the two of them.

That night Kai dreamt that he was at Hauanu, the plateau near Kōrihi's home. In the dream his arm convulsed as he tossed a spear towards his foe. The next morning, perplexed, he described his dream to Tui, who was also unable to make sense of it. Kai spoke to old Kaiora and the tohunga gave his interpretation.

'He nui hoki ngā tū āhua o te tākiri. E kore e puta noa ēnei tohu; nā ngā atua anō.' *There are many different manifestations of convulsive twitching. As signs they do not appear at random; the gods prompt them.*

'So what is the meaning of this one?' Kai asked.

'If you dream of throwing an object and it results in a twitching, it means that you will eventually be diverted to the place you dreamed of.'

'Hmm. That settles it,' Kai said to Tui. 'Hauanu will be the ground where we do battle with Kōrihi.'

'Will it be a night attack?' Kaiora asked.

'Am I a slave that I should need to take such an advantage? No, when we strike, the sun's rays will be glistening over Hauanu.'

Kai sent one of the kai-rākau to notify Kōrihi that Haere's brothers intended to fight him at Hauanu on the day the moon was next full.

+

In the days immediately before the fray there was heavy rain in the hinterland. Pona, Te Ika and their nephew Tūhoro-Paku, wearing raincapes, arrived at Kō Pā from Ahu Point where they now lived. Kai, Tui and Kaiora stood waiting in the porch of the whare puni.

'Me āta titiro ki te hiko,' said Kaiora. *Observe carefully the lightning in the distance.*

The men watched the mountains until three flashes came in succession.

'He tohu tērā. Nā tātou taua hiko i tuku atu hei mihi hei tangi ki a te Kōrihi, mea ake ka hinga i a tātou,' said Kaiora in a low voice. *It is a sign. That lightning is sent from us as a greeting and a weeping for Kōrihi, for he will soon fall before us.*

The others were all pleased with the tohunga's interpretation.

'Remember when Tukua taught us the omens of the rainbow gods Uenuku and Kahukura?' Kai asked his friends.

'He aha?' Te Ika shook his head. *What do you mean?*

'If the lightning springs from our side, it would be we who would fall before our enemy.'

The next morning, the skies had begun to clear and Kai selected twenty kai-rākau to join them. They spent a few days rehearsing at Kirikiri-tatangi. Two days before the full moon the war party, accompanied by a group of women, set out for Kauae-nui Pā. As they neared the Matā River, the lead kiore noticed a line drawn across the track. He halted the party. Kai and Pona came to the front of the taua to look at what the scout had found.

'Call for Kaiora,' Kai said.

After observing the furrow, the tohunga spoke. 'This spot is bewitched.' A nervous reaction rippled through the ope taua.

'Kōrihi's tohunga has cast this magic to destroy us, or at least delay us,' said Kaiora. 'Should any warrior pass over the line, he will surely meet death in the coming fray.'

'Can you do anything about it?' Pona asked.

'My atua is greater than that of the one who laid this obstruction. I can recite an incantation to clear the path.'

'All right, do that,' said Kai, 'but to be doubly safe, we will backtrack to the last stream and follow it into the river.'

They walked back about a kilometre. Tui brought up the rear, sweeping away their footprints with a mānuka branch. If Kōrihi's tohunga had been able to capture the spiritual essence left by their footprints, Kaiora told them, he could have consigned them to the other world.

Once they reached the Mākarika they dropped into the stream's bed and stayed in the water until its junction with the Matā, where they crossed to the other side.

At Kauae-nui Pā, Kere and a dozen more warriors, including his and Kai's brother-in-law Tāmō, had been readying themselves to join the ope taua.

'You will bring up the rear,' Kere told them. 'Everyone else will watch the fighting from inside the pā.'

The next morning the taua crossed the Matā River. Pona, with the tohunga alongside him, led a column consisting of ten kai-rākau up on to the Hauanu flat facing Kōrihi's home. Kōrihi's warriors were gathered on a plateau ahead of them.

Pona and his men jogged with short strides up to the edge of the plateau with the tohunga before turning and signalling to Kai and the rest of the taua to approach.

'Tukua te kawau mārō!' Kai shouted to his men. *Advance in column!*

The solid column of thirty-six warriors with weapons in hand fell into a triangle formation and advanced as one. Kai, Kere, Pona, Te Ika and Tui stood at the head. Kaiora preceded them, waving a branch to and fro and reciting incantations.

'What's he doing?' Te Ika asked Tui.

'Weakening them by causing them to lose their nerve,' Tui answered. 'Let's hope his power is greater than their tohunga's.'

'If it's not?'

'Prepare for a long fight.'

Kai halted the ope taua fifty metres from Kōrihi's men and Pona, patu in hand, began the kaioraora. As he pranced up and down in front of the taua, yelling the aggressive words of the haka, his warriors thundered out the response. They worked themselves into a frenzy, the stamping of their feet resounded with their cries across the plateau.

When their display reached a crescendo, Pona called: 'Tau ki raro!'

At those words, all but Kai and Tui dropped to one knee.

While they were catching their breath, they watched Kōrihi's men respond with their own haka. Their movements were just as frenetic, just as insulting, their eyes rolling back, their mouths frothing as they spat out the words. They advanced several metres during their haka, which drew shouts of abuse from Kai's taua. Pona ordered their men to stay where they were.

When the haka finished, Kai stepped forward a few paces and surveyed his opponents. He eyed each of those along the front rank, glaring at the best of Kōrihi's warriors, two of whom he recognised as being with him when he killed Whiwhi-rangi. The tohunga was still waving his branch and chanting. In a moment Kai had counted their number — forty in all.

'What do you think?' Tui asked his brother.

'We have their measure,' Kai replied. 'They may have a few more than us, but at least a dozen of ours are expert warriors. I smell fear.'

'So do I,' Pona said, 'but I bet they won't back down. Look at Kōrihi in his māhiti.'

'The audacity of the man,' Kai said. 'That's Ihumātao's hide!'

Kai called out: 'He tau-mātaki-tahi, e te Kōrihi!' *I challenge you to single combat, Kōrihi!*

Kōrihi accepted Kai's challenge, no doubt keen to atone for his previous defeat all those years before.

Both men left their parties and walked to meet each other, accompanied by their piki or seconds. Kai's piki was Tui. His task was to guard his brother and, if necessary, assist or avenge him.

Kai had his favourite taiaha, Te Atua-pūhohe, the one Kākahu had made for him. Kōrihi carried a huata made of mānuka, the point of the spear hardened by fire.

'He aha rawa tāu māku e te tama a te hamo pango?' Kōrihi asked smugly as he stroked his māhiti. *What have you brought for me, son of the black-back-of-head?*

Kai clenched his jaw. It was a reference to someone running away from a battle, as his opponents would only see the back of his head.

Baring his teeth, Kai quoted a proverb in reply: 'He ihu kurī, he tangata haere.' *Just like a dog following its nose, so you too are a wayfarer.*

'Mmm, mehemea he kurī,' Kōrihi retorted, 'te reka hoki.' *And if it be a dog, the sweeter indeed.* He licked his lips and rubbed his stomach.

'Since we were children, you've always known how to incite my rage,' Kai replied. 'You should be afraid. Wehe is no longer here to save you.'

'Kaua te toa e haere atu ana ki te whawhai e whaka-mana-mana e pērā me te tangata e wete-wete ana i te whītiki.' Korihi replied. *The warrior going forth to battle should not rejoice as the victor who loosens his war belt.*

The sparring began, with Kōrihi making several attempts to jab Kai with his huata, but the chief was too quick for him, each time blocking Kōrihi's moves. Then Kai began to force his old rival backwards, making contact with every blow. Kōrihi stabbed repeatedly at him but the chief blocked, and with his own counter-stroke caught Kōrihi with a blow to the gut, unbalancing him.

Kai then cut his right leg from under him and Kōrihi, who was still fighting to stay alive, fell with a thud. The chief levelled the point of his taiaha at Kōrihi's throat. Kōrihi's piki moved to save his man but he was attacked and kept at bay by Tui.

Kōrihi, realising he was a dead man, looked along the length of Kai's taiaha, and taunted him. 'How sharp is the tongue of Te Atua-pūhohe?'

'Sharp enough to sever the throat of the son of Marua,' Kai replied, pushing the taiaha further under Kōrihi's chin.

'Sharper than Kōrihi's huata?'

Kai looked to the weapon lying at Kōrihi's side and saw that his fingers were stroking the long hair tied to its butt end. It was the tail of Ihumātao. Kuruki, whakataha, he whispered to himself before replying. 'Much sharper.'

'Then prove it,' jeered Kōrihi.

'Soon enough,' Kai replied. 'But first, as you breathe your last, know this. After you are dead, your people will be exiled, your homes sacked and your land, along with your head, will be counted among the possessions of my sister.' With that, Kai lunged forward, forcing the taiaha home.

Once Kōrihi's people saw that their leader was dead, they began withdrawing from the field of battle. Kai called after them that he would let them live but their land would be forfeited.

The corpse of Kōrihi was taken to nearby Umu-tangata and cut up on the huge flat rock while large stones were heated in a fire. The body parts were placed in flax baskets and, when the stones were red hot, they were wrapped in leaves and covered with dirt in a single pit. Kai instructed a party of food-bearers to hurry to Kō Pā with some of the roasted flesh.

'Take these morsels to my sister so she may sample her antagonist and lift her spirits.'

Kai and Tui traversed Kōrihi's land, marking out the areas that would now belong to their sister.

'This land will serve as recompense for the loss of Ihumātao,' Kai told Tūhoro Paku and the others with them. 'But I shall keep for myself the Hauanu flat up to the top of the hill behind it. Lest I forget my adversary Kōrihi.'

The group climbed the hill and descended to the Mākarika Stream on the other side. Then they headed up another ridge, at the highest point of which they were met by Kai's cousin Meha, a grandson of Te Tau.

'Tēnā koe, e Meha,' Kai said.

'Tēnā hoki koutou, e Kai,' Meha replied.

'He aha te take i whanga mai nei koe?' *Why are you waiting here?*

Meha took out his adze and struck a tree, planting the toki firmly in the trunk.

'Because the land beyond this point is mine. This far you may go, but no further. I shall leave my axe in this tree as a sign of the boundary between my cousin Haere and me.'

'Agreed,' responded Kai. 'Let Meha's axe mark the limit of our sister's land.'

He turned to Tūhoro Paku. 'Brother-in-law, this is now your wife's land. It is essential that she physically occupy it if she is to retain authority over it. Come and live here with your family.'

PART

FOUR

CHAPTER THIRTY-ONE

I orea te tuatara ka puta ki waho.
The reptile continues to bore until it is out.
(A problem is solved by continuing to look for solutions.)

'I don't want you in my life any more!' she screamed. 'Don't want to ever see you again! Don't want to have anything to do with you!'

Ngāheru, now eight, was woken by the sound of a woman in hysterics.

'What's going on?' he muttered to his mother, rubbing his eyes.

It was still too early for the whare to be opened up to the new day. A shaft of light from the doorway enabled Ngāheru to identify the outline of his pregnant mother who was sitting up beside him, listening intently to the fracas going on outside.

'Someone is fighting,' Wairere said. Ngāheru recognised his father's voice outside trying to calm the situation down. He could also hear the sound of someone crying in the distance, punctuated by bouts of yelling. Then there was a sudden thump on their porch and they both jumped. The sobbing was much closer now.

Ngāheru wondered if their family might be under some kind of attack.

Wairere wrapped a garment around her belly and told her son to stay put. Then she crawled out the door opening. Ngāheru crept over and peeked out, squinting as his eyes adjusted to the bright light. A young woman he didn't recognise was curled up in a corner of their porch crying. She was dirty, and her arms and back were cut and bruised. Wairere was crouched beside her, trying to calm her. The young woman began to quieten down.

'Ngā, bring my cloak,' Wairere called. He complied, then retreated quickly inside.

Wairere threw the korowai over the young woman just as an angry-looking man approached. Ngā recognised him from a neighbouring pā. Seeing the chieftainess's cloak covering the distressed woman, he stopped in his tracks.

'You'll be safe now,' Wairere reassured her.

Suddenly there were the sounds of a fight. Ngā looked through the doorway in the direction of the huts of the kai-rākau who lived at Kō Pā, where a fight was indeed in full swing. His father was trying to mediate.

'You beat our cousin!' somebody yelled as Old Hara was repeatedly struck by several others.

'It was bad enough you brought that low-bred girl into your whare, Hara,' a woman shouted, 'but now you dare to throw out your first true wife in favour of her?'

With weapons poised, the angry mob turned to Kai.

'Give us payment!' they yelled as they gesticulated wildly.

Ngā was astonished when a woman tore a greenstone pendant from the neck of one of his playmates. Soon his father was striding back to the whare.

'What's happening?' Wairere asked, her arms still wrapped protectively around the young woman on the porch.

'He taua muru. *They're a plundering party.* Hara kicked his wife out of their house and moved the pononga in. The wife tells a story of abuse, which Hara claims is false. He says she knocked herself about the head with a stone, then accused him of assault to cause trouble. Now his wife's relatives have come from their pā to demand retribution.'

They stood looking back in the direction of the disturbance just in time to see people descending on Hara's raupō hut.

'They'll take anything they can lay their hands on,' Kai said.

'Why aren't the other kai-rākau stopping them?' asked Wairere.

'You know as well as I, if he wants to keep this pononga as his wife, then restitution must be awarded to his in-laws.'

Suddenly there was another roar from the crowd as Hara's wronged wife, Rōpā, grabbed a child by the arm and tried to wrest it from Hara's sister. The little girl was screaming.

Kai stepped back into the fray. He spoke to Hara, who was lying beaten on the ground before him.

'Hara, your wife's family demand that you hand over your youngest as payment for your offence. Best you do that, or your troubles will continue.'

Hara lifted his bruised head, looked meekly up at his sister, and nodded.

'No! No!' the woman shouted as the niece she had raised was forcibly pulled from her grasp and thrown over the shoulder of one of the men like a kete of kūmara. Only then did the angry mob depart, leaving a cloud of dust in their wake.

Ngā watched them wend their way out of the pā, elated at their good fortune, including Rōpā, for each had secured a souvenir of the morning's proceedings. The only resistance came from the child, who continued to cry heartily, her hands outstretched towards her distraught aunty, who was being restrained by two kai-rākau.

Wairere returned to the porch and managed to coax the young woman to her feet. She stood with her head bowed.

Kai called out to the bruised and bloodied Hara.

'Come on, Hara, take your new wife and put your house in order.'

Ngā noticed how cool his father had remained throughout the disturbance, and the protective role his mother had played for the pononga. *This is how chiefs behave,* he told himself. It was his first real experience of leadership in action.

Later, when the dust settled and normality resumed, Ngā asked his father, 'Pāpā, why is Hara smiling as if nothing happened?'

'Muru is a long-practised tradition, son. Had Hara's in-laws not come to exact payment, they themselves would have been subject to muru by the rest of the tribe.'

'I felt sorry for him, Pāpā.'

'Don't worry, son. Hara would have felt disgraced if his bad behaviour had been ignored. He'll see it as a high honour that his most treasured possessions have been taken. Now everything is set to rights and life can go on.'

'But they left him with nothing, Pāpā.'

'He has the woman he wanted, doesn't he?'

'I guess so.'

'Honour holds top place in the estimation of all but outcasts. Anything that might disturb it is met either with muru or a crack on the base of the skull. Which do you think Hara would have preferred?'

And it was true. Everyone was happy and smiling and seemed to feel that justice had been served. The young pononga became Hara's wife. Though she was still referred to as his junior wife, and scorned by a few, from that day onwards she was generally accepted as a legitimate member of the Kō Pā tribe.

+

'Squawk! Squawk!' the shrieking of the weka awoke Kai from his reverie. The chief got up off the log he'd been resting on, took in a lungful of ocean air, and turned to see where the noise had come from. He ran his eyes along the bushline. A gentle breeze tickled the dark green trees and he almost missed them.

'Tiro atu, e tama mā, he weka.' *Look, boys, some weka.* He pointed to two birds, necks outstretched, scurrying out of the undergrowth. It was just on dusk, the close of a clear spring day. Kai, now twenty-six, quickly stripped a blade from a nearby flax bush, tied part of it into a running noose and fixed it to the end of a long stick while Ngā and his friends watched the large brown rails making a foray onto the beach.

'Watch and learn,' Kai said as he strode briskly down the beach. Placing the flax blade between his lips and breathing in, he began imitating the shrill cry of the weka. '*Squawk! Squawk!*' He slowed as he neared the birds and the boys could hardly believe their eyes when one of the birds came towards him.

Kai crouched down and repeated the cry until the curious weka was within reach. Then he slipped the noose over its neck and tightened it, walking back towards the boys with the weka in tow. The boys' faces were gleeful, especially when they saw its mate following at a distance. Kai gave Ngā the flax lead, while the other boys tried to stroke the trapped bird's soft feathers.

'That'll make for a tasty dish,' Wairere said to Kai. She and her mother had been leaning against the log watching. Poka, who had been widowed for over a year, had come to be with her daughter in the final months of her pregnancy.

'Every man must learn to be a provider for his family,' Kai replied. 'There's no time like the present to show the boys how to hunt.'

The boys now had a strip of flax each and were trying to entice the other weka towards them. When one of them received a peck from the bird's strong beak, Poka and Wairere laughed.

Kai took his stick and with a swift downstroke he broke the neck of the captured bird. Ngā let go of the flax as the weka spasmed and flapped violently around him. He looked shocked.

Once the weka was still, Kai sat back down.

'That is the way of things,' he said to his son. 'Birds are man's provision, just like the fish in the sea and our enemies on land. You must train yourself not to feel sympathy for them when their lives are taken to sustain yours.'

The boys chased the other bird down the beach. It let out its peculiar cry before darting back into the bush.

'We have good kai for tonight.' Wairere smiled affectionately at Ngā and rubbed her palm over her puku. 'May the gods continue to look kindly upon us.'

She was nervous about this pregnancy, which is why her mother had come from Kauae-nui to be with her. Wairere had bled heavily after Ngā's birth and to Kai it had seemed like forever before she was removed to the whare kōhanga.

At times Wairere felt as though her body had turned against her. The moon had waxed and waned six times before she had fully recovered from her first pregnancy and childbirth. She was worried about trying again and when, after two years, she eventually became pregnant a second time the child was a stillborn. It was another three years before she felt ready to try once more. This time Kai consulted the tohunga, just as his father had done to enable his own conception.

Kai had reservations about the role of his mother-in-law in all this. He had been so impressed by Wairere's confidence in the beginning, but after Ngā was born she seemed to retreat into herself. Kai felt Poka was undermining her confidence. Poka was very opinionated about her daughters' entitlements. If Kai ever opposed her she simply ignored him and carried on. She even told him what she felt was best for him sometimes.

One day he overheard Wairere and her mother in conversation.

'Kei te mau koe i tēnā? *Are you wearing that?*

'Aē rā, Māmā, kei te mau au i tēnei.' *Yes, Mother, I'm wearing this.*

Silence.

'He aha te raru?' *Is there a problem?*

'I know you like to express yourself, Wai, but I don't know how your husband is going to feel about that type of thing.'

'What type of thing?'

More silence.

'*What* type of thing?'

'Wai, don't raise your voice; it's very unbecoming for a chieftainess.'

Kai couldn't stand it any longer. 'Hey,' he called to them from outside the whare. 'Her husband doesn't mind what she wears. She looks beautiful in anything.'

Poka turned and walked off without a word.

The only thing Kai and Poka agreed on was that Kai and Wairere needed to produce more children.

That night when they were alone, Kai broached the subject of Poka with Wairere.

'Be careful you don't let your mother influence your thinking too much.'

'Why do you say that?' Wairere asked.

Kai placed his hand on her belly.

'When I was young, my mother told me that in her womb I had kicked often, and she urged me to do so. "E ea i a koe te mate o tōku pāpā." *Your role in life will be to avenge the death of my father.*

'Throughout her pregnancy she said she had sung me one single oriori, and that lullaby was about her father and the retribution she was committing me to. In this way, she said, she sought to influence my character from before I was born.

'From the time I was a little boy she led me up Kai-namu-namu every day, pointed to the ranges and explained that the Aitanga Nui lived on the other side. "Your goal in life," she said, fixing her eyes on mine, "is to kill as many people at that place as you possibly can. That is your purpose and why you are here."

'My mother's need for revenge could only be sated by the infliction of maximum pain on those people and, as far as she was concerned, it was through me, the fruit of her loins, that it was to happen.'

Kai paused.

'What I'm saying is that if you continually fill a child's mind with that sort of talk you will influence and control him. He will in time become as cold-hearted as you are. And that's what's happened to me. The same spirit of hatred that had power over my mother soon possessed me,' he continued. 'I lived for the day that I would travel to Pātete Pā and avenge my grandfathers and granduncles for my mother's sake and for my own peace of mind. I spent my entire youth preparing for it.'

It was unclear whether Kai was giving his wife advice or exorcising himself of something he had carried for too many years. Perhaps it was both.

'You are your own woman, Wai. Consider your mother's advice by all means, but you're not a child any more. You can make your own decisions.'

293

CHAPTER THIRTY-TWO

———

Ehara taku toa i te takitahi, he toa takitini.
My success was not mine alone, it was through the work of many.

The old lady had been told she would find her nephews — Kai, Tui and Whai —training at Kirikiri-tatangi. Flinging back her cloak, she raised her arms and closed her fists as she approached, her beautiful feathered kākahu held about her neck by a bone pin.

In the early days of his leadership, after his success at Pātete, Kai was frequently sought out to avenge various grievances for members of the Whānau-a-Mate hapū. He didn't mind.

On this occasion it was his Aunt Ēpa who needed help. She found her nephews with the kai-rākau, deep in conversation. Kai was the last to notice her approach. As one by one the others stopped talking, he raised his head at the sudden hush and saw her. Ēpa could not walk right up to her nephew because he was a warrior chief, so she stood and waited for him to initiate the conversation, as was the traditional way.

'You're a long way from home, daughter of my grandfather's brother,' he said as he pressed his nose to hers. 'Why do you seek me out, Aunty?'

Ēpa glanced at the ocean. 'It's always refreshing to watch the sea caress the sand again,' she replied, before turning back to him, 'and to see my coastal relatives.' She paused as Tui and Te Ika also greeted their aunt.

'I have come to you for help. You and your men are known in all the Ngāi Haere pā for what you have achieved. I acknowledge you for avenging the death of my brother-in-law, Te Rangi-tike-tike. After Te Maniaroa, your Uncle Kuharu and I raised his orphan son as our own. When Kuharu took to wife his grieving, widowed sister-in-law, I said nothing. It is custom and expected under our lore. But now your uncle has left both her and me for another woman.' The young chief, who was stroking his beard, raised an eyebrow but let her continue.

'That is bad enough,' she scoffed, 'but he continues to bring this woman's relatives onto my land to procure food. I will not stand for such humiliation.'

Kai looked at Te Ika and Tui, who appeared as surprised as he was. Suddenly Ēpa drew from inside her cloak a pounamu mere and, holding its flat spatulate end, offered the handle to Kai. Through gritted teeth she said, 'I would rather see him dead than let this carry on.'

Her fury seemed to set off a reaction through the watching kai-rākau, who shifted around restlessly, pretending not to be listening.

Ēpa pushed the mere further towards Kai. 'This belonged to my father, Kō. My family have always prized it highly after having regained it in battle from our enemies.'

Kai knew she would not be parting lightly with such a valuable heirloom.

'Let it serve as a lasting witness of our pact,' she said.

Kai's long fingers curled around the greenstone handle and he replied.

'I have always been fond of you and my Uncle Kuharu. It is disappointing to hear what has happened between you two. I shall try a peaceful settlement first. Tui will carry a message of warning to our uncle. Unless he agrees to stop going on to your land, and to recompense you for what these people have taken, then it shall be as you have spoken.'

'You will do this for me, nephew. I know you will, and I will reward you with land. The morning mist vanishes and disappears, but the land endures.'

Tui, accompanied by Te Ika, left with the ultimatum the following day, and on reaching Kuharu's home, explained the situation to their uncle and outlined his choices.

Kuharu was one of those tough, wiry men who, though now about fifty, was still a match for anyone. 'An attack on an unsuspecting and unprepared enemy,' his deep voice growled, 'is a far cry from making an open threat upon us, your whānau.' Tui knew he was referring to Pātete.

One of his sons, Whakapiki, stepped forward.

'What chance do you boys have against seasoned campaigners like us?'

'You're not much older than us,' Tui retorted as he stepped forward. 'And what campaigns have you seen lately?'

Te Ika grabbed Tui's arm, murmuring under his breath, 'We're only here to deliver the message, cousin. There is plenty of time for fighting if words have no effect.'

'I rule my household with an iron fist,' boomed Kuharu. 'I do not cower to the words of a boy. I understand only the language of weapons. Tell your brother we will go to Taitai mountain to hunt at the start of winter as we have always done. If he tries to stop us, it will be on his head.'

Kai was furious when Tui and Te Ika reported back. He took a stick and threw it angrily on the fire.

'It is decided, then. I promised my aunty that our uncle will never return to her land and we will make sure of that.'

'I'm with you, brother,' said Tui.

'Come the end of autumn we will strike out to Ēpa's kāinga on Taitai mountain,' Kai told his men. 'But we will not build a pā there. I will not huddle like a kererū on a branch while our foe spears us from below. No, I will go out and meet him at his camp.'

He unfurled his dogskin cloak, took the flaming stick and burnt several holes in the garment. He shook out the smouldering māhiti and called a runner to him.

'Take this to Ōkau Pā and lay it before my brother-in-law, Whai. If he accepts, tell him when, and at least thirty warriors.'

Whai received Kai's māhiti wordlessly and indicated his consent to joining the fight by placing it over his shoulders.

+

Mist and drizzle were keeping each other company on the summit of Taitai mountain. Ēpa's kāinga sat on a huge plateau above a razorback ridge, which was even more treacherous in the slippery conditions. Yet there was plenty of room for the sixty warriors and their women who almost always accompanied Kai whenever he set out on the war trail. Tui's wife Hinewehi had stayed back with her sister, Wairere, who was due any day now.

The ridge opened out along a triangular hillside, a natural defence against would-be attackers. Kai's kiore reported that Kuharu's people were camped on the edge of the dense bush at the foot of the mountain, alongside the Aorangi-wai Stream.

Kai consulted Parakore, medium of Uenuku, asking whether the war god had warned him of any imminent danger. Parakore delivered his reply through a song, the lyrics of which suggested that it would bode well for the success of their mission if a life were taken that night. Kai, Tui and Whai pondered the words of the song, and the glint in the tohunga's dark, malevolent eyes suggested to Kai that if it were not to be one of the enemy, Parakore expected him to sacrifice one of his own men.

'No man should predict what the day might bring forth,' said Whai uneasily.

'It is not a mortal that makes such forecasts,' Parakore snapped back.

Evil omens had the potential to weaken chiefs and reduce their force by half their fighting power. But if Kai was alarmed, he gave no sign of it.

'We should get some rest,' he advised Whai and Tui. 'It will be an early start.'

Later, Kai told Tui he could not sleep and was going out for air. When he grabbed his tao, Tui threw him a troubled glance, then forced a smile and said, 'Of course.'

Kai took the tao and set out alone. The short wooden spear was perfectly plain, about a metre and a half long, six centimetres in diameter at the thickest part and tapering to a sharp point at both ends.

The night was warm and Kai wore only a puapua, a flax garment wound several times around his left forearm — padding to protect him from blows. He made his way by the light down the ridge until he reached the bush-fringed stream, which he followed for half the night. The ground underfoot was soft and wet with dew, and the stream's rapids winked in the moonlight. Then he climbed its bank and crawled like an insect through the trees until he reached a little nook in the bush that housed Kuharu's campsite.

With his strong thighs outspread, Kai lay quietly for some time until he worked out where the sentries were positioned. One was asleep at his post. He crept closer until he could see the glow of fires. Then with crazed war cries of 'Riria! Riria!' *Assault! Assault!* the warrior chief sprang past the sentries and into the camp, thrusting his tao at anything that moved. He came upon a group of men sitting around a fire, completely unprepared. In seconds he ran four of them through before he himself was the recipient of two spear wounds. He had not wanted to, but he also stabbed a woman who came screaming at him with a patu and a terrified boy who surprised him as he was running into the bush.

The camp was in a panic, thinking a whole taua was attacking. Then, as quickly as he had arrived, Kai was gone. He raced towards the stream bed, ran back along its path, stooping low to avoid being seen, and scrambled towards the incline which led back up the mountain ridge. The element of surprise had given him an unassailable lead over any pursuers. He climbed back up to Ēpa's kāinga while it was still dark.

The adrenaline of the attack and flight to safety had left Kai unaware of his wounds, but he now discovered he was bleeding from the stomach in two places. When his companions heard what he had done, many were impressed, though some of the more superstitious kai-rākau began murmuring about the effect of having a wounded chief lead them.

Sitting on a flax mat, Kai summoned Tui.

'Patch me up so that I'll be ready in the morning.'

Te Ika interceded. 'You may be able to fight, but you're in no condition to lead.'

'Kao!' Kai stormed. 'Ākuni taui ana tēnei ringa i te patunga.' *No! Soon this hand will ache with the slaughter.* 'I will not stay back licking my wounds, while you have all the fighting to yourselves!'

He braced himself as Tui applied a poultice to his wounds.

'Uncle Kuharu has heard my weapon speak,' Kai continued. 'Tomorrow he must taste it.'

Sensing that a compromise was needed, Whai intervened. 'I will take charge.'

'I have answered Uenuku,' Kai replied. 'His favour is with us now.'

'Please let Whai lead,' said Tui. 'Our men may lose heart when they see your wounds.' His younger brother was probably the only person who could have risked saying this to Kai, and the only person Kai would listen to when it came to fighting. In this way, temporary authority of Kai's men was given over to Whai.

Later that morning, after the kai-rākau had eaten the meal the women had prepared for them, Kai came out of his wharau, Te Atua-pūhohe in hand, and walked among them.

'Ka kī te puku, ka ora te tangata.' *When the stomach is filled, man is content.* He touched each man on the shoulder.

'Nā, ka mau tonu mai te rā, ka tū tonu mai hoki te marama, kia tūpono tātou ki te hoariri.' *Now the sun will stand still and the moon will stop until we come upon our foe.*

Whai assembled the group and gave a rousing speech. He finished, 'Whītiki! Whiti, whiti, e!' *Put on your war belt! Rise up, Rise up!*

They clutched their weapons and performed the tūtū ngārahu. Kai, Whai, Tui and the women watched carefully for evidence of any mistakes that might serve as ill omens and make them second-guess the plan to attack. But there was nothing obvious, so Kai delivered his own speech to further excite the warriors' passion.

Then Whai led them down to the ridge, from where he sent kiore ahead of the main body. As the eyes of the force, they were to look out for ambushes.

As each fighter filed past Parakore, the tohunga recited a karakia asking Uenuku to ward off the blows of their opponents' weapons, to render their foe powerless, and to deprive him of strength.

'Remember,' Parakore cautioned Whai and Kai, 'a man under the influence of Uenuku must be extremely wary in his demeanour and actions. Should you commit any act that pollutes your tapu condition, the protection of the war god will be withdrawn from you. Then you will find yourselves in a very dangerous position.' The chiefs needed little reminding of the seriousness of what they were about to do.

They took the route Kai had taken the night before, and eventually they found themselves scrambling from the Aorangi-wai Stream into the bush near Kuharu's camp. Brown figures flitted like pīwaiwaka from cover to cover so that only naked arms and topknots showed themselves, and only fleetingly.

When they came to the campsite they found the fires doused and the inhabitants gone. Whai ordered the kiore to spread out to the edge of the bush to find them. A distant medley of voices soon reached the scouts' ears. They reported back that their opponents were waiting in a clearing for them.

They approached the clearing and Whai called his warriors out of the bush. They spread out behind him, Kai and Tui, a slow-moving ripple of taiaha, tao and tewhatewha until the kai-rākau formed one single line facing the clearing. Each man selected an adversary and readied to engage. If his opponent was considered an expert fighter, two kai-rākau were assigned to that warrior.

Kuharu was a big, forbidding man, well into his fifties. He stabbed the tongue of his taiaha into the ground and yelled to Kai.

'A rat comes at night to ferret out its food, nephew, but the brother of Te Rangi-tike-tike is no rat. He appears in daylight, unafraid. Before the sun has set, it is the rat that will be eaten.' The call was intimidating, but Kai was unfazed.

'See, Uncle, that's twice now that you have insulted me with your words,' Kai called back. 'Soon you will have no more words, for your mouth will be closed forever.'

Whai called the kai-rākau to advance and the whole line moved forward so that they were well clear of the bush. They had not gone more than a few metres when Kuharu's daughter, Taonga, sallied out to meet them. She raised her taiaha and called out: 'Are you Kai?'

'I am he.'

'I challenge you to single combat.'

Kai was holding Te Atua-pūhohe with the blade on the ground and his hand on top. He turned around and addressed his men: 'Look at this. A woman dares to challenge me to fight. I will not lower myself to fight someone who seeks to make a name. I can easily kill her, but what good will that do to my reputation? Tui, chase her away.'

He raised his taiaha and shouted out to his cousin, 'Make your escape while you still can.'

Tui stepped forward to answer the challenge, but before he could close with Taonga, her brother Whakapiki ran forward.

'Don't concern yourself with my sister. She doesn't know what she is doing. I am here.'

Taonga slowly withdrew to her father, all the time watching the bush behind Kai and his men.

'That was a bit strange,' Tui said to Whakapiki. 'Sending a woman out to represent your army.'

'My father did not send her out to fight, but to create a diversion,' Whakapiki replied as they began jousting.

A diversion? Tui didn't like the sound of that.

Whakapiki grinned as blood-curdling shouts erupted from the

bush behind them. Kai turned to see dozens of naked brown bodies, previously camouflaged by the trees, rise up like the dead. The scouts had missed them entirely.

Some of Whai's kai-rākau were new graduates who had never before encountered an enemy in the bush. He could see that the terrible yells unnerved them.

'Whakatangata kia kaha! Kōkiri rā!' Whai shouted. *Conduct yourselves like strong men! Charge!*

Kuharu's women waved their mats while screaming encouragement from behind his main force. 'Kua akitu te hoariri kia kore ai tētahi e rere. Patua rātou! *The enemy are hemmed in so that none can escape. Kill them!*

Whai's men fought valiantly and soon had the upper hand. One warrior fell to Kai's tao, on his knees and gurgling after receiving a strike to the throat. As Kai leapt forward to finish him off, he speared another man on the way through.

Whakapiki's spear flashed out at Tui's chest — once, twice, three times — but Tui blocked every thrust with his taiaha, continually deflecting the point of the tao. On his fourth attempt Whakapiki overextended himself and lost his balance. Tui didn't hesitate. *Whack!* He belted the muscle of Whakapiki's upper thigh with his weapon. The injured limb gave way and, with a bellow, Whakapiki crashed on his back. He managed to push himself up to a sitting position, grimacing as his thigh trembled with pain, and one hand crept down his side toward the handle of his stone club. *Smack!* Tui struck Whakapiki's lower arm with the blade of his taiaha.

Despite the agony of his throbbing thigh and broken wrist, Whakapiki looked up at Tui and jeered, 'You hit like a girl.' Those were the last words he uttered.

Several kai-rākau tried to slay Kuharu, keen to claim the big man among their trophies, but he evaded them all until Kai, who was bleeding from his earlier wounds, called on them to stop.

'That is no way to treat my uncle,' he said, and challenged Kuharu to one-on-one combat.

The old chief was armed with a patu and Kai had his trusty taiaha.

A skilful warrior armed with a patu would usually have the advantage over an opponent using the longer-thrusting spear, especially one who had recently been wounded. However, in this fight the two men looked well matched.

Twice Kai successfully stabbed his opponent, sending him tumbling to the ground. Gathering himself again, Kuharu tried to strike Kai's head, but the chief's agility saw him avoid being hit. The skirmish continued until Kai felled Kuharu for a third time. The older man was visibly beginning to tire. This time he did not try to get up but from his prone position he handed his patu to Kai.

'Since I have made a home of the ground, here, take Kanae and finish me off. Let it be remembered that Kuharu was killed by a weapon worthy of his head.'

'Kanae will indeed dash out your brains,' Kai replied. He took the patu and gripped the handle so tightly his knuckles turned white. 'You are a man who understands only the language of weapons,' Kai declared, 'but you desert your wives at a cost. Now, let Kanae forever speak for you, for you have no more words.' He loosened his grip on the patu and drove it home.

The loss of Kuharu and Whakapiki spread instant fear among the remaining men and women, who broke and began to run.

The final act before Kai's men removed their slain was for the tohunga to take a māwe from the field of battle. Parakore cut a lock of hair from the head of Kuharu, explaining for the benefit of the younger kai-rākau, 'The māwe is not a spirit, but something physical that we can use to hold on to the mauri of this place.' He began chanting a karakia.

+

As she had promised, Aunt Ēpa gave land as payment to the army's leaders. To Whai she gave Taitai mountain, and to Kai and Tui she gifted the surrounding flats below, including the clearing upon which they had fought.

CHAPTER THIRTY-THREE

Ki te inumia weratia te tutu, ka rore.
If the juice of the tutu is drunk while it is hot, it is intoxicating.
(Consider possible consequences before acting.)

'How's my wife?' Kai asked Oha as he approached his whare. His wife's youngest sister was outside the chief's house playing with his son, Ngāheru. One of the younger kai-rākau, looking like a lovelorn puppy, had been beside her, but as soon as he heard the chief, he went back to his guard duties.

'No change; she's still in the sick house. Hinewehi is putting baby Tuameko to bed. I'm just playing with Ngā.' She smiled. Oha had a natural beauty, though she also had quite a spirited temperament.

Poka had sent her youngest daughter from Kauae-nui Pā to help out when Wairere was carrying her first child. That was eight years ago and now the adolescent had been brought back to help out again.

'Dinner,' Kai said as he passed Oha a kete. He had the smell of fish on his hands. She pulled apart the handles and looked inside to see four scaled and gutted tarakihi. Ngā wanted to see too and when he peered into the kete, Oha pulled it up towards his face, sending him reeling back. Kai and Oha both laughed.

'How long will you stay this time?' Kai asked, sitting down on the porch and pulling his son onto his lap.

'I'm not sure, but I am happy to be here. It's nice to be by the sea again.' She walked over to the tree reserved for drying fish. 'I'll hang these at once.' Oha's voice was husky and seemed somehow as if it should have belonged to a much larger woman. She was small-boned and petite, with a long mane of straight black hair that she wore to her waist.

Kai watched her as she worked. She forced the sharp, hard end of a flax strip through the mouths of two of the tarakihi so she could tie them to a branch. He noticed that her hands were muscular and that her once skinny legs were more shapely now. How old she was he could not say for certain. He knew she was young, perhaps sixteen — no more than seventeen. She wore a threadbare little maro of flaxen cloth which barely covered the contours of her hips and buttocks.

When she reached up to tie the fish to the branch, Kai felt an overwhelming urge to reach out and stroke the soft flesh of her breast. It was obvious to Kai that Oha was no longer a child, and he was clearly not the only one who had noticed. When another kai-rākau offered to give her a hand, Kai got to his feet.

'You'd better take Ngā in and I'll finish that,' he said to her, glaring at the kai-rākau, who hastily beat a retreat.

+

Sun and cloud were vying for dominance in the sky when Kai went to visit his wife. Wairere was sitting up in the hut that had been built for her convalescence. The internal injuries she suffered during the birth of Tua were still causing pains two months later. Kai found her singing a waiata she had composed about her constant bleeding and her inability to respond to her husband's sexual approaches.

He sat down next to her, thinking back to when she was pregnant. In Ngāpō the ideal of feminine beauty was a woman who was expecting a child, especially if it was her first. But Wairere was looking far from her best at this moment, Kai thought with dismay. Her whole being seemed dull and indolent. She had lost her lively radiance, her once pert breasts now sagged and her skin had lost its sheen. Childbearing obviously didn't suit her, he thought. But it wasn't only that — lately Wairere had seemed distant from him. Where once her eyes had sparked with passion and happiness whenever she saw him, now she barely even acknowledged him when he returned from hunting or training.

Kai looked into her eyes and spoke at last.

'When a woman becomes too busy and distracted and doesn't look to her husband for anything, a man can become lost.'

Wairere was silent for a moment as she pondered her husband's words. 'It will be some time before you can take me to your bed,' she eventually said.

'I don't mean that,' Kai snapped. 'You hardly talk to me these days.'

'What is it you would have me say, husband?' she retorted. 'My thoughts and opinions are not valued around here. You would think they might be, as I am high born just as you are. But you're the one with all the glory. There is only room for one hero in our house.'

Kai was taken aback. Lately Wairere had been so quiet he had almost forgotten his wife had inherited her mother's oratory skills. When she spoke with passion, her manner of delivery commanded attention. For a moment he saw a flicker of the woman who had so bewitched him more than a decade before.

'Do you recall the words of our tipuna, Hau, when his senior wife left him?' Wairere asked.

'Of course.' Kai knew the story well. There were hills at Hautanoa to commemorate the event.

'And what did his junior wife say to him to console him?'

Kai knew the answer but struggled to see its relevance. '"Tahuri mai ki a au, ki tō wahine iti."' *Comfort yourself in me, your lesser wife.*

Perplexed, he lifted her chin with his fingers and asked, 'And?'

She looked him squarely in the eye. 'You are chief. You should take another wife.'

Kai pulled his hand away, clearly shocked. 'That is my decision, not yours. If I wanted another wife, I would have had a house erected next to ours a long time ago.'

'I will not soften the truth for you,' Wairere continued. 'I have done my duty as a chief's wife. Have I not given you two sons?'

Kai couldn't believe what he was hearing. He rose and stormed out of the whare. Sun had won the tussle in the sky, mirroring the burning rage that coursed through the young chief's veins.

It was another week before Wairere was well enough to venture out of the whare, and a further week before the hut was demolished. The morning after she returned to her husband's bed, she raised the matter again.

'Kai, listen to me. Will you be willing to go and fetch the daughter of Te Rehu to become a wife for you?'

Kai's heart sank. He had thought it might have been the pain she was suffering that had prompted Wairere to say what she had said before. But she was clearly not going to let the matter drop.

'I will not hear of it,' Kai replied curtly. 'And anyway, she has a husband.'

'Are you not a great chief? You may have any woman you wish.'

'I will hear no more of this.'

'Didn't you tell me, "Be your own woman, Wai. Make your own decisions, Wai." Well, Wai has made her decision, damn it!'

He raised his hand to strike her, but instead muttered, 'Kuruki whakataha,' and walked away.

+

It was a somnolent spring day. By mid-morning most people in the village and pā were looking for shade and the children were at the swimming holes. It was too hot to do much else.

When Kai returned from a visit to the village he approached Wairere, who was cradling baby Tua. 'The tide will be out in a little while. I'm going down to the water. I came to ask if you wanted crayfish or eels.' He grabbed a kete from the porch.

'Kōura would be nice,' she answered quietly. 'We could have them for dinner tonight. My mother is arriving this afternoon.'

Kai scowled. His mother-in-law was all he needed right now. Since Poka first brought her daughters to Ngāpō it was abundantly clear that she expected him to treat her with respect bordering on reverence. Who did she think she was? He was the chief!

Kai had always had an issue with his mother-in-law's interfering ways, and after the tragic loss of his own beloved mother he found himself even more intolerant of Poka. On her previous visit he broke out in boils. Parakore, the tohunga who treated him, told him it was a symptom of the way his mother made him feel — boiling with anger.

'Can I help gather the kōura?' Oha asked.

'No, you stay and help your sister,' Kai barked. 'She needs you more than me.'

'She can go,' Wairere overruled him. 'She can hold the kete for you.' Kai turned and left, grumbling under his breath about these women around him who had no respect for his authority. He headed off down the track without waiting for Oha.

When he reached the stream, Kai decided that instead of turning right towards the mouth down at the beach, as he usually did, he would turn left and head upstream. When Oha reached the stream she almost missed him. She was turning towards the beach when she heard a whistle from the bush. She looked upstream and caught sight of Kai rounding the first bend. She ran to catch up with him.

'I thought you were going for kōura?' she said, panting, as she finally reached him, her face flushed.

'Your sister wants kōura, so I'm getting tuna,' he said petulantly.

Oha ran ahead and, turning to face him, she blocked his path on the track.

'Why are you angry with my sister?' she challenged him.

'You're slowing me down,' he growled, ignoring her question.

'You're taking bigger strides than me.'

'Get behind me then.'

Oha stopped and turned side on to let him pass. As he moved past her, his forearm brushed against her, sending a shiver across her skin.

'How far are we going?'

'There and back,' said Kai.

'How far is that?'

'You talk too much. If you don't like not knowing, then go back to Kō.'

There was silence between them for some time after this. The only sound was Oha's shallow breathing as she tried to keep up with the chief.

The further they went, the more isolated they became. The high growth along this part of the narrowing stream shut out any cooling breeze.

'Are we close?'

Kai gave no reply. For the next quarter of an hour they walked several hundred more metres along the overgrown track. The afternoon was growing hotter and they were both sweating.

'I'm hot,' Oha called.

Finally Kai stopped. 'We're here,' he said. He handed her his patu, dropped his kete, stepped off the path and trod carefully down a slight bank before wading into waist-high water. Oha longed to be in the water too. Kai must have sensed this because he called, 'Stay on the bank.' The pool had become muddied by his presence.

'I'll throw them up to you. Make sure you stun them before putting them in the kete.' He crouched and ran his hand under the bank. His beard dripped water each time he rose. At times she lost sight of him entirely but it wasn't long before there was a splash and Kai tossed the first eel onto the bank. 'Get it!' he yelled.

Thud! Thud! Oha missed the slithering tuna twice as it made for the stream again. As it slid over the bank, she dropped the patu and kete and dived in after it.

'It got away,' she gasped when she came up for air.

Despite himself, Kai burst out laughing. His sister-in-law looked like a drowned rat.

Oha started laughing too. 'You're not angry?' she asked cautiously.

'Happens to me too.'

Oha slowly got to her feet, her wet hair clinging to her shoulders and arms. When her full, high breasts appeared out of the cold water, Kai noticed her dark nipples stood erect.

'It's cold when you first get in, eh?' he said. 'You'll soon warm up.'

Oha was aware of his eyes on her body. She pulled back her shoulders and stretched then twirled and dived like a dolphin.

When she emerged a second time, Kai smiled.

'Warm now?'

'Yes.'

'Then let's get on with it before you scare all the tuna away.'

Oha climbed up onto the bank, grabbing the kete and patu once again. 'I'm ready.'

Kai began feeling under the banks, sometimes using his feet in the muddier parts. While he worked his way upstream, his thoughts returned to the conversation he and Wairere had had that morning.

So, she wants me to take a second wife, he told himself. Perhaps I will do just that. But I won't take one who is already married. Kai thought back to how regularly he and Wairere had made love in the first years of their relationship. Usually in the early mornings so they could wash themselves in the sea afterwards. It was often Wairere who initiated it. That was so many moons ago now.

He compressed the next eel between his fingers and passed it to Oha. As soon as Oha laid it on the ground she thumped its head hard with the patu.

'Now you're getting the hang of it.' They both laughed. 'Feeling for eels in muddy water is full of surprises,' he said, not taking his eyes from her face. 'You never know what is going to bite.' Oha blushed and looked away demurely.

It took some time to fill both kete, then Kai tied the tops to prevent the tuna escaping. The afternoon was humid, quiet and heavy with heat.

'I need to cool off again,' said Oha.

'Well, we've got what we came for,' said Kai, 'so hang the kete on a branch and come back in.'

After she had done as he asked, he reached his hand out to her. She took it, her own hands still sticky with eel slime, and stepped down into the water. She crouched down so that only her head was above the water. Then she went under.

'Oooh, that's better,' she gasped as she popped up again.

Kai just stared. It was all he could do not to grab her there and then, so overcome with desire was he.

Oha pushed off into the deeper part of the stream, turning onto her back. Then she stopped and trod water, returning his gaze. He glided towards her and disappeared. Then he swam up from underneath her, brushing against her body.

Oha had never before been intimate with a man but Kai could see that she wanted him as much as he wanted her. He grabbed her by the hand and pulled her to him.

He nuzzled her neck and she tilted her head back as he pressed his body against hers. In an instant Kai grabbed her buttocks and lifted her onto him. She instinctively locked her legs around him and began grinding against his hardness.

Oha moaned with pleasure then she suddenly stopped and whispered into Kai's ear, 'On the bank.' She uncoupled herself and swam away from him.

He followed like a dog on heat. That morning she had been someone to growl at, but now she was giving the orders and he was obeying. She lay flat on her back before him on the shaded grass. He looked at her for several moments, drunk with the sight and the scent of her. Then he ran his huge hand from her throat to the base of her belly, where he ungirdled her maro to reveal her dark triangular patch.

Oha was flushed and panting, her heart fluttering in her breast. As she drew her knees outwards he positioned himself over her, resting his palms on the ground and covering her nakedness with his muscular body.

With his arms outstretched and his face above hers, he whispered, 'You will be my wife.'

Oha knew this wasn't a question. She nodded. Then she let him place her legs on his shoulders and he thrust himself inside her. It was then that she began to understand the pleasures of love her aunt had told her about. Their union was a mix of many things: the soft warmth of a fire ignited; pain — sharp and brief, as quick as the movement of scampering pūkeko; the triumphant surge of a waka bursting through the surf of a wild sea; and, finally, the most intense pleasure she had ever felt — like climbing on an albatross's wings and soaring across the sky.

When Kai cried out in his final spasm of delight, their fate was sealed. Oha held him captive in the depths of her pool, startled at the sense of her own power.

CHAPTER THIRTY-FOUR

Te Ao Hurihuri
The Ever-changing World

Kapu Fishing Ground, October 1769

The famous hāpuku fishing ground, Kapu, was so far out to sea that Kai could no longer see Ngāpō village, only the high ranges of hills behind it and the chain of mountains in the interior.

'You all right?' he asked Ngāheru.

'Āe,' his son replied. 'From this far out the land looks like a big island.'

From the bow of the waka, nine-year-old Ngā watched his father and uncles recite a prayer to the atua of the sea before they baited their large shell-lined, wooden and human-bone hooks. Ngā did likewise, then dropped his finely bound twine line over the gunwale of the waka, holding tightly to the stick at the other end. Only four lines were let down at one time. The crew of seven sat silently, awaiting a nibble. About thirty metres away from them, their companion waka with a crew of five dropped its own anchor.

Ngā held his line with one hand. The light played around his outstretched fingers as he touched the water's surface. The day could not have been more perfect. He yawned, causing his father to give him a steely look.

He couldn't really be blamed for being tired. For several nights Ngā had sat with his father on Kai-namu-namu. Together with his uncle Tui they had studied the night sky, looking to see if the coming days would be calm and without wind. Before dawn that morning they had set sail for Kapu. His last meal had been the previous evening and he knew there would be nothing more to eat until they made landfall again. That was the way.

Kai's expression was typically unreadable. He just looked at his son, then turned his attention back to his line, gazing at the water.

Like his father before him, Kai felt at home at sea. To him the ocean was a dazzling enigma: as much bounteous resource as unpredictable force, with the power to enrich lives and to destroy them. He felt at his most energised and most inspired the further out to sea he travelled. At sea, devoid of the distractions, the noise, and the issues of tribal life, his mind was free to roam and simply dwell on the people and places he loved. As he held his line between his thumb and forefinger Kai's thoughts drifted again to his sister-in-law Oha and their escapade of a week earlier.

'Do you remember that time we got caught out here?' Tui's question brought his brother back to the moment.

Kai nodded as he let out a little more line.

'What happened, Uncle?' Ngā asked Tui.

'We were very young at the time,' Tui replied. 'We were with our father and a group of fishermen.'

'Ka tae ki te tahora,' Kai chimed in, 'ka kaha ake te hau tuawhenua, arā, te Tāraki. Kātahi ka pūawhehia mātou ki te moana waipū.' *When we reached the open sea a strong wind sprang up and we were blown further out.*

'I think I got a nibble,' an excited Ngā piped up. Then a moment later: 'Oh, maybe not.'

'We were then caught in a storm,' Tui continued, 'and there was nothing for our crew to do but anchor the stern and ride out the gale.'

'We all moved to the stern,' Kai added, 'to lift the bow and allow it to swing around so we wouldn't capsize. We managed to balance the vessel, but there were moments when I thought we were done for.'

'I got a bite,' one of the fishermen said, clearly delighted as he watched his line tugging over the gunwale. Soon Kai and Tui felt nibbles at their hooks also.

'Yep, I got one too,' Ngā concurred. 'Definitely.'

Ngā felt the power of the big fish as he began pulling his line hand over hand into the waka. As Tui looked over the side he could see a grey groper with a silvery-white underbelly coming to the surface. He helped Ngā drag it in and stunned it with a short wooden pounder.

'There's another one!' Ngā cried, pulling up more of the line. They had clearly hit a sweet spot — lines were hauled up, hooks were rebaited, weights checked and lines dropped over the side again. Kai looked across at the other waka and saw that they were doing well too.

After a while the bites started to be less frequent and the conversations started up again.

They had been fishing for a little over an hour when something unusual occurred. A strange apparition was spotted on the horizon towards the south. No one had seen anything like it before. At first, Kai thought it was a distant island, but as the fishermen watched it they realised it was moving.

'It looks like it's coming from Hautanoa,' Tui said. 'But what is it?'

'Remember the news of the visitors at Ōtama?' Kai replied. 'Perhaps it is them?'

Ngā felt nervous but his father seemed completely calm so he tried to imitate him. Those with lines out carried on fishing, but their eyes kept returning to the strange object. As it got closer, theories began to be tossed around. The consensus was that it must be some kind of huge bird.

The sun was high when the object stopped several hundred metres away.

The fishermen continued to watch, speechless, as a canoe left the floating bird and began paddling towards them.

'Pull up your lines,' Kai ordered his men. He was not afraid, but he made sure he knew where his patu was should he suddenly need it.

They could now make out the crew of the canoe. All were fair-skinned and wore odd garments.

'You were right, brother. These must be the visitors from Ōtama,' Tui remarked.

The unusual canoe was almost alongside them now. They did not appear hostile but the fishermen knew that may have been a trick.

'Hūtia mai tā koutou punga,' one of the strangers called to Kai and his men. *Pull up your anchor.*

The vessel paddled closer to where the smaller fish that the groper were feeding on were flapping on the sea's surface. Kai's two waka came alongside each other and everyone watched the strangers carve and chop bait before putting down fishing lines.

'He aha aua mea?' Ngā asked. *What are those things?*

'He tūrehu,' Tui replied. *Mythical beings.*

'He patupaiarehe,' one of the other fishermen suggested. *Fairies.*

Another offered his opinion. 'He atua kahukahu.' *Spirits of the stillborn.*

'Tēnā pea he kō-whio-whio?' said yet another. *Perhaps they are whistling spirits?*

'He apa-a-rangi, mōhio tonu ki tō tātou reo,' said Kai. *They must be spirits of the dead, for they know our language.*

While the strangers fished and conversed with each other in their bizarre spirit language, one of their number, who was brown-skinned like the Ngāpō people, greeted Kai and called to him with questions.

'Do you know the great chief Tare?'

'We know him, and we know his people. But who are you? And where are your people?'

'I am Tupaea, chief and tohunga. These fair spirits are my people.' He went on to explain that he was from the home islands, what they knew as Tawhiti-nui.

Kai told him that their forefathers had met spirits like Tupaea's people many, many years before.

The tohunga wanted to know more about the earlier visitors but Kai was not keen to tell the story because he knew his tīpuna had killed and eaten them and placed their bones in the limestone shafts in the Ngāpō hills.

Through Tupaea, Kai came to understand that the great entity from which they had come was in fact not a bird but a huge canoe with many more sails than theirs.

When the strangers had caught enough fish the man at the bow of their canoe stood to pull up the anchor and all the men in the middle seized the main rope.

And then, just as quickly as they had appeared, they returned to their mother vessel and the huge waka moved on. The fishermen gazed at the ship until it disappeared, each man contemplating what the encounter foreshadowed.

'He maha hoki nga kitenga i ngā rā o mua atu. I kitea e o tātou koroua me ngā kuia he tipua pēnei nā i te wā i a Rau mā,' Kai said. *There have been such sightings in former days. Our own old men and women saw such strange beings in the time of Rau and others.*

He let this sink in before he went on.

'It was said that a group of such beings came to this coast when Rau was chief of Whānau-a-Mate. They were fair and spoke another language. My father told me that, at first, they also took the strange vessel for a great bird. The beings were crafty and wise — the fashioners of a strange type of stone, much stronger than ours. By their wiles they stole some of the women and children from our great-grandfathers and from other tribes of this coast. In the end our waka rammed their vessel and fighting broke out. Our people set their giant waka alight and killed the beings, hiding their bones in one of our caves.'

The fishermen sat quietly for a long while after. Then Ngā broke the silence.

'Where do they come from, Pāpā?'

'An unknown place.'

When the fishing party returned to shore that evening, word of the floating island had already reached Ngāpō from the south.

'Our relatives at Hautanoa saw it offshore,' Te Ika told Kai. 'E ai ki ā rātou kōrero, kia hoe atu rātou i runga i ō rātou waka ki te mātakitaki, ka tere atu taua mea.' *They say that when they paddled towards it to investigate, the apparition floated away.*

Kai broke a dried grass stalk and tapped it on his lips. 'It was not an apparition.'

'Seems not,' said Pona. 'Word has it that the vessel belongs to the atua. The people of Ōtama saw the occupants close up. It appears they were, as you said, white-skinned.'

'Me he pū-nehu-nehu?' Te Ika asked Pona. *You mean, like the beings with fair skin that resemble people?*

'He urukehu rānei, pērā i a Whiwhi-rangi. Heoti, ko te reo he hoi-hoi, he kihi,' said Kai. *Perhaps like our fair-headed, lighter-skinned brethren, as Whiwhi-rangi was. However, these ones speak a noisy, hissing language.*

Pona and Te Ika were wide-eyed as Kai and the others told them about their encounter.

There was a lot of interest in the chief of the fairy people. 'A great tohunga from the ancestral homeland accompanied the atua,' said Kai. 'Tupaea, they call him. We couldn't understand the spirits' language, but that tohunga could interpret it.'

'Well, that explains it.' Te Ika breathed a sigh of relief. 'Inā rā ngā tohu i kitea e te matakite a Tauātia, e rua ngā reo tauhou ka rangona ki te tai-rāwhiti, he "kihi" tētahi e hoihoi ana.' *Remember the prophesy of our late seer, Tauātia? He predicted the coming of two curious forms of speech to this coast, one being an indiscernible, hissing language.*

'I have other news,' said Pona. 'Tare, the great chief at Poko Pā, has invited us to Ōtama. All the chiefs of note throughout the district are being asked to gather at his pā.'

'Āwhea?' Kai asked. *When?* 'Remember we have the annual Ngāi Haere sports tournament coming up.'

'Āmuri i tēnā. Kia tau ki raro a Rūhiterangi,' Pona replied. *After that. When Rūhiterangi, the summer star, goes down.*

Tui nodded. 'Makes sense, when the fruits of the earth, of the fresh water and of the sea are plentiful.'

'He wants to show us the gifts that these supernatural beings presented to him.' Pona smiled.

'To persuade us what a great chief he is,' Te Ika joked.

'No doubt,' Kai said. 'Even though his kāwai rangatira speaks for itself.'

'As our fathers taught us,' Tui added, 'we must always proceed with caution if we expect to retain life.'

'Of course,' Pona replied, 'but his messenger said that the taonga were like nothing to be seen anywhere in this land.'

Kai and Te Ika exchanged a wide-eyed look.

'Tare has clearly called this meeting mainly to discuss what this might mean for the local iwi. I shall take Ngā along. You all may want to do likewise with your families. It's time our children were involved in inter-tribal affairs. The Ōtama people hardly know my sons, yet Ngā is almost of age.' Ngā's face lit up.

Kai's thoughts returned to his first visit to Poko Pā. The childhood memory of consuming part of a man's heart, there on the sand, would forever be seared into his memory. He had tasted many men's hearts since, but he would never forget his first. He prayed that his son's first visit to an enemy tribe would not be such a brutal encounter.

CHAPTER THIRTY-FIVE

Kāre he koa o te ao hei rite mo te mea i tangohia atu.
There is nothing so pleasing in the world as that which it takes away.

The day began like a graceful poi dance. Black-winged gulls climbed away from the sprays of the crested waves into an ambient sky. Each soaring arc they made resembled the elegant dip and twist of the poi in motion.

The annual sports tournament at Ngāpō was always an exciting occasion for Ngāi Haere and people had turned up in their hundreds. Competitors from each of the iwi's six pā, including Kauae-nui, were spread out along the beach. Above the sand, makeshift shelters had been raised. Although the sun's heat was pleasant early in the day, come midday everyone would be looking for shade.

Kai and Wairere, along with Poka and baby Tuameko, took their places among the elders in the main shelter. Ngā sat on the sand with his cousins, eagerly watching proceedings. The warm ocean breeze swept over them in playful ripples, bringing the taste of salt with it each time.

The parade along the beach opened proceedings. It was led by sixty kai-rākau, stripped to the waist, veterans of many battles now. They were of varying heights and ages, some athletically lean, others extremely muscular, their skin coated with a light layer of brine from the sea spray. They marched in pā formation, their fingers curled around their favourite weapons, each group more impressive than the last.

Following them were the youths still in warrior training, chests out and heads held high — the unsung heroes of the future and sons of a hundred proud mothers and fathers. Then came the women and girls, dressed in as many colours as could be found. Some were feathered with the whitest of white; others in capes of brown, green, yellow or black feathers; while others again wore the multi-dyed tāniko-bordered kaitaka — displaying not just their beauty, but also their braiding abilities.

The first event of the day was dart throwing. Oha had somehow managed to get herself selected as a competitor.

'I've never seen you this interested in the games before, sister,' remarked Hinewehi.

'Well, look at how many boys are competing!' said Oha. There were plenty of boys Oha's age and other young men whom she had not met before.

'Since there are so many competitors, you'll only get two throws each,' announced the kai-rākau conducting the event. 'Select a teka from that pile and make your way over to this line,' he continued. 'When it's your turn, throw it as far as you can. The reed that travels the furthest is the winner.'

The first competitor took up a reed and walked over to the line in the sand. He spat on the teka, recited a charm over it, then launched it into the air with all his strength. It flew a great distance upwards, then the head of the dart turned towards the sand and it fell fifty metres along the beach. A cheer went up from his supporters.

Oha was fifth in line in the second group and in due course she went up with the girl in front of her to select a reed and wait her turn.

'Is this one any good?' she asked the tall, wiry kai-rākau standing nearby, batting her eyelashes coquettishly.

'That one will be fine. Your turn.'

Oha strode up to the line. Her throw was a poor one, but she hadn't intended to compete seriously — not in this game anyway.

She threw a glance towards the main shelter, where she knew Kai would be watching.

The next event Oha entered was pou toti or stilt-walking. The stilts were made from mako saplings, a light wood when dry. The footrests were cut from the heavier base of branches. Oha's were poorly made but that did not deter her. She asked a handsome young man if she could borrow his pou instead when he had finished his race.

He happily acceded. 'Will you be at the feast tonight?' he asked.

'Depends on my appetite,' she said, flashing him a broad smile. The boy stood there blushing as she strode away on his stilts.

After the race, in which she once again failed to shine, Oha declared to Hinewehi, 'Tonight is going to be exceptional.'

'Why's that?'

'The moon's in Ōmutu,' Oha said as she pointed at the waning crescent visible in the morning sky. The day that Kai deflowered her the moon had also been in Ōmutu. He had not touched her again since then — a full four weeks. He had certainly tried, but Oha had rejected his advances. Discovering her sexuality had awakened in Oha a desire for freedom and independence. She did not want to be a junior wife to any man, least of all to one of her sisters' husbands. She planned to choose her own life partner.

'What do you mean by that? Ōmutu is bad for everything: fishing, eeling—'

'But the nights are dark, which makes it good for catching boys,' Oha cut her sister off and gave her a mischievous smile. 'Look how many are here? They're like a massive school of kahawai feeding on krill.'

'Well . . . take my advice and don't be the krill. Sex out of marriage is for the common people, Oha. You are high born and you will be ceremonially betrothed like your elder sisters.'

Hinewehi had noticed Oha's recent interest in the opposite sex. She'd noticed her little sister flinging her black mane and opening her eyes wide, knowing that her admirers would be caught in her trap in an instant.

'She's like a bitch on heat,' she had recently observed to her mother.

'Does she remind you of someone else at the same age?' Poka asked wryly.

Sex was considered a normal and healthy part of everyday life in the Ngāpō community, with few taboos around it. Carvings depicted copulating couples and Poka and her female relatives often told salacious stories and sang waiata that talked of sexual exploits or the size of men's penises. Yet while most young people might have more than one partner before settling down, as far as Poka was concerned, her daughters were not most young people.

'We'll need to keep a close eye on her,' Poka said.

'We might have to do more than that. We might need to tie her up!'

When Oha was preparing for the evening's activities Poka went to have a serious talk with her youngest. Mother and daughter were soon embroiled in a fierce argument.

'Haramai te koroua a Noho ki te tono i ahau hei wahine mā tana mokopuna,' Poka said. *You have a suitor whose grandfather, Noho, has approached me about a betrothal between you and him.*

'E kī, e kī! Kāre mā kōrua. E kao, māku tonu e rapu he tāne māku,' came the spirited reply. *The cheek of it! It's not for you two to decide. I will find my own man!*

The last of her brood had always been the most headstrong. Poka wanted her daughter to be happy, but not at any cost. Ancient conventions could not be flouted.

'I can't believe you said that,' she replied. 'It flies in the face of everything we stand for! When it comes to the chiefly class, parents decide their children's partners. And as your father has passed on, it is my decision.'

'Then was it you, Mother, who agreed I should become a wife to my sister's husband? I'm telling you now, I will not take second place to my sister.'

'What are you talking about?' Poka was taken aback. 'Which sister?'

'Kai wants a second wife and he has decided it will be me.'

323

'Who told you that?'

'Oh, Mother! Who do you think?'

Poka was silent as she contemplated this sudden turn of events. This was not the path she would choose for her youngest daughter, but she would need to be cautious. Her son-in-law was the chief, after all. 'I will speak to Wairere about it,' Poka said eventually.

'If Kai approaches you to ask for me as his junior wife, please do not agree, Mother.'

'It will happen over my dead body, my dear.'

Poka went directly to Wairere's house. She was even more shocked when Wairere told her it was she who had encouraged Kai to take a second wife. If he had chosen her younger sister to warm his bed, then so be it.

'It's not as if it's an uncommon thing, Mother. How many chiefs do we know of who have married sisters? Not just a few.'

Poka was not impressed. 'You should see a tohunga before giving up your bed to another woman.'

'Why do you care? You've never really liked Kai.'

'He's only interested in himself, always has been,' Poka said tersely. 'Anyway, I have plans for your sister, and I will simply not allow this. Oh, that your father were here.'

+

At sunset Oha appeared, beautifully dressed, wearing a headdress of long, pointed, light-coloured leaves with a single white kōtuku feather over the black sheen of her long hair. She knew plenty of young men would be looking at her, but by this time she had set her eyes on a young man named Tāu, son of Hara, one of the Kō Pā kai-rākau. She wasn't the only one — Tāu was the object of many girls' affections — but Oha was confident she would win him.

Other girls were clearly intimidated by Oha's stunning beauty. She glowed in the twilight, the whites of her deep-set eyes as bright and as dazzling as the perfectly plaited paepaeroa that ran from her armpits all the way to her ankles. Her white teeth gleamed as she laughed with her female cousins.

The smell of several unearthed umu wafted across the marae. Endless baskets of steaming fish, eels, kūmara and other local delicacies were transferred from the cooking area and laid out on mats by pononga. Children watched with hungry anticipation. There was a strict order of eating based on age, but food was not on Oha's mind. She broke away from her circle and headed over to where Tāu was standing, leaving the other young women to watch from the edge of the courtyard.

'Tēnā koe, Tāu,' she said, her heart pounding.

'Tēnā koe, Oha.'

Oha stepped aside to make way for the people behind her. Three young women from another pā sashayed past. On the way through, the tallest one looked back over her shoulder and gave Tāu a wink. Oha suppressed a frown. Perhaps this would be harder than she'd thought.

Oha worked hard to maintain Tāu's gaze, pushing her shoulders back and regularly flashing her beautiful smile, but she needn't have been concerned. After chatting for some time he leaned forward and whispered in her ear, 'Meet me on the beach after the feast.'

During the meal, groups from the different pā responded to their hosts' hospitality with songs and dances. There was something particularly enchanting about the poi — the young women's soft voices, the perfectly synchronised motion, the bright colours of their costumes, every movement fluid.

Something stirred in Oha's chest when it was her pā's turn to perform; she felt Tāu's brown eyes on her. She stood tall, lifted her chin and aimed her eyes, her smile and the delicate movements of the stringed ball at him. But he was not the only one drawn to her rhythmical movements. Kai was also watching. Fury raged in him when he realised Oha was directing all her attention to one of his men.

Poka was rocking baby Tua, alongside a group of other grand-mothers. She also could see what her daughter was up to. Her eyes darted back and forth between her youngest daughter flirting with a suitor, and her son-in-law, whose rising anger was plainly evident.

As soon as the next party replaced the Kauae-nui performers, Kai stood and strode directly over to Oha. He grabbed her by the arm and spoke to her in an angry whisper.

'Come to my bedside tonight,' he ordered.

Standing there, staring up at Kai's eyes, Oha recalled their intimate encounter and was briefly tempted, but she was committed to the decision she had made to choose her own future. And — she was determined to have Tāu tonight.

Be polite, she told herself. You don't want to hurt his feelings.

'I'm afraid I have other plans tonight. What's more, my mother has told me I'm spoken for already.'

'I told you you would be *my* wife,' Kai said through clenched teeth.

'Ah, but you neglected to ask my mother.' Oha's thick lips twitched in a petulant smile.

'I don't need to ask anyone. I'm the chief.'

'It is not my place to go against my mother's wishes,' Oha said demurely, and looked away.

Kai returned to his seat fuming. He was reluctant to openly challenge his mother-in-law, but he had to have Oha as his wife. He sat down next to Wairere in a glum mood. He had felt less dejected when he was sleeping outside Wehe's whare as a boy, beaten and bruised.

When next he looked up, Oha was gone.

CHAPTER THIRTY-SIX

———

Kei muri i te awe māpara e tū ana he tangata kē.
Nōna te ao, he mā.
Shadowed behind the tattooed face a stranger stands.
He owns the earth; and he is white.

Poko Pā, January 1770

During the moon's last quarter, Kai, Tui, Pona and Te Ika readied themselves to travel by sea to Ōtama. They left on *Te Rūrū* with a retinue of kai-rākau aboard and several pononga. The air was light and the feel of the sun on their skin seemed to put everyone in a good mood. As they entered the cove at Ōtama they saw several waka already drawn up on the sand in front of Poko Pā. Soon other canoes arrived.

The pā gradually filled with men and women of all ages and from across the land. Most were strangers to each other, though some men had their chiefly status in common.

'On another occasion we might well be meeting to fight some of these people,' Kai said to his cousins. 'We mustn't let our guard down. Make sure the kai-rākau are alert at all times.'

They were soon seated. Kai instructed Ngā to sit beside him. Kai recognised that some of the chiefs had come from as far south as Tūranga. His relatives from Hautanoa were there, as were his sister

Manu and her husband Whai with their children. Some inland chiefs and many others were in attendance.

Tare had welcomed his visitors, speaking to each one in the same manner, asking about their health and the progress of their cultivations, which was the primary focus for all at this time of the year. The ones he knew little about he acknowledged with silent approval.

Kai was not particularly interested in Tare but was keen to see the gifts he had received from the strange people and to learn the strength and resources of his place. He was distracted, however, because some of his relatives he had not seen for some time, and politeness prevented him from showing any impatience with proceedings.

Kai remarked to Pona at how healthy and numerous the people of the district looked.

'Ko ētahi he tino kaumātua rawa, ōtira kāre i piko ngā tīnana.' *Some of these elders are very old, but their bodies are not stooped in any way.*

Tare invited a visiting chief from further south to explain the unhappy circumstances of the pake-pakehā visit to the Tūranga district.

'They killed nine of our men without laying a hand on them,' the younger man started, and immediately he had everyone's attention.

'He mahi mākutu?' someone called out. *Was it bewitchment?*

'Kāre e kore. He pake-pakehā no te tūrehu.' *Without a doubt. They are fair-skinned and resemble humans, but they are mythical beings.*

'Just like the ones we saw, Pāpā,' Ngā whispered.

'When the huge canoe appeared, our people were amazed,' the young chief continued. 'They mistakenly thought it was the island of Waikawa, which had floated there from beyond Māhia. So they shouted from the beach, "He motu, he motu tere mai nō tawhiti! Inā e tere mai nei!"' *An island, an island that drifts here from afar! See how it floats!*

'Once the sails were furled and reefed they called out again, "E i, me he uru rākau tonu nō tahaki hikitia ai ki te moana te motu tere e tū mai nei."' *Eek, they are like a grove of trees lifted from the shore and placed on the sea, on the floating island.*

The young chief strode back and forth within the circle created by the large audience, becoming more and more animated as he recounted the peculiar experience, which ended with the deaths of those of his kin who were killed by pake-pakehā magic.

'The visitors had long sticks they held up at shoulder height,' he explained, 'which they pointed at people. Then there was an almighty bang, and some smoke from the end of the stick, and someone ten metres away fell down dead! They may have befriended you, oh Tare, but they came as enemies among us.'

Young Ngā sat open-mouthed, clearly stunned at what he was hearing.

As soon as the young chief sat down, Tare was on his feet again. He wanted his guests to know that his experience of the pake-pakehā had been quite different, with no killing.

'Tupaea and the pake-pakehā spent a long time getting to know us. In the six days that they were among our people we were able to see clearly what these beings looked like,' he said. 'He mā, he mā kōrako, he whero tākou, pērā tonu te āhua o ngā kanohi.' *White, albino, red ochre-like; such was the appearance of their faces.* His audience was enthralled with his description and nodded as he spoke.

Tare wore a bright red scarf which he said had been presented to him by the chief pake-pakehā. It was from Tupaea's island. Red feathers from the home islands were now so rare along this coast that seeing this scarf led the people to endorse the statement apparently made by the chief pake-pakehā: 'Tare, Tare te rangatira.' *Tare, Tare is indeed a chief.*

Tare instructed his wife to display her gift and she willingly paraded around the circle. Her flax necklet bore three blue beads of a colour the chiefs had only ever seen in the sky or sea. A sharp, spike-like object, about a finger's length and with a flat head, was driven into wood and passed around. Still, more was yet to come. Everyone had heard by now about Tare's hatchet, formed from a block of a heavy substance given him by Tupaea. The pake-pakehā called it lead, and it had recently been fastened to an intricately carved handle.

'I have had the blade sharpened,' the chief assured everyone. 'Nothing was ever so sharp.'

A log of wood was brought before Tare and all the chiefs prepared to admire the hatchet's capabilities. But at Tare's first attempt, the blade bent sideways.

'What?' Te Ika whispered to Kai. 'Not so impressive!'

Tare was mystified, and said he had watched the visitors effortlessly chopping wood with just such a tool. He spoke to his people and then said someone had observed one of the pake-pakehā tempering iron by heating it in a fire. One of them called out, 'Auē, tahuna ki te ahi kia mārō ai!' *Oh, it needs to be put to the flame to be hardened!*

Tare ordered a fire to be lit, using wood that would give the most intense heat. But when the lead was placed in the flames, to everyone's dismay it began to melt.

'Kapea ki tahaki!' Tare called. 'Me āta whiriwhiri marie he tikanga mō te toki nei.' *Pull it from the fire! We must work out some way to perfect this adze.*

Te Ika and Kai grabbed sticks and tried to pick out the hatchet head but it melted and they soon abandoned the rescue.

Everyone was amazed, for no one had seen stone behave in this way.

'Nō wai te hē?' Ngā asked innocently. *Who's to blame?*

'Kāre noa iho he take o te uapare,' said Tare. 'Ka tutuki hoki ki tōna tutukitanga a te kūare.' *No one's to blame. It's the natural consequence of ignorance.*

'He's right,' Kai said to his son. 'These are new things, and without the knowledge of the white beings, how can anyone know the correct way to use them?'

'I have one further gift to show you all,' Tare said.

To see this gift they all had to walk over the hill to the Paremata flats, which gave them an opportunity to see the extensive plots that Tare's people had under cultivation. A small fire was burning near the neatly ordered plots. One small garden grew an unusual plant that none of the chiefs had ever seen before. The few plants were mounded in the same way as kūmara.

'Ka hōmai e te pake-pakehā ko te para, ka tohutohu mai i te mahinga, me te kī mai a Tupaea he kai pai,' Tare explained. *The pake-pakehā gave us this vegetable, with instructions for its cultivation. Tupaea told us it was good food.*

He ordered one of his men to uncover one of the mounds. While the earth was being cleared away, Tare described the new food.

'We have called it "para" because it is like the fern of this land. It tastes like the para-tawhiti.' *The starchy-based fernroot.*

The potatoes were unearthed one by one and laid out for all to see.

'Anana, he para nunui!' Ngā cried out. *Wow, a big para!*

'Aeha, he para kaitā,' said Te Ika. *Gosh, a large para.*

'He para whakahara kē,' Tui remarked. *A huge para indeed.*

The potatoes were cleaned, taken to the fire and placed in the ashes. When they were cooked, Tare's men used sticks to extract them. They tossed them from hand to hand to cool them, then squeezed them so that they broke open. The potatoes were passed around for the chiefs to sample.

'He para māngaro,' Kai gave his seal of approval to the new food. *It tastes starchy.* Other chiefs offered their opinions, all of which were favourable.

'Āe, he para pai tonu.' *Yes, this para is really good.*

'He para kakara.' *The para has a nice fragrance.*

'Kātahi te para-reka.' *What sweet para.*

Raw potatoes for growing were distributed among the group. Kai and Tui were keen to get theirs back to Ngāpō to plant.

'Kātahi anō ka ora ngā wāhine me ngā tamariki,' said Kai, 'ka ngaro hoki te kōpura kai ki te whenua! *The sustenance of our women and children will be taken care of once these tubers are in the ground!*

One furrowed row in the garden had not produced any shoots. It contained what they had thought to be seeds for another new vegetable from the pake-pakehā. Clearly dismayed, Tare ordered the ground to be turned to see if the seed had rotted. When the seed was uncovered it appeared exactly the same as when it was planted.

'Throw it in the fire,' Tare said. 'It's worthless.' When the fine grain was collected up and tossed into flames it exploded and Tare's audience jumped back in fright.

'What magic is this?' Kai asked his friends.

'The pake-pakehā gave us this seed along with a stick that was as long as a taiaha. It produced a puff of fire and smoke,' Tare told the chiefs. 'When I was given the fire stick and told to put it against my shoulder, it gave me such a shock when it puffed its smoke that I let go of it and it fell on the rocks and was broken.'

'Those are the weapons that killed our people!' cried the young chief from the Tūranga district.

Back at Poko Pā, a feast was served to the visitors, after which the chiefs were invited to discuss what the visit of the pake-pakehā might mean for them.

'He tino tohunga a Tupaea, he mōhio ake i ōku tohunga,' Tare began. 'I tapaina ko tōna ingoa i runga i ngā piripoho.' *Tupaea is a well-informed tohunga — more knowledgeable than any of mine. Some of our newborns have been given his name.* There were tohunga present who frowned at Tare's comment, but those of them who had met with the Tahitian wayfinder could hardly deny it. One of Tare's most powerful tohunga had spent days with him, testing his knowledge, and agreed that the visitor's training and travels were far superior to anything he had experienced.

'There is another remarkable thing about him and his white friends,' Tare added. 'None of them eat human flesh. They were surprised to learn that we eat our enemies.'

'Not just our enemies,' Te Ika jested, earning frowns all round.

'They have equipment far superior to ours too,' the Tūranga chief said. 'The fire sticks are powerful, magical and can kill at a distance. Our men are from warlike stock and they like a good fight but they were no match for the fire sticks.'

'Speaking of superior equipment,' Kai said, rising to address the gathering, 'our men witnessed first hand the pake-pakehā's exceptional fishing techniques.'

'Nō nāwhea? I whea hoki?' Tare asked. *When? And where?*

'Nō tō rātou wehenga i Hautanoa. Kei Kapu,' Kai answered. *After they left Hautanoa. At Kapu fishing ground.*

Kai spoke of the long boat that had come out of what they had thought was a giant floating bird. 'Ka rere mai taua autaia nei.' *That strange vessel sped towards us.*

He looked around at the chiefs. The Tūranga and Ōtama people who had seen the longboat nodded in agreement.

'Kōrero mai, Koroua,' Tare said as he leant forward. *Speak on, Sir.*

'It was long, with many people paddling on each side. Rows of fair-skinned people in the middle, and the fugleman and the man in the stern were standing. They headed straight to our canoes and rested by us.'

All eyes were on him, and Kai was enjoying the attention, drawing out his oratory accordingly.

'Our fishing party were curious. Once the visitors had baited their hooks they threw them into the sea. And almost straight away they hauled up hāpuku — four, five or six fish on the hooks of one line. It was the same for both sides of the vessel.'

'Ka mau te wehi! Ehara rātou i te kai-haoika, he atua kē!' Tare commented. *Incredible! They are not fishermen; they are indeed gods!*

The tohunga who were present were silent, keen to hear more before drawing conclusions.

'He tohu nō te aha?' Kai asked the gathering. *What does this mean?* 'Before he died,' he went on, 'the seer from the Waiapu Valley, Tauātia, predicted that when the roots of the slow-growing hinahina tree had spread over his grave, he would hear the clattering of a strange tongue and the noise of numbers. Are these the beings he foresaw?'

People exchanged wide-eyed looks and soon everyone was chatting excitedly with those around them.

'Now, listen up!' Tare called the meeting back to order. 'Ka riro te mātauranga o te matakite ki tēnei iwi kē, mātau atu ai, mōhio atu ai, rangatira atu ai.' *The knowledge of what the seer prophesied is in the possession of these strange beings; with them lie wisdom, understanding and prosperity.*

Then he added, 'I say this as a caution, for Tupaea warned me that we have not seen the last of them.'

CHAPTER THIRTY-SEVEN

He hinganga tokānuku, he terenga tōtara.
When a person of importance dies, that is where the mighty will converge.

'Wairere should be back at Kauae-nui by now,' Kai said to Te Ika as he inhaled the pristine mountain air.

'Perhaps they may not seek utu.' Te Ika tried feebly to cheer his friend up. 'They all know how her mother treated you.'

'If there is one quality more highly cultivated by our people than vengeance,' Kai responded, flexing his neck from side to side, 'I am yet to learn of it.'

'Let's take a short stroll around Pā-o-te-Kī,' said Te Ika by way of distraction.

The top of Aorangi mountain rose majestically from the forest-clad hills. The peak was covered with bush, some of which had been burned, leaving the approach to Pā-o-te-Kī bare. The apex of the pā was girded by a triple line of parapets, the inner two of which stood three-and-a-half and five metres high respectively. The area around the pā was denuded of trees of any height, which not only afforded Kai a splendid view of the plains below, but also allowed warning of any approach by intruders.

They walked around the newly built stockades. Every three or four metres Kai placed his hand against the stout pūriri posts that supported the sharp stakes between them.

'Good and solid,' he murmured.

'We're going to need it,' said Te Ika. 'Not many of the kai-rākau have sided with us.'

'I know. They'll either go to be with Tāmō at Kauae-nui or they'll stay out of it with Tui at Ngāpō. Choose a side, I say.'

'You can't blame Tui for returning to Ngāpō. Kere will find it difficult too when he hears. After all, Poka was the mother of their wives too.'

'Do you know why I picked this spot to build my pā?' Kai changed the subject.

'Why?'

'Do you remember when we first came across the tarn on Hikurangi?'

Te Ika struggled to recall.

'Well, I spotted this peak from there. Like a rock standing in the sea, I thought. Unmoveable. One time when I was bird-snaring in the bush below here I came up to check it out and I thought, if I ever need an impregnable spot from which to defend myself, this will be it.'

'You mean you built this pā knowing you were going to kill your mother-in-law?'

'No, of course not. I built it because I have many enemies out there who want to get even with me for killing their fathers. It was only a matter of time before one or more came calling.'

He stood at the entrance to the pā and looked down the trail that led up from the bush.

'My mother-in-law should never have come here,' he sighed. 'This would never have happened if she hadn't!'

Te Ika sensed that Kai might be feeling some regret for what he had done. He let his cousin continue.

'After we got back from Ōtama and Poka refused to let me take Oha as my wife, my only thought was to get away from her and her daughters. So I came up here but I missed my children so much, I had Wairere and the boys brought here. When Wairere requested that her mother visit, I should have refused but I am too soft.'

Te Ika raised an eyebrow but said nothing.

It had happened only three days earlier. Kai had gone to speak with Poka who was plaiting a kiekie basket in the shade at the edge of the bush. Tuameko was fast asleep at her side. Kai hated having to go cap in hand to his mother-in-law; it was not a chiefly thing to do. But it was tikanga — she too was high born. He strolled right past her at first as if he was heading off into the bush. She kept her head down but he knew her snake-like eyes would be following him. When he turned back and went to speak, she growled like a dam preparing to defend her litter.

'I have given you my answer already.'

'You don't know what I was going to ask!'

She went on with her work. He stood there studying her, his temperature rising.

'I . . . I—' he started, but she cut him off again.

'You're too late. I have betrothed her to Noho's grandson.'

Kai was furious and before long the two of them were engaged in a heated argument that could be heard from the farthest corners of the pā. As he raged, Kai took his stone patu from his belt and turned it this way and that.

The old lady was unfazed by her son-in-law's intimidatory tactics, glaring back at him as each tried to be heard over the other. Baby Tua, rudely awakened, began to scream, adding to the commotion.

Kai clenched his patu, set his jaw, and took a swift intake of breath between parted lips. That should have served as a warning to Poka, but she got to her feet and started pointing her finger at him as she continued to list the chief's character flaws at the top of her voice.

A look of pure hatred flashed in Kai's black eyes. The strike to her temple was clean and sharp. It felt to Kai as if he was moving in slow motion, but in fact it was as quick as a lightning strike. The ugly sound of the patu striking bone rang through the pā, which had fallen eerily silent. Even the baby had stopped his screaming.

Poka dropped like a stone. The next thing Kai remembered was her three daughters — Wairere, Hinewehi, Oha — wailing, screaming, clutching at their mother's body.

'I don't know what came over me,' he told Te Ika now. 'It was as if I heard my wife's taunting in my ears: "Are you not a great chief?" and after that I was no longer in control of my own actions. Before I knew it, I had struck her, and of course with my years of training, the death blow was instantaneous.'

'At least you did the right thing in letting Wairere take her mother's body back to the burial ground at Pā-pōhatu,' Te Ika said in a conciliatory tone.

'Yes, and I sent Oha's lover, Tāu, with her, in the hope that Tāmō might kill him, because he is one of my men. But I don't suppose the gods will even allow me that. His father Hara was always kind to me, and this is how I have repaid him. I must face the consequences of my actions.'

'Are you afraid?'

'The last time I was afraid was when I came face to face with the laughing atua below Kōrau-whakamae. What can a mere mortal man possibly do to the great chief Kai?'

+

Wairere had her bearers stop on a grassy plateau some distance from Kauae-nui. The litter in which she was carried, enclosed by woven mats and borne on the shoulders of four pononga, had been a gift from Kai, no doubt in an attempt to ease his conscience.

After they placed it on the ground, the fatigued pononga vanished with a wave of Tāu's hand. Wairere was aware of the young warrior standing there, apparently waiting for her to draw back the screen. She had tried to avoid speaking to him since leaving Pā-o-te-Kī, except to give him commands. He was loyal to her husband and she didn't trust him.

As soon as she climbed out, Tāu moved off while Wairere seated herself beneath a large rātā tree in full bloom, a short distance from

337

the pā. The place had a tranquillity about it, she thought, as if nothing bad could happen to her here.

Tāu, at Wairere's request, had the other bearers place the wrapped corpse before her. Her contact with it rendered her tapu until the supernatural condition was removed by karakia. She could not approach any person or pā and had to refrain from receiving food, only eating what she could forage. The grieving daughter wore a sacred red kura or plume that blended with the scarlet flowers of the rātā. She had placed another on the outside of the litter to warn people that she was tapu.

As a further precaution, when descending from Pā-o-te-Kī, Tāu had made sure to use the less frequented tracks to avoid meeting anyone who might be out hunting or on their way to Kai's mountain fortress. But they met no one. The weather was beautifully fine and no streams were flooded; this good fortune Wairere put down to the incantations she recited and the protection of the spirit of her deceased mother, whose sacred pounamu tiki she now wore around her own neck.

Wairere gazed at distant Kauae-nui, the pā of her birth and child-hood, which held so many fond memories. She recalled how boyish Kai had been that day her brother defeated him at wrestling, but how she had fallen for him the moment she set eyes on him. She tried to remember when those intense feelings had started to diminish. She certainly had no love for the man now. The man who had murdered her beloved mother.

She had come here to give her brother and half-brothers news of their mother's murder. She stood and called out to the watchmen on the palisades.

'E Tāmō! E taku tūngane! Haramai ki a au!' *Tāmō! Oh my brother! Come to me!*

Hearing her cry, some of the women came out of the pā, saying, 'He is at Pua-o-te-Roku snaring birds. He will return later today. Will you not come into the pā and wait?'

'I cannot,' she replied. 'I will wait here.' The women went to

338

approach her but when they saw the red plumes they promptly withdrew back into the pā.

Wairere had not washed since the day her mother died. The dirt on her skin felt like some sort of penance and she welcomed it. She wanted to hurt her husband as he'd hurt her, to remind him that she was a chieftainess, not because of him, but in her own right.

She had tried when she saw what he had done to her mother. In a frenzy she had gone at him with an adze, but he, still consumed by fury, had beaten her until she was bloody. The ochre on her face, even now, went some way towards hiding the bruises.

While she lay injured and semi-conscious, Kai had approached her sister. Oha was shaking with fear, her eyes wide but unfocused.

'Now, you have no excuse,' Kai told her. 'Your mother is gone. There is no one to ask. Or if there is, tell me who they are and I'll deal with them in the same way.'

Later, when he had calmed down, Oha said to him, 'How do you expect me to ever love you? You killed my mother!'

'I did it swiftly,' came his cruel reply. 'And I don't need love. I need a wife.'

Oha wondered how she could ever have thought him handsome. And that night she took off — escaping into the bush.

Strangely, as well as anger, Wairere also felt guilt. If she had not put the idea of a second wife into her husband's head her mother might still be alive. For two days she sobbed herself to sleep, woke weeping and cried herself back into a slumber, until the morning when Kai suggested it was time she took her mother's body to Pā-Pōhatu. They both knew she would stop at Kauae-nui and that her husband would soon face the wrath of his brothers-in-law and their kai-rākau.

'Perhaps my brothers will give me your head to place at Pā-Pōhatu,' had been her parting words to her husband.

The orange-gold expanse of sky as the sun set behind the mountains heralded the faint conversation of hunters who appeared out of what now resembled an enchanted forest. The hunting party emerged from the bush and Tāmō, on seeing his sister on the plateau, ran up to her.

'Wai, what are you doing here?' Tāmō asked, knowing from her face and the wrapped corpse on the ground that it was bad news.

Wairere choked back sobs and, without words, unveiled the face of the corpse.

Tāmō stepped back, stunned into silence.

'Who committed this foul deed?'

'My husband.'

'Where is he?'

'He is waiting for you on Aorangi mountain at Pā-o-te-Kī.'

Tāmō did not weep but immediately sent for a tohunga and a party to carry his mother's remains to Pā-Pōhatu, where he could perform a karakia over the corpse to remove the tapu. The tohunga said it would be dark by the time they reached the burial ground so they should wait until the morning. So Tāmō himself recited some incantations. Finally, he allowed himself to weep over his mother.

'Go back now, sister,' Tāmō said to Wairere. 'We will see that our mother rests at Pā-Pōhatu. Leave vengeance to us.'

He then sent runners out in the night to their relatives in the various Ngāi Haere pā to assemble at Kauae-nui.

+

When Tāu and the pononga returned to Pā-o-te-Kī they set down the litter in the inner court of the newly constructed pā.

Kai put his head inside the screen and smiled at Wairere. 'I am pleased to see you have returned, wife.'

Wairere thought of how his eyes, which had once mesmerised her, now seemed hard and cold. I hate you, she said to herself.

She made him wait a while before she climbed out. As she opened the screen she caught the aroma of cooked food. Kai had ordered a meal to be prepared for her. A futile effort, thought Wairere. From now on nothing would give her the pleasure it once had. Except for her children. She was filled with emotion when she saw nine-year-old Ngā and eighteen-month-old Tua standing next to their father, obviously happy to see her.

'Waiho mā ngā tūpāpaku e tanu ō rātou nā tūpapaku,' said the chief, his smile now more of a smirk. 'Ko koe ia me whakatipu i a tāua tamariki.' *Let the dead bury the dead, for you have our children to raise.*

Wairere climbed out of the litter, opened her arms and her boys ran and hugged her. I must live for these two, she vowed to herself.

'Tāu,' Kai called, 'you will be the first line of our defence. After you have eaten, take a guard of kai-rākau — you'll have to make the numbers up with pononga. Take them down to our forward redoubt and keep watch for Tāmō. At the first sign of him, send a runner back to me.'

+

It was another four days before Tāmō was ready to attack. The autumn air was cooler than usual, even at that dark morning hour. The bush was quiet except for the footsteps of his warriors and the sound of the soft breeze in the trees that surrounded them.

They were at the base of Aorangi Mountain and seemed to be wandering directionless in the dark through the broken foothills, climbing over large boulders and crossing small streams until the scouts picked up the start of the wide path that led to the top.

Out of the pre-dawn darkness a messenger came rushing out of the bush and up to Pā-o-te-Kī.

'They have been spotted, e Rangi.'

'A dawn attack,' Kai said to Te Ika, who had joined him as soon as he heard their voices. 'How many?' he asked the runner.

'Hard to tell, but we estimate about sixty of them.'

'We have only half that number here manning the pā,' said Te Ika. 'And fewer again at the redoubt.'

'It's me they're after,' Kai replied. 'I will go down to the redoubt and challenge Tāmō and his brothers to single combat.'

'How far away are they?' Kai asked the runner.

'They will be at the redoubt by the time I get back.'

'They know what a good fighter you are, Kai,' said Te Ika. 'You know what they'll do. They'll set four or five warriors on to you, and only when you tire will they let you fight them one on one.'

'Go back and tell our men at the redoubt to withdraw back here,' Kai told the messenger, who took a last sip of water and took off back down the trail.

The rising sun spread a rosy hue across the morning sky. The air was cool and invigorating, full of songbirds.

Before long, voices could be heard and then shouts. Birds took flight from the bush at the sound of a fight in progress. It ended as quickly as it had started, and the air fell silent again.

Kai and Te Ika stood outside the pā scanning the bush, waiting for their men to appear. But it was not Tāu or any of his party who walked out of the trees. It was Tāmō and his brothers, fronting their ope taua, which was much larger than the runner had estimated.

'There's at least a hundred of them,' whispered Te Ika. He saw Kere with them.

'Go back inside and shut the gate,' Kai ordered Te Ika.

'No, I'm staying as your second,' said his loyal friend.

Tāmō's army spilled out of the bush and fanned out into three ranks on the gradual slope in front of the pā, about fifty metres from Kai and Te Ika. Kai recognised warriors from each of the Ngāi Haere pā, many of whom he and Te Ika had trained. Only Kō Pā was not represented.

Then out from the taua stepped a group of warriors who held their long tao high. Impaled on the ends of their spears were fourteen bloodied heads. One was Tāu's. The others belonged to the kai-rākau and pononga who had tried and failed to defend the redoubt.

Tāmō rallied his men for the final assault.

On bended knee, Kai called to them.

'E Tāmō! E Kere! He aha tā kōrua māku nā ō tāua tīpuna?' *Hey Tāmō! Hey Kere! What have you brought me from our ancestors?* Tāmō and Kere knew what he meant. He had led them in many battles over the years. He had saved some of their lives and he was asking that, while they might fight and kill him, the defenders of his pā might be spared as they were all relatives.

'Anā tā te ururoa,' he said as he stepped forward. *Behold the strength of the great white shark.* It was a warning but he was grandstanding; Kai knew he had no chance.

Tāmō consulted with Kere. Everyone else was silent, including those in the pā who were watching from the parapets. The morning sun cast shadows from the edges of the bush.

Kere got to his feet. Kai and Te Ika watched their old friend raise his taiaha horizontally above his head and then, using both hands, deliberately break it across his knee. Then without a word to Kai, Kere turned his back and walked down the path towards the bush. Twenty warriors from his pā stood and followed .

'You were once our leader,' Tāmō called to Kai. 'For that reason only, we will spare your life. These men of yours,' he pointed to the impaled heads, 'will serve as part payment for the murder of my mother. The rest we will take in land. Your land. All those areas that you inherited from your father and grandfathers, from Ēpa, are from this day forward forfeited to my family. We leave you only this mountain. You will no longer be one of our chiefs and if you ever set foot in Kauae-nui again, it will be the last time you do. You are banished to live here in your fortress. You built it to keep people out; now it will serve as your own prison.'

Tāmō turned and looked at his men. 'E hoki, tātou.' *Let us return.*

CHAPTER THIRTY-EIGHT

He tao huata e taea te karo. He tao nā aituā, e kore.
The thrust of a spear shaft may be parried. That of death, never.

Kai took a deep breath, inhaling the earthy scent. Everywhere he looked, it seemed fungi had sprouted from the soft, damp forest floor. White kōpurawhetū or basket fungus peeped through the undergrowth, light brown toadstools stood out from dead trunks, and creamy grey-capped mushrooms with pinkish gills, some as slippery as eels, shoaled along the heavy root buttresses of the trees.

'Those are the ones to eat, boys,' said Kai. The four boys crouched down near Kai and Tui and began plucking the mushrooms at their stalks. Kai's sons, Ngāheru, now sixteen and Tuameko, almost nine, enjoyed their Uncle Tui's visits because he had two boys of similar ages. Their uncle would also bring a supply of kaimoana — dried fish and lots of fresh kina, pāua and crayfish. Wairere also looked forward to Tui's visits because she got to see her sister Hinewehi and their four little girls. With no daughters of her own, Wairere loved to spoil her nieces.

Every year, during the long sigh of autumn, Tui and his family came for three months. The kererū and kākā were fat during this period. The two families usually stayed at Ōtūtū, above the Matā River, to be closer to the pua manu and do some bird-fowling. This year they built their wharau alongside a grove of miro, whose berries were just now reaching a bright red plum colour.

A light, cold drizzle was falling, and insects whirred about their heads. The boys pulled their raincapes over their shoulders and rubbed some more ngaio infusion onto their skin to repel the mosquitoes. As they filled their kete with mushrooms, flocks of kākā invaded the misty canopy with their shrieks, and kererū whooshed slowly through the trees. Cackling tūī added to the cacophony.

'It will be a feast of mushrooms and kererū tonight!' said Kai as they turned back towards their wharau.

+

Seven summers had passed since his exile and Kai had spent nearly all that time in the mountain hinterlands, hunting in the foothills about Aorangi and Hikurangi. He had fed his family on eels, birds, the fruit of the kāuka or cabbage tree, mushrooms, aruhe and pikopiko, the spiral shoots of the mamaku or black tree fern. Kererū flew about in great numbers, as did several species of kārearea, kākā and a multitude of other singing birds. Down in the wetlands of drowned bulrushes, pārera or wild ducks crowded together. Their tameness enabled Kai and his boys to catch several at a time.

This had been their home for so long now that they had grown accustomed to the bounty of the bush.

Whenever Wairere took the boys to see their relatives at Kauae-nui or Ngāpō, Kai stayed behind at Pā-o-te-Kī, with his taiaha and patu never far from his side. He had become like his Uncle Wehe: he would sleep in his bed for no more than two nights running, and if he noted bad omens he would sleep under the stars, always in a different place on his land, always ready to defend himself. It was not distant enemies he feared, but rather his wife's relatives or even one of his own tribesmen, all of whom lived within a day's travel. He knew his death would occasion celebration for hundreds so he stayed away.

Oha had married the man her mother had betrothed her to and they lived in Kauae-nui under the protection of her brother.

'There is change in the wind,' Tui told Kai as they walked. 'The prophecies of the seers since the visit of the pake-pakehā foretell much that is new.'

'What do you mean?'

'Well, for one thing, the roads and seaways seem safer to travel, so that even our distant neighbours visit Ngāpō more frequently.'

'Be careful of their motives,' said Kai, ever wary. 'They may be staking out your resources and the strength of your defences.'

'Ngāi Haere's leadership has been weakened,' Tui went on. 'At a recent tangihanga our closest neighbours asked us to give them a pononga to eat. I said, "No, we have none except ourselves." Their chief replied, "That will do." He didn't push it, but it shows how disrespectful the weaker iwi have become in the time that you have been in exile.'

Kai said nothing.

'You are the true-born leader of our people,' Tui continued, 'as our father was before us. Once you were expelled, others were quick to vie for the role. You know the old saying — "Hinga atu he toa, ara mai rā he toa." *When one warrior falls, another takes his place.*

'But there was no single chief that everyone would follow. Not even I could pull in all the Ngāi Haere hapū as you were able to do. The iwi is breaking up, with many moving away from Kauae-nui and Ngāpō to settle land nearer the food resources. Kere and his people have built a new pā, Te Ika and Pona are at Ahu; only Tāmō and his brothers' families remain at Kauae-nui.'

Tui left his older brother to ponder his words and walked over to join his sons and nephews.

Kai sat on a log and quietly sang a lament. He sang of his grief for his people, now fragmenting and dispersing. Not all of what Tui had said was news to him. He had heard rumours of the state of things among Ngāi Haere from those few who still visited him. Yet he was powerless to do anything for his people while he was banished.

As Kai finished his song he heard someone heading through the bush towards them. It was Taha, one of Kere's men. The messenger was making his way up the track from the Matā River.

'Kere instructed me to bring news to you,' Taha said to Kai and Tui. At that moment the rain began falling harder, drumming loudly against the ground.

'Come, let's go up to the wharau to talk,' Kai suggested. The three men retired, leaving the four boys sheltering under a rātā tree.

'Tēnā koutou,' the messenger began as soon as they were inside.

'Wait, have something to eat first,' said Kai. 'You've come a long way.' Wairere removed a broth from the fire, which they now stoked to warm the abode.

The warrior ate hurriedly as he delivered his message. He had brought the startling news that the Aitanga-Nui had made a foray into the region south of Wawe-ki-uta and were intent on settling old scores with pā right along the coast, including Kauae-nui and Ngāpō.

'The Ngāi Haere pā have all emptied out and the people have gone north,' Taha continued urgently. 'Everyone is staying with neighbouring tribes in the Waiapu Valley to await the enemy's approach. But Kere is still in his pā across the river from Kauae-nui, very near Pā-pōhatu. He refuses to leave.'

'I know the one,' nodded Tui. 'He calls it Ōrongo-iri.'

'He says he will not be scared off,' Taha added, 'and that he would rather die fighting on his own land than desert his pā.' For the first time in a long while, Kai thought back on the numerous battles and assaults he had instigated and fought in in his younger years, most of them with Kere at his side. The old burning intensity flashed in his eyes.

'What do you know about the strength of the Aitanga-Nui ope taua?' he asked Taha.

'They are about sixty strong and led by a young warrior named Hae. He was just a boy when you raided Pātete Pā and killed Whiwhi-rangi. He was made to stand on the parapet and watch as our Ngāi Haere warriors taunted his relatives with haka after haka. Since then his life has been devoted to studying the art of fighting. Now that he has

347

come of age, he seeks to avenge the insults and defeats his people have suffered.'

'How do they say he performs?'

'His fighting technique is apparently excellent. His weapon of choice is the taiaha. Some say he is as quick as you were at his age. He has already led a war party through the southern territories, challenging chiefs and their best warriors to single combat.'

'And how has that gone for him so far?'

'Well, he's still alive. He went first to Tūranga to avenge his grandmother. The giant albino warrior Kurī was his target. He set a group of his warriors on to him and when he saw that the great chief was tiring, he challenged him to a one on one and killed him. So some of the chiefs, once they realised what kind of warrior he was, brought their iwi together in one pā and told him, "If you want to kill the chiefs, you must first take all of us." Since they outnumbered his small party he backed down.'

'Where is he now?'

'Probably nearing Hautanoa — no more than two days south of here as he's travelling overland. Word has it he intends challenging Kauae-nui and Ōrongo-iri if he finds anyone there.'

Kai could hardly believe that his kai-rākau — with whom he had served in numerous campaigns and some of whom he had trained — had apparently scurried away to safety like frightened rats.

'War was my trade for so many years,' he told the two men. 'Life seemed like a continual series of battles, and death was my constant companion. What's the old saying? "Ko tēnei taonga ko te mate he tīno kākahu nō tēnei hanga nō te toa."' *This prized treasure death is ever the garment of the warrior.* He sighed. 'And then came my exile.'

He stood, looked at them both in turn, and said decisively, 'Enough is enough. It's time I returned. We must drive these invaders from our land and this madness must cease! Go and tell my friend Kere to expect me tomorrow.'

After the messenger had left, Tui turned to his older brother. 'You must make them look to you again as their chief.'

Kai nodded gravely, grateful for his brother's confidence in him. 'We both know my men have lost respect for me,' he said matter-of-factly. 'Only the most loyal remain here at Pā-o-te-Kī and you can count those men on two hands.' He put his hand on Tui's shoulder. 'I need you to accompany our wives and children to the kai-rākau at Pā-o-te-Kī.'

'No, I'll go with you to fight.'

'Not so, my brother. If the gods are with us, I shall return. But if I am killed, someone must make sure my sons avenge my death once they reach maturity.'

Tui was clearly unhappy with Kai's request but he could never defy his brother.

'Should I die, promise me you will keep with custom and take Wairere to wife. She and I have had our differences but I have never stopped loving her. I need to know she will be looked after if I am gone.'

Tui clutched both Kai's arms and pressed his nose against his brother's. As they parted, Kai said, 'And I want my boys to serve our people as warriors, just as we did.'

'You have my word, brother,' Tui said.

+

That night, in the warmth of their wharau, Kai spoke to his sons. Wairere sat against the back wall, listening. The chief's fist was closed, palm up.

'Pay attention, boys,' he whispered. 'When I open my hand, you'll see the strangest thing.' Ngā and Tua leaned forward with their faces almost over their father's hand.

'Sit back and give us light from the fire or you won't be able to see what it is,' Kai said. Then he slowly uncurled his fingers to reveal a shiny bone in the shape of a cross, set into a piece of oiled tōtara. The two boys stared, perplexed, at the strange object.

'He aha tēnā?' asked Tua. *What is it?*

The cross glistened in the firelight. The object was no bigger than their father's thumb. It reminded Ngā of the wooden crossbars outside palisaded pā.

'This is the object that a pake-pakehā used to try to scare our tīpuna,' Kai said in a low voice, 'before it was wrenched from his neck five generations ago.' Shadows from the fire leapt along the walls. 'Since then, this taonga has been passed down from father to son. My father gave it to me when I was about your age, Ngā. I had the bone shape set in wood so I would not lose it.' He let the two boys feel its texture.

'My sons,' he continued, 'the Aitanga Nui are expected to arrive soon. They are not the first to invade us, nor will they be the last. There will be other tribes in future; you may even have to fight them yourselves. But fear not, for the invaders will be like the tide — they will come and they will go.'

The two boys gazed spellbound at their father as they all sat in front of the fire.

'The ones to fear,' Kai continued, 'are the ones who come bearing gifts, for they will never depart. The owner of this taonga prophesied their coming, and you yourself, Ngā, saw them when we were fishing at Kapu. He told our ancestors, "They will be fair-skinned like me and they will speak a language you do not understand. But you will know them, for they will bear objects like this one."'

With that, Kai placed the taonga in Ngāheru's palm and closed the boy's fingers around it. 'You and your brother are its keepers now.'

+

No tears were shed by Kai or any of his whānau the following morning. That was not their way. His parting farewell to Wairere was a simple hongi. Despite the dangers that awaited him, she still expected him to return in a few days as promised to retrieve them.

Kai set off alone down to the Matā River, while Wairere, Tui, Hinewehi and the children headed up the mountain.

'You are brave, but you are not stupid,' Wairere said to Tui. 'Your brother, on the other hand, is fearless. As long as I have known him, I have never seen him afraid of anything. And he can be very impetuous. I wonder which of you is the wiser?'

'You know, Wai, when I was a boy I heard it said many times that Kai would grow up to become both hero and rogue. The old tohunga had prophesied it. My mother told us, my sisters knew it, the whole village spoke of it openly. After we returned from Pātete with Whiwhi-rangi's head he became that hero and fulfilled the first part of the prophecy.'

He paused and looked at her. 'Somehow, after that, no one mentioned the tohunga's prediction any more. Only when he killed your mother did we remember. Perhaps now he is going to help Kere in order to atone for his mistakes?'

'Perhaps, but evil deeds cannot be undone.'

+

Kere's pā was atop a rocky cliff face overlooking the Mākarika Stream, one of the many tributaries of the Matā River. Ōrongo-iri was a small fortress, no bigger than Pā-o-te-Kī, facing Kauae-nui. As he climbed a bank to the side of the rock face, Kai could see that the front parapet was well manned. Every four metres a warrior stood on watch, the wind blowing the feathers in his hair.

Maybe enough kai-rākau have remained to give us a fighting chance, he thought to himself, feeling a little more hopeful. As he climbed closer, one of the warriors appeared to nod at him and Kai returned the gesture.

He was soon at the gate and walked through. When he looked back at the eight warriors supposedly standing on the front parapet he saw to his surprise that they had no bodies or legs. The heads were all stuck on poles with a cross-stick tied on to represent the shoulders, and a flax cape thrown over to deceive anyone approaching. Well, it had fooled him!

Taha, the messenger from the previous day, stood before Kere's house waving him forward. He bowed as the chief passed.

'Where is everyone?' Kai asked.

'Save Kere and his priestess, myself and four others, this pā is manned by the dead,' Taha replied as he drew away.

Kai left his raincape on the porch and crept through the small aperture of Kere's house and down into the dimly lit dwelling on all fours. The space inside was no more than three metres by four, hot and humid. The old friends locked themselves in an embrace, noses drawn together and tears streaming down their faces.

When their hongi was over, Kai removed his heru and unbound his topknot to let his hair dry. He reclined on the mat. A grey-maned kuia, Kere's tohunga no doubt, was sitting against the back wall of the wharau with her knees drawn up to her chin. Once Kai was comfortable she began a chant honouring his visit.

In one corner of the house a preserved head was placed on a pole. In the middle of the enclosure a small fire burned fiercely in a shallow hole ringed by four flat rocks. The air was hazy with smoke.

The elderly priestess, whose entire body below her slitted eyes was hidden by a kaitaka, delivered the names of their illustrious dead in a low and constant monotone. Kai cast his eyes over her shoulder at a cobweb on the thatched roof. A spider was descending on its web line and he remembered his father telling him, when he was a little boy, that such a thing was a bad omen.

'It has been a long time, e hoa,' Kere said with a smile. He offered Kai some tāwhara juice and a basket of hot kūmara and dried eel. 'I knew you'd come.'

'How could I not? You saved my life when Tāmō and his men were bent on taking it,' Kai replied as he took a bite of kūmara. He was ravenous. 'How are your fighting limbs these days?'

'Older and slower — can't be helped. But win or lose, who doesn't like a good fight, eh?' Kere said, pointing with his short hani at the preserved head.

'Ha, remember Uncle Wehe?' Kai said. 'War was his sole pleasure, just as it was for old Tukua. It ought to be so for our children, too.'

'Speaking of our children, I hope you have not forgotten that our eldest daughter is betrothed to your eldest son. That has not changed.'

Kai was pleased. Ngāheru had been betrothed to Mahuru when they were scarcely able to walk and well before Kai had committed the act that saw him exiled. It was nice to be reminded that some men honoured their promises. He drank deeply, then looked at his old friend.

'They say this boy Hae is a good fighter.'

'Good enough to have sent our kai-rākau retreating to the Waiapu with their tails between their legs.' Kere shook his head. 'As menacing as the Aitanga-Nui party sound, I refuse to leave. Tāmō tried to convince me to go. I told him, "Ki te mate au, me mate ki te kāinga, kia heke aku toto i ngā wairatarata o Mākarika."' *If I'm going to die, I will die at home, so that my blood will flow in the sparkling waters of the Mākarika.* 'And what of you, my friend? What will you do?'

'Do you remember our first bird-fowling days at Pua-o-te-Roku?' said Kai. 'You gave me some advice back then. You said: "We're all willing to give our lives, but for the right cause. Not because of someone's selfish arrogance. You might not like some of us, Kai, and some of us might not particularly like you, but we need to know we can rely on one another."'

Kere smiled at the realisation that Kai had carried his words with him all these years.

'If we are to die,' Kai's voice dropped, 'let it be defending what is ours, side by side, as brothers.'

+

The following afternoon Taha came to tell Kere that Hae and his party were in the stream below the pā. Kai, Kere and their five other warriors had been preparing for the impending clash.

'A pā manned by seven warriors and an elderly tohunga is no match for a party of fifty,' said Kai, stating the obvious.

353

'I'll go down to him,' said Kere.

'No,' said Kai, 'let's not make it easy for them. Make them come to us.'

At that moment, as if they had heard them, eight of Hae's warriors appeared on the banks, four on either side of the cliff face. When they reached the outer palisade, three engaged Kai, Kere and Taha and four took on the other kai-rākau.

The eighth soon scaled the inner palisade and, quickly realising the pā was empty, headed for the various wharau. Far from involving himself in the fighting, this warrior, they discovered later, was intent on acquiring some booty. Ignoring the frail-looking priestess, who sat outside Kere's hut, apparently in a deep trance, he eagerly crawled inside. He gathered together the preserved head, some mats, a whalebone necklace and a few other small valuables and threw them in a pile outside, along with his patu and adze, freeing his hands to collect more loot.

Now unarmed, he pushed his head out through the small opening of the hut only to come face to face with the old woman, fully conscious now, uttering a wild incantation. Quick as a flash the kuia seized his adze, raised her arm and *smash!* Down came the sharp edge of the weapon on the back of the warrior's neck. She continued chopping frantically until she had severed his head from its body.

His fellow scouts, who had both given and received wounds in the meantime, saw this and withdrew to report back to Hae.

'So, your warriors are a ruse!' boomed Hae from the stream below.

Again, Kere said to Kai fiercely, 'I need to go down there!'

And for a second time Kai replied, 'No, let them come to us. We'll give them a fight they never expected.'

Kere nodded. 'Come up!' he yelled to Hae. 'I have opened the gate!'

When Hae and his party eventually reached the entrance to the pā they found the seven warriors armed with taiaha, bleeding from wounds but in their fighting stance, their tohunga chanting behind them.

Hae called out a single word, chanting it over and over as he gestured his men forward: 'Kōkiri! Kōkiri! Kōkiri!' *Attack! Attack! Attack!*

Kai pranced out to meet them, Taha and one of the kai-rākau behind him either side, and the tohunga finishing the diamond shape. Kere led out the other three, also in diamond formation.

'Ki te mate tātou,' Kai shouted to his companions. 'Kia kotahi, hei whakamahara mā te hoariri ki te ao tūroa.' *Should we die, let us fall together and forever be remembered by the enemy before the world.*

And with those words resounding in the air, seven men and one old woman raced fearlessly towards the sea of warriors.

'Kōkiri rā te Aitanga Nui! *Oh, the Aitanga Nui, attack!*' yelled Hae, rushing forward to meet them.

Despite the disparity in numbers, it was a battle for the ages.

EPILOGUE

––––––

'Cattle, Koroua!' I warned as we rounded the corner and were enveloped in the dust from a hundred plodding hooves. The drover, on horseback, whistled at his dogs while I wound up my window. With minimal guidance from the drover, the dogs cleared a path for our vehicle. As we chugged through, the koroua, not especially good at judging distance, now and again nudged a recalcitrant steer from behind. Several animals promptly kicked back at the vehicle and I realised why he had so many dents in the front bumper.

The drive back to Nūpe Pā was long, the day had become even hotter and the dust lingered behind our vehicle. When we struck Highway 35, the ammoniac stink of melting tar was so strong I had to close my window once more.

How much of what the koroua had told me was true? I had doubt about some of it — like the bit about the pake-pakehā and the family heirloom Kai gave to his sons. My academic training, though only just beginning, had taught me to question the validity of oral records. Not wanting to distract the old man from his driving, however, I decided I would not ask any questions until we were back at the pā.

After unloading his car we sat down to a cup of tea in the cool of the house. At this point, I decided to ask him straight out.

'What proof do you have that this story about Kai is true?'

'Proof?' he spluttered, almost choking on his tea. 'What *proof* do I have?'

I immediately deeply regretted asking the question.

'I have spent the last three days recounting to you the history of our tipuna, the great chief Kaitanga, whose name this house bears and whose history is etched into its very walls. I have relayed it to you as it was told to me by my grandmother, who in turn heard it from her own grandmother, who lived at Pā-o-te-Kī with her father Tuameko. And you are asking me about proof?' He was really angry.

I sat looking at my feet.

He walked off and began rummaging through some drawers. After several minutes he seemed to have found what he was looking for. He stood there with something in his cupped hands, examining it, slowly turning his back to me.

I felt terrible that I had upset him. I certainly hadn't meant to seem ungrateful.

After a long pause he took a deep breath, turned around and walked back to me. He stretched out his cupped hands as if he were holding a newborn child.

'This is my proof!'

In his hands lay a white cross set in a piece of wood, which sat inside a little black box.

'Is that enough for you?'

I was suddenly struck dumb, staring at what I knew must be the taonga that Kai had given his sons. It was difficult to tell what the cross was made of, but I suspected whalebone. I suddenly wondered if it might be human bone. Surely not, though after all the accounts of cannibalism I had just heard, it was not beyond the realms of possibility.

The koroua encouraged me to take it from the box. I did so, placing it in my palm and studying it. As I turned it over and over, I wondered how many of my tīpuna had handled this taonga over the hundreds of years of its existence. How many of them had understood what it represented?

Recognising the huge honour the old man had paid me, I placed it back in its box and gave it back to him. 'Sorry, Koroua. I shouldn't have asked about proof. But this is amazing. How old do you think it is?'

'Well, when you consider it was Old Ue's grandfather who took it from the pake-pakehā, oh . . . maybe about four hundred years.'

'Wow.'

+

That night as I lay on my mattress in the meeting house, it took me ages to fall asleep. My head was full of stories — of my history. The koroua had brought my ancestors to life. He had given life to the wooden carvings and the old portraits and allowed me to get to know them.

As I stared up at the kōwhaiwhai on the ceiling I imagined the wharau, the whare puni and the other places my tīpuna had slept. I was grateful for my blankets and pillow . . . but still I couldn't sleep. My mind kept coming back to the cross. What was its provenance? Who was the pake-pakehā that my ancestors had taken it from? Who else in our whānau knew about it?

After breakfast the next morning I went out onto the veranda and stood looking at the name above the door. KAI-TA-NGA. I wondered who else knew his story. Surely no one of my own generation. They were all more interested in looking forward than back. In making their way in the modern world.

I waited for the old man to join me, my overnight bag and my aunty's kete at my feet.

'I'm afraid I have to return to the city today, Koroua,' I said. 'I need to make some money before university starts.' We shared a hongi and a handshake, then before I knew it I had blurted out, 'May I come and see you again in the next university holidays?'

'I'm not going anywhere, boy,' he said with a smile.

As I latched the gate behind me, I looked back at the whare. The old man was squinting through his thick black-rimmed lenses, one hand raised in a wave. For a moment I thought I saw a figure standing behind him, mirroring his pose, though the upheld arm was holding something like a taiaha.

I rubbed my eyes and looked again. It was only his shadow.

GLOSSARY

Some words and phrases have several meanings. The meanings listed here relate to their use in this book.

aē	yes
ahi-tautai	ritual fire where the tohunga conducts special rites. Below Kō Pā the fire was lit alongside a tributary to the Ngāpō Stream
akapirita	supplejack, *Ripogonum scandens* (also kareao)
aruhe	edible root of the bracken fern, *Pteridium esculentum*
atāhu	love charm, spell
atua	spirit, deity, god or goddess
aute	paper mulberry, *Broussonetia papyrifera*, once cultivated to make cloth
awe māpara	tattoo on a person's face, body or limbs
e tā/e tama	originally e tā mā *oh sirs*, a Ngāti Porou expression of exasperation. When addressing a lad, 'e tama' can also mean 'boy'
haka	vigorous posture dance with actions and rhythmically shouted words
haka pōhiri	posture dance of welcome
haka taparahi	haka without weapons
hākari	feast
hani	carved wooden weapon more commonly known as a taiaha
hapū	subtribes
hāpuku	groper, *Polyprion oxygeneios*
harakeke	flax
hauhake	harvest
heru	comb
hika / hika mā	wow, gosh
hinahina	whiteywood, *Melicytus ramiflorus* (also māhoe)
hīnaki	wicker eel basket
Hine-nui-te-pō	'great woman of the night' who receives the spirits of humans when they die
hoeroa	steering paddle
hoewai	broad-bladed paddle
hua	gut of the pāua
huata	long spear, pointed at both ends
iho	umbilical cord (middle portion)

Ika-a-Whiro	war veterans, experienced warriors
iwi	tribe
kahawai	a common fish, *Arripis trutta*
kāheru	wooden spade-like implement, sometimes carved
kahikatea	white pine, *Dacrycarpus dacrydioides*
kahu	cloaks, garments
kaihautū	fugleman, coxswain in a canoe
kaihoe	paddlers
kai kōtore	marriage feast involving chiefly families
kaimoana	seafood
Kaipō	star that heralds the lunar month of April
kaioraora	song of derision, cursing or abusive song, venting haka
kai-rākau	warriors or band of experienced warriors
kaitaka	special cloak with an ornamental border
kai-whakatere	waka navigator, helmsman
kākā	large native forest parrot, *Nestor meridionalis*
kākahu	cloak
karae	seabird (species unknown)
karakia	prayer / entreaty
karakia hono	entreaty that binds
karamū	small tree with large glossy leaves and edible fruit, *Coprosma lucida*
karanga	ceremonial call to welcome visitors onto a marae
kareao	supplejack, *Ripogonum scandens* (also akapirita)
kārearea	New Zealand falcon, *Falco novaeseelandiae*
kāretu	scented holy grass, *Hierochloe redolens*
karo	small bushy tree, *Pittosporum crassifolium* and *P. ralphii*
karoro	seagull, *Larus dominicanus*
kauae nui	large jawbone
kāuka	cabbage tree, *Cordyline australis* (also kōuka, tī kōuka)
kāuta	cooking area
kāwai	line of descent
kāwai rangatira	chiefly lineage
kawakawa	pepper tree, *Macropiper excelsum*
kawanga whare	to lift tapu from a house
kehe	marblefish, *Aplodactylus arctidens*
kēhua	ghost or spirit that lingers after death
kete	flax kit or basket
kina	sea egg, common sea urchin, *Evechinus chloroticus*
kinaki	relish
kiore	rat, also scout
kiri mate	bereaved family
kō	wooden implement for digging
koha	gift, offering, donation, contribution — has connotations of reciprocity

kōkiri	attack
kōkopu	cockabully, *Galaxias fasciatus*
kōkōwai	red ochre
kono kai	flax food basket
kōpara	bellbird, *Anthornis melanura* (also korimako)
kōpura kao	kūmara that has been steamed and sun-dried
kōpurawhetū	white basket fungus
kōrero	to speak, talk, address
kōrero tuku iho	oral traditions
korimako	bellbird, *Anthornis melanura* (also kōpara)
koroī	orange-red fruit of the kahikatea tree, *Dacrycarpus dacrydioides*
koroua	elderly man, grandfather, male elder
korowai	cloak often ornamented with black twisted tags or thrums
kōruru	carved face on the gable of a meeting house
kōtuku	white heron, *Egretta alba*
kōtukutuku	tree fuchsia, *Fuchsia excorticata*
kōura	crayfish, freshwater and saltwater species
kōura mara	crayfish fermented in fresh water
kōura rangi	krill
kōwhaiwhai	painted scroll ornamentation, commonly used on meeting house rafters
kuia	elderly woman, grandmother, female elder
kūmara	sweet potato, *Ipomoea batatas*
kurī	dog
māhiti	cape covered with long white hair from dogs' tails – a superior garment sometimes worn over a cloak
Mahuru	fourth lunar month of the Māori year, approximately equivalent to September
maioha	naming ceremony
makariri	winter, to be cold
mākutu	to bewitch, cast spells
mamau	wrestling
mana	authority, prestige
māngaro	floury, starchy fernroot (the term was used to describe potatoes when Māori first tasted them)
mangō ururoa	great white shark, *Carcharodon carcharias*
manuhiri	visitor
marae	area immediately in front of the whare tipuna where visitors are formally welcomed
maramara kai	scraps of food
maro	short kilt, loin cloth, apron-type garment worn by men and women
maro huka	type of apron, preferred garment in wartime
maro tūhou	apron worn when conducting rites

mātāika	someone's first kill in battle
matakite	to see into the future; prophesise, foretell
mauku	filmy fern, *Hymenophyllum* species
mauri	life force
māwe	significant object used to represent someone or a place, or to defeat an enemy
mere	a short, flat stone weapon often made from pounamu
mimi	to urinate, urine
miromiro	white-breasted tomtit, *Petroica macrocephala toitoi*
moho	small fish taken by net
moko	tattoo
moko kauae	chin tattoo
motu	island
muru	plunder
nohu	southern burrfish, *Allomycterus pilatus*
noke	earthworm
ohāki	dying speech, parting wish, last words
ope taua	war party
oriori	song composed for a chiefly child about his/her ancestry and tribal history
pā	fortified village, now the modern-day marae
pā tuna	eel weir
paepae	dish or open shallow vessel
paepaeroa	fine dress cloak
pake-pakehā	mythical beings with fair skin, resembling people
Pākehā	English, European
pakokori	baby's playpen
pākūwhā	traditional wedding ceremony
papa kāinga	original home, home base, village, communal Māori land
para	fern tubers (the term was used to describe potatoes when Māori first tasted them)
parakore	pure, uncontaminated
para-tawhiti	a starchy based fernroot that was a traditional food
para whakawai	parade ground
parāoa rēwena	Māori bread made with yeast
pare	lintel, carved slab over the door of a house, also headband
pārera	grey duck, *Anas superciliosa superciliosa*
parera	north-west wind, nor'wester
pātio	thickened skin, calluses from walking barefoot
pato	a heavy wooden tool used for beating, crushing and grinding fernroot
patu ōnewa	dark-grey stone club
patu parāoa	whalebone hand weapon
patupaiarehe	fairy people, also referred to as 'tūrehu'
pāua	abalone, *Haliotis species*

pekerangi	small stage or platform attached to each main palisade post of a stockade
pīkau	backpack
piki	second or supporter in a fight
pipi	shellfish, *Paphies australis*
piripiri	creeping native plant, *Acaena anserinifolia*, 'bidibid'
piupiu	knee-length skirt with free-hanging strands made of flax
pīwaiwaka	fantail, *Rhipidura fuliginosa* (also pīwakawaka)
pōhatu	stone
ponga	tree fern, *Cyathea dealbata*
pononga	people captured in battle and retained as slaves
popotahi	position in which the taiaha is held vertically in front of the body, tongue end down
pō-rakaraka	traditional bassinet
pounamu	greenstone
pūhoro	tattoo on thighs and buttocks
pū kōrero	a powerful orator
pua manu	bird reserve
puapua	garment wrapped around the arm as protection from weapon blows
pūkeko	purple swamp hen, *Porphyrio porphyrio*
puku	stomach
punga kārewa	bow anchor of a waka taua
punga whakawhenua	stern anchor of a waka taua
pūtātara	conch shell trumpet with wooden mouthpiece
rāhui	restriction, ban, closed season
Rākau-nui	full moon, time to plant
rangatira	chief
rāpaki	flax kilt
rape	tattooing on the buttocks
rauawa	gunwales – the upper edges along each side of a waka
raupō	bulrush, *Typha orientalis*
raurākau	large-leaved coprosma, *Coprosma grandifolia*
rehu	premonition, extra-sensory perception, foreboding
Ringatū	a Māori Christian faith founded in the 1860s
Rongopai, Te	the Gospel
rua	storage pit
rūnanga	village leadership group
tahā	calabash, gourd
taiaha	spear-like weapon of hardened wood with a long narrow blade
takapau wharanui	marriage mat
tākiri	convulsive twitching
Taku Kare-ā-roto	my soulmate
tamāhine	daughter

tāmaki	omen
tāmoko	tattoo
tāmure	snapper, *Chrysophrys auratus*
Tāne	god of the forests and birds
Tangaroa	god of the sea and fish
tangihanga / tangi	funeral ceremony
tāniko	woven border on cloaks
taniwha	dangerous water creature
taonga	treasured item
tapu	sacred, special, forbidden, untouchable
tapuhi	attendant
taramea	speargrass, wild Spaniard, *Aciphylla species*
taro	starchy edible plant, *Colocasia esculenta*
tāruke kōura	crayfish trap
tatau pounamu	peace agreement
tātua	belt
tau-ihu	carved figurehead at prow of canoe
tau kai	year of a bounteous food supply
tau-mātaki-tahi	to engage in single combat
taumau	betrothal / arranged marriage
taunga ika	fishing ground
taurapa	stern-post of a canoe
tāwhara	succulent flowers of the kiekie tree, *Freycinetia banksii*
teka	dart
tewhatewha	long wooden or bone weapon with a flat end like an axe
tikanga	custom, protocol
timo	grubber
tīpapa kererū	flock of woodpigeons
tipu	kūmara shoots; to grow, sprout, increase
tipua	supernatural being, not human
tipuna	ancestor (plural tīpuna)
tohu	omen, sign
tohunga	skilled person, expert, priest, healer
tohunga tāmoko	tattoo expert
tohunga whakairo	master carver
toka	rock
toki-pou-tangata	weapon like a battle-axe
tokotoko	walking stick carved with figures and intricate patterns; staff used in close-quarter combat
toma	shrine for bones
toroa	albatross, *Diomedea species*
Tū-mata-riri	Tū, the ugly-faced war god
Tū-matau-enga	Tū, the angry-faced war god
tūī	tūī or parson bird, *Prosthemadera novaeseelandiae*
tūmau	cook, chef

tuna	eel, *Anguilla* species
tūpāpaku	corpse
tūrehu	fairy folk, mythical beings of human form with light skin and fair hair
tutu	*Coriaria arborea* var. *arborea*, a native shrub that is extremely poisonous, except for the juice of the purple-black fruit
tūtū ngārahu	war dance – haka prior to battle
uku	clay receptacle
umu	earth oven
umu kōtore	wedding feast
ure	penis
uri	descendants
urukehu	fair-skinned, red-headed or auburn-headed person
utu	revenge, payback
wahaika	short club of whalebone with a carved figure on one side of the blade
waka taua	vessel carrying a war party
weka	flightless wood-hen, *Gallirallus australis*
whai	string games
whaiāipo	sweetheart; to be in love with
whakamomori	to pine oneself to death. In traditional Māori society spouses or close relations might express their profound grief by taking their own lives.
whakapiri	to fasten together, remain close to
whakataukī	proverbial saying
whānau	extended family group
whanaunga	relative
whāngai	adopted
wharau	low-arched, thatched hut or house with its floor sunken in the ground
whare kōhanga	house for childbirth
whare paku	outside toilet like a long-drop
whare puni	principal guest house, forerunner to the modern day ancestral meeting house
whare rauhi	birthing tent
whare tapere	house of recreation, community centre
whare tīpuna	ancestral meeting house
whare wānanga	traditionally, places where tohunga taught the sons of rangatira their people's history, genealogy and religious practices
whāriki	flax woven mat
whata kai	elevated stage for storing food
whatu manawa	inner eye, intuition
Whiro	god of things associated with evil, darkness and death

NOTES

1 A Māori Christian faith founded in the 1860s with adherents mainly from the Bay of Plenty and East Coast tribes.

2 Mate Māori is an illness thought to be caused by an infringement against tapu.

3 Gisborne.

4 As far as is known, Aotearoa New Zealand was first spotted on 13 December 1642 by Dutch navigator Abel Tasman. But he did not land. His only encounter with the local people ended badly, when four of his crew were killed and the locals were fired upon in retaliation. The British explorer Captain James Cook, who is referred to here, arrived in Poverty Bay in October 1769.

5 Lines from Chief Taki-o-te-rangi's composition 'Rūaumoko'.

6 Rūaumoko, Ngāti Porou's famous haka taparahi, was once described by its tribal leader, Sir Apirana Ngata, as 'a masterpiece of the phallic cult'.

7 Te Ika-a-Māui is the North Island of New Zealand.

8 A general term for lizards, skinks and geckos, which were feared because of their association with the atua Whiro, whose realm was evil things.

9 Maru-ā-nuku was a place at Hawaiki and this is the story of Pourangahua, according to Ngā Rauru. It is likely on the island of Raivavae, mentioned in the Horouta 'karakia' tradition as 'sacred hollows'. Maru-ā-nuku is also one of the two furrows dug in the ritual first planting of kūmara. (Translation by Barry Soutar.)

10 Elsdon Best, *The Maori as He Was: A Brief Account of Life as it Was in Pre-European Days,* Dominion Museum, Wellington, 1934, p. 186.

11 'Chow lega' is a linguistic corruption of the Māori expression 'Kia reka', which literally means 'How Sweet' but is translated more colloquially as 'Neat' or 'Too much'.

AUTHOR'S NOTE

This novel, the first in a series, is inspired by the life of our tipuna, Rongo-
i-te-kai, the name of our whare puni at Pēnu Pā, near Ruatōria. The pā was
renovated in the early 1980s and again in 2017. The pine trees described in
the prologue have gone, as has the old homestead. Today no one resides in the
meeting house, but Parekura's memorial and the hill cemetery are still clearly
discernible.

For Such a Time as This is loosely based on accounts recorded in my hapū's
oral traditions, which, when I was a teenager, were concealed in the memories
of a caring few, in meticulously compiled manuscripts that whānau members
jealously guarded, and in the early minute books of the Native Land Court.

The genesis for wanting to write this story goes back to my youth. In the
late 1970s *Roots*, an American television miniseries, captured the attention of
many New Zealanders, myself included. It told of author Alex Haley tracing
his ancestral roots to a young African boy kidnapped and sold into slavery.
It planted in me the seed of desire to know my own family's history.

I did nothing immediately to work towards that goal, but in hindsight from
that moment, I was moving towards it. The prologue, for example, is very
much a recounting of how I started my inquiry at age nineteen, first with my
mother and then with the koroua. The old man's character is an amalgam of
elders who, in 1980, were in their seventies — Ruahuihui Makarini (Peter
Mac), who lived in the whare puni, Tamati Kupenga (Tom Sherwood), Moni
Taumaunu and Tipene Ngata. I should also mention here Sherwood's son,
Tautohe (Mae) Kupenga, Amster and Mokena Reedy, Waho Tibble, Apirana
Mahuika, Koro Dewes, Sir Tamati Reedy, Mate Kaiwai (née Ngata), Hopaea
Kerr (née Taewa), Keita Walker (née Ngarimu), Matere Reedy (née McLean),
Manu Stainton, Phil Aspinall, Wiremu Parker and Sir Henare Ngata. They were
some of the people who instilled in me a deep-seated interest in our history.

In 1987 I became a full-time researcher with the Department of Māori
Affairs. I pored over tomes that recorded oral testimony given by my forbears
and other witnesses before the Native Land Court in the late nineteenth
century. After two years of tedious examination, combined with hikes across
terrain below Mt Hikurangi, I compiled my voluminous notes into what
became *The Origins and Early History of Te Aitanga Mate.* This unpublished
manuscript was circulated among the hapū and it provides the basis from which
this novel was created.

The idea of writing a novel was ignited in me in 1994 when Professor Ranginui Walker gave a keynote address at the New Zealand History Conference. He said that, in his opinion, the Great New Zealand Novel had not been written and that when it was, it would challenge the grand narrative of New Zealand historiography.

The following year I attempted to write my first novel, but I never produced more than a page or two. On reflection I had neither the training nor the experience at that time.

How I came to eventually write it was this: In July 2019, after I launched my latest non-fiction work, I took a well-earned break and, with my wife Tina, went to visit friends in Greece. Taking a trip or introducing a change of scene and environment often replaces old thought patterns with new ones.

Before we departed, the old familiar idea of writing a novel kept pulling at me. So, I pitched the idea to my publisher.

'If you write a novel,' he said, 'I'll publish it.' His positive reaction surprised me, given I had never written fiction before and, at the time, Bateman Books only published non-fiction.

In Greece Tina and I spent two months with our friends at the seaside town of Kalo Nero, in which time I read historical novels and the idea of writing fiction grew in me.

The last two weeks of our European sojourn was spent in France. It was during our stay in the picturesque village of Connelles that I first shaped the plan for the *Kāwai* series. It was bold, ambitious and it involved risks. But nothing in life is worthwhile unless you take risks.

I prayed about it, then trusting the voice of intuition, I wrote out a strategy for how I would approach the project. When we returned to Aotearoa New Zealand, I gave up full-time employment and I focussed my life on that one main thing — the novel series. I first met with Paula Morris, Director of the Masters of Creative Writing at the University of Auckland. She steered me in the right direction, then I enrolled in a couple of online sessions, and the rest was trial and error. I had only just made a start at writing when the country went into its first lockdown because of the Covid-19 pandemic. It took me one year of hard study and intense practice to teach myself how to write a novel and then another year to complete the manuscript for this first book.

The *Kāwai* series is based on my own antecedents to limit the criticism to my whānau. *For Such a Time as This*, the first novel in this series, reveals a way of life in pre-colonial times that was both beautiful and raw. But it was not the utopia that we would so readily go running back to. For it was often shaded by seemingly cruel and pitiless behaviour among iwi, hapū and even members of the same whānau. Utu, mākutu and kaitangata had long been so much a part of traditional society that by the time Captain Cook arrived it was firmly embedded in the culture.

Historical accuracy is vital to my kind of writing and I undertake every measure to ensure the correctness of my facts. In *Kāwai* I have taken certain liberties, however, by changing the chronology and sometimes the location of various actual events. For the sake of the story, some of the narrative draws on speculation and some scenes have been intentionally created. Take the one in the whare kōhanga (Chapter Three) where Tāwae visits his young wife and newborn son. I wanted to show intimacy between the couple, yet in reality males, even a chief, could not break tapu and enter the kōhanga. Instead, Tāwae would have spoken to his wife from outside the temporary structure.

In this sense, *Kāwai: For Such a Time as This* is a work of fiction, and I am solely responsible for any errors or deliberate alterations of the facts. That said, some of what appears in the novel happened in real life in the exact way it is described.

This series is engaging and more than a little confronting. It's the counter-narrative of Māori history we know so little about. Those who do know about it have tended to confine their talk within closed circles.

I envy those of you discovering this history, for I will never forget the impact these stories had on me the first time I heard them.

Monty Soutar
Tūranga-nui-a-Kiwa
December 2021

ACKNOWLEDGEMENTS

Prov 3:6

We are each blessed with talents and abilities and with opportunities to develop them. I acknowledge that mine are God-given. Throughout this journey I have received flashes of inspiration from the voice of intuition. I once read that prayer is the way we phone God, and intuition is the way God phones us.

So many people have been involved in my journey. To begin with, I received help in my daily life from my wife, Tina. Not only did she give me ideas and the subtitles for this first novel, but she took me to sample the berries of native trees, she was always on the lookout for books that might help me, and she was never afraid to tell me when my writing wasn't cutting it. Together with our youngest daughter, Aohuna, the other person in our household, they bore witness to the single focus I gave to creating this work — my dogged determination, struggles and jubilations. Nei rā te mihi ki a kōrua.

I think with special gratitude of our other three adult children, especially Te Tuhi, who came up with the idea for the cover and produced the original coloured version for the book. Oriwia and Eparaima also had small parts in it. The three of them always believed in what I could do and never doubted I'd come through with *Kāwai*.

I would never have managed to produce this book if not for everyone at Bateman Books. I did test the waters with other publishers, and while they showed genuine interest in what I was trying to achieve with the series, I opted again to follow the direction of that small, still voice of intuition.

To Paul Bateman, thank you for supporting a book that fell outside your traditional wheelhouse, even when it existed only in my mind.

My major thanks has to go to Louise Russell, my editor at Bateman, for making everything possible in the impossible circumstances of Covid-19. For your encouragement, for so generously sharing your time and counsel, and like Paul, for seeing the *Kāwai* series as books of critical importance, thank you very much. Truly, I could not have done it without your guidance, your gentle persuasion and, at times, your tough talking. I have never felt disappointed after receiving one of your emails.

Once Louise had helped me with the hard, structural work — building and refining the framework, she engaged a freelance editor, Rachel Scott, who applied her keen eye and attention to detail to the final manuscript. Rachel, you focused on the finer textual detail and asked some essential questions. The novel is all the better for your input.

In 2021 I was awarded the prestigious Creative New Zealand Michael King Writer's Fellowship to support me in the completion of the *Kāwai* series. I am indebted to Creative New Zealand and the judging panel who saw fit to award the fellowship to me. I am also grateful to Copyright Licensing New Zealand (CLNZ) who awarded me a grant from its 2020 contestable fund.

Many experts gave me their help and time in the writing of this book. Among them I may mention my brother Barry Soutar, my good friend Victor Walker, Dr David Butts and his wife Fay, as well as Kim Pittar, Leanne Tamaki and Wananga Walker. They read and commented on the early drafts and left me with my own judgements, and headed me off from several grave errors. Not only did Barry help me translate many of the ditties, haka and karakia, but also, through his company TORO Studios, I had the assistance of both Dan Witters, who has a background as a media lawyer and script editor for television, and graphic artist Raukura Riwaka, who worked tirelessly on the elements for the front cover. Te Ohorere (Jossie) Kaa gave valuable feedback on the Māori text, words and macrons. She too asked for no assurances and scrupulously left me with my independence. Ngā mihi maioha ki a koutou.

I must also express my gratitude to Campbell Dewes who arranged for me to see the pā referred to in the story as Ōkau, my nephew, Te Hemara Rauhihi, who modelled for the cover, Siobhan Houkamau who produced his photograph, and Zandria Taare and Fran McGowan, both of whom were assiduous in helping me obtain the books I needed through their respective libraries.

I also want to thank those others who read parts of the manuscript. I won't mention names for there are so many, but you know who you are, and I am so grateful to all of you. In your own individual ways, you helped make this book possible.

Kia ora koutou katoa.